For the girls:
Denise, Lyndsey, Felicia, Kristen and Megan.
You make the trials and tribulations of daily life
easier to bear.
Here's to dinner, coffee, play dates and whinging!

Author's note

Dear Reader,

This story follows the antics of two best friends who swap lives. Half of the story is set in Perth, exploring the fast-paced legal profession. The other half is set in the south-west region of Western Australia in a quiet town called Yallingup – a place very dear to my heart.

Yallingup is a small slice of the Margaret River wine region, most famous for its world-class wine, surfing and gorgeous natural limestone caves surrounded by beautiful jarrah and marri forest. If you ever have time to visit this part of the world I highly recommend you do, if only to enjoy the organically grown produce and delicious wine. I have family there, so it's where my husband and I always choose to spend our holidays.

While I wanted to keep the book as real as possible for readers, I want to clarify that Rickety Twigg Road, which cuts from Bussell Highway to Yallingup, is not a real road, nor do any of the estates mentioned on it, such as the Oak Hills Winery, exist. This road and the surrounds, however, are based on Wildwood Road – the real gateway to Yallingup.

The Grass is Greener

LORETTA HILL

BANTAM

SYDNEY AUCKLAND TORONTO NEW YORK LONDON

A Bantam book
Published by Random House Australia Pty Ltd
Level 3, 100 Pacific Highway, North Sydney NSW 2060
www.randomhouse.com.au

First published by Bantam in 2016

Random House Books is part of the Penguin Random House group of companies whose addresses can be found at global.penguinrandomhouse.com.

National Library of Australia
Cataloguing-in-Publication entry

Hill, Loretta, author
The grass is greener/Loretta Hill

ISBN 978 0 85798 432 6 (paperback)

Best friends – Fiction
Families – Fiction
Life change events – Fiction

A823.4

Cover images (woman) © Tomas Rodriguez/Corbis, (vines) © logoboom/Shutterstock.com
Cover design by Christabella Designs
Internal design and typesetting by Midland Typesetters, Australia
Printed in Australia by Griffin Press, an accredited ISO AS/NZS 14001:2004 Environmental Management System printer

Loretta was born in Perth, the eldest of four girls. She enjoyed writing from a very early age and was just eleven years old when she had her first short story published in *The West Australian* newspaper.

Having graduated with a degree in Civil Engineering and another in Commerce, she was hired by a major Western Australian engineering company and worked for a number of years on many outback projects. She drew upon her experiences of larrikins, red dust and steel-capped boots for her bestselling novels *The Girl in Steel-Capped Boots*, *The Girl in the Hard Hat* and *The Girl in the Yellow Vest*. Her fourth novel, *The Maxwell Sisters*, was set in the Margaret River wine region, where she returns for her fifth novel, *The Grass is Greener*.

She lives in Perth with her husband and four children.

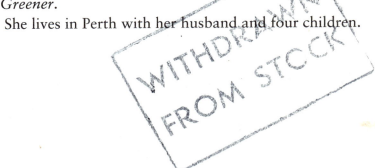

There are so many other gorgeous wineries in this region similar in operation to Oak Hills and definitely worth the visit. I've tried to keep the winemaking part of this story as real and authentic as possible; to do so, I drew on the experience of my good friend Ben Gould, who owns and runs vineyards in Wilyabrup and Quindalup, also part of the Margaret River wine region. His winery is called Blind Corner.

If you would like to taste Ben's label – and you should, it's delicious! – you can find his wines in many fine restaurants throughout Australia. Or check out Blind Corner's website to order at www.blindcorner.com.au.

Apart from great food and wine, this book is about starting again. I think at one stage or another we've all been stuck in a rut. You feel like your life is going around in circles and you're never going to get out of it. It's easy to look at our friends, neighbours or work colleagues and wish we had what they have. The grass is always greener on the other side, right? I really wanted to write a book exploring that theme because I felt that, like all great theories, it was definitely flawed. Someone else's life would never perfectly suit. You'd always have to adapt to it or make it adapt to you. True happiness doesn't come from being someone else but from being our best selves.

I really enjoyed pushing my two heroines, Claudia and Bronwyn, to discover just that. I hope you enjoy their journey too.

Happy reading,
Loretta Hill

Chapter 1

'So?' Claudia cupped her hands around her steaming mug. 'Now that we've finished lunch, tell me how you've *really* been.'

For Bronwyn Eddings, looking into her best friend's kind eyes over a comforting cup of tea was the straw that broke the camel's back. It had been too long since she'd seen a friendly face, and the mask that she'd worked so hard to keep in place began to crack.

'I hate my life,' she said firmly, her fist thumping on the polished timber tabletop in their favourite Perth cafe.

'Okay,' Claudia blinked in surprise. 'I wasn't expecting so extreme an answer, but go on.'

'I *hate* it,' Bronwyn repeated, glad finally to get what had been going through her mind for months off her chest. 'I hate all of it. Every single, commercial, materialistic piece of it. I hate my boss . . .' she ticked off on her fingers, 'I hate my job. I even hate my apartment. It's cold, empty, lonely and completely unwelcoming. *And,*' she added with a purse of her lips, 'I hate wearing skirt suits. They're so stiff. I feel like a funeral director in them, and with all the bad news I'm constantly delivering I –'

'Okay, okay, okay.' Claudia held up a hand to stall the complaints. 'I get the picture. What's brought this on, Bron? I know it's been a while since I saw you –'

'Over six months.' Bronwyn drummed impatient fingers on the table.

'Yes, more than six months since I've been able to drive up to Perth,' Claudia continued calmly. 'And that is definitely my fault. I've been a bad friend to you. Totally MIA. I'm sorry.'

'I know you've been having a hard time with your dad and everything.' Bronwyn smiled with understanding. 'And it's not like I couldn't have driven to you.'

'Why didn't you say anything in your emails?'

'Emails are so impersonal.' Bronwyn blew her blonde fringe out of her eyes as she dropped her chin in her palm dejectedly. 'Besides, I didn't want to send you a ten-page rant. Not that my schedule would give me time to write that. It certainly isn't billable.'

'Ten pages, huh? Surely things haven't all turned to shit since I last saw you. Has something happened at work to make you feel this way?'

'You don't understand, Claud. It was shit when you were last here. And the time before that, and the time before that. I just didn't know how to tell you. I didn't want you to think less of me.'

'Why would I think less of you?'

'Because I brought this on myself.' Bronwyn slumped in her chair. 'And I know you. You'd be the first one to point that out.'

'Okay, I'm really not getting this.' Claudia frowned. 'What is so terrible about your life? You work for one of the most prestigious law firms in town, your career is exactly on track and you're making more money than you have time to spend.'

Bronwyn bit her lip. *That's exactly what's wrong with it.*

At her telling silence, Claudia folded her arms. 'Bron, you

have everything you ever wanted. Hell, you have everything we both ever wanted. The kickarse career, a stake in stuff that really matters . . .'

'I'm not passionate about the law the way you are,' Bronwyn tried to explain. 'I suppose I can get the job done. But I don't like it.'

'Seriously? You don't feel the power of the justice system coursing through your veins as you right wrongs, save the innocent and put the bad guys away?'

Bronwyn grinned at her best friend. Claudia had always been an environmental crusader, a human rights activist and completely Left politically. At uni, she had been a member of all the community groups. Save the whales. Feed the orphans. Keep the arts centre open! And while you're at it, don't eat meat, don't drink dairy and plant a tree once a year.

Bronwyn laughed. 'Come back to earth, supergirl. That's not what it's like for me at all.'

Claudia leaned back in her chair thoughtfully. 'Better than driving from one hotel to another, giving the same boring spiel about why they should have Oak Hills wines in their cellar.'

Bronwyn shook her head. 'There is nothing boring about Oak Hills or their wine.'

'There's nothing earth-shattering about it either.' Claudia thought about the business that had supported her family for at least two generations. 'I'm completely over it.'

'It's better than my job.'

'Are you kidding me?' Claudia exclaimed.

Bronwyn winced. 'Do you know where I was this morning?'

'Court?'

'I wish,' Bronwyn sighed. 'I was at Casuarina Prison, meeting one of my clients.'

Claudia's eyes lit up like a little kid in front of a cupcake. 'You got to go to a maximum security prison? Damn, girl, how exciting!'

'Yes, with all those lovely murderers and rapists inside. What an adventure! My client was as terrified as I was. He can't wait to be shifted.' She shuddered as she recalled the sweat beading on Peter Goldman's brow as he had pleaded with her to do something . . . anything . . . to get him moved on. She didn't blame him. She'd been awake to every sound in that place as she'd walked through all the checkpoints, even with a massive guard leading the way. What would it be like to be on the other side of those bars? She didn't want to think about it. Peter was a white-collar criminal. She very much doubted he'd be able to hold his own against other, more physically imposing types. However, he had to wait in prison until his sentencing. That was just procedure.

It was times like these that made her hate working as a lawyer even more – moments when she involuntarily caught herself actually feeling sorry for the criminal. Peter Goldman was a con man. He had stolen the life savings of hundreds of honest middle-class families to service his life of luxury – big house on the hill, boat in the bay, a gambling debt the size of Bronwyn's mortgage, and all the happiness fraudulent funds could buy. His only regret was that he'd got caught. He deserved to be punished for this. So why did she feel sympathy for him? Her mother would have a fit if she knew that she'd been affected by his pleas.

What was the first rule of thumb? Professional perspective with your client was paramount – never care personally for them, simply look after their affairs.

She was too soft to be a lawyer – she couldn't seem to switch off her emotions when the occasion demanded it. Peter must have sensed that weakness in her when he'd hit her up with that inappropriate proposal.

'What happened?' Claudia demanded when Bronwyn fell suspiciously silent.

'Oh, nothing,' she tried to end the subject. 'It's a long story.'

'I've got time. Tell me.'

She glanced up at Claudia. There was a little glint of steel in her best friend's sharp blue eyes. Now *that* was the look of a lawyer. It was ruined, of course, by the streaky honey-brown hair that cascaded over her shoulders in gentle waves – nothing a French roll and a bit of dark lippy couldn't fix, though.

She figured Claudia would get it out of her one way or another so she might as well save herself some time. 'Now that my client is in prison, his wife is divorcing him. She's taking their kids and leaving Perth to go live in Melbourne.'

'That sounds understandable.'

'It is, only his dog no longer has a home. His wife is refusing to take the dog with her.'

'And that's your problem because . . . ?'

'His wife wants to put it down and he's distraught. He doesn't want that.'

'So he can call a dog-rescue place. I don't see how this is your drama.'

Bronwyn smiled at Claudia's impartial logic. *Why can't I be like that?* Her best friend was a great lawyer. It was unfortunate she was unable to practice.

'So what's his next move?' Claudia asked.

'He's asked me to take the dog.'

'Take the dog where? To a kennel?'

'To my home.'

Claudia gasped. 'He wants you to keep his dog for him?'

'Just till he gets out.'

'That could be years!' Claudia's eyes widened. 'Bronwyn, you didn't say yes?'

'Well, no, not really.'

'What do you mean, *not really*? Did you agree to take the dog or not?'

'You should have seen him, Claud,' Bronwyn moaned. 'He loves that dog. He says, in this traumatic time, his Elsa is the only thing that has kept him sane. His wife couldn't give a shit. She wants to kill it. An *innocent animal*, Claud! Snuffed out,' she snapped her fingers, 'just like that. I thought you of all people would get why I empathise.'

'You do realise that the traumatic time he is talking about is the fact that he got sent to jail. And the chicken you had in your sandwich five minutes ago was also innocent but you ate it anyway.'

Claudia had eaten a grilled vegetable salad, and Bronwyn winced guiltily. 'Yes, but –'

'Bronwyn,' Claudia slapped a hand to her head, 'he's a criminal, not your friend. You can't trust him and you *cannot* take that dog. It's not your responsibility.'

'Just because he committed fraud doesn't mean he can't have a genuine love for an animal.'

Claudia rolled her eyes. 'Bron, I'm not questioning his love for the animal but why can't he call the RSPCA? I'm not advocating that this dog just be handed to the wife and put down. If it's as loving and wonderful as he says it is, I'm sure someone will provide it with a good, *permanent* home. This request for you to keep the dog till he gets out is completely inappropriate and it's unprofessional of you to even consider it. Honestly, this reminds me of the time you let that guy who got evicted for not paying his rent sleep on your couch.'

'He was a nice guy,' Bronwyn protested. 'Just a little misunderstood.'

'Bronwyn, he stole all your credit cards.'

'That was my fault,' Bronwyn quickly jumped to his defence. 'I left my purse on the kitchen counter. It was just too much of a temptation for him.'

'So now you're blaming yourself for his thieving?'

'He was going through a rough patch. He wasn't thinking clearly.'

'Honestly,' Claudia briefly closed her eyes, 'sometimes I don't know how you get through your day.'

'There! You see!' Bronwyn stabbed the table triumphantly as Claudia hit upon the crux of her problem. 'I'm just not cut out to be a lawyer.'

Claudia pressed her lips together. 'That's not what I said.'

'Damn it, girl, I'm not offended.' Bronwyn threw up her hands. 'You're absolutely right. I'm hopeless.'

'Bronwyn, you are *not* hopeless.'

'Well, I'm not good either.'

'You're an Eddings.'

'And what a curse that name has been to me since the day I was born,' Bronwyn returned bitterly. With her mother at the bar, her father a judge, one uncle in parliament and the other running one of the most prestigious law firms in town, what chance did she have of ever doing anything else?

'You don't mean that.'

'Of course I do. If I hadn't become a lawyer, my parents would have disowned me.'

In hindsight, that might not have been a bad thing.

'So you're saying you did five years of study and four years of work just to fit in?'

Bronwyn shrugged. 'I knew this was how you'd react.'

'Do you blame me?' Claudia's eyes boggled.

'You don't understand,' Bronwyn protested. 'My mother is very controlling. You know how ambitious she is. She has all these plans and hopes for me. What was I going to say?'

'No! Bron, you say *no*!'

It was Bronwyn's turn to get cross. 'Well, if that isn't the kettle smoking pot, I don't know what is!'

'You mean the pot calling the kettle black.' Claudia grinned.

'Whatever.' Bronwyn tossed her head indignantly. 'I'm not the only one at this table who caved in to family obligation.'

'Good point,' Claudia conceded, then cunningly changed the subject. 'But you still haven't answered my question. Did you agree to take his dog or not?'

Bronwyn veiled her eyes. 'I said I needed a couple of days to think about it.'

'Bron.'

'The animal is on death row, Claud. What would you have done?'

'Any number of things, but not that.'

Bronwyn straightened her shoulders. 'He said I was the only one he trusted.'

'That's what worries me,' Claudia's eyes narrowed. 'Don't take the dog, Bron. Promise me.'

'Okay, okay.' Bronwyn held up her hands. 'I won't take the dog. It's not like it would be an easy thing to do anyway. My apartment building doesn't allow pets.' She frowned. 'Just another reason why I hate it.'

'I love your place,' Claudia protested. 'It's small enough to have character but big enough to feel luxurious. It's perfect.'

'It's numbing.'

'Numbing?' Claudia choked. 'Honey, you want to talk numbing? I still live with my parents.'

Bronwyn sighed, watching the traffic outside the window but not actually seeing it. 'Yeah . . . in the most magical place on earth.'

Claudia impatiently took another sip of tea. 'Did you hear me? *With. My. Parents.*'

'In a gigantic house, on a huge property,' Bronwyn continued. 'You probably barely even see each other.'

Claudia snorted. 'I wish. Believe me, all of Yallingup isn't big enough for the three of us, not to mention dear brother Chris as well.'

Yallingup.

Bronwyn felt an immediate pang of both envy and longing as her friend named the place she had, for years, considered her private sanctuary. Not that she'd ever told Claudia that. It would have been too much pressure to put on their relationship, especially in the beginning.

Bronwyn dropped her gaze. 'I miss it, that's all.'

'Then come and visit, like you used to. I could use the distraction.'

A mere three hours' drive from Perth, Yallingup was a haven of organic produce, gorgeous beaches and sweet country air. It was no wonder Claudia had grown up with a strong desire to save the planet and everyone on it. It was also a popular holiday destination for many city dwellers. For Bronwyn, however, it represented freedom – a place to escape.

A place to hide.

It had been her alternate reality – a life that Claudia took for granted and that Bronwyn would never have.

'Claud,' she said softly, 'didn't you ever wonder why I was always so keen to come home with you on our uni breaks?'

Claudia grinned. 'Because you're a good friend and you wanted to help out even though you knew my family couldn't afford to pay you.'

'Unfortunately I can't say that's the whole reason.'

Grape-picking in February, working in the cellar door in June – she had loved every minute away from her parents' world. Oak Hills Winery was a family-run business with a family-run flavour. It felt more like home there than any of the mansions her parents had shifted her through during her choppy childhood, which was characterised mostly by their contentious and long-winded divorce. The memories she had of Oak Hills were more meaningful than anything she'd experienced in the city. It had been the best sort of therapy, squished as she was between stressful study and the nagging of ambitious parents. If anyone deserved to be envied, it was Claudia.

'Claudia, you have a family. A real family.'

Claudia's large blue eyes rolled. 'Tell me about it. Can't bloody get away from them.'

'You don't know how lucky you are.'

Claudia had two brothers and two parents who interfered in her life as much as they loved her. Sure, the Franklins had their problems, but they talked about them bluntly or fought like cats and dogs. Bronwyn couldn't imagine speaking her mind to her mother. Ever.

'Believe me, my family takes as much as they give,' Claudia remarked bitterly. 'You know where I would be right now if it weren't for them? Here in the city with you.'

After her graduation and before she had been called back to Oak Hills, Claudia had worked for two years in Perth as a lawyer. She had loved every second of it. Bronwyn remembered whenever they'd caught up for lunch Claudia would be high on the case she was working on. Eager to discuss what hole in the evidence there might be, the missing link in her circle of witnesses or the latest gossip from the bar, when all Bronwyn had wanted to know was what was going on in Yallingup.

Once they started working, neither of them made it back to Oak Hills often. Bronwyn even less so than Claudia. In fact, she was sure she'd only been back a handful of times since becoming a lawyer and that was in the early years. She emailed the family regularly, of course, and often made plans to visit but then always seemed to have to cancel at the last minute. Law was a profession that more or less swallowed your life.

To make her feel even more guilty, just before they graduated there had been an accident in Yallingup and one of Claudia's brothers had become permanently disabled. When Chris Franklin had been sentenced to life in a wheelchair after a stupid prank, it had hit everybody hard. Bronwyn often thought of him and the events leading up to his terrible trauma. Not that Claudia didn't. But she was more positive about it and proud to tell Bronwyn about how Chris was handling it.

'He's amazing, Bron. If it had been me,' she shook her head, 'I'm not so sure I would have bounced back like he has.'

'It's your family,' Bronwyn had reasoned. 'The support and encouragement you've given him.'

Claudia had snorted. 'Everyone except Jack, that is.'

Pain throbbed in the centre of Bronwyn's chest whenever Claudia mentioned her other brother.

The black sheep of the family.

The outcast.

The man who had broken Bronwyn's heart and abandoned them all when it counted the most.

Not that she didn't feel partially responsible for that. It was the one reason she couldn't put her time in Yallingup to bed. She had to know news of Chris's progress, if only to assuage the terrible feeling that it was her fault the two brothers had never fully reconciled and Jack hadn't been home in years.

Two years ago, tragedy had struck the Franklin family again. Horace, Claudia's father, was diagnosed with glaucoma and had to pull back on his workload. With Jack gone and Chris unable to fully take the reins, Claudia had been called home to help out. If she hadn't, Oak Hills most definitely would have gone under.

The problem was, Claudia's return was only supposed to be temporary.

Weeks had turned into months.

Months had turned into years.

Somehow, in it all, Claudia had become stuck.

'It's never going to end, Bron.' Her friend's shoulders slumped now over her tea. 'With Dad retiring completely this year because of his illness, I'm needed more than ever. I don't know what to do. I don't think I'm ever going to be able to leave Oak Hills to practice law again.'

'What about Jack?' Bronwyn was surprised at herself for asking the question. Claudia rarely mentioned him and when she did, it was always with resentment.

'Are you kidding me?' Claudia retorted. 'We haven't seen him in years. And I have no expectations of him doing the right thing anytime soon.'

'You don't hear from him at all?' Bronwyn asked tentatively.

Claudia shrugged. 'The occasional vague email. He contacts Mum sometimes. Probably because she's the only one who doesn't judge him.'

Bronwyn smiled. 'Of course.'

'No, it's just not fair, you know,' Claudia said crossly. 'He gets to go off and tour Europe while I'm stuck juggling the business he was born to run. I don't think I'll ever forgive him for taking off when he did.'

'Jack did love Oak Hills,' Bronwyn whispered.

'Not as much as he hates Dad.'

'I see.' Bronwyn didn't meet her eyes.

'Hey,' Claudia eyed her knowingly, 'what's up with you? You always get like this when we talk about Jack.'

'Like what?' Bronwyn tried to lighten her tone.

'Cagey as hell.'

Bronwyn started. She had forgotten she was speaking to the most skilled cross-examiner on the planet. 'You know, you're right, you really are wasted on that vineyard.'

'And yet you still haven't answered the question.'

'I don't know what you're talking about.' She was never more glad that she had refrained from telling her best friend the full details of the tragic love story of her and Jack Franklin.

Claudia's eyes narrowed shrewdly. 'It wouldn't have anything to do with that kiss you two shared in the gazebo when everybody wasn't looking?'

'Puh-lease.' She tossed her head a little too indignantly. 'That was a big fat nothing.'

'I don't know.' Claudia shrugged. 'You were awfully upset about it at the time.'

'I was nineteen,' Bronwyn scoffed. 'And incredibly idealistic. Ripe for lessons in love.'

Claudia laughed. 'Oh, but now you're all worldly and sophisticated. Nobody could pull the wool over your eyes.'

Bronwyn shoved her shoulder playfully. 'Stop it. That's not nice.'

'I apologise.' Claudia said with a grin. 'The truth is, I'm jealous of your busy love life.'

If she meant that Bronwyn dated a lot and no one ever stuck, she was right on the money.

'I don't know what there is to be jealous of.' Bronwyn rolled her eyes.

'Come on, you're talking to the girl who hasn't been out on a date in months. Don't leave me in suspense when I'm supposed to live vicariously through you. Who's the latest?'

Bronwyn grinned helplessly. She knew Claudia was hopeful of a story involving longing looks and tantalising flirtation. However, the latest – if you could call him that – had been more her mother's choice than hers.

Phillip Bilson.

Son of a judge

Nephew of a QC.

He was a federal court barrister who had been born rich but now earned enough to do without his inheritance. He was good-looking, if you liked slick, pale and well-dressed. Her mother had introduced them at court one day and gently but firmly pushed her in the right direction.

'Darling, if you want to marry well you have to date well, and he's just the sort of feather I want in your cap.'

She was beginning feel that this so-called 'cap' she was wearing was more like a shackle round her ankle.

'So tell me all about him,' Claudia urged.

'He's, er . . . nice.' He had no sense of humour to speak of and was far more interested in himself than her, but perhaps that was just being too fussy. She'd only seen him twice, after all. Maybe she hadn't given him a good enough chance.

'*Nice*?' Claudia repeated, her expression so horrified that Bronwyn felt compelled to add with a slight cough, 'Very nice.'

'Like a hot cup of tea?' Claudia raised her eyebrows.

'No, not hot. More like lukewarm.'

'Okay, girl,' Claudia flattened her palms on the table, 'you know when you said before you hated your life? *Now* I believe you.'

Bronwyn grinned. 'Why? Because I'm not desperately in love?'

'Well, you need to feel something more than lukewarm,' Claudia protested. 'Remember when we were in university and we made a list of things we wanted in our ideal man?'

It was Bronwyn's turn to laugh. 'The Checklist. You still remember that?'

'Hey. It's all I have to keep me warm at night at the moment. You remember the fantasy, right?'

'No,' Bronwyn lied.

'Come on, The Checklist's only got five things on it.' Claudia tapped her chin. 'He has to be one of the boys, a real lad but deep down incredibly romantic; smart, like wickedly intelligent; easygoing; great sense of humour and, of course, chronically good-looking.' She tilted her head with a secret smile. 'I've added blond specifically to that last point, because I do like a man with a fair head.'

'You always have, haven't you?' Bronwyn smiled. Claudia's last three boyfriends had been blond, all lads, smart and funny. 'You definitely have a type,' she nodded seriously. 'I don't know why it's not working for you.'

Claudia sighed. 'Because lads want to be lads. They don't want commitment or a serious relationship. Is it so wrong that I want the whole nine yards?'

'Don't we all,' Bronwyn groaned wistfully. 'But honestly, I don't have much time for falling in love. I don't have much time for anything really.' She worked nearly twelve hours most days and usually all weekend. Her apartment was sparse, not because she couldn't afford to fill it with stuff but because she had no time to shop. Her fridge was empty but her freezer was full of microwave meals. And she was the thinnest she'd ever been due to a lack of food, not exercise.

She couldn't remember the last movie she'd watched.

The last book she'd read.

Or the last walk she'd taken.

The thing with law was, once it got a hook into your life, it started worming its way into every aspect – all in an attempt to be impressive.

Bring in new clients.
You're impressive.
Have no life.
You're impressive.
Stay back later than everyone else.
You're impressive.

The problem with being an Eddings was that you were expected to be more impressive than everyone else. Sometimes, the pressure of living up to the assumption that she was a cut above the rest became too much. In fact, the expectations of her colleagues were occasionally more gruelling than the actual casework itself. If she'd known that this was what her life was going to be like after she left university, she probably would have rebelled earlier.

'Still,' Claudia shrugged, 'I'd trade places with you in a second. Do you know how difficult it is to meet guys when you live with your parents and your father has a shotgun?'

Bronwyn smiled. 'I'd be lucky if my father cared where I was, let alone who I dated.'

'My father knows where I am every second of every day,' Claudia groaned. 'I swear everyone from Yallingup to Margaret River is in on his little spy network. Last week, I went to this little gathering in a bar in Dunsborough, you know, with Phoebe Maxwell and the usual set? I thought maybe if I put myself out there a little more . . .' She sighed.

'Go on.'

'I got all dolled up for it. Wore a dress and everything.'

'A dress!' Bronwyn widened her eyes. 'That's a big statement for you.'

'Damn straight!' Claudia tossed her head, her heavy mane gleaming as it rippled over the shoulders of her plaid shirt. Bronwyn would have bet anything that she had looked absolutely smoking. Claudia didn't have much occasion to dress up as she was constantly working the land but when she did – wow! She turned heads. Bronwyn was almost certain that she'd turned more than a few when she'd walked into that bar in Dunsborough.

She grinned. 'Get some attention, did you?'

Claudia's eyes twinkled. 'Sure, maybe. Then, surprise, surprise, my father walked in right after me and gave everyone the evil eye.'

Bronwyn had seen 'the eye' on Horace Franklin many times before. 'He didn't.'

'Oh, he did,' Claudia nodded. 'And he followed it up with a little announcement.'

'*No!*'

'He said, "Okay, gentlemen, now that I've got your attention and you've seen my daughter walk in, you will notice that *Death* has followed her."'

Bronwyn gasped. 'You're kidding me.'

Claudia glared at Bronwyn. 'Do I look like I'm joking?'

Bronwyn had often been jealous of Claudia's ability to inspire a super-protective streak in Horace Franklin. Who wouldn't want a father who cared? But this sounded a little over the top, even for him. 'That's insane,' she whispered.

'Will you tell him that next time you see him? Because no one else thinks it's worth the mention.'

Bronwyn laughed.

'I just feel like if I could get away from them, I could finally have a life.' Claudia threw up her hands. 'And a career to boot. It's not like I haven't earned it.'

'You have,' Bronwyn agreed.

'I'm just sick of doing –'

'What everybody else wants,' Bronwyn finished for her with a triumphant smile.

'Okay,' Claudia conceded, reaching out and squeezing her hand briefly. 'Maybe I do get where you're coming from.'

'Hallelujah.'

'You should have been a Franklin and I should have been an Eddings.'

Bronwyn grinned. 'That would sure solve a lot of problems.'

'So what are we going to do about this?'

'What can we do? Book in for therapy?'

Claudia grinned. 'Fake our own deaths?'

'Swap places,' Bronwyn joked.

Claudia paused thoughtfully. 'That's actually not a bad idea.'

'If only we were twins.'

'I'd be the evil one,' Claudia said with a wink.

Bronwyn laughed. 'I sure have missed you, Claud. Don't leave it six months till you come visit me again. You don't know how lonely I am out here.'

'Well, you could always visit me, you know. You haven't been to Oak Hills in over two years. What's up with that?'

There were a lot of reasons, none of which she wanted to go into. So instead she said, 'You know they'd make me take work with me. It would ruin the experience for everyone.'

As if on cue, Bronwyn's mobile rang. Frankly, she was inclined to ignore it but Claudia indicated her bag.

'It's okay, go ahead. Answer it. I wouldn't want you to get in trouble for taking a long lunch break.'

She pulled the phone from her bag and lifted it to her ear, immediately regretting taking the call.

It wasn't work. It was her mother, which was actually even worse.

'Good afternoon, Bronwyn. Can you talk?'

'I'm kinda in the middle of lunch.'

'Excellent. How did your meeting go this morning?'

Bronwyn bit her lip, thinking about the dog proposal. 'Not that great actually.'

'Oh good. I also have some wonderful news.'

'Okay.' Bronwyn blinked, not knowing whether to be relieved or insulted that her mother didn't actually care about her answers. 'What is it?'

'My colleague Francis Aldermon had a heart attack last week.'

Bronwyn gasped. 'Mum, that's terrible. Is he all right?'

'Absolutely fine,' Bianca returned airily. 'But the mishap did give me a chance to visit him in hospital and talk to him in a less formal setting.'

Only her mother would find a hospital visit an opportunity to network.

'I was able to direct the conversation in your direction . . .'

You mean, away from the fact that he almost died.

'. . . and he said he would be very pleased to sponsor you to the bar.'

Bronwyn choked. 'But I've had no thoughts about going to the bar. I'm fine where I am.'

Or should I say, less miserable.

'Nonsense. There's no need to play coy with me, Bronwyn. I'm your mother. I know how stressed you must be getting about your situation.'

'I have a situation?'

'Well, we both know that Simon Bantam is not going to promote you for another year, Bronwyn. I went to uni with the man, he's a stickler for the trenches. He'll keep you there as long as he can, particularly because you're such a good little worker. Why not move across to the bar where all the movers and the shakers are? Including,' she gave a slight titter, 'myself.'

'I don't know, Mum.'

Her mother–daughter relationship with Bianca Hanks was not good at the best of times. She couldn't imagine working near her as well. Best not to tempt fate.

'I'm happy where I am.'

'Happiness, Bronwyn, is a commodity you know nothing about.'

Okay, you caught me.

'When I was your age,' her mother continued, 'I thought I was happy too. That's why I married your father. Look what that got me.'

A child neither of you wanted?

'A very expensive divorce,' her mother rattled off.

Bronwyn's brow wrinkled. She knew that to speak her mind here would be a mistake. 'Mum, can I talk about this with you later?'

'All right,' said Bianca briskly, 'we can park that opportunity for a minute and talk about the family firm.'

Bronwyn opened her mouth and then shut it again. 'Huh?'

'Hanks and Eddings. Your Uncle Cyril is always looking for good junior lawyers and I hear he's short at the moment. It might be a good opportunity to take your rightful place.'

'Mum, I haven't worked at the family firm for a reason.'

'Yes, yes, to avoid the stigma of nepotism,' her mother offered valiantly, like a trainer throwing fish to a seal. 'To prove yourself on your own terms.'

Actually, that wasn't the reason.

'Well, you are an Eddings. And if you're not going to the bar, then I think it's time you explored your birthright.'

As though I was ever allowed not to.

'Then you can really spread your wings and soar.'

Or cut my tail feathers and crash.

'Why don't I call your uncle and get an interview time for you next week?'

'Mum, don't –'

'It's no trouble.'

'Mum!' Bronwyn cried, almost with relief, 'I have to go. I have another call coming through.'

She actually wasn't lying about that. Before her mother could reply she hung up on her, mouthing 'Sorry' to Claudia. Claudia dismissed her apology with a swat of her hand and a broad smile. Clearly, she was relishing eavesdropping far more than Bronwyn was enjoying active participation.

'Hello?'

'Bronwyn!' An abrasive voice barked down the line.

It was Simon, the stickler for the trenches. If she wasn't so surprised by his tone she might have laughed, because he did sound like he was standing in the middle of a war zone. Was that a crash in the background or the thump of a rolling head? Did his secretary Lulu just scream?

'Sir, are you okay?'

'Where the hell are you?' he demanded, the volume making her pull the phone slightly from her ear.

'Just finishing lunch, sir.'

'Then get back to the office right now! We have a situation here.' With orders given, the phone went dead.

Great.

'What the matter?' Claudia asked.

'Everything, by the sound of it.' Bronwyn stood up. 'I'm going to have to cut lunch short.'

'No worries.' Claudia stood up too. 'We can talk tonight or tomorrow.'

'I assume you're staying at my place as usual.'

'Is that all right?'

'Of course.' Bronwyn tutted. She reached into her bag and removed a gold key from her car keys. 'Here, take this. You'll probably get there before I do.'

Claudia's eyes lit up. 'Thanks! I'll see you tonight. Dinner's on me.'

'Perfect, cause there's absolutely nothing in the fridge.'

Bronwyn hurried out of the restaurant and up St Georges Terrace. It was a gorgeous day, blue skies with only the gentlest breeze. The sunlight winked off the windows of office towers and cars creeping past in the busy lunch-hour traffic. Luckily, her firm was not far away. All the same, she hitched her shoulder bag higher and increased the pace, her black shiny heels clicking like a train on the pavement. After walking one block she flew into the lobby of Bantam, Harvey and Grey, nearly bowling over the janitor as he was carrying out one of the bins.

'Sorry, Henry.'

'No worries, Bron. Simon losing his shit again?'

'Hope not.' She jabbed quickly at the elevator button. 'But I wouldn't place any bets on it.' The doors opened and she scuttled inside.

She watched Henry laugh as the doors slowly shut. Seriously, if she had to name one friend she worked with in this building, it would be him. The rest of them were all sharks.

The ride to the eighth floor seemed interminable. But pandemonium erupted as soon as the lift doors opened, along with some very loud, very raucous barking. There was a dog in reception – a large, angry bullmastiff with a squashed black snout and big sunken eyes surrounded by black fur. The rest of its body was that beautiful tawny brown, glossy and silken. Not that this was the sort of dog you would want to pat. In fact, Bronwyn started to move back into the lift.

'Don't you dare!' A woman, as angry as the dog on her leash, slammed a palm on the lift buttons, causing the silver doors of freedom to glide shut. 'Are you Bronwyn Eddings?'

'Y-yes.'

'At last!' She released the leash, allowing the dog to charge upon Bronwyn, who gave a startled yelp of terror. She backed away only enough to land on the waiting area couch when the bullmastiff leaped upon her person and pinned her there. Its front paws rested on her shoulders, its doggy breath on her face.

'Meet your new dog.' The woman's satisfied voice came from her left as she sat frozen in fear. 'Her name is Elsa.'

Chapter 2

A meeting with Bronwyn Eddings always left Claudia with mixed emotions, which was probably why she'd been such a terrible friend to her this last year. *Honestly, you're just as bad as Jack!*

She loved her friend. Bronwyn was one of the kindest, sweetest people on the planet. She didn't have one wicked bone in her body, but catching up with her always made Claudia feel just a little less.

A little less successful.

A little less rich.

A little less connected.

And even a little less pretty.

Bronwyn was so pristinely perfect in a Nicole Kidman kind of way. Her skin was like porcelain. It just glowed with an apricot radiance that was only enhanced by her blonde hair. It was pure gold uncompromised by any streaks or inconsistencies of tint that usually characterised the colour.

By contrast, Claudia's hair was fifty shades of brown and not in a sexy way. More like it couldn't make up its mind what it wanted to be, which was almost a metaphor for her life really. Tall and thin, if Bronwyn ever wanted to give up law, she'd definitely have a career in modelling. Whereas Claudia was always trying to make up for her shortness by being extra feisty. Not that it had helped so far.

She was still running a business that was on its last legs.

Money was tight.

Work was tough.

And life . . . life was a truckload of crap she never wanted to do.

She kept telling herself if she could just pull Oak Hills out of the river and keep it on dry land for a while then maybe she could entrust the running of the place to someone else and move the hell on.

The problem with Oak Hills was that it had lost its reputation. And with wine, ratings were everything.

Who wanted to buy into a drop that had sadly seen better days? When her father had started to lose his eyesight, she had thought assuming the throne would be short term. However, it looked like for every disaster she managed to steer them around, another would crop up in its place, making it even harder for her to leave.

The latest, of course, was her father's retirement. She could hardly blame him. There was no way he could continue on as their winemaker if he was struggling to see. The new guy they'd hired hadn't done them or their clients any favours either. It had been the first time in two generations that someone who was not a Franklin was allowed to take the helm. Her father had descended into a depression no one had yet been able to pull him out of.

Claudia bit her lip.

She loved the man. She really did. And she hated seeing his life's work slowly withering away, but was it really her job to keep his dream alive at the expense of her own?

Damn you, Jack!

She wouldn't be in this mess if it weren't for her brother's negligence. However, there was no use crying over spilt milk. She was in Perth to give a presentation at the Oceanic Hotel in the centre of town. Oak Hills was now targeting mid-level restaurants rather than the upmarket ones. She was hoping that branching into this new area of business might compensate for the clients they had lost. Fingers crossed, she could secure some contracts to supply the 'house wine'. This was trading down on past reputation, but what other choice did they have? She had invited maître d's, front of house managers and sommeliers from all over town to attend her free presentation, involving tastings and gorgeous slides depicting images of Oak Hills vineyard and winery taken four years ago.

She felt like a fraud taking them through pictures that no longer portrayed current conditions. But how else was Oak Hills supposed to get their wine back out there and start making money again?

We need customers.

At the end of the presentation, she handed out samples from their best vintage. Cabernet Merlot 2011. Her father's pride and joy. He hadn't done it that good since. There were nods all round and she scored a few orders that would keep them ticking over for the next vintage at least.

Saved the day again, Claud.

Maybe if she just stopped trying so hard she wouldn't have this problem year after year. She immediately dismissed the defeatist thoughts.

If Mum and Dad lose Oak Hills, it'll kill them.

And the guilt will haunt you forever.

After all the chefs and restaurant owners had left the function room she packed up her things, taking her last three bottles of wine, one half-empty, into the Oceanic main restaurant and bar, Seashells.

'Hey,' she said to the girl behind the front desk, 'is Rinaldo about?'

Rinaldo was a friend of the family. He had worked at Oak Hills in his late twenties as their cellar-door manager. After he'd married and had two children he'd moved to the city for more pay as bar manager at Seashells. In a way, it had been a blessing for them, because he always ordered Oak Hills wine for their bar and he managed to get them thirty per cent off the Oceanic function room where Claudia liked to hold their presentations. In the financial situation her family was in, every saving counted.

'I'm sorry,' the girl behind the counter said, 'I think he's in a meeting with the hotel manager. Did you want to leave a message?'

Claudia held up the bottles. 'I just had a few freebies for him and his family as a thank you.' She smiled.

The girl nodded just as an almighty crash sounded in the kitchens behind her. She glanced worriedly over her shoulder.

'Look,' Claudia suggested, 'how about I just put this behind the bar and you go deal with that. I'll leave him a note.'

'Thanks,' the girl said gratefully and scurried off.

Claudia made her way across the room towards the bar, noticing that there were only two men sitting there. She knew straight away they were lawyers by the tailored cut of their suits, the square black document bags at their feet and the telltale yellow notepads sitting beside empty glasses.

A little recess in between court appointments, perhaps? She smiled wistfully.

Why is everyone having fun but me?

As she walked behind the bar holding the wine, one of them lifted his finger at her, clearly calling her over.

He thinks I work here.

He was a severely handsome man. Severe because his features were so well defined they were unforgettable. Dark black hair, dark brown eyes, an expressive, sensuous mouth and high cheekbones. His shoulders were broad and square, the perfect shape for the suit he was wearing, which was cut so perfectly to his impressive form that it creased in all the right places. She pegged him at late thirties in age. His colleague, clearly the younger and less confident of the two, also wore a tailored suit, just not as well. And it was pinstriped instead of black.

An unfortunate choice, Claudia noted absent-mindedly. *Trying much too hard.*

Then again, he couldn't be that much older than her. Maybe a couple of years younger, even. His weak chin wobbled too eagerly, his fingers fidgeted with the pen on top of his yellow pad as though waiting for the next axe to fall. His jacket was off and on the back of his stool, and there were sweat patches at his armpits.

His companion, however, lounged beside him, cool as a cucumber. 'Excuse me, miss,' the older man said, as she was about to walk past them. 'We need a top-up.'

Not one to ever miss an opportunity to market her wine, Claudia decided that this was a chance to make another impression and prevent her open half-bottle from going to waste.

'I'll do you one better,' she said with a smile, taking two fresh wine glasses off the rack and placing them on the counter in front of the men.

'Oak Hills's best vintage. Cabernet Merlot 2011, classic dark fruit tones with a hint of vanilla, spice and nougat.' She poured them each a glass slowly so that they would enjoy the tinkling sound of the wine and appreciate the aroma of mulberries and cedar that immediately filled the air around them. She leaned in. 'Best served with grilled pork, pistachios and green pepper sauce.'

The lawyer in the black suit raised an eyebrow and said in a baritone that was both low and silky, 'We were drinking whisky.'

Claudia winked at him. 'Oh, you'll like this much better and, don't worry, it's on me. No charge.' She waved her hand airily. 'You'll be back for more, trust me.'

She pushed the drinks towards them and walked through the open staff door behind the counter. There was a large storeroom here full of bottles, glasses, cutlery, napkins and other supplies. There was an office in one corner that belonged to Rinaldo. She went in there, left the other two bottles on his desk, scribbling a quick note to leave with them.

Thanks for everything. Hope to catch you next time. C xo

As she came out of Rinaldo's office and walked back to the door she'd come in, she heard a bark of laughter.

'I can't believe she just came on to you like that, Seb. Out of nowhere.'

The silky voice she recognised from before replied, 'How do you know she wasn't coming on to you?'

'Women never buy me drinks.'

'Give it a couple of years.'

She stopped walking, and slowly backed up against the shelves so she was out of view of the doorway and the two men, who were clearly talking about her.

'A couple of years? What do you mean?'

The older lawyer seemed amused. 'I'm going to let you in on a little secret, Nelson, that will ensure your success in any bar of your choice. *Women want to marry lawyers.* The only man, in fact, more desirable than a lawyer is a surgeon.'

'But –'

'I know,' his tone seemed quite disappointed in the female sex, 'it seems to be a useless ambition given both professions work such long hours. If they do indeed manage to pull off this amazing feat they spend the rest of their lives trying to entice their husbands away from their work.'

'So what you're saying, Seb, is that I should pretend I want to get married,' Nelson asked carefully.

Seb chuckled. 'There's no need for you to state your intentions true or otherwise, my friend. Take that waitress who just bought us both drinks, for example. I saw her walk in.'

'You did?'

'Immediately. She glanced first at our bags and then at our notepads. I saw her smile.'

Claudia covered her mouth.

'So, she knew we were lawyers?' Nelson seemed stunned at the predatory fashion in which he had been hunted.

'Of course.' Seb's tone was bland. 'What she didn't know was that I had her number too.'

'You did?'

'Nelson,' Seb seemed disappointed by his lack of faith, 'we are trained profilers and that witness was very easy to read.'

'She was? I mean, of course she was.'

'The white shirt, a little grey from over-washing, buttons not done up high enough to be modest . . .'

Claudia grasped her shirt at her chest, noticing for the first time that an extra one had indeed come undone.

Damn it!

She did it up.

'She's fallen on hard times. That thin gold chain with a diamond pendant so small it might be a grain of sand indicates she has a taste for jewellery but she just can't afford it.'

Claudia fondled the chain around her neck. *My parents gave me that for my sixteenth birthday!*

'She's working in a bar, so clearly left high school when she was sixteen. Probably lives with friends in a unit housing three or more people. She's down on her rent so she's looking for a benefactor. And we both know what she's offering.'

Claudia gasped.

'Are you saying one of us should take her up on her offer?' Nelson asked nervously.

'Are you calling dibs?' Seb was faintly amused.

Okay, this has gone on long enough!

Claudia stepped away from the shelves and walked back through the open door, her face wreathed in a fake smile that was perhaps a little too bright.

'So, gentleman, did you enjoy my cabernet merlot?'

Nelson reddened, clearly worried that she might have heard what they were talking about. Seb, however, appeared completely unfazed by her sudden reappearance. His lip curled slightly as his thumb and forefinger played with the stem of his glass.

'Delicious.'

'Thank you.' She tossed her head. 'I'll be sure to tell the winemaker that he's doing a marvellous job, next time I'm on my estate down south.' She knew she sounded completely snooty but just couldn't help herself.

Nelson cleared his throat nervously. 'You own a winery down south?'

'My family does. But for me it's really just a hobby on the side.'

'Is that so?' Seb's lips curled even more.

'Yes.' Claudia glared at him. 'When I finished high school I went to law school. Graduated top of my class.'

'Really?'

'And I supposed you passed the bar exam too?'

'With flying colours,' she shot at him.

'Let me guess,' Seb smirked, 'you found law too boring to practise so you went home to play.'

She lifted her chin. 'It's more complicated than that.'

'Why? Because now you're back in town to work at a bar. Just not the one you qualified for.' He polished off his wine. 'A plausible story.'

'Oh, I don't work here.' She shook her head. 'I just came to visit a friend.'

Seb stood up, dropping a fifty-dollar note on the counter. 'Sweetheart, just keep the change.'

Claudia saw red. A vein near her temple began to throb as Nelson stood up quickly too, grabbing both document bags from the ground.

'You really think you're a good judge of character, don't you?' she said quietly.

'My attention to detail has often been remarked upon,' Sebastian admitted without modesty.

'So has mine.' Claudia's eyes narrowed, indicating his person with flick of her hand. 'The tailored suit, a little too expensive for the B-grade executive because you've had it specially made to show you're a cut above the rest. You need that because you've got no friends to tell you so, no free time to spend with them even if you did. And why black? It's the colour of your soul and your complete and utter loss of faith in humanity.'

She did gain a lot of satisfaction at the way his eyes rounded as each of her little darts found home. There was a pause, but he wasn't done.

'Ah,' he returned in a patronising tone, 'don't try and play games that are above your grade.'

She knew in that moment that her temper was about to get the better of her and she was going to do something rash.

But to hell with it.

She was mad enough to spit fire.

'What did you say your name was again?'

'I didn't.' He looked back over his broad shoulder as he began to walk away. 'You are unlikely to need it, given we move in completely different circles.'

And that's when that rash action she had dreaded took hold.

'You're completely right, of course. I doubt my Uncle Cyril or Uncle Robert would ever have heard of you.'

At these words, Seb stopped and turned back.

That's it, prick. Take a second look.

At this stage, she was feeling not in the least bit guilty about borrowing Bronwyn's family for a couple of seconds. In fact, she was sure her best friend would approve.

'The Eddingses?' Sebastian raised an eyebrow.

'That's right,' Claudia lifted her chin. Somebody needed to take this guy down a notch.

'You really have no shame, do you?'

Claudia drew in a sharp breath as Seb and Nelson walked out. She thumped her forehead with her fist.

Seriously, girl, your uncles?

She shut her eyes as hot embarrassment streaked through her. It was no wonder he didn't believe her. She'd gone too far.

Lying about being an Eddings!

Dumbarse.

Chapter 3

It was a scene from a nightmare. Bronwyn was pinned down by a ferocious beast, unable to run or scream. Fear paralysed her. She was only able to turn her head away as the dog barked loudly in her face. Just when she thought it was going to rip her head off, it stopped and licked her face from chin to hairline.

Oh, grooosss!!!

The real owner of the dog, who reminded her very much of a lion tamer in her tight back leggings and red jacket, walked over to the side of the couch.

'You're lucky. She likes you.'

Bronwyn eyes boggled at the woman as she pushed on the chest of the dog, which did not budge. 'Help me.'

'I can't believe how young you are,' the woman continued contemptuously. 'Though in hindsight I should have expected it. What are you? Twenty-five, twenty-six?'

She was twenty-seven actually.

Bronwyn gasped as the dog began to bark at her again. 'Please, can you get your dog off me?'

'Oh no, honey,' the woman smirked, 'it's not my dog.'

Mercifully, however, she grabbed the dog by the collar and pulled it from Bronwyn's lap. It bounded onto the floor. She was a rather impressive creature, standing nearly a metre in height with a very muscular chest. Bronwyn scrabbled off the couch, putting the coffee table between her and the over-eager canine. She tried to wipe the doggy spit off her face with the sleeve of her shirt . . . but she could still smell rotting meat.

'Who are you?' she demanded breathlessly of its owner.

'Peter Goldman's wife. Well,' the woman shrugged in correction, 'ex-wife, you'll be pleased to know. I can see exactly what he sees in you.'

Bronwyn wrung her trembling hands as Mrs Goldman gave her the once over, as though she were a stripper in a gentleman's club. Was this mad woman implying that she was having a relationship with her husband?

'Mrs Goldman –'

'Call me Freya.' The woman flicked her hand as her dog loped off to stick its head in a wastepaper basket behind the reception desk, rattling it around and knocking it against the desk. Several papers were scattered on the floor along with thousands of little white dots from a haphazardly emptied hole punch. It looked like Jenny, the receptionist, had retreated from her post.

'To be honest, I didn't think you were really out at lunch,' Freya went on to say conversationally. 'I thought you were hiding behind there with the rest of them.' She jerked a thumb over her shoulder. 'But they refused to let me and Elsa through to check your office.'

Bronwyn didn't blame them. She glanced across the room, which was divided in half by a glass wall. In front was the vandalised reception desk, behind were the offices. Sure enough, there was Jenny and a few other wide-eyed staff members barricaded behind the glass doors, which were locked with a chair back inserted under the handles. They were all watching her. There were cracks around the door handle as though someone had been rattling it . . . or pushing hard.

Her eyes swung back to the lion tamer.

'What have you been doing?'

'I needed to see you, so sue me,' Freya said and then laughed vulgarly at her own joke. 'You probably will, won't you?'

Bronwyn coughed. 'It seems likely.'

She looked at her colleagues, who continued to watch from the safety of their glass enclosure. Were none of them going to help her? Had the police been called to deal with this invasion? Or were they all just waiting around to serve her up as their peace offering? She must have been staring at that door too long because Freya felt the need to comment.

'It's just a door, and it's not like you don't owe me for messing up my husband's case and my marriage as well.'

'I didn't mess up either.'

'Honey, I know my husband screws around.'

'Good for you,' she retorted. 'Now go get the rest of your information before accusing other people falsely.'

Freya's eyes narrowed. 'Maybe you're not as dumb as you look, but you still messed up our lives.'

'I hate to break it to you, Freya,' Bronwyn said coldly, 'but Peter Goldman did that all on his own.'

'Lovely,' Freya's face twisted cruelly. 'I'm almost happy he wants you to have Elsa.'

Bronwyn's eyes swung sharply back to the dog, which lifted its head from the bin and barked at her again as though in acknowledgement.

There was no way in hell she was taking that dog!

All things considered, Claudia was absolutely right. She never should have agreed to think about anything.

'Please remove the dog from our premises and tell Peter that I have come to the conclusion that –'

Freya seemed to read her expression correctly and interrupted with sugary satisfaction, 'I don't care what conclusions you've come to. I'm not keeping her. I've got a plane to catch in a few hours and Peter promised me I would not be left with any remnants of his life.'

Freya walked over to the lifts again and pushed the button.

'You can't just leave that dog here,' Bronwyn gasped.

'Peter said you would look after her.'

'I didn't agree to that.'

The lift doors opened and Freya stepped in. 'Frankly, it makes no difference to me what went on between the two of you. Take it up with Peter. I don't have time for this.'

Bronwyn raced over to stop the doors from closing but got there too late. She jabbed frantically at the buttons but could only watch in horror as the lift lights showed Freya had well and truly escaped.

Shit and biscuits!

The dog began to bark loudly behind her again. She spun around with a hand to her temple. What the hell was she supposed to do now?

As if in answer, someone thumped loudly on the glass doors across the room to get her attention. Some assistance maybe? She glanced their way.

It was Simon.

And he was furious.

'Bronwyn,' he shook his finger at her, 'get that dog out of here!'

'But –'

As she was talking, Elsa bounded to the glass where Simon was standing, jumped up on her hind legs and pushed on the handles, rattling the door. Simon took a step back but continued to glare at Bronwyn.

'You brought this problem into the firm,' he said harshly. 'Now you remove it!'

The hairs on the back of her neck stood on end. 'But what do I do with it? I don't know anything about dogs.'

What if she bites me?

The dog didn't appear to be vicious but nor was it sedate or quiet either.

'Check it into a kennel and then go see your client and sort this shit out!' Simon threw back at her.

'But –'

'Bronwyn, I want that mutt out of my office right now! We will discuss your situation later.'

My situation? Why does everyone keep saying I have a situation?

He turned and walked away from the glass wall, becoming absorbed back into the safe confines of the firm. The other staff continued to glare at her and the dog through the glass.

He didn't honestly think she was having an affair with Peter Goldman, did he? Or perhaps he thought she'd agreed to accept the dog. You would think her colleagues would at least have had a kennel address ready for her. If they couldn't bother helping her that much, she wasn't going to worry about what further damage Elsa did to their workspace while she googled 'kennels'. They had literally left her to the dogs.

Unfortunately, at this point Elsa lost interest in the glass doors and came bounding back across the room, her leash trailing behind her. This dog was strong enough to crack glass, so Bronwyn knew one of her femurs wasn't going to faze Elsa. She quickly scooted behind the armchair on the opposite side of the coffee table, having no desire to be pinned down again. Glancing around for her handbag, she saw it discarded on the couch. Elsa tilted her head curiously at Bronwyn, as though amused at the defensive stance she'd taken.

'Is there any way you'll come with me quietly?' Bronwyn asked.

Elsa gave a mocking bark and trotted back to her new favourite toy – Jenny's wastepaper basket. Bronwyn used the chance to pull her phone out of her handbag. She went to work locating several kennels not too far from the city, some of better repute than others. Finally she settled on her choice. It was only just in time. Elsa came loping back towards her again.

'Okay, Elsa,' Bronwyn tried to keep her tone soothing, 'perhaps we can negotiate an agreement. I'll buy you some doggie biscuits if you let me take your leash.'

Elsa whined, sat down and happily began to thump her tail loudly on the carpet.

Bronwyn swallowed and ran sweaty palms down the front of her jacket. 'That's more like it.'

Slowly, she inched her way around the armchair and then around Elsa so she was standing looking at her lead curled on the floor behind her tail. She snuck forward, reaching carefully. Her fingers were just about to grasp the leather strap when Elsa jumped up and spun around, barking loudly in protest.

Bronwyn flew back, her bum hitting Jenny's desk.

'That's not fair! I would have given you those dog biscuits.'

Elsa ignored her and walked over to the coffee table. She stuck her head underneath it and pulled out a stray cushion, which must have fallen there. With a growl, she began to shake it vigorously, a long glob of drool hanging low from her chin. The cushion flopped around, hitting her on the side of the head. Funnily enough, she appeared to enjoy that. Bronwyn bit back a grin.

If only my clients were this easy to placate.

Slowly, she inched her way forward again and finally managed to get close enough to stoop and pick up Elsa's lead.

'Got you.'

Elsa immediately dropped the cushion and raced towards the lifts, nearly causing Bronwyn's arm to pop from its socket. 'W-whoa!'

At least Elsa was going in the right direction. She jabbed at the lift button while Elsa ran in circles, winding the leash around her body, causing her to almost topple over.

'Elsa! No!'

She didn't dare contemplate how they were going to fare in the street, especially in her three-inch black heels.

Carefully, she unwound herself and then pushed the lift buttons again. The doors swung open almost immediately.

'Excellent.' She had her car parked in a bay under the building. It was only a matter of minutes before she'd have this dog inside and strapped down. The ride to the basement was fine, but she shouldn't have counted her chickens on the rest. Once out of the lift, Elsa seemed to want to walk in any direction but the way in which she was required to go. They did a couple of laps of the car park before they circled back to her car.

Her feet were already killing her.

She managed to put a seatbelt on Elsa and hoped this would keep her from jumping into the front seat while Bronwyn was driving. Somewhere between the city and the dog kennel, Elsa freed herself from confinement and jumped into the front passenger seat. Thankfully she seemed content to sit there for the rest of the ride to Doggy Haven.

When they got out of the car, however, Elsa was keen to run off into the surrounding parkland. Perhaps it was a mistake on Bronwyn's part not to let her do so. If she had, Elsa might not have released her bowels on the floor of Doggy Haven's reception.

'Er . . . excuse me,' the woman behind the counter said before Bronwyn could even ask for any forms. 'What the hell is your dog doing?'

'She's, er . . .' Bronwyn spun around. '*Elsa!* Oh crap.'

As she named it, the turd detached itself cleanly from Elsa's butt and dropped onto the tiled floor. 'Do you have a bag or a paper towel?'

With pursed lips the woman behind the counter handed her a small shovel that was hanging on the wall.

'Is your dog toilet-trained?'

'I assume so.'

'What do you mean, you assume?'

'Well, the dog isn't mine.'

'So you're a dog-sitter.'

'Sort of. Not really.' She tried to smile, hoping for some understanding but finding none in the face of stone regarding her. 'I – I'm more of a middle man.'

The woman behind the counter began to look very wary.

'So do you know whether this dog has been vaccinated or treated for fleas?'

Bronwyn hedged. 'Is that a standard thing? Because if it is then probably. I mean, this dog is from a good home.'

'So why can't the owner take care of her right now?'

'Um, does it matter?'

'Try me.'

'He's in jail. When I said good home, I meant expensive decor.'

'I see.' The woman was now looking very stern. 'So the likelihood of the owner coming back for the dog at a later stage and paying his account isn't very high.'

'Well,' Bronwyn put on her most professional voice, 'the owner is very attached to his dog and I'm estimating that he won't get more than a three-year sentence.' The woman lowered her chin to look at Bronwyn over the top of her glasses.

'All right,' Bronwyn winced, 'four years tops. I'm his lawyer, you see. So of course, I'm aiming for the best possible outcome but I can only work with what I have. In the meantime, I could put up a reasonable deposit for the dog's stay here. Would that help? Please, I'm desperate.'

Apparently, desperation wasn't a factor that strengthened her argument. Doggy Haven did not take dogs from sitters, only from owners. Nor did they take dogs that hadn't been treated for fleas, vaccinated or toilet-trained. Five minutes later, Elsa was in the front seat of Bronwyn's car again, on her way to Paradise Paws.

As it turned out, kennel managers were almost as difficult to negotiate with as high court judges. She spent the remainder of the afternoon driving all over town.

The man at Paradise Paws said, 'We require all Elsa's vaccination documentation before we will accept her.'

The granny at Kennels for Kings said, 'We don't take aggressive dogs.'

'But she's not aggressive,' Bronwyn protested as Elsa barked at the other dogs, all of which cowered in one corner of an outdoor play pen.

'There's a vicious looking scar on her back,' remarked the administrator. 'Explain that to me.'

To be honest, Bronwyn had not had the time to notice it, but now that it had been brought to her attention she tried to block it from view at Pet Play House and Hound Hotel. It was to no avail.

'We don't take pitbulls, mastiffs, or staffies.' The teenager with dark-purple painted nails that matched the streak in her hair drummed her fingers on the counter. 'Or any breeds known for their aggression. They just put too much wear and tear on the premises. And we aren't willing to risk the liability.'

Surprisingly, Elsa was best behaved when riding in the car. Happy to gaze quietly out the window at the blur of passing buildings with her tongue lolling.

'Why can't you be like this when we go inside?' Bronwyn demanded.

Elsa whined slightly and scratched her ear.

'You know, it's for your own good. If we don't get you into a place soon I don't know where you're going to sleep tonight.'

Elsa barked, her tail thumping against the seat.

'Not at my place,' Bronwyn said sternly. 'I live in very nice apartment in Subiaco. No pets allowed.'

Elsa seemed pleased with this and the tail only thumped harder.

Finally, about five o'clock that afternoon, Bronwyn found Canine Comfort. It was a large property, further out of the city than all the rest. Situated, in fact, in the outer coastal area of Yanchep, a suburb home to one of Perth's national parks. She had to drive over an hour to get there but figured it was probably worth it. If ever there was a perfect spot for a dog kennel, this was it. She just hoped the patrons might be more 'relaxed' than the others she had tried.

Across the road was a large park, which Elsa tried to run off to the second she bounded out of the car. Luckily, Bronwyn was now getting quite used to her spontaneity and had managed to wrap the leash twice around her wrist before it pulled taut.

'Nice try,' she smirked triumphantly and pulled Elsa towards the doors of Canine Comfort, chanting all the way, *Please don't turn me away. Please don't turn me away.*

By now at least she had a bit of system going and some good lawyer spiel to increase her credibility up front. Before the girl at the counter could even greet her, she opened her argument.

'Hi, my name is Bronwyn Eddings. I'm a lawyer from Bantam, Harvey and Grey and I'm here on behalf of my client. How are you?'

The young girl behind the counter removed the lollipop from her mouth and sat up straighter. 'Er . . . good.'

Bronwyn passed her card swiftly across the counter and as the girl picked it up, she continued talking. 'This is his dog, for which we require a temporary holding. Unfortunately, I do not have Elsa's vaccination or flea treatment papers on my person but if you give me your email or fax number I can have those directed to you within twenty-four hours. How does that sound?'

'Er . . . good.' The young girl nodded slowly.

Bronwyn curbed the urge to dance on the spot before saying, with a complete lack of emotion, 'Fantastic. Do you have some consent forms I can complete for you?'

'Sure.'

The girl pulled these from a pigeon hole. While Bronwyn was filling them out, she walked around the counter so that she could look at Elsa.

'She's a mastiff,' she observed.

'A very placid one,' Bronwyn hastily added, relieved to note that lightning did not strike her dead as the white lie tripped easily off her tongue. 'Most of the time.' At least for once Elsa was sitting calmly at her feet, panting happily.

'Hey, girl.' The teenager got down to Elsa's level and rubbed a hand over her glossy coat. 'Aren't you good-looking.'

'Yes, she is,' Bronwyn added for good measure. 'Very well groomed by her owner. I'm sure she'll be no trouble to you at all.'

'How long will you leave her here for?'

'A few months, maybe more. Where do I sign?'

The girl, whose hand had slowed over the side of Elsa's belly, frowned. 'Actually, nowhere. I don't think you should.' She stood up.

Bronwyn froze. 'Huh?'

'We won't be taking her today.'

'*What?* Why?' Bronwyn cried. 'She's been so well behaved and not in the least bit aggressive.'

'Yes, poor thing,' the girl nodded. 'Being a bullmastiff she must get lumped with that stereotype a lot. But that's not why I'm passing.'

'Then why? I don't understand. Haven't I considered all of your requirements? Vaccination? Fleas? Grooming? Behaviour? There can't possibly be something else you object to.'

The girl shrugged. 'She's pregnant.'

'*She's what?*'

'Pregnant. And pretty far along from the look of things.'

'No, that can't be right. She doesn't look that fat.'

'Her nipples are quite prominent. I wouldn't think she's more than a few weeks away from popping, if that.'

'Seriously?'

'I'm sorry, but we can't deliver puppies here, we don't have the liability insurance for it.' She glanced meaningfully at the card on the counter.

Bronwyn glared at Elsa, who put her head down between her paws as though to stave off the lecture. 'What did you do?'

Elsa made a slight whiny noise.

'Does your father know about this?'

Elsa barked.

'How could you do this to me? How could you do this to *us*? This place was the last kennel on my list within driving distance. What am I supposed to do now?'

'Er . . .' the young girl interrupted, 'could you take her back to your client?'

'I would,' Bronwyn retorted, 'only the bastard's in jail, isn't he?'

'Oh,' the girl smiled uncertainly. 'So did you want your card back then?'

'*Damn it!*' She tugged on the lead. 'Never mind. Come on, Elsa.' She stomped all the way back to her car. 'I've just wasted five hours of my life on a wild goose chase.'

She lifted her keys to remotely unlock her car when Elsa happened to notice the park across the road again. She barked ferociously and then tore off in this direction, pulling Bronwyn across the bitumen with her. When they were off the road, Bronwyn had the good sense to simply let go of the leash. As Elsa ran to the far end of the park, she dropped her hands to her knees to catch her breath. Her feet were two lumps of pure agony. She reached down and yanked off her high heels, throwing the shoes away from her. Sighing with relief, she hobbled over to the kids' play equipment and sat down on the swing. Elsa did laps of the surrounds, stopping to sniff the ground at intervals.

Bronwyn was sure if she looked at her phone there would be at least a dozen missed calls from Simon. No doubt he expected her back at the office by now, dog-free and ready to explain herself. Instead, she was still here with Elsa, with red blistered feet and the unwelcome discovery that yet another person had managed to take advantage of her.

As if refusing to be ignored, her phone buzzed in her handbag. *Great.*

She supposed she couldn't avoid him forever. Fishing the phone out, she closed her eyes and said, 'Hello?'

'Bronwyn, what's your status? I need you on the Hayman case. You should have been back hours ago.'

What, no 'How are you, Bronwyn? Do you still have all your fingers or did that dog take one?'

Frown lines appeared at the bridge of her nose and the first pin of rebellion stuck in her spine. 'My status is busy. I still have Peter Goldman's dog with me.'

'Why?'

'Because no kennel will take her. She's pregnant.'

Simon groaned. 'For fuck's sake, take the dog to the pound.'

'But they'll put her down if they can't give her away.'

Pregnant and aggressive. Bronwyn did not like Elsa's chances.

'That's not our problem. That dog is a fuckin' imposition. Not to mention the damage to our property, which I fully intend to add to Peter Goldman's bill. Get rid of that dog, Bronwyn, and get back here now. We can't waste any more of your time on this.'

'No.'

There was a heady pause in which she felt all her senses go on high alert. The sound of the crickets in the grass grew louder, her upper lip moistened. She licked it, tasting her own sweat as she waited. Claudia was right. There was the perfect answer to all her problems.

'*What did you say?*'

'I said . . . er . . . No, sir.'

'And what exactly do you intend to do instead?'

Bronwyn licked her lips again. 'I'm going to keep the dog, sir. And I need a little bit of time this afternoon to sort that out.'

Simon laughed. A laugh that was neither humorous nor warm. 'Perhaps you'd like to take tomorrow off too to buy it a dog bowl and blanket?'

'Actually, that would be perfect.'

'Bronwyn!' he barked. 'I don't care if you are an Eddings or not. I will have no hesitation in firing you if you do not get back to your desk immediately.'

Her heart sank. 'Oh.'

'The truth is, despite your very impressive pedigree, you lack the qualities I admire the most in your mother and father.'

Bronwyn's slumped shoulders lifted. 'Really? I do?'

'Definitely. While you are competent, I expected so much more grit in the daughter of Bianca Hanks.'

'Of course you did.'

'In fact, I don't think you should have become a lawyer at all!'

Bronwyn laid a hand on her chest. 'Sir, that is the nicest thing you have ever said to me.'

'Are you being sarcastic?'

'No.' She frowned. 'Of course not.'

'Good, because we stand to incur penalties if you don't get the Hayman documents filed in court by tomorrow. You need to get back to the office now. Do you understand me?'

'I understand you perfectly, sir.' Bronwyn's features hardened as another pin of rebellion was driven home. 'But I am not taking this dog to the pound.'

'Then you're fired.'

'Thank you, sir, I was hoping you'd say that. I would have quit but I didn't want to work notice.'

'*What?*'

'I'll come and pick up my things another day,' Bronwyn said. 'Like I said, I have a dog to sort out.'

Elsa barked happily at her as she cut the line with shaky fingers. She put the phone back in her handbag, trying to process what had just happened.

Surprisingly, her panic was subsiding and she was feeling good.

Really good.

She began to swing slowly, backwards and forwards.

Up and down.

The wind whipped her hair, causing strands to come out of her stylishly loose bun and brush against her face. She could hear wild birds tweeting in the trees and the roar of the occasional car from the main road in the distance. It had been a long time since she'd been to a park and sat on a swing.

Life was one long rat race and there was no time for anything but the game.

This was her defining moment.

This was the point where she realised it all had to change.

She'd been such a coward up until this point, more concerned about hiding who she was than revealing it. But the truth was she'd been moving towards this moment for a long time.

She let the sides of the swing go and flung herself out. Jumping into the sand like a symbolic leap of faith. She rummaged in her bag again for her phone. It only took her a second to find Claudia's number and only another five for her best friend to answer the call.

'Hey, Bron, I'm just heading to your place now. Had a hellish day.'

'Me too. I'm coming home as well.'

'Oh really? Isn't it early?'

'Yeah. I sort of have a bit of problem.'

'Okay. What?'

'You know that dog you told me not to take at any cost?'

'Y-es.' Claudia's tone was deeply suspicious.

'I kinda . . . did.'

Chapter 4

When Claudia arrived at Bronwyn's super-slick Subiaco apartment building, it was not to be greeted with the luxuries of inner-city living. Instead, the vision that greeted her was of Bronwyn streaking across the car park, being dragged by a dog the size of a small pony. Her friend looked a mess. Her hair was out and windswept, her skirt suit in crumpled disarray and her feet bare and dirty. It was like she'd been bitten by a pixie and gone wild.

'*Bron?*'

'Hey.' Bron stopped next to Claudia's ute, completely breathless, her bright smile indicating that her current state caused her none of the unhappiness that you might expect. 'Glad you finally got here. This is Elsa. Beautiful, isn't she?'

'Sure.' Claudia slowly lowered her hand to the dog's head, giving it a tentative pat. 'If you discount the fact that her father's in jail, she's pregnant and by association you're currently ineligible to stay in your own apartment.'

'And I got fired because of her as well.' Bron merrily shook her finger.

'*You got fired?!*'

'Did I forget to mention that? I guess in the information offload over the phone, it got missed out.'

'Yeah, right,' Claudia retorted. 'You didn't tell me on purpose.'

Bronwyn rolled her eyes. 'Maybe because I knew you would react like this and really there's nothing to be worried about.'

'How can you say that?' Claudia gasped. 'What are you going to do?'

'Do?' Bronwyn's eyes lit up like Christmas lights. 'What can I do but enjoy it?'

'Which part exactly?'

'All of it. This is one of the best days of my life and it's shortly to become the best day of yours.'

Claudia frowned. 'I'm not seeing it.'

'You will.' Bronwyn nodded as she struggled with Elsa, who clearly wanted to take off again. 'Perhaps if we take a walk down to my local park I can tell you all about my cunning plan.'

'You've got a cunning plan?' Claudia raised her eyebrows. 'Okay. Who are you and what have you done with my friend?'

'Stop it,' Bronwyn laughed. 'Simon reckons I have no grit either, but maybe it's just with law. Maybe I can be brave at something else.'

'There's bravery and there's stupidity.'

'Come on, don't be like that. I'll explain on the way.'

'You're going to take a walk without shoes?' Claudia looked down at her feet.

'Good point.' Bronwyn handed her the dog lead. 'I'll be back in a jiffy.'

As soon as she was gone, Elsa clearly recognised Claudia as the inferior authority and ran circles around her, winding the lead about her body.

'Hey,' Claudia cried with a half laugh, half groan. 'Quit it! You've already caused enough trouble as it is.'

She had no idea how Bronwyn was going to keep this dog, especially living in a two-bedroom apartment on the second floor. It was just no place for an animal, especially one of this size. She ran a hand down Elsa's back, pausing curiously at a scar on her right shoulder. A thought distracted Claudia.

Maybe Bron's decided to move.

Her eyes widened.

Was that the plan? After all, she had just lost her job. Claudia felt a pang for the place. She'd always loved Bronwyn's fancy digs but knew it would probably be too expensive to keep without the fancy job as well. Whatever the case, change was coming and it was going to be drastic.

It took Bronwyn about ten minutes to return, so Claudia figured she was probably getting changed as well. She used the time to imagine all sorts of harebrained schemes that her best friend might have in mind to fix her life. Bronwyn was such an idealist and often far too trusting. Claudia had never heard her say a bad word about anyone. Even her own parents, and it wasn't like they didn't deserve it.

Claudia remembered one summer she had signed them both on to a Big Sister program that hooked up well-adjusted young adults with teenagers who 'needed new role models'. They had taken two sixteen-year-olds to Adventure World, Perth biggest fun park. One of them told Bronwyn she'd left something in the car and Bronwyn had just given her the keys to go and retrieve it. They'd been left stranded in Bibra Lake all afternoon.

Unsurprisingly, Bronwyn's shock was not at the girl's dishonesty but her age. 'She's only sixteen,' she had said. 'Who knew she could drive?'

Claudia sighed at the memory. She really hoped Bronwyn hadn't bitten off more than she could chew this time as well.

'Ready to go?' her friend asked brightly when she returned, holding out her hand for the leash.

'Ready as I'll ever be.'

They took off down the street, Bronwyn's arm stretched out before her as Elsa tried to increase the pace. 'Heel, Elsa, heel,' she chided gently.

'Okay, I'm sick of waiting. Tell me what you've got in your head, because imagining the worst is driving me crazy.'

'Well, it's really quite simple.' Bronwyn grinned. 'We both hate our lives right now. It's just making us both miserable. I think one of the ideas we came up with earlier would really work.'

Claudia gasped. 'You want to fake our own deaths?'

'No, doofus! I want to swap places. It's the perfect solution.'

'Yeah,' Claudia rolled her eyes. 'Perfect if I had your DNA. Bronwyn, you're dreaming.'

Bronwyn ignored her friend's response. 'It's not only possible, it's actually perfect timing.' The excitement in her voice stepped up a notch. 'I've lost my job and gained a pregnant dog. I can't live in this apartment. I need a big country house with lots of open space. You, on the other hand, need to start working in law again.'

'Are you suggesting I apply for the job you just got fired from?'

'No,' Bronwyn shook her head immediately, 'I'm suggesting you apply for a job at Hanks and Eddings.'

Claudia sucked in a breath. 'You want me to work for your family?'

'Well, Mum sent me an email today saying she'd set up an interview for me with Uncle Cyril tomorrow. So I called his secretary and notified her that you'd be attending instead.'

Claudia gasped. '*You did what?*'

'Ten am. Don't be late.'

Claudia choked. 'But you can't do that. Your mum isn't recommending me.'

'Who cares?' Bronwyn swatted her hand. 'Uncle Cyril's secretary doesn't know that. All she knows is that I'm an Eddings, so I must know what I'm talking about. I told her that I was leaving town and couldn't make the interview so my mother was recommending you instead.'

'And your uncle will be fine with that?'

'Most likely he won't know about the swap till tomorrow morning,' Bronwyn assured her.

'And that's a good thing because . . . ?'

'Once you're in the door, you'll impress the hell out of him and he'll forget who came with what recommendation.'

'I think you're reaching a bit there, Bron.'

Her friend only laughed. 'I know you, Claud. You've got the grit that everybody wants. Just use it.'

By this time they had reached the park and Bronwyn bent down to unclip Elsa's leash. The second the dog was free, Elsa tore off towards the tree line.

'Bronwyn, your mum will be furious when she finds out I took the job that was meant for you.'

'Don't worry,' Bronwyn promised. 'Once you're working there, she won't say a word. If there's one thing my mother hates more than anything, it's being made to look like a fool.'

'I was afraid you were going to say that,' Claudia groaned.

'You worry too much.'

'You worry too little.'

'Isn't that what you like about me?' Bronwyn smiled.

'I wish I had your blind trust, Bron, but I really don't think it's that simple.' Claudia shook her head. 'Why would your mother recommend me of all people?'

'Because you're a close friend of the family, of course.'

'Your close friend maybe, but she never liked me. I was always the bad influence who used to steal you away to the country. I remember she used to resent the hell out of it whenever you'd bring me to an Eddings family function.'

'That's only because she was secretly annoyed that I didn't have a boyfriend of good pedigree to bring instead,' Bronwyn retorted as she sat down on a nearby park bench, watching Elsa sniffing at an invisible trail that weaved into a bush. 'I absolutely hated those events. I would have been so miserable without you there.'

While Claudia deplored high society fluff, wasteful amounts of food and needless condescension, she was by no means immune to the opportunity to play Cinderella for a night with her best friend. She winced guiltily. In fact, she had secretly loved attending Bronwyn's family events, just to see how the other side lived – all those high-profile guests she read about in the media, and the gorgeous venues she'd never have set foot in but for their invitation.

She'd actually seen, though not formally met, Bronwyn's Uncle Cyril, who headed up Hanks and Eddings. She'd been to his daughter's wedding. It was the last event she had attended with Bronwyn, over two years ago. It had taken place on a yacht and Cyril had given an entertaining speech full of humour and goodwill. It had lacked only one element to reflect the significance of the occasion – depth.

Cyril struck Claudia as someone who was good-natured as long as it didn't in any way inconvenience him – the very embodiment of the 'fairweather friend'. She doubted he would remember her, but then she was sure that people such as herself who hung upon the fringes of his family's society like desperate band groupies did not make it into his memory bank. Not that she thought this was malicious or mean. She just suspected that his primary concern, like most Eddingses and lawyers alike, was the firm.

Claudia sat down beside Bronwyn. 'I'm still not completely comfortable walking into an interview that came from a fake recommendation.'

Bronwyn sighed. 'Look, my family has never cared what I wanted. They have manipulated me my whole life to be who they want. What we're doing is nothing. Besides, what's the worse they can do? Not hire you? Come on, Claud, you know this is what you've always wanted.'

It is.

And then some.

She felt her will wavering. 'And what will you do?'

'Elsa and I will hop in your ute and make for the hills. Oak Hills. I will take on your role as manager of your father's winery. You know I could do it, right?'

Claudia nodded slowly, wincing as she went. She had seen Bronwyn in action on her parents' property before. Her best friend knew a lot about their business and how they ran things. However, there was a big difference between helping out and managing the place full time.

'I mean, I know it's a little more responsibility than your family ever gave me but if I have any problems you're just a phone call away, and I figure Oak Hills is already on its last legs, so it's not like I can do any real damage.'

Claudia's mouth twisted as she thought of her family. 'You'd be surprised.'

'Well, I have a hankering to show you what I can do!' Bronwyn announced passionately.

'What are you saying?' Claudia asked dryly. 'That you'll succeed where I have failed?'

'I didn't mean it like that,' Bronwyn eyed her worriedly. 'I just meant I'm going to give it my all.'

Claudia rubbed her temple. 'I know. You love that place more than your own home. But I think you're oversimplifying the situation. You've forgotten the most important part of the Franklin Estate. *The Franklins.*'

Bronwyn's gaze dropped to her hands, which were clasped firmly in her lap. 'Your family won't like it?'

'I think there would definitely be some unease,' Claudia said slowly. 'I mean, you know they love you, Bron. They talk about you all the time. Ask when you're coming to visit and all that. But . . . you coming home *instead* of me? They'd be shocked and probably a little hurt too.'

Bronwyn's shoulders drooped. 'That's true. I guess I wouldn't want to go somewhere I'm not welcome.'

'Not welcome?' Claudia blew on her fringe. 'No, it won't be like that. Chris will love having you around. And Mum, you know her, she'll be too consumed with excitement to see the wood for the trees at first.'

'It's your dad I have to worry about, isn't it?'

Claudia frowned. 'To be honest, he's been grumpy since his retirement. Hasn't agreed with most of the changes I've implemented at Oak Hills over the years. So that'll be nothing new. But are you prepared to deal with him?'

Bronwyn raised her eyes slowly. 'I think I can certainly give it a shot if you'll let me. Come on, Claud, take a chance.'

A light, airy feeling entered Claudia's chest, almost like it was filling with butterflies. To hand over all her obligations to another so that she could pursue her own dreams? It seemed too good to be true.

Did they dare risk it?

'When were you planning on leaving?' she asked breathlessly.

Bronwyn leaned forward. 'First thing in the morning. I can conceal Elsa in my apartment for one night perhaps, but not for much longer.'

Claudia thought hard. It was all happening so fast, her head was beginning to spin. For so long, she had been trapped by what her family wanted. Bronwyn had too.

Did they dare be selfish?

It was such a fantasy. Such a risk to both their situations. And to Oak Hills as well.

Her family would think she'd gone off the rails.

Maybe she had.

'Don't overthink it, Claud.' Bronwyn grabbed her hand. 'If you do, you'll never agree. We just need to take what we can and prove that we deserve it later.'

Claudia squeezed her best friend's hand in return. 'Are you sure you're up for this? You don't know how bad it's become at Oak Hills. It really is a sinking ship.'

'Then maybe fresh blood is exactly what they need.'

For a while they held each other's gaze, caught in a rip of their own needs versus those of their families.

Claudia knew the right decision was to say 'no.' Her obligations to her family were hers and hers alone. It was callous of her to pass them off to somebody else, wasn't it?

How many years have you already given to Oak Hills, Claudia?

And how much more are you prepared to sacrifice?

She knew how trapped Bronwyn had felt for so many years because the feeling was so close to her heart. Here was a chance for them both to get what they wanted and needed.

'All right, Bronwyn.' She held her arms open for a hug. 'You win. Let's do it.'

Bronwyn squealed and hugged her back.

'But remember,' she added sternly, 'at the first sign of trouble we call it quits, all right?'

'Of course,' Bronwyn agreed.

If only Claudia could have predicted then how impossible that would be.

Chapter 5

Bronwyn stepped out of Claudia's old ute, closed her eyes and lifted her nose to the wind. Who knew that freedom smelled both fresh *and* fruity?

After a moment she allowed herself to take in the ramshackle home she was parked in front of. It was two storeys tall and leaning against the side of a hill, much like a tired old man catching his breath. In its heyday it must have been rather grand and stately. Now it looked a little too rickety to still be standing at all. Most of the building was timber and the beige-coloured paint was old and peeling, especially near the roof gutters. The porch sported a ramp rather than steps, which may have seemed odd-looking to some people but made perfect sense to her.

Bronwyn sighed quietly. Even in its dilapidated state, the house still had the power to take the chill off her troubled heart. She had so many memories of this place and the surroundings. All wonderful.

Hot sausage rolls.

Lazy days on the beach.

Spicy shiraz.

My first kiss . . .

She shook away the daydreams.

This visit is not going to be quite as relaxing.

It was one thing to drop by and visit old friends. It was quite another to move in and take over their business. The plan, which had looked good in her mind's eye, was now starting to pinch at every nerve.

Elsa barked from the tray of the ute as though in agreement.

She turned. 'Yep, girl, this is it. Your new home.' She ran her hand between Elsa's ears, looking across the vineyard behind her. Rows and rows of vines rolled over the hills, divided by the gravelly dirt track that cut a path from Rickety Twigg Road to the winery and then to the residence. She had just driven up this track to the house and the wheels of the ute were covered in a rich film of red-brown dust.

'Here, let me get you a drink.'

She walked round to the side of the porch where there was a hose and a bucket. She filled the bucket with water and brought it back to the ute for Elsa.

'Do my eyes deceive me?'

Bronwyn spun around as the creak of something that wasn't quite footsteps sounded on the timber floorboards behind her. 'Chris!'

The flyscreen door swung closed behind him as he came out. 'Well, if it isn't my long lost love, come to break my heart all over again.'

Her eyes widened as he came fully into view. 'Wow, Chris, you look fantastic.'

Chris Franklin was in a wheelchair. But if there was anyone out there that thought they had more vitality than him, she'd dare them to come forward. He wore a loose tank that showed off his impressive biceps and sun-kissed skin. His hair was streaked with gold, further evidence that he spent plenty of time outdoors. He wore shorts and sneakers, so she could see that his legs were skinny from lack of use, but there was nothing limp about the arms resting lightly but with complete control over the top of his wheels. A mischievous dimple in his right cheek appeared.

'That makes two of us. I didn't know you were coming to town.'

'Neither did I, till yesterday.'

His eyes moved beyond her. 'Where's Claud?'

Guilt, a familiar companion, slung an arm across her shoulders and drew her close. This was definitely going to be harder than she thought. 'Do you mind if we hold off on that? It's kind of a big conversation and I need to get Elsa settled first.'

'Elsa?'

'My new dog.' She pointed at the tray.

'Wow, Numbat, she's big.'

She flinched at the old nickname and her eyes involuntarily lowered as they always used to do. 'I can't believe you still remember that stupid name Jack used to call me.'

'Actually, neither can I.' He sounded amused, almost like he was mocking himself, not her. 'Sorry. I have a feeling it doesn't really suit you anymore.'

'Well,' she took a breath and raised her head, 'I'm not that shy teenager I once was who was too afraid to say a word.'

He gestured at Elsa. 'You've certainly got a very impressive bodyguard now. No one will mess with you again.'

The reason why Jack called her Numbat, apart from the fact that he just liked to be annoying, was because when they first met she used to go all quiet whenever he was around. Like she'd gone into a torpor, a state of semi-hibernation that numbats often achieved in the winter. Not that Jack would know what that really looked like. Numbats were an endangered species after all, and she doubted he'd ever seen one around, even in these parts.

Didn't stop you reading up about them, did it?

The truth was, back then she'd had the biggest crush on him. She felt her face warm at the memory. It was no wonder he'd likened her to a spooked marsupial. He was the gorgeous older guy with all that awe-inspiring worldliness, and she the self-conscious teenager struggling to be accepted by her parents. It had taken her ages to respond to his teasing with any sort of coherence. It was no wonder he'd enjoyed it so much. She shrugged off the thought. The past was the past.

She'd grown up since then.

A lot.

Chris seemed to read her mood correctly. 'You know what, you look different too. More self-assured. Maybe it's the hair. It's shorter. But I suppose that's what women do from time to time.'

'Yes, that's what we do,' she inclined her head with a slight smile, 'especially when we're looking for a new start.'

He grinned. 'Mum will be so pleased you've come to visit. How long are you staying?'

She licked her dry lips. It seemed a little premature to say 'indefinitely'. After all, this was their house and she hadn't even asked their permission yet.

Damn it, Bron! Why on earth did you think this would be easy?

She should have asked Claudia to call first. Pave the way, so to speak. She just hadn't wanted to stress her best friend out further this morning. She knew that the job interview had already kept her up half the night with worry.

'Er . . .' she stalled. 'I'm not really sure.'

Chris's grin broadened. 'Very cagey, aren't you? Should I be worried?'

'Not yet,' she smiled back.

'At least let me take you out to dinner while you're here. I hear the Maxwells might be reopening their restaurant. It overlooks their lake. Could be very romantic.'

Bronwyn laughed as she unclipped Elsa's leash and opened the back of the tray, allowing the dog to jump down and bound around the car to sink her snout into the refreshing liquid in the bucket. 'I'd love to go out with you, Chris, but not as a date, okay?'

The sound of water slapped against Elsa's parched tongue.

Chris gasped. 'Seriously? You just said I look fantastic.'

She shook her head with a wry grin. 'Yeah, but you're like a brother to me.'

'Was that how you felt about Jack too?' His eyes narrowed.

She put her hands on her hips crossly. 'Are we really going to go there?'

'No,' he grinned, 'I suppose not. But old habits die hard.' He sighed. 'Come on, we better go inside. If we stay out here much longer we might start hugging and agreeing to just be friends.' He looked so disgusted by the concept that she had to laugh again as he did a quick twirl on his rather sporty-looking chair so that he could hold the door open for her. Bronwyn noticed the slanted wheels that looked like they were built for speed rather than stability.

'See something you like, sweetheart?' he enquired, clearly flirting again. What was it about Franklin men having thick skin?

'I admire you, Chris,' she said softly and sincerely. 'I really do.'

His grin widened even further as he took in the whole of her. 'Don't sweat it, darlin', the feeling is perfectly mutual.'

With a slight smile, Bronwyn walked into the house. Despite the obvious need for repairs in various nooks and crannies, the house was very welcoming. Wooden floorboards gently groaned as they made their way across an expansive foyer. An old oak barrel that had been cut in half and topped with a slice of polished tree trunk sat in the centre. This made a very earthy-looking hall table. The only other piece of furnishing in the room was a giant oriental rug. From here, there were four doors they could have taken. Bronwyn would have taken the first one on her left but Chris stopped her.

'My parents are in here.'

*

60

He led her through the second door, the entrance to a large study occupied by two desks, a worn-looking couch and a couple of filing cabinets. The desk by the window had a computer on it and there was a woman in her sixties seated there, peering at the screen over her plastic pink glasses.

'Ah, Chris,' she said without looking up. 'I'm glad you're back. Can you get your father out of here? He's not helping me with these bills at all.'

'What are you talking about?' a man of similar age protested from the couch. 'All I'm doing is helping. It's you who won't listen.'

She waved a paper bill at him crossly. 'But we can't get rid of the free cheese and crackers on the bar. Everyone in town will say we've fallen on hard times.'

'Er, Mum,' Chris pointed out from the sidelines, 'we *have* fallen on hard times.'

'Well, there's no need to be so bloody blatant about it,' his mother replied, finally allowing her gaze to find him, and then his companion.

'Bronwyn!' she exclaimed, whipping off her glasses. She had the same vibrant eyes as her daughter. As she rose abruptly to her feet some papers that had been on her lap fell off and joined the many others littering the floor about her desk. 'We've missed you so much, sweetie. You never come to visit us anymore and, believe me, you were the sanity in this house, let me tell you.' She grabbed Bronwyn just above the elbows, so that she could examine her carefully. 'You haven't changed one bit. Oh . . . except for the hair, but that's to be expected.'

'Absolutely.' Bronwyn caught Chris's mischievous look before she allowed the older woman to envelop her in a huge hug.

She pulled back to observe her hostess. 'You haven't changed either, Lydia. You're looking as well as ever.'

'Aren't you a flatterer,' the older woman chided, but looked pleased nonetheless.

'Bronwyn?' Chris's father stood up. He had turned his head left and was squinting out the corner of his eye at her. 'Sorry, I can't see as clearly as I used to.'

She left Lydia's side and came closer, knowing the distance didn't help. 'That's okay, Horace.'

The glaucoma had caused a gradual loss of sight, which would lead to eventual blindness – an age-related illness that was also incurable. She knew he was on some sort of medication to slow the process but he would never regain the eyesight he had already lost. Her heart went out to him. The last time she'd seen him, he'd been much more lively. Time and the disease had not been kind. It was strange to see him step forward with hesitation in his movements. Although he was only around five years older than Lydia, the gap seemed closer to ten now. His hair and eyebrows were more white than brown and his skin was riddled with sunspots.

She hugged him. 'It's good to see you –' She cut herself off awkwardly as she realised what she'd just said. 'I mean –'

'There's no need to walk on eggshells with me,' he grunted. 'I've got a thick skin. Too thick, according to my wife. So, how's life been treating you, anyway?' He seemed to visibly buoy himself to ask. 'Still in the fast lane?'

'Er . . . sort of.'

Where do I start?

Lydia waggled a finger and then said to Chris, 'This girl always had a terrible poker face.'

'Tell me about it.' He grinned. 'What's going on, Numbat? You promised me an explanation at some point.'

Bronwyn shifted from one foot to the other. 'It's about Claudia.'

Lydia's smile disappeared. 'I hope nothing bad has happened? Is she okay? She hasn't hurt herself, has she?'

'She's fine,' Bronwyn hastily reassured her. 'In perfect health, actually.'

'But . . .' Chris prompted.

Come on, girl. Just rip it off like a band aid.

'She's not coming home.'

There was a moment of silence.

'As in, she's not coming home *today*?' Lydia suggested tentatively.

'As in, she's not coming home . . . indefinitely.'

Lydia gasped.

'What does that mean?' Horace demanded.

'It means,' Chris chuckled, 'that she's finally had enough and she's jumped ship. Wish I had her gumption and the legs to do it with.'

'Oh no,' Lydia shook her head, 'Claudia wouldn't do that. She wouldn't leave us high and dry.'

'That's right –' Bronwyn tried to seize the opportunity to explain further but Horace wouldn't let her.

'Yes, she would. You know she's been dying to get out of here for years. Wants to live in the city.'

Lydia's mouth pulled. 'Yes, to practice law, of course.' She turned back to Bronwyn. 'Is that what she's doing?'

Bronwyn nodded apologetically. 'She's trying to get a job with my family as we speak.'

Lydia sank back into her desk chair, her voice wistful. 'She's pursuing her dream. I guess it's about time.'

'About time?' Horace snapped. 'Just after I've retired and can no longer work? Surely she's got more responsibility than that.'

Lydia sighed. 'You honestly can't blame her, can you? She trained for all those years at university and we've been holding her back. Keeping her here against her will . . .'

'Oh, don't be so melodramatic!' Horace cried. 'We did no such thing. She knew what she owed to her family.'

'It was wrong of us to put that on her,' Lydia protested.

'But we can't run Oak Hills without her,' Chris spoke up. 'What'll happen to the business? The least she could have done was arranged for someone else to take her place. Though how we would pay them, I have absolutely no idea.'

'Actually,' Bronwyn managed to stem the flow of conversation at last, 'she did arrange for someone to take her place.'

All eyes swung to her.

'Who?' Lydia enquired.

Damn! Can I really do this?

'Well, don't leave us in suspense, Numbat,' Chris protested. 'Spit it out.'

'Well, it's,' her gaze shot from one to the other before she spread her hands hopefully, 'it's, er . . . me.'

For a moment they all just stared at her in stunned silence and then Horace let loose a roar of laughter.

'You're going to run Oak Hills Winery! No bloody way!'

'I . . . I beg your pardon?' Bronwyn stammered.

'As much as I like you, Bronwyn, we are not packaging up our business and handing it over into your untried hands. Why would we? It's too risky, not to mention ridiculous.'

'Ignore him.' Lydia came forward, clasping both Bronwyn's hands between hers. 'He's being rude.'

'So you think I could do it?' Bronwyn eagerly pounced on this.

It was Lydia's turn to stall. 'You're a wonderful girl, sweetie. Smart too, with all those degrees behind you. But . . . this is our . . . everything.'

'I totally get that.' Bronwyn squeezed Lydia's hands. 'And I would fight for it with my . . . everything, and not ask for payment except food and a roof over my head. I would replace Claudia exactly.'

Just like I was your daughter.

She groaned inwardly at her teenage fantasy that was unexpectedly coming to life.

Lydia's expression became rather bewildered. 'But don't you have commitments back in Perth, Bronwyn?'

'Not really.' Bronwyn winced. 'I kinda got fired and I can't stay in my apartment anymore because of Elsa.'

'Her new dog,' Chris informed his mother, tapping his fingers thoughtfully against the wheels of his chair. 'Big bullmastiff, the size of a small pony. Can't say I would have picked her as your type, Numbat. But I guess you're full of surprises today, aren't you?'

Bronwyn stuck out her tongue at him as he grinned at her.

Horace, however, was not to be distracted.

'And we're supposed hand over our livelihood to someone who has no experience of managing a winery, who just got fired from their job and encouraged my daughter to flake out on her responsibilities?'

'Come now, Horace,' Lydia scolded him, 'that's not fair.'

'No,' he declared, 'it's just the truth.' Closing his eyes, he rubbed his fingers over his temple. 'Why do the people I count on the most always let me down?'

It was this gesture of true despair, more than his words, that hurt Bronwyn.

She licked her lips. 'I got fired because I refused to give Elsa up to be put down, not because I was incompetent. The whole situation made me realise that I don't want to practice law anymore. In fact,' she glanced at their faces earnestly, 'I actually think I hate my old job. I don't want to ever go back.'

She braced herself for the protests her mother would no doubt have voiced . . . had she given her the opportunity to do so.

Why?

What happened?

You were so good at it!

Why quit now when you're at the top of your game?

Don't be silly. You love what you do!

As for her father, Robert Eddings hadn't ever taken that much of an interest in her life, so why on earth would he start now?

'Well,' Lydia nodded contemplatively, 'I guess one can't do the same thing forever, but are you sure this is what you want to do instead?'

'Absolutely,' Bronwyn replied firmly, both relieved and grateful for Lydia's response. 'Claud told me you guys were having problems here. All I want to do is help you get your reputation and sales back on line. I love this place. I want to restore Oak Hills to its former glory as much as you do.'

'Okay,' Horace nodded. 'So you've got passion and ambition. I admire that, but winemaking is not corporate law. This business is as much art as it is science. It requires a delicate balancing act, a love of the land and an intuitiveness that Claudia doesn't have and neither do you.'

'Then who does?'

To Bronwyn's surprise it was Chris who had jumped in. She had never seen him so affected. His face was pale, his voice rough with anger. He'd always approached life with an air of whatever will be, will be. When he'd lost the use of his legs, his easygoing attitude had remained. She'd always admired him for that and his willingness to give anything a go. Even today, for most of the conversation he'd sat quietly in his chair contemplating everything that was said without a shred of the panic his parents were clearly feeling. And it wasn't to say that he too shouldn't feel some sort of upheaval. Chris was by no means the family freeloader. He managed the cellar door, organised tastings and sometimes gave tours in the summer, explaining to wide-eyed tourists and winemaking experts alike their process from harvest to fermentation. He was good at it too. Chris knew how to play up the romance of it all, and his cheeky good humour had always been an asset to the family.

However, there was none of that in play now. 'Is it Jack you have in mind, Dad?' he asked sarcastically. 'What a pity you drove him away.'

'Jack!' Horace spat out the name like a mandarine pip. 'That boy had ability but no discipline, apart from being a downright disgrace to this family.'

'A disgrace because of what he did to me?' Chris demanded. 'Or how he disappointed you?'

'I don't see how that has any relevance.'

'Of course it has relevance.'

Horace glared at him. 'I don't want your opinion. Didn't ask for it.'

'That's right. Doesn't count, does it? Never did.' Chris lifted his chin. 'And that's what's so ironic about this whole mess. You got rid of the one guy who could bring this place back to life because of me, the son you never loved as much.'

His words were like hot oil spitting from a pot, leaving everyone scalded.

Bronwyn's gaze flew to Chris. He was clearly just as shocked by his outburst as everyone else. He probably hadn't meant for it to come out but now that it had, he couldn't snatch it back.

Oh dear.

It was in this moment that Bronwyn realised she might have been blindsided by her own need. She had been so determined to get out of law, she'd jumped headfirst into this escape plan. The Franklins were no longer the happy family from her uni days. There was a reason Claudia had been so miserable at Oak Hills, and now she was about to discover firsthand why.

'I think it's time I took a walk,' Horace remarked and, with an unsteady gait, left the room, shutting the door behind him firmly.

'Sorry about that,' Chris remarked with a humourless smile. 'I don't know what came over me.'

'No, it's my fault,' Bronwyn tried to patch things over. 'I didn't realise this plan Claudia and I have hatched would open old wounds.'

Chris snorted. 'Who said they were shut?'

Lydia laid a hand on Chris's arm, her face a picture of concern. 'Perhaps it is time we sorted through our dirty laundry. We've let this all fester for too long. I'm just sad that it's taken Claudia leaving for us to realise it.' She looked up and met Bronwyn's eyes. 'On reflection, Bronwyn, I think you have come at an excellent time. We are definitely going to need you around here. In fact, you're the perfect distraction for the storm about to break.'

Alarm bells began to ring in her head. 'What storm?'

Lydia spread her hands. 'Oak Hills can't sustain my husband's dissatisfaction for much longer.'

'What do you mean?'

'Honey, it's not just you or Claudia or me or Chris he doesn't trust to run Oak Hills.'

Chris groaned. 'He doesn't trust anyone.'

Lydia pursed her lips. 'My husband is finding the concept of retirement rather difficult to process.' She sighed. 'Winemaking has been his life for so many years now, it's hard to just chuck it in and let someone else take over. Especially a stranger. He won't admit it but he always thought Jack would take the reins when he retired, and in truth he doesn't really want anyone else. His pride is standing in the way. As for me, I never thought this feud between them would last so long.' She tapped her fingers restlessly against her arm.

'Well,' Chris pointed out, 'he can't keep firing every wine-maker we take on just because he doesn't like his way of doing things.'

'Is that what's been happening?' Bronwyn's eyes rounded.

Chris nodded. 'Can you imagine what kind of wine we're getting with three different winemakers having a hand in the one vintage? That's why our reputation is gone.'

'Too many cooks spoiling the broth?'

'Exactly. Claud and I have told Dad again and again to lay low but he won't listen. Even the fact that he's nearly blind now doesn't stop him. We're basically at our wits' end.'

'Well, I'm not,' Lydia responded firmly.

Chris glanced at her in surprise. 'What do you mean?'

'You were right about Jack. He *is* the one person who can save Oak Hills. He's every bit as talented as your father was.'

'That doesn't mean I want him to come home,' Chris added.

'He's been shunning us for years, Mum. He has no incentive to help. It won't work.'

Bronwyn went still. 'What won't work?'

Lydia reached out and squeezed her hand. 'Bronwyn, we'll need you here to keep the peace, you'd do a much better job than Claud ever could. She's as bitter about Jack abandoning us as your father is.'

Her heart sank. 'Lydia, what are you going to do?'

'Something I should have done a long time ago.' Lydia nodded. 'I'm going to ask Jack to come home.'

Chapter 6

Sebastian Rowlands was both busy and frustrated.

He had court appointments booked to his eyeballs, at least half a dozen affidavits to finalise and ten witnesses to interview. His junior lawyer, Nelson, was already fully loaded with work and his secretary, Juliet Nesbitt, had taken a personal day. Not that she didn't deserve it. Of all the secretaries he had known, she was definitely the best. Honest, trustworthy and methodical to a fault. Juliet ate through his paperwork like termites in a timber roof. He couldn't ask for better. Of all the women who had guest-starred in his life, his relationship with Juliet was singularly the most longstanding and meaningful.

Did he find that sad?

No.

He'd much rather have a good secretary than be married. Low maintenance, high rewards.

No bullshit.

Nelson, on the other hand, required a lot of attention. The young lawyer did try his best but his efficiency was low because he was still learning. In turn, being a mentor to him was a time-consuming process that took longer than if he actually did the work himself.

He tutted as he flicked though the brief in front of him written by Nelson, which was full of errors. He was going to have to sit down with the boy again, putting them both further behind. Not that there wasn't something to be said for having another human being look at you with envy, respect and doe-eyed wonder.

That he liked.

Not because he saw himself in Nelson, but because he didn't.

Nelson had grown up in a stable family environment, well supported by his parents, and still lived at home. He had no notion of independence because there had always been someone there to pick him up should he fall. He had moved smoothly from high school to university without a care in the world.

No, he liked Nelson because he was earnest.

He was good and he was kind, untouched by the jaded cynicism that years of getting to know the frailty of man's honour brought to your life. He loved shocking him with the hard advice and 'war' stories; startling him when Seb pointed out Nelson's mistakes just in time to pull him back from the brink of liability and disbarment. Unfortunately for Nelson, this seemed to occur on rather a regular basis.

Seb chuckled to himself as he flicked through more of the young man's work, seeing a number of flashing danger lights in his phrasing. He circled these with red pen.

And so you've adopted him.

Much like an old man takes in a stray puppy.

Wasn't that what you were when Cyril gave you a leg up?

He shook his head at the thought. He always knew when he was stressed because he started reminiscing about the past. When he was seventeen, already supporting himself because the discontinuous nature of foster homes had started grating on him, he hadn't dreamt of becoming a lawyer. Honestly, he had just wanted to get by, pay his rent and maybe buy an old bomb that someone was trying to flog so he could get away to the coast for the weekends. He was a loner. Still was. There was no one in this world he trusted more than himself.

Until he met Cyril.

The phone on his desk buzzed, rousing him from his musings. He hoped it was Juliet, calling to say she was coming in after all.

It wasn't.

'Morning, Seb.'

'Cyril.' Genuine pleasure coloured his voice. 'Don't tell me you have another case for me.'

'Something better than that, son. Get over here, will you?'

'Right now?'

'Right now.'

Seb put the phone down. Standing up, he threw on his jacket and walked out of his fish-tank style office and straight into a pool of cubicles, mainly occupied by graduates and paralegals. They kept their heads down as he strode past, hoping not be flicked another one of his files, no doubt. The thing was, he needed more help. He was going to have to get it somewhere.

He reached the main foyer of Hanks and Eddings. The receptionist there fielded all calls, but particularly Cyril's. His office was directly behind her desk, a double-doored entrance with stark silver handles. It looked ostentatious, just as it was meant to.

'Morning, Seb,' smiled the receptionist. 'I was just about to put Mrs Matheson through to your office.'

'Tell her I'll call her back,' he nodded. That was likely to be a very long phone call. Mrs Matheson tended to cry a lot whenever they went over the facts of her case, which he supposed was understandable. She stood to lose her home, her beach house and the ability to pay her children's private school fees because her husband had dared to avoid paying taxes. Ah, the benefits of spousal dishonesty. Yet another reason he had no intention of getting married anytime soon.

He strode on and the receptionist didn't stop him. She was used to him coming and going from Cyril's office as he pleased. It was a privilege not enjoyed by many. When he walked in, the old man was already seated on the couch in the alcove off to one side, a mug of coffee resting on his knee.

'Help yourself.'

Seb definitely didn't have time for a break. But he'd learned very early in his career that you refused the founding partner of your firm nothing if you could help it. He filled himself a mug from the Nespresso machine on the bar behind the couch and then walked around to sit next to the man whom he regarded more as a father than a boss.

'I've got a surprise for you,' Cyril nodded with pleasure, his bushy eyebrows lifting cheekily. 'A present, if you will.'

Seb took a fortifying sip of his coffee. 'You haven't set me up on a blind date again, have you?'

'Lord, no!' Cyril shuddered. 'Given the last three were such disasters, I wouldn't risk my reputation with my female friends further.'

'Disasters? Really, they said that? I thought I gave all of them a good time. Who was that last girl I dated, Lisa, Lilly, Lee-anne . . . ?'

'Her name was Lani and she *was* my personal trainer.'

'Ah yes, we spent a wonderful week together. Good food, expensive entertainment, great sex.' Seb permitted himself a ghost of a smile. 'Most dates didn't wrap up till the next morning. It was very nice. I don't know what she could possibly be complaining about. '

'Perhaps the fact that after you reeled her in for a week of paradise, you never called her again,' Cyril groaned as though he didn't know whether to laugh or scold. 'Do you know how difficult it was to find another personal trainer when she quit on me? She was so good, too.'

'Ah well, that's a shame. I'm terribly sorry.'

Cyril raised his eyebrows again. 'No you're not. You're not sorry at all.'

There was a flash of white teeth. 'Well, I can't help it if you don't believe me.'

'I just don't know why you do it, Seb.'

'Do what? Apologise?'

'No, always put an end date on your little affairs before they've even begun.'

Seb snorted as he took another swig of coffee. 'Hardly. I usually don't know until at least after the first date.'

Cyril, however, was not to be put off by humour. 'You've never had a long-term connection to one woman since I've known you. Even your own mother.'

'In my defence,' he pointed out, 'that isn't entirely my fault.'

His mum had been in contact only a handful of times in his teenage years and twice in his twenties. None of those times had been an enriching experience. The connection had been more about her than about him and after he turned twenty-five she had ceased to reach out to him at all. That was more than ten years ago now. He definitely had no desire to reconnect with her in the present. Not after she'd abandoned him at six years old for her drug problem. He did sometimes wonder where she was. Just out of curiosity, of course, but never for any great length of time.

'Yes, I suppose that's true,' Cyril agreed. 'But you shouldn't judge the values of every woman you meet upon your mother's.'

Unbidden, the pretty face of a smart-mouthed waitress intruded upon his senses.

Why black? It's the colour of your soul and your complete and utter loss of faith in humanity.

He banished the vision of her immediately. Why the comments of someone he was never likely to see again should affect him this much, he had no idea. It was Cyril's fault. Sometimes the man pushed all the wrong buttons, and yet . . .

He had nothing but love and respect for the man. Cyril had given him the guidance and support he'd needed at just the right age. Their friendship had begun in response to a favour – a favour that was pretty much unforgettable, though neither of them had spoken of it since.

He had just started working at Hanks and Eddings as the mail clerk; the only job there that didn't require some sort of qualification.

He walked into Cyril's office with papers for his in-tray. The managing partner was seated behind his desk, but his chair was pushed out at a comfortable position so that he could peruse the document he was reading. He didn't look up as Seb leaned across the desk to place the new mail and remove the ones to go out. Mail clerks were tantamount to furniture at this firm.

As Seb straightened to move away, he heard Cyril's soft gasp. He looked down in time to see a wet patch growing on the crotch of Cyril's pants. Cyril was also watching it in shock and mortification. The incident was so odd that it took Seb a couple of seconds to realise that the managing partner was actually wetting himself involuntarily. Cyril glanced up, his eyes watery with humiliation. 'It must be my prostate, I can't control the fuckin' thing.'

Since then Cyril had had an operation and thankfully no longer had this problem. At the time Seb remembered feeling deeply sorry for him. Before he could offer any assistance however, the door opened and Pam, Cyril's secretary, poked her head in. 'Your ten o'clock, sir.' Then she stepped back and three people walked in – a client and two partners from the firm, one of whom was Bianca Hanks.

Thinking fast, Seb knocked the glass of water sitting on the edge of Cyril's desk into his boss's lap. The fluid went every-where and then the glass smashed on the floor at their feet. The cracking sound caused the three people entering the room to pause in confusion.

'Oh shoot, I'm so sorry,' he said, particularly to Bianca Hanks, who was eyeing him like she would like to serve him up for dinner.

It was a well-known fact around the office that Bianca Hanks was dying to knock Cyril off his perch and usurp his position. Since they had both started at the family firm as young lawyers, they had competed neck and neck to become managing partner, a position held until just recently by Cyril's older brother, Robert. Bianca had gone so far as to marry the man to increase her chances of being his successor. However, when Robert had left the firm to become a judge, he had chosen his brother instead of his wife to take the reins, giving further proof to the old saying, 'Hell hath no fury like a woman scorned.'

Bianca Hanks took any opportunity she could to undermine Cyril's authority. Seb may have been low in the pecking order but he was well versed in reading people . . . particularly the dangerous kind.

He grabbed the box of tissues beside the in-tray and passed it to Cyril. 'Here you go, sir.'

Cyril met his eyes gratefully for a second longer than necessary. 'Thank you.'

'Oh, for goodness sake, Sebastian,' the other partner at Bianca's elbow reprimanded him, striding past the client, who was looking rather bewildered. 'How could you be so careless? He's soaked.'

'It was an accident,' Seb apologised. 'My hand slipped.'

'So I saw,' Bianca threw at him. 'It seemed almost deliberate.'

'Hardly,' he said quietly. 'Shall I go source you another pair of pants, sir?'

'That would be ideal,' Cyril nodded tightly before turning to Bianca. 'Your abrupt entry startled him, my dear. Next time please ask my secretary to summon me to the boardroom. In the meantime, I think we might have to reschedule.'

'What are you waiting for?' Bianca had snapped at Seb. 'Those pants aren't going fetch themselves.'

'Of course.' Seb nodded and dashed from the room.

After that Cyril had taken a great deal of interest in Sebastian's progress at the firm. He noticed he was smart, he noticed he was fast and he noticed his phenomenal attention to detail. He'd given him advice and encouraged him to realise his potential. Before Seb knew what was happening he was being sponsored through a law degree and offered a job too. Cyril had been far more paternal towards him than the biological father he had barely known.

And, yes, because of all that he did permit the old man certain liberties, but there were some boundaries he didn't like anyone to cross.

'Is there a point to this conversation?' he demanded.

'Don't you want the comfort of companionship? Someone who actually cares if you don't come home at night?'

He folded his arms. 'Why do I need someone to care if I don't come home?'

'Everybody needs that, Seb. When I was your age I was married with two kids.'

'Good for you.'

'Damn straight. Nothing makes this job easier than a good wife, Seb. You need a support system with the hours we do. I don't know what I'd do without Maggie.'

'Believe me, Cyril, if I wanted to get married there are plenty of women out there who would help me out.' He shuddered. 'Just the other day I met an interesting piece of work at Seashells on Clarabel Terrace.'

'Did she propose to you?'

'No, but when she found out I wasn't interested, she insulted me.'

'Insulted you?'

'Said I clearly had no friends on account of my lack of faith in humanity.'

Cyril chuckled. 'She might be onto something.'

'Subterfuge is what she's onto,' Seb retorted. 'Said you were her uncle, too. Haven't got any hot brunettes in your family, have you?'

Cyril eyed him shrewdly. 'So she was good-looking, then?'

'Like a Venus fly trap.'

'Then, no, she can't possibly be a member of my family.' Cyril laughed. 'None of us has that allure. Of course, I wouldn't risk any of my loved ones on you after the care you've shown my female friends.'

Seb rolled his eyes. 'You really think I'm that dangerous?'

'Yes,' Cyril said simply. 'You're not just heartless, Seb, you're indifferent. I've never seen a woman get under your skin. I doubt one ever will, and for that I am very sorry.'

The seriousness of his tone was sobering. 'Come on, Cyril. You don't need to worry about me. I know how to enjoy life.'

'The most enjoyable thing about enjoyment is sharing it with someone else, son,' Cyril said softly.

'Have I just stepped onto the set of this year's Christmas special?' Seb shook his head at Cyril's sentimentality.

'All right, all right,' Cyril waved his hand. 'I can tell I'm losing your interest so I'll explain to you why I called you in here in the first place.'

'Hallelujah.'

'You need help.' Cyril jabbed his finger at him. 'As in more staff. And I might have found you someone. Another junior lawyer. She'll be here any minute for her interview.'

Seb couldn't have been more delighted with this news. 'Perfect timing, Cyril.'

'Don't get too excited just yet.' Cyril leaned forward to replace his mug on the coffee table. 'She comes as a gift from my ex-sister-in-law, Bianca Hanks.'

Seb raised an eyebrow. 'Is Bianca in the habit of sending you gifts now?'

Cyril snorted. 'What do you think?'

'What's she up to then?'

'I'm not precisely sure, but I have reason to believe that Bianca is unaware of the true nature of the gift she has given me. So we shall see this girl for ourselves and make our choice from there.' Cyril shrugged. 'Let the battle of wits begin.'

Chapter 7

Despite the air-conditioning maintaining the temperature of the room at a very mild twenty-two degrees, Claudia was perspiring like a glass of cold Coke on a hot bench. She had been in the waiting room of Hanks and Eddings for the last half hour. Stiffly seated with her knees pressed together on their white leather couch, not daring to take off her jacket because she knew there was a high chance of sweat marks. Luckily, some of Bronwyn's suits roughly fitted her. They were a little tight around the bust and the skirts were slightly long for her diminutive height but otherwise she had no complaints. The shoes on her feet were of the safe black court variety. She'd bought them in a rush that morning on the way over. They weren't great but were so benign that they wouldn't give anyone cause for comment.

She clutched her résumé on her lap but was less focused on this document than the looming suspicion that 'Uncle Cyril' was going to be disappointed with whose name he saw on it.

So far there had been no hiccups. The receptionist had accepted her name without any surprise. She was definitely going in for this interview. But could she score the job?

She had tried to outline her skills in her résumé without too much embellishment. Given her limited time in the workforce, there wasn't that much to add. Coupled with Bianca's supposed 'recommendation', Claudia really wasn't sure what Bronwyn's Uncle Cyril would make of it all.

'Mr Eddings will see you now.'

With a start, Claudia looked up at the receptionist, who was sitting at the desk opposite the couches, the words 'Hanks and Eddings' in big block letters on the wall behind her. She was beckoning Claudia to walk through to her left, leading into what could only be described as the firm's throne room. Claudia stood up, nervously smoothing her skirt with sweaty palms.

'Er . . . thanks.' She straightened her shoulders as though shrugging on a cloak of confidence, and walked briskly through the double doors and into a gorgeous-looking office. The back wall was glass from floor to ceiling, with panoramic views of the city. Cyril Eddings's desk was centre stage, large and charcoal in colour. Surprisingly, he wasn't seated in the high-back leather chair behind it, but was standing in front of the desk. He held out his hand to her in greeting.

'Ah, my dear, thank you for coming. Claudia Franklin, isn't it?'

'Yes.'

'Sorry to have kept you waiting. I'm Cyril Eddings, pleased to meet you.'

Claudia felt herself relax a little as she shook his hand. Remembering quickly the man she had witnessed at the wedding, mild-mannered and easygoing. He had not changed much since she had last seen him. He was still portly, with a full head of salt and pepper hair and a smile that was both sharp and engaging.

'Oh.' Her lips stretched into a smile. 'That's absolutely no problem at all.'

'I believe you come to me from Bianca Hanks.' He tilted his head to one side. 'How do you know her?'

A bark of laughter erupted from left field, startling Claudia, as she had not previously noticed anyone else in the room.

A low baritone sounded. 'I'd be surprised if she knows her at all.'

Claudia's wide eyes veered away from the man in front of her to the one on a couch in a pocket of the room that was out of her direct field of vision. She only just managed to stop her jaw hitting the floor.

The man from the bar.

You've got to be kidding me!

He lounged there on one of the couches, one arm stretched out along the back, one leg crossed over the other. He regarded her steadily and without any outward sign of threat. Yet instinctively she knew that she'd be a fool to regard that slight twist to his mouth as anything but suspicious. She glanced quickly at Cyril, who did not seem perturbed by his companion's statement.

'Do you know Sebastian Rowlands?' he asked her, in tones more curious than accusatory.

'Yes,' Sebastian answered for her, with predatory satisfaction. 'She does. This was the woman I met at Seashells. I'm surprised you don't know her. After all, she is your *niece*.'

Double crap.

Claudia glanced quickly at Cyril, expecting to be outed immediately. However, he was watching Sebastian with more enjoyment than shock on his face. The man on the couch stood up unhurriedly, buttoning his open jacket and walking towards her, his eyes trained on her face. 'Are you sure you're in the right place, er . . . Claudia, is it?'

The sarcastic lilt to his voice indicated that he believed she was both liar and fraud, and was expecting her to turn tail and run. Her spine stiffened, making her temper flare anew.

'Definitely. Perhaps you'd like to see my résumé too so that you can satisfy yourself that I am indeed qualified for this position.'

She fished the spare out of her slim, soft leather briefcase and practically shoved it into his hand.

He didn't look at it.

'You do realise that this job requires not only university qualifications but admission to the bar and registration as a practitioner with the High Court of Australia?'

'I satisfy all of those requirements,' she declared truthfully.

He snorted. 'You don't look old enough to have finished uni.'

'And you don't seem well mannered enough to speak in corporate circles but you do, don't you?' She snapped crossly before she thought better of it.

At Sebastian's gasp, Cyril barked with laughter, making her cringe.

'Well, this is all very intriguing.' Cyril rubbed his hands together. 'Please, Claudia, don't stand there by the door. Come in, come in, I want to hear all about you.'

In truth, she would much rather continue giving Sebastian a piece of her mind, but that wasn't going to get her this job anytime soon.

Better to pull back.

She allowed herself to be led over to the couches where Cyril handed her a cup of coffee.

'I have to apologise for my colleague's rudeness,' he said. 'It looks like you've made quite an impression on him.'

She took a sip of her coffee as she sat down. The warm, dark liquid mollified her somewhat as it slipped smoothly down her throat. 'The complete wrong one, obviously.'

Cyril sat beside her. Sebastian, however, continued to stand there, towering over them like a black cloud, threatening to spoil their party. No doubt her bum wasn't good enough for the furniture either.

'Well, I for one am most impressed with your credentials,' remarked Cyril, refilling his own mug. 'Tell me, my dear,' he ignored Sebastian, 'why do you want this job?'

'Because I'm passionate about the justice system and believe that Hanks and Eddings is a firm at the forefront of legal expertise. I would be honoured to join your team.'

Claudia looked up to meet Sebastian's glare. His deep brown eyes bored holes in her like the drill bit of a power tool, which did seem a rather apt description given he was a tool on a definite power trip.

'Excellent, that is all I needed to hear.' Cyril nodded.

Sebastian choked. 'Cyril, this *lawyer*, if she is one, claimed to be a member of your family among other things.'

Claudia bit her lip. He had her there. She *had* lied about that, after all – in a fit of rage, of course, but it was still a lie.

She braced herself for the humiliating questions to follow. 'I am so sorry, my dear.' Cyril leaned towards her. 'I'm shocking when it comes to names and faces. My family, large as it is, is no exception.'

Claudia's eyes widened and she said carefully, 'Oh, I don't expect you to recognise any connection between us at all, sir. Especially for the sake of this job.'

'Oh no.' Sebastian refused to let her escape retribution, slotting himself back into her field of vision so that she had to raise her eyes to his. 'Cyril's far too polite for that. I think we should get right to the bottom of this so-called family connection right now.'

Oh, for goodness sake. What did he want from her? An open confession? So that he might dance to the tune of her humiliation.

What did it matter whether she was a member of the Eddings family or not? She was still completely qualified for this job. With a sigh, she moistened her lips. There was no way to avoid it. She would just have to come clean.

'Cyril is not my uncle exactly.'

'That's right, Seb,' Cyril nodded jovially, 'she's my second cousin.'

Huh?

'*What?*' Seb demanded.

Both their gazes swung to the older man.

'You're one of Adriana's girls, aren't you?' Cyril exclaimed. 'I swear I haven't seen that cousin of mine in years.'

'Cyril.' Seb's tone was stern, but the reigning partner of the firm didn't seem to notice he was being addressed. He threw himself back on the couch, his expression one of reminiscence. 'Why, the last time I saw my cousin Adriana was at my daughter's wedding. You have the look of her, you know.'

'I do?' Claudia squeaked, wondering what the hell was going on.

'Same shade of hair. Wonderful girl.'

'Are you sure it's the exact same shade?' Seb demanded curtly. 'Not too dark by any chance?'

'Oh no,' Cyril said brightly, 'it is the exact same shade.'

What is happening right now?

Does Cyril actually think we're related?

Do I dissuade him?

Do I change the subject and try to leave?

As though reading her mind, Seb said to her darkly, 'You need to go.'

This may have been good advice, but coming from him as an order rather than a request, it did more to put her in a dangerous mood than any shot of alcohol ever could.

'I'm sorry,' she sat up straighter, 'is this *your* office? Because last time I checked it belonged to my uncle.'

He blustered. 'Your uncle –'

'My uncle will ask me to leave when he wishes me to go,' she said sweetly.

'Well said, my dear,' Cyril patted her arm encouragingly. 'Well said.'

Seb switched tack. 'Tell me about the last time you saw your cousin, Adrianna, Cyril.' He turned to the older man, much like he was in court conducting a cross-examination. 'It was at your daughter's wedding, wasn't it? You must have invited her whole family.'

Claudia sat up straighter, anger stiffening her spine. 'Are you asking if I was there?'

'What do you think?' Sebastian's eyes shot daggers at her.

She lifted her chin. 'Well, I was.'

The room went silent as both men regarded her with different degrees of surprise. Nothing was more exhilarating to a lawyer than having the one piece of information that nobody else had. And, unfortunately, she was not immune to the spike of adrenaline that went straight to her head. The temptation to hit a home run was simply too overwhelming.

'You gave a wonderful speech,' she said to Cyril. 'It was very entertaining.'

'You thought so, did you?' He leaned forward with a grin.

'You told so many great jokes. I loved the one about the wedding cake and how it was so big you hoped no one was going to jump out of it.'

Cyril was pink with pleasure. 'I did say that, didn't I? Seb,' he turned back to the lawyer, who was still standing, 'you really should have been there.'

'Ah yes,' she turned in sympathy to the fuming man still looming over her. 'I don't recall seeing you at the reception. Given it was a river cruise, I would have to say,' she added with a mocking twinkle, 'you really missed the boat.'

Cyril laughed out loud. 'My dear, you must work for this firm. I insist.'

The triumph she felt as he made this announcement didn't take long to go cold.

You can't be hired as an Eddings!

'Oh.' She stood up, shaking her head. 'I couldn't possibly take a job based on our relationship.'

'Who said it was based on our relationship?' Cyril demanded. 'We need more people like you. Attitudes like yours kick goals.' He swiped a fist through the air. 'Seb, sort out the paperwork, will you? I've just realised I have another meeting to attend in the boardroom.' His gaze flicked to his watch. 'For which I am now late.'

'But –' Claudia tried to interrupt him, to no avail.

'Congratulations, my dear.' Cyril lightly kissed her cheek, stunning her into silence. Then he patted the spot his lips had been as any uncle would. 'Welcome to Sebastian's team.'

'Wait. Sebastian's team?'

'He'll tell you all about it.' He gave her both pointer fingers as he backed out of the room. 'I'll see you tomorrow.'

A second later he was gone.

What have I done?

Shell-shocked, she turned round to find Sebastian Rowlands watching her. This was why he had been present for the interview, because he was to be her new boss. If only she'd put two and two together a few seconds earlier. His eyes glinted and she could tell immediately that he was enjoying her slow realisation. Just as he was going to enjoy having control over her in the workplace.

'I'll be working with you?' Her tough veneer faltered a little.

'*For* me.' His smile was sadistic.

Of course.

'Congratulations.'

'I think,' she swallowed hard, 'that if I were to take this job it would be best if we didn't tell anyone about my relationship to Cyril. After all, it's not the reason he hired me. I wouldn't want to give people the wrong impression.'

'Of course not,' he purred knowingly. 'I wouldn't dream of telling anyone. In return, I will require your absolute compliance with all my instructions.'

The balance of power had already shifted.

She lifted her chin. 'Of course.'

Chapter 8

After Lydia made the announcement that she was calling Jack back into the fray, one could say that everything went to shit. The last person Bronwyn wanted raining on her parade was Jack Franklin.

'Mum, it's a bad idea,' said Chris. 'Dad will never allow it.'

Lydia looked at him. 'Who says I'm going to tell him?'

'Even worse.' Chris shook his head. 'Besides, Jack won't agree. He hasn't been at Oak Hills in five years. Why would he come back now?'

'We've never asked him to before.'

'With good reason,' Chris retorted angrily.

'Because there's too much bad blood?' Lydia enquired softly. 'After the accident, we all treated him like some sort of outcast. Myself included.'

Chris's face seemed to close off. 'Bronwyn didn't.'

To her alarm, Lydia's gaze swung in her direction. 'No, that's right. When he moved out, you were the only one who kept an eye on him.'

A fat lot of good it did me.

Lydia continued, 'It has always been my shame as a mother

that I was so focused on Chris that I forgot about my other son. Jack was okay physically but he must have been going through hell.'

Bronwyn bit her lip. 'He wasn't far off it.' She'd always been mad at Lydia for that, but she guessed the older woman had punished herself more for her lack of insight than words ever could. After all, she hadn't seen her older son in half a decade.

'I always thought he'd cool off and come home, you know,' said Lydia. 'I never thought we'd be standing here five years on, wondering why he's still angry with us.'

'*He's* angry with *us*!' Chris scoffed. 'That's rich. What about me and Dad? Who's to say we're not still angry at him?'

On these words, he pushed his hands on his wheels and exited the room, leaving Bronwyn awkwardly alone with Lydia.

'There's something you've got to understand, Lydia.' She chose her words carefully. 'I may have felt sorry for Jack all those years ago but it made no impression on him whatsoever. If you're thinking of bringing him back here, I think you're making a mistake.'

'Why would you say that? You used to adore Jack. I remember speaking to your mother about it.'

The room tilted on its side for a second. '*You spoke to my mother about that?*' She couldn't stop her voice from trembling.

Lydia swatted her hand. 'This was years ago. You know, just a mother to mother chat. She was concerned about how the accident was affecting you.'

My mother doesn't have 'mother to mother' chats.

Bronwyn swallowed hard as pieces of a puzzle she'd long given up on started to fall into place.

'What's the matter?' Lydia eyed her with concern. 'Have I said something wrong?'

Several things, actually.

'It's nothing to be embarrassed about, Bronwyn.' Lydia touched her arm. 'I always knew there was something going on between you two. It was the way you spoke to one another.'

Bronwyn tried in vain to clear the lump in her throat. 'I think you got the wrong end of the stick, Lydia. Jack and I were always fighting.'

Lydia looked surprised. 'Whatever about?'

'Anything and everything. Don't you remember how much he used to tease me?'

'Really?' Lydia squinted at the ceiling.

Bronwyn folded her arms crossly. 'He was always playing pranks and hiding my things. He called me a "numbat", for Pete's sake, and then everybody else caught on.'

'Oh, I'd forgotten about that. But he did care about you in his own way, you know.' She sighed. 'He was always being nice to you and Claudia. He lent you his car that one time, so you could go on that day trip to Augusta, remember.'

'That car was a bomb and it broke down on a lonely stretch of Caves Road right in the middle of the Boranup Karri Forest.'

'Such a beautiful part of the region.'

'He left us waiting there for hours before he came to rescue us!' Bronwyn found she was still annoyed by his behaviour.

'At least he did that,' Lydia protested. 'Didn't he take you sandwiches as well?'

'Yes, and ate most of them on the way over.'

'He always did have a good appetite,' Lydia smiled. 'Perhaps that's not such a good example. What about the time you accidentally deleted a uni assignment and had to redo it all? He stayed up all night with you retyping certain bits so you could still get it in on time.'

Bronwyn threw up her hands. 'That's because it was his fault I lost the work! He renamed the file "Jack's got balls" as a prank, and that's why I deleted it!'

'Well,' Lydia tried again, 'you have to admit at least he was very protective. He didn't like any of the other local boys taking an interest in you. He always used to pick you and Claudia up if you went out partying late, which I thought was very sweet of him.'

There was that, she supposed.

Along with a nice generous dollop of arrogance.

Sprinkled with nosiness.

And smothered in presumption.

Quite the sundae was Jack.

'Personally,' Bronwyn snapped, 'I think he just enjoyed patronising us. Putting his two cents in where it wasn't wanted.'

'If you say so.' Lydia shrugged. 'I always thought there was more to it. Call it a mother's intuition.'

To her annoyance, Bronwyn felt her face heating up. It was a good thing that no one but Claudia knew about that 'out of left field' kiss she and Jack had once exchanged. A kiss that had left her embarrassed and angry with herself for having let it happen. Because it was her first kiss. It should have been something special.

Who are you kidding?

It was special. Too bloody special to forget.

Also crazy, insane and completely random. She didn't know what had come over her, letting it affect her the way it had. Reading into things that weren't there. Hoping there was something more to it when there wasn't. Give Jack Franklin an inch and he'd take a yard and then leave you with nothing in return – which was exactly what he'd done.

He was a cheeky rascal.

Easy to fall in love with. A devil to forget.

He had a wicked sense of humour that you didn't want to be drawn in by, but sometimes you couldn't seem to help yourself.

Throughout the entire time she'd known him she'd always been so careful to guard herself when he'd seemed inclined to flirt with her. It was that one stupid moment, when she'd let her guard down for a second.

Stupid, stupid, stupid.

The world knew all Jack had ever seen her as was Claudia's dorky little friend from the city. Another girl in half a dozen.

He had a reputation in these parts as the womaniser of the South-West. Kissing girls indiscriminately was a very 'Jack' sort of thing to do. When she'd known him he'd dated but never had a girlfriend. During her university holidays with Claudia, she'd met a string of his conquests and witnessed the fickleness of his attitude firsthand. Some of them were heartbroken when they realised they weren't going to get more out of Jack than he'd already given them. Some knew the game and were happy to play. It would have been so easy to get caught up in his charisma. He had a smile that could melt steel, eyes that could make you feel like you were his whole world, and the undeniable talent of being able to make world-class chardonnay out of backyard grapes.

Whatever you said about him, Jack was good at what he did. He was very in tune with his art, just as talented as his father, and tipped at the time to take Oak Hills to even greater heights. Nothing was more attractive than a man's bond with his passion, and she knew that Chris often lamented his lack of creative skills.

'It's like a chick magnet,' he used to tell Bronwyn. 'When they find out he makes wine, they think he's God's gift. I don't get it.'

'That's because,' Jack had walked in on their conversation with a devious smile, 'I work in mysterious ways.'

There had been a snort and shoe thrown across the room but, all the same, she imagined Chris must miss Jack a great deal, because they had been such good mates.

Best friends as well as brothers.

So alike in some ways. So different in others.

They'd done everything together.

Both impossible flirts, though Chris had not been quite so callous with the ladies as Jack. Often getting ribbed by his brother as the one they could 'bring home to Mum'. Chris had taken this in good part, accepting his role as the more reliable one with good humour.

Now, Bronwyn wasn't quite sure how Chris's attitude had changed. It didn't seem like the two brothers had reconnected at all.

Claudia said she emailed Jack from time to time, but she wondered if Chris did. Bronwyn bit her lip. Could it be possible that they hadn't communicated with each other at all during Jack's time away? Sadness tore at her heart. This was never what she would have wished for either of them, though she could see how it had happened.

After the accident, Jack had left, leaving both Chris and Oak Hills to fend for themselves. He'd done a terrible thing under terrible circumstances. Dealt with it in a terrible way too, as only Jack could.

'So what about Chris?' Lydia enquired. 'You must have noticed the crush he had on you back then.'

Bronwyn lowered her eyes. She *had* noticed but things had never been like that between them, and Oak Hills was her sanctuary. She hadn't wanted to do anything to jeopardise that.

'Well?'

'I have never felt anything for Chris beyond friendship, before and after the wheelchair.'

Lydia shook her head sadly. 'And there lies the crux of the matter. Well, I don't suppose there's much point debating the past when we have so many problems right now.' She rubbed her hands together. 'Should we get you settled in a bedroom?'

Bronwyn thought she'd never ask. There was one thing she needed to do first though.

'How'd you like to meet my dog?'

They went outside and Bronwyn breathed in the air, allowing the tranquillity of her surroundings to take away some of the fallout from the emotional conversation she'd just had. A blue fairy-wren and a New Holland honeyeater danced in Lydia's garden alongside the house. She'd planted a few varieties of kangaroo paw, Pincushion Hakea and choisya there. Bees buzzed around the wildflowers, giving Bronwyn a sense of a whole other world she'd been missing out on all these years.

They found the large bullmastiff asleep under a gum tree. She was lying on her side, paws straight out, panting. Her heavy belly was very noticeable against the flat ground and her nipples more prominent than ever.

'This is Elsa,' Bronwyn told Lydia proudly. 'Trust me, she's not normally this restful. I fully expected her to be trotting through the vines right now, not sleeping under a tree.'

She watched in fascination as Elsa's tummy jerked slightly and moved from within. Bronwyn knelt down and patted the dog's head. 'I keep forgetting she's pregnant, poor thing.'

Lydia knelt as well. 'She looks like she's almost due. Do you know how long she's been pregnant for?'

Bronwyn screwed up her nose. 'Absolutely no idea.'

Lydia's eyes twinkled. 'And I suppose you don't have any experience with delivering pups either.'

'Me?' Bronwyn put a hand to her chest, wide-eyed. 'No.'

'Well, that's something to look forward to, isn't it?' Lydia grinned.

'Er . . . I guess so.'

Lydia laughed. 'You'll have to make a nest for her some-where. Maybe out the back of the house on the patio.'

'A nest?' Bronwyn's eyes widened.

'Just out of old blankets and stuff. I'll help you. She's got to have somewhere comfortable to deliver her babies.'

'I really don't know anything about birthing pups. Shouldn't we get a vet involved or something?'

'*Pfft.*' Lydia blew on her fringe. 'Completely unnecessary. Dogs are much better at giving birth than humans. She'll do most of the work.'

'Are you sure?'

'Almost positive,' Lydia winked, not really improving Bronwyn's faith in her earlier statement. 'We'll just keep a good eye on her for the moment. Let me know if you see her shivering. That's when she's real close.'

'Okay,' Bronwyn agreed nervously. 'I was actually going to take her for a walk now but if she's asleep then maybe I'll spend a bit of time unpacking.'

They grabbed her two bags from the boot of the car and went back inside the house.

'I was thinking it might be best if I put you in Jack's old room temporarily,' Lydia mused as they mounted the stairs. 'No one's slept in there for years but I always keep the bed made up. Wishful thinking, I suppose.'

Bronwyn's steps faltered. 'I thought I'd be in the guest room like when I used to stay.'

Lydia shook her head. 'Sorry, dear, we've been using that as a storeroom. It's full of boxes now. We'll need a few days to clear it out for you.'

'What about Claudia's room?'

'I guess you could take that, if you can find the bed. You know what Claudia doesn't lack in brains she makes up for in untidiness.'

This was true. Bronwyn smiled. Her apartment was certainly going to get some character over the next few days.

'Jack's old room is huge with nothing in it,' Lydia went on. 'You'll have your own balcony and a much nicer view.'

The thought of braving her best friend's messy room with two suitcases of her own didn't really appeal, and she supposed a balcony was a definite advantage. She never got tired of the views from the upper storey. You could see straight over the vineyard to the winery from there, not to mention the small glimpse of the ocean on the horizon. Her heart warmed to the idea.

'Okay,' she agreed.

If it was just till they cleared the guest room out, there was no point in being coy.

At the top of the stairs they took a left turn and arrived at Jack's room. It was large and airy. A queen bed with a pair of bedside tables dominated one wall. The doona was a pale olive green with matching pillows. A couple of beige cushions had also been thrown on the bed to break up the colour. The room had both its own bathroom and an empty walk-in robe. A desk near the entrance held a few of Jack's personal belongings. Some text books, a photo of him at the MCG with a couple of mates, a few stationery items and a rather worn-looking football. On the wall beside the desk, in a silver frame, hung his degree in Viticulture from Curtin University.

'I'll let you rest and see you downstairs in a bit,' Lydia suggested, exiting the room.

Bronwyn wheeled her suitcase into the walk-in robe. Just as she started unpacking, however, her mobile phone buzzed from her handbag on the bed. She answered it before looking at the number.

'Hello?'

'Hello, this is Casuarina Prison, will you accept a phone call from Peter Goldman?'

'Oh, er . . .' Clearly Bantam, Harvey and Grey had not informed her client that she'd left the firm. 'Okay fine, put him through.' She'd have to tell him herself.

'Bronwyn, thank you for taking my call. I –'

'Peter, I'm going to have to stop you there. I'm sorry that the firm has not told you but I am no longer your lawyer. I've left my job; you're going to have to speak to someone else. If you like I'll shoot Simon an email and ask him to get in touch with you.'

'No, I don't want him to get in touch with me. I want to talk to you.'

'Peter, as I said –'

'It's not about my case, it's about my dog. Has she had her pups yet?'

'No, and thanks for telling me she was pregnant.'

He ignored her reprimand. 'Well, I need her back now.'

Bronwyn frowned. 'That seems like an odd request given you're still in jail.'

'I meant . . .' he corrected himself hastily, 'someone else is adopting her.'

'Why? What's wrong with me?'

'Nothing's wrong with you. You were only ever meant to be a temporary caretaker until Elsa had her pups. However, now the man I've sold her pups to might want their mother as well.'

Alarm bells starting ringing in Bronwyn's head. 'But I thought you loved Elsa. Who is this guy?'

'Names don't matter. I can give you the address of a pub in Northbridge, The Quiet Gentleman. You should take Elsa there as soon as possible. If not tonight, then first thing tomorrow morning.'

Rock up late at night to a pub in Northbridge, to hand over a dog to a person he couldn't name. *Yeah right.* Even she wasn't that dumb. 'I'm sorry, Peter, but I'm out of town right now. I'm not going to be able to do that anytime soon.'

'You're out of town!' He seemed unnecessarily angered by this statement. 'Why the hell would you go out of town?'

'I don't see how it's any of your business.'

'You need to get back to Perth immediately and you need to bring my dog with you, or things are going to get ugly.'

'Ugly how?' Bronwyn demanded.

There was a lengthy pause, probably because Peter had just remembered that all calls put through the prison telephone system were recorded. With a groan of frustration he hung up. Bronwyn pulled the phone from her ear as the dial tone sounded loudly. A feeling of unease slithered down her back.

Elsa, what other trouble have you got me into?

Her phone buzzed again. With relief she looked down and saw that it was Claudia. Lifting the phone to her ear, she walked out onto the balcony, the smell of earth and vine calming her somewhat as she gazed out over the property just as the sun was setting. 'Hi.'

'Bron, I think I'm trouble.'

'Ha!' she snorted. 'You and me both. Okay, you go first.'

'I got the job.'

Bronwyn squealed. 'Yay! That doesn't sound like trouble. That's excellent.'

'I don't think I should take it.'

'Why not? This is all you've ever wanted. Our plan is working out perfectly. You can't give up now.'

'It's not about confidence.' Claudia took a deep breath. 'You see, for some reason, don't ask me how this happened, your Uncle Cyril thinks we're family. He reckons I'm an Eddings!'

'But that's insane. Your name's Claudia Franklin. You had that clearly stated on your résumé, didn't you?'

'Of course, but apparently that's just my mother's married name. I'm a long-lost second cousin come back to the fold,' Claudia's words tumbled out like dominoes set up to fall. 'I wanted to tell him he'd made a mistake but he gave me a kiss and told me to shut up.'

'He kissed you?'

'In a business meeting, like I was his niece.'

'Well, that's odd.'

'Tell me about it!'

Bronwyn's brow wrinkled thoughtfully. 'Does anyone else know about this?'

Claudia groaned. 'Just another lawyer, my new boss, Sebastian Rowlands, who said he won't say anything but I don't know. Do you know him?'

'Oh yeah, incredibly handsome, disgustingly smart and never lost a case to date.'

'And you didn't think to tell me about him before?!'

Bronwyn started at the scolding. 'I, er . . . didn't think he would be a problem for you.'

'He's a right pain in the arse, is what he is. And this whole mess is entirely his fault.'

'How so?'

'He made me so mad that when Cyril made the relationship mistake I kind of backed him up just to put Sebastian in his place.'

Bronwyn's hand went to her hip. 'So what you're really saying is that this is all about your inability to control your temper.'

'You should have seen him, Bron. Grilling me about my qualifications like I had none. You would have done exactly the same thing.'

'Actually,' Bronwyn raised a finger, 'I don't think I would have.'

'Okay. Maybe not *you*, but anyone else on the planet. Trust me.'

'Well, I think I'm going to have to, because I really need you to take that job.'

'What do you mean? Has something happened?'

Bronwyn winced. 'I think I just received a threatening phone call from Elsa's owner.'

'The guy in prison?' Claudia was quick on the money.

'Peter Goldman. He wants his dog back, or else.'

'Or else what?' Claudia snorted. 'He'll break out of jail and stalk you?'

'It's not him I'm worried about, it's his dodgy connections in Northbridge. Who knows who this new person is he wants me to drop his dog off to. You haven't told anyone where I am, have you?'

'No,' Claudia said quickly. 'Geez, Bronwyn. You're not in trouble, are you?'

'I hope not.' Bronwyn's gaze stretched to the horizon with a silent prayer. 'But it would be great if you could have a chat with Peter for me. It'll be easy if you're a lawyer working at a reputable firm. No one will bat an eyelid at you wanting to talk to a prisoner.'

'So now you're saying I *have* to take this job.'

'Just till we get Peter squared away at the very least. Besides,' Bronwyn added cheerfully, 'that little mix-up with you being the niece is nothing to worry about. You did say no one except Sebastian knew and he's not going to tell anyone.'

'Yeah, but what about your mum? When she finds out you used her recommendation to get me a job she's not going to be happy.'

Bronwyn smiled wryly. 'My mum being happy has never been one of Uncle Cyril's top priorities. I think you're pretty safe.'

'I'd feel safer if you called her and tried to smooth things over.'

'I don't know, Claud. My mum is not like yours. I can try, but she's never taken any direction from me. I don't know if I'll just flag a situation she might want to ruin.'

There was a groan. 'But you've got to tell her you've left town sometime. Why not now before things really blow up?'

Bronwyn had hoped to be firmly entrenched in her new role before she brought Bianca Hanks into her confidence.

After all, you know what she's capable of when you do something she doesn't like.

She didn't, however, want to cause Claudia any extra stress when she was already taking this job for her. 'All right,' she agreed. 'I'll give it a go.'

Claudia's breath whooshed out. 'Thanks. So apart from the threat from prison, how are you going in Yallingup?'

'Not as great as I hoped.' Bronwyn sighed. 'You never said how tense things were here. No one was overjoyed with our plan and your dad and Chris had a bit of a stand-off this afternoon.'

'Don't worry, it'll blow over. You know how Chris is, Bron, as easygoing as the wind.'

'I don't know, Claud. He's changed a lot since I last saw him. He's definitely got a bitter streak now and your mum's talking about getting Jack home.'

'Ha. Jack has absolutely no incentive to come home. Don't forget, he has his pride. Dad fired him and kicked him out. He's not going to come home without some dire reason or an apology. So I don't see it happening anytime soon.'

'I guess you're right.'

Men and their pride. It had broken up more families than Bronwyn cared to think about. As a lawyer, she'd seen so many divorces for similar reasons. She'd even got in trouble one time for leaving a couple together in the conference room for too long, secretly hoping they'd just work it out. Yes, it was one more dumb thing she'd done in the legal profession.

'Okay.' She took a deep breath. 'But what about your dad? He hates that I'm taking over your role. In fact,' she added in a small voice, 'he said it was ridiculous.'

'Bron, he's all bark and no bite. He'll expect you to prove yourself no doubt, which I'm sure you will.'

'How?' Bronwyn asked. 'I have no idea where to start. I feel like you've sent me unarmed into the Colosseum.'

Claudia laughed. 'Honestly, Bron. This is your forte. You've got this.'

'I don't see how.'

'People skills,' Claudia said firmly. 'You've got them in droves. Everybody loves you. Or haven't you noticed? Just be yourself.'

'Thanks, but I'm going to need a little more direction than that to bring this winery out of the morgue.'

'Okay.' Claudia cleared her throat. 'In my humble opinion, there are three things holding this winery back: my dad, my mum and Chris.'

'Well, that's very complimentary.'

'Yeah, well, they don't get it but they're killing their own business, and no amount of talking on my part has got them to realise it.'

'Your mum and Chris have already explained to me your dad's issues with retirement. But how are your mum and Chris sabotaging Oak Hills?'

'Just get into my office and go over the bills. You'll see what I mean.'

'Okay.

'But don't forget to call your mum first.'

'On it.'

'And I'll see if I can find out more about Peter Goldman.'

'Thanks.'

Bronwyn put down the phone. The truth was, the very last person she wanted to call was her mother. Bianca Hanks was not going to take this well. Nevertheless, with a sigh she rang the number and was ridiculously relieved when it went straight to voicemail. She hung up.

Maybe I'll write her an email instead.

She could be much less confrontational and much more vague. Lying down on her bed, she tried several times to write the message.

Dear Mum,
You'll never guess what happened this week

Delete, delete, delete.

Dear Mum,
Funny story

Delete, delete, delete.

Dear Mum,
So I've got good news and bad news.

With a wince, she clicked her phone off. It wasn't going to work. For Claudia's sake she had to gauge her mother's reaction, and sending an email would not allow her to do that. Perhaps she should try calling her mother again before she went to bed.

She could smell dinner downstairs and it was making her stomach roil in hunger. As a uni student she'd always looked forward to the family meal. It had been the best part of the day. There was a closeness the Franklins had then that she had always envied. They argued like cats and dogs, made fun of each other's choices and didn't have the least respect for privacy. But there was such warmth between them . . . then.

On the other hand, dinner with her mum had usually been pre-prepared gourmet meals home-delivered by Lite n' Easy, eaten on stools at the kitchen counter while her mum lectured her on all facets of her personality from her looks to her grades. Dinner with Dad was always from the local Chinese takeaway and generally eaten in front of the news – no talking allowed.

She really didn't know which was worse: the parent who didn't engage or the one who engaged too much.

Her father tended to call her twice a year, once on her birthday and once at Christmas, their conversations no more than five minutes and mainly about work. On Father's Day she usually went to visit him and each time she hoped they would bond over something else – the gift she'd given him, the latest political news or the last book he'd read. But the truth was the only connection they had was the law, and maybe that was in part why she'd held on to it for so long.

Bronwyn put aside the sad memories and went downstairs, allowing her nose to lead her straight to the kitchen. For Lydia, cooking was as much hobby as it was necessity. She was a messy cook who loved to taste as she prepared. She usually put as many of the ingredients in her mouth and on the floor as she did in the dish. She had more cookbooks than Bronwyn cared to count but mostly didn't follow them. They were mainly for ideas. She threw together her own combinations with a flair that always resulted in delicious dishes that went well with wine.

That night, they were having grilled salmon seasoned with lemon pepper and thyme, served with a garlic mash and steamed vegetables. Horace had brought out sauvignon blanc from his personal cellar downstairs, because the Franklins had wine with dinner every night.

As the delectable meal melted in her mouth, Bronwyn couldn't help but notice how quiet everyone was. The clinking and scraping of cutlery was the loudest sound at the table. There was none of the laughter or raucous debating she had experienced in the past. Perhaps it was because both Claudia and Jack weren't there, two siblings who were more alike than they knew, especially when it came to pride. Or perhaps because the trouble that had been festering in the Franklin family for years was now running too deep to talk about anymore. She had her job cut out for her, that was for sure.

If she hadn't been thinking about it so closely she might have enjoyed her meal more. And she also might have remembered to call her mother before she went to bed that night.

Chapter 9

A law firm wasn't exactly the safest place for an identity fraudster like her. Swimming with corporate piranhas, she knew there was more than a few who would like to take a little bite out of her . . . if only they knew how.

On her first day she recognised a couple of faces from law school. Unlike Claudia, they hadn't taken two years out of their career to work in their parents' vineyard. Instead, they had been building solid reputations at Hanks and Eddings, hoping for a promotion like the one that had been handed to her on a silver platter. Claudia cringed inwardly when she discovered that working exclusively for Sebastian Rowlands was the position most coveted by the young bloods of the firm. They were not happy to see what they considered their opportunity handed over to someone new and, in their opinion, less deserving.

If Cyril was number one at the firm, then Sebastian was most certainly number two. He brought in the most clients, handled the most cases and was the source of the most work in the office. It didn't take Claudia more than a day or two to discover that sucking up to Sebastian Rowlands was a matter of course. The lawyers did it, the secretaries did it, even the mail clerk went above and beyond to look good to the man. It was no wonder he was so full of himself. He had people falling arse over tit to please him. There were more than a few looks of jealousy that followed her in when she took her seat beside Nelson Rubin, Sebastian's other protégé.

Luckily, Nelson seemed genuinely pleased to see her.

'You'll take the pressure off me,' he confessed. 'I don't think I've been working fast enough for Seb. I can feel his frustration through the glass walls sometimes.'

There was certainly *something* coming through those glass walls. It was strange to be able to fully observe Sebastian in his fish tank of an office without being able to converse or communicate with him. That first morning, when she arrived, he didn't even come out to greet her, just kept fielding calls. His jacket was off, hanging on a hook by the door. His white shirt moulded around his broad shoulders when he reached for the phone and outlined his generous bicep. It looked like Sebastian's strength was physical as well as corporate. Blinking fast and turning away to halt this unsettling train of thought, she refocused on Nelson.

'So what do I do?' she whispered. 'Do I knock on his office door and ask for work?'

Nelson looked horrified. 'You never interrupt Sebastian unless invited to do so. I reckon, if you want to know what's going on, ask Juliet. The secretaries know everything around here.'

It was a universal truth of most law firms that if the partners ran the show, it was the administrative staff who held the balance of power. A secretary was a lawyer's right hand. He or she handled all his files, knew all his secrets and was closer to him than a spouse . . . if he had one. Most lawyers were divorced or in the process of becoming so.

Claudia sighed. That was one aspect of this career she wasn't planning on adopting, but it didn't mean she didn't get the rules. Juliet Nesbit sat on the other side of Nelson. She'd had a set of earphones on while they were talking and was busy typing a document. Claudia tentatively approached her desk.

Juliet's eyes remained on her screen, but she held up a finger to Claudia while she inserted a full stop and then a comma into the text, before pulling off her earphones and addressing her. 'You must be Claudia.'

Claudia held out her hand cheerfully. 'Yes, very nice to meet you.'

'Likewise.' Then Juliet cut to the chase. 'Seb wants you to look at these.'

She drew three huge black foolscap files from under her desk and placed them on top with a loud thwack. Claudia took a breath.

Day One. Three cases.

'Wow,' her eyes widened. 'That's a lot of work.'

'What were you expecting?' Juliet's eyes narrowed.

Rule number one when it came to this profession was that work was your friend.

Your best friend.

A good caseload meant good billables, good billables meant a healthy timesheet, and for a lawyer who wanted a positive career trajectory, the numbers were *all* that mattered. She hadn't thought Sebastian would be this kind to her, though she wasn't going to tell his secretary that.

'Okay.' Juliet leaned heavily on the files. 'Let me give you some idea. You work for Sebastian Rowlands. That means long hours, no weekends, no boyfriend, no social life to speak of except for the occasional takeaway dinner in a meeting room with myself or Nelson or the man himself, *if* he deigns you smart enough to keep up with him. You live work, you breathe work. At no point in the day do you not think like a lawyer because that's the point you will get screwed. And if you get screwed the firm gets screwed and we all suffer. Get it?'

'Absolutely.' Claudia stood straighter, unable to keep the grin from her face. She was definitely not complaining. This was why she was here, to submerge herself in the profession she loved, like it was a nice hot bubble bath. 'Thanks.'

Juliet Nesbit sniffed as though she were hoping for a little more snivelling and Claudia quickly scraped the files off her desk, turned tail and made her way back to her desk.

She worked solidly for the next couple of hours before lunch. Then when the other lawyers left their desks to buy sandwiches, she rang Casuarina Prison. Bronwyn had, after all, charged her with the task of dropping in on Peter Goldman. She had better see what she could do. When she tried to make an appointment to see him, however, she got a rather disturbing piece of news from one of the prison officers.

'Peter Goldman went into hospital this morning with a couple of broken ribs after being attacked at breakfast by one of his fellow inmates.'

Claudia did not like the sound of this at all. She sat up straighter. 'Was the attack provoked?'

'We are still investigating but from what we know of Bruce Carle, the attacker, he's a loose cannon. He picks fights like this all the time. He said he didn't like the way Peter looked at him.'

'Right,' Claudia swallowed. 'Thank you for your time.'

She put the phone down, chewing hard on her bottom lip. *What now?*

Her fingers brushed over her keyboard and she brought up Google. Fifteen minutes and several old news articles later, she had a much clearer picture of who Bruce Carle was. The man was in prison for murder, though it wasn't the only death he was suspected of causing. Bruce Carle was a minion of Leon McCall, an organised crime boss who had fingers in all sorts of illegal pies. Drugs, prostitutes, smuggling. Claudia knew his name as soon as she read it. His face was always being splashed over the media. He was one of those celebrity criminals who shamelessly flaunted his ill-gotten gains with extravagant and eccentric spending. Leon McCall had interests in precious gems, luxury cars and women half his age. He'd been married at least five times. She'd heard the latest spouse was an ex-swimsuit model eager to make a name for herself on the charity scene.

As for Leon's illegal activities, the police hadn't been able to nail him because he hid behind his legitimate businesses, letting his followers, such as Bruce Carle, dirty their hands instead.

Any connection to Leon was not good news.

She looked up the court documents that detailed Peter's trial and sentencing, which were now part of public record. His crime was fraud. Setting himself up as a land developer, he'd siphoned money from his clients' investments. There didn't really seem to be any connection between him and Leon McCall . . . yet.

She sent Bronwyn a brief text message which read, 'Is there any way Peter Goldman could be connected to Leon McCall?'

A second later her phone rang. It was Bronwyn, so she quickly picked it up. 'Leon McCall!' her best friend cried. 'Are you trying to freak me out?'

'Sorry. There's just been a bit of a development here.' She quickly outlined for Bronwyn what had happened.

'Oh.'

'So you see, it's just one path of investigation I have to rule out. Please tell me I can.'

'I . . . I *think* you can,' Bronwyn said slowly, as though she were ticking off boxes in her head. Just as Claudia was starting to breathe a sigh of relief, Bronwyn corrected herself. 'Wait! He's a gambler.'

'A what?'

'Peter is a high-stakes gambler. He used his fraudulent earnings to fund his habit. Loved the casino, was there all the time when he wasn't ripping people off. It's no wonder his wife hates him.'

Great.

Leon McCall was notorious for this vice as well. His wins and losses at the Crown were legendary.

'Do you think they ever played each other?' Claudia asked.

'I have no idea.'

'It still makes no sense. If Peter owes Leon money, then what does that have to do with Elsa?'

'Well, we're just guessing here,' Bronwyn suggested. 'Maybe we're guessing wrong. Maybe it has nothing to do with Elsa. Maybe it's all just a big coincidence. After all, didn't the prison officer say that Bruce Carle had a quick temper and was notorious for causing trouble just because?'

'Yes.'

'Then?'

'Then I hope you're right, but the only way to know for sure is to question Peter myself. I'm going to have to go to that hospital and ask him.'

Bronwyn sighed. 'I'm sorry I'm putting you through all this, Claud, especially on your first week at work. Maybe you should just leave it alone.'

'Why on earth would I do that?'

'Well, I'm perfectly safe here. Nobody knows where I am, except for you. I haven't been to Oak Hills in a couple of years so it shouldn't fall under immediate suspicion, *especially* with those people who don't even know me.'

Claudia snorted. 'I'd rather be safe than sorry. Don't give it another thought, I'm doing this. So you better let me get back to calling Casuarina Prison. I'll have to see if I can schedule that appointment with their inmate, after all.'

They said their goodbyes and rang off.

'Hitting the ground running, I see?' Nelson smiled as he returned to his desk, a ham and salad roll in one hand, a juice bottle in the other. 'Already working through lunch.'

'Er . . . yeah.' She clicked the article about Leon McCall she'd been reading off her computer screen, hoping he hadn't heard her mention Casuarina to Bronwyn either. As she drew a large black file to the front of her desk, he bent his head to read the spine.

'The Cornwall case. That's a good one.'

'Yes it is,' she agreed, glad to have diverted his attention.

'So where did you work before this?' Nelson asked as he sat down. 'I haven't seen you around town before.' He flushed. 'I mean, at court that is.'

She knew he was referring to the day they'd first met at Seashells under very different circumstances.

Nelson winced. 'I should, er . . . probably apologise for my behaviour that day. Seb and I . . . we were out of line.'

He's apologising!

Claudia couldn't help but see the irony in this when his boss, the main culprit, had offered her no such courtesy at all.

'That's all right. I know *you* didn't mean to insult me.'

Nelson paused, eyeing her uncertainly. 'I know you were furious at Seb and probably still are but I'm sure he feels bad about his mistake.'

Claudia choked.

'He's not really that mean a guy,' Nelson rushed on. 'He's been really kind to me and . . .' He trailed off, reddening again, which piqued Claudia's interest.

'And what?' she prompted gently.

'It's just that,' Nelson shrugged rather self-consciously, 'I'm not quite sure why he picked me.'

If Claudia was brutally honest with herself, she wasn't sure why Sebastian had picked Nelson either. Of all the junior lawyers she had met so far at Hanks and Eddings, Nelson was actually nice, which was an attribute that didn't work strongly in his favour. He'd been friendly, charming and extremely helpful since she'd arrived, if a little anxious. Until now, she had thought that Nelson had been allocated to Sebastian perhaps by Cyril, to lift the young man's self-esteem. She had heard Nelson speaking several times on the phone and winced. He stammered hopelessly through his instructions with clients.

He apologised far too often to people he was suing and he seemed to be driven by nerves all the time. She'd even seen him jump a couple of times when the email alert sounded on his computer.

It was very odd that Sebastian had chosen Nelson to mentor. The knowledge did kind of mess with the two-dimensional image of him she had in her head.

'I mean,' Nelson wrung his hands self-consciously, 'you should meet some of the other lawyers on this floor.'

Claudia already had.

There was one girl called Anna Mavis who fancied herself the alpha of the group and had already tried to make sure that Claudia was aware of her place in the pecking order.

After introducing herself, Anna pointed out how lucky she was that *her* desk was facing a window. It wasn't a particularly good view, Anna could only see into the building next door. However, by contrast, Claudia's desk faced a wall. A wall on which hung a fire extinguisher and the safety warden's helmet. There was no comparison.

Like Nelson, Anna too tried to dig deeper into Claudia's past, though with more sinister intent. Claudia told her exactly what she had told Nelson. She named the firm she had worked for as a graduate and then said she'd taken a couple of years off to spend time with her family.

All of which was perfectly true.

There was no need to go into details and, given Cyril's mistake, she hoped to steer clear of that topic as much as possible. As for the interview mix-up, Sebastian had so far made good on his word. There was no hint of her deception floating around the office. And she was finally starting to feel safe that it would never come out.

It was unfortunate that she had completely forgotten that the lie about being an Eddings had not started in Cyril's office. The first time she'd told it was at Seashells, when Nelson had also been present.

And sadly no one had sworn him to secrecy.

Chapter 10

Sebastian always grabbed his morning coffee from the street-corner cafe, Costello's, a five-minute walk from Hanks and Eddings. Thursday morning was no exception. What he didn't expect was to bump into his junior lawyer, Claudia, in the line.

He refrained from bringing his presence to her notice immediately, content to just study her for a moment in dissatisfaction. He still hadn't quite decided what he was going to do with her. When she had started yesterday he'd sent her a few files and decided to wait and see if she sank or swam. This time they were going to play by *his* rules, not hers.

Watching her unguarded movements was actually quite liberating.

Since their second meeting, in Cyril's office, he had noticed that she only wore her hair up, in a loose but professional chignon. Almost as though dressing in that way improved her chances of being taken seriously. It was definitely a far cry from the sexy disarray she had sported in the hotel bar the day they'd first met, yet it did not detract from her youthful beauty. He certainly felt the age gap between them when the barista, a good ten years younger than him, started flirting with her. He gritted his teeth.

Despite having been served by the same young man almost every day for the past two years, this was the first time Sebastian had bothered to read his name tag.

Tom Rubin. Assistant Manager.

He wore a dark T-shirt printed with the words 'Ten cents from every coffee bought here goes to the Lucas Foundation.'

'So I haven't seen you around before,' Tom said to Claudia as he held his silver milk jug under the steamer. 'Have you just started working in the area?'

'Hanks and Eddings,' Claudia responded shyly.

'A lawyer.' Tom raised his eyebrows as though impressed. 'You must be super smart.'

'I get by.' Claudia shrugged. 'I like your T-shirt. What's the Lucas Foundation?'

'It's a charity dedicated to helping young people with drug and alcohol addictions get off the streets and return to their families.'

'That's really great.'

Tom pressed a lid onto her takeaway cup. 'Yeah. We're having a big fundraiser in a couple of weeks actually. A special breakfast here.' He grabbed a flyer off the counter and passed it to her. 'You should come.'

'I think I will.' Claudia smiled.

She turned around then and almost walked straight into him. 'Sebastian!' she gasped.

He inclined his head. 'Claudia.'

She hesitated, as though unsure whether to continue the conversation, then said finally, 'I'll see you back at the office.'

'You will,' he agreed and stepped forward to order his own coffee, but Tom was busy waving at her.

'See ya, Claudia!'

'Er . . . yeah,' she said quickly under Sebastian's hard stare. 'Catch you later.'

They met again in the foyer of Hanks and Eddings outside the lifts. She seemed uncomfortable by the silence that stretched between them so he made no effort to break it. She was probably wondering why he hadn't come to see her yet, welcomed her to the office, so to speak.

Ha! Did she deserve a welcome?

'Thanks for the files yesterday.' She sipped her coffee. 'Let me know if there's anything you want me to go through with you.'

'Of course.'

She shuffled from foot to foot when he said nothing more. To his amusement, she then tried to engage him in small talk.

'So I think I might put this on the noticeboard in the kitchen.' She lifted the flyer she was holding. 'Might be a good thing for everyone to attend.'

'I'm sure, though I think Tom was extending the invitation mostly to you rather than the entire firm.'

'Tom?'

'The barista you were flirting with.'

'His name was Tom?' To his annoyance her eyes lit momentarily with interest. 'He didn't mention –' Hastily she cut herself off, cleared her throat and glared at him. 'I mean, I wasn't flirting with him.'

'My mistake,' he said drily.

She frowned. Inwardly, he was wondering why he cared so much that his inference had been right. Those two were well suited to each other. Similar in age, and if the fundraiser was anything to go by, both carrying backpacks of idealism on their shoulders.

As if to prove his point she said, 'I happen to believe in this cause, it sounds like an extremely worthy charity.'

'Is that so?'

The lift doors opened and they both stepped in. 'Drug addiction, any sort of addiction really, places a lot strain on families.' She pressed the number of their floor. The lift doors closed.

Unwilling to get into a conversation he knew all too much about, he turned the topic back on her. 'Family means a lot to you, I take it.'

'For many years,' Claudia nodded, 'it's been my everything.' Belatedly, she seemed to realise to whom she was talking, squared her shoulders and cleared her throat. 'I mean, with things like addiction, those important family relationships are the first to break down. Bringing people back together after trauma –'

'Is not always a good thing,' he said involuntarily.

'I beg your pardon?'

'You can't force things like that, especially with just a lot of high ideals from people who have never been in that situation.'

'So don't even bother to try?' she demanded, and then muttered under her breath, 'I might have known you'd say something like that.'

It was his turn to get angry. 'You know absolutely nothing about me, Claudia. And if I were you I would stick to your case files rather than saving the world at large.'

The lift doors opened and he was relieved to step out.

Damn it, Seb! That was a complete overreaction.

Why did this girl have the power to rile him so badly? He had to stop thinking about her as the sexy temptress he met in a bar and remember she was a lawyer he was now supposed to manage.

It was what Cyril wanted. Though damned if he knew why.

'I thought you said you were giving me a gift,' he'd said to Cyril when he'd come back after Claudia's interview.

'I have.' Cyril had winked at him. 'Exactly the sort you need. You haven't had a decent challenge around here in a long time.'

'It sounds to me like this present is more for yourself,' he had retorted angrily.

'What can I say?' Cyril had shrugged. 'Any excuse to make Bianca Hanks wiggle like a worm on a hook.'

Seb's eyes had narrowed. 'So you admit it, you don't think this girl has come from Bianca Hanks.'

'She's my niece,' Cyril professed even more cryptically. 'Why would she have?'

There was no use talking to the old man. He seemed to think his bizarre actions were completely justified. Not only was he going to settle old scores with Bianca Hanks, he was going to teach Seb a much needed lesson about women, which only served to incense Seb further.

If Claudia taught him anything about women, it was that they should never be underestimated. If they were smart enough, which this girl obviously was, they could get away with just about anything.

It was perhaps unfortunate that he had a meeting with Nelson later that morning and was still in this rather acrimonious mood. Nelson was in fine spirits and had only nice things to say about the new addition to their team.

'She's so efficient,' he sighed. 'You should see her. Not an ounce of fear. I bet she'd be awesome in court. I always find it so demanding.'

Sebastian pursed his lips, trying to soften his words but not quite succeeding. 'Trials are trying, Nelson. They define the word. No one finds them easy.'

'I guess so. Is there anything else you need help with today? Or perhaps you'd like me to assist Claudia? I heard her talking on the phone to Casuarina Prison yesterday about interviewing an inmate. '

Sebastian's mind had already started wandering towards to his own cases but Nelson's words jerked him right back.

'What? Casuarina Prison?'

'Yes,' Nelson nodded.

'That's not one of my cases.'

What the hell was she doing working on files that weren't from him? Which of the other partners was already trying to poach her?

Surely she wasn't that good.

Would you really be surprised?

He ground his teeth again.

Meanwhile, Nelson was beginning to look a little guilty. 'Maybe I heard it wrong. I was just impressed by her gumption, calling them.' He sighed as he reflected on his own flaws. 'Some people just have a gift. She's going to be hugely successful.'

Tired of hearing him sing Claudia's praises, Sebastian's fingers curled into a fist and he said, a little too tightly, 'You don't own success, Nelson, you lease it. And trust me, payments are due every single day.'

'Even though she's one of the Eddingses? I thought they were born with it or something.'

Sebastian's eyes widened. He had forgotten that Nelson had been there that day at Seashells. 'No,' he responded, 'success isn't genetic either.'

'You know, when we first met her in that hotel,' he remarked, 'I was kind of sceptical about her claim, but having seen her in the office . . .' He looked up trustingly. 'What did Cyril say? You would know. Is it true?'

If the local TAB was taking bets, Sebastian would have withdrawn his entire life savings and put it on 'false'. And yet, he suddenly found himself addressing Nelson with a tone as deadpan as his face.

'Of course. Absolutely.' He shuffled the papers on his desk. 'It was a surprise to me too.'

Not as surprising as what's coming out of your mouth right now!

An endorsement from him would carry weight around the office. He had Cyril's ear and his confidence. Everybody knew how close they were. If he backed up the rumour then it would be believed.

Nelson heaved a sigh of relief. 'You know, she hasn't mentioned it to anyone else. Do you think I shouldn't either?'

Sebastian debated with himself momentarily – on one hand was the honourable urge to rein Nelson in and on the other, the unmistakable desire to teach Claudia Franklin a much-needed lesson.

She'd brought this on herself.

Shouldn't she reap the fruits of her own misbehaviour? He had already kept his side of the bargain and told no one. It was up to Cyril to protect his project. And if Claudia felt the discomfort of uncertainty until then, it was no more than he had felt after being pushed into a corner he had no desire to stand in.

'It seems a silly thing to keep a secret,' he said to Nelson. 'After all, who wouldn't want to be part of the Eddings family?'

'Too true.' Nelson stood up to leave.

As soon as Nelson was out the door, Sebastian threw down his pen and sat back in his chair, trying to decide if he'd made the right move. He picked up his phone. 'Juliet.'

'Hi, Seb, what can I do for you?'

'I just had an interesting conversation with Nelson. He told me that Claudia is working cases for another partner at the firm. Who is it?'

There was a startled pause. 'No one, as far as I'm aware. Claudia only has the three files I gave to her yesterday.'

Odd.

He frowned. 'Can you please monitor her phone calls? And if any of the other partners ask to see her, please let me know.'

'Sure.'

He put his phone down, unease spreading through his veins. What did they really know about this girl? Honestly, the only thing that was absolutely certain was that she couldn't be trusted. She was masquerading as Cyril's niece and was now wanting to make contact with an inmate at Casuarina Prison.

He thought about their run-in that morning and her judgemental comment about *his* values.

As with all young, pretty girls, she thought she had the world on a string. That no one would see through her fake veneer and false attempts at morality.

This time, however, Claudia Franklin was poking a stick at the wrong man.

Nobody made a fool out of Sebastian Rowlands and got away with it.

Chapter 11

Claudia should have known that her first day was far too easy and that things were only going to get worse from there.

Day two started off with Sebastian witnessing her flirting with a cafe barista and somehow making her feel bad about it. How was it any of his business who she took a fancy to? Tom had been rather good-looking – blond, easygoing, with a great sense of community responsibility, practically all the things on her checklist. Wasn't it about time she stretched her dating muscles, especially now that her father and his shotgun were nowhere in sight? She'd always been so envious of Bronwyn's freedom and choices.

So incensed by the ridiculous way he'd made her feel, the first thing she did upon arriving in the office was head up to the kitchen to stick the flyer that Sebastian had condemned onto the noticeboard.

'Anybody with half a heart would approve,' she muttered darkly as she stuck pins into the corners.

'Who doesn't approve?'

She spun around, her hands self-consciously going to her throat. 'Oh, hello, Mr Eddings. Er . . . Cyril.' She quickly made her tone less formal. 'Great to er . . . see you.'

'How are you enjoying your first week?'

'A lot,' she smiled.

'I'm sorry I didn't come to welcome you yesterday morning.' Cyril filled a glass jug from the water cooler. 'I had back-to-back meetings and today is much of the same.' He looked her over thoughtfully. 'I take it you and Sebastian are getting on well?'

'As well as can be expected,' she said, with a sheepish glance at Tom's fundraiser advertisement. He followed her gaze.

'Sebastian has a very close connection to addiction,' Cyril commented, seemingly out of left field.

Claudia started. 'He has a drug problem?'

Cyril laughed. 'With the amount of work he turns around, you'd think he was on something, wouldn't you? No,' he shook his head sadly, 'his mum was an addict. Left him at a police station, aged six. I don't think he's ever forgiven her.'

Sebastian's words came back to her, making her want to bite her own tongue in shame.

You know absolutely nothing about me, Claudia.

So now it appeared she owed him an apology as well.

'Sebastian may appear to be heartless,' Cyril said, 'but that's only because few people have showed him theirs. Good luck, Claudia.'

With his full jug, he walked out of the kitchen, leaving her standing there.

She spent most of the morning trying to figure out how she was supposed to rectify her faux pas. However, sometime after lunch a new development had cause to distract her.

The mail clerk came by her desk to stick an envelope in her tray. 'So you're Cyril's niece, are you?' she said.

Claudia's hands stilled over her keyboard, her mouth went dry. 'Who told you that?'

'Nelson.' Her colleague was conveniently absent from his desk. The mail clerk tilted her head to one side. 'I've never seen a brunette in Cyril's family before.'

Claudia had no idea what she was supposed to say to this, unless the woman's pointed gaze indicated that she should fish out her birth certificate and an accompanying family tree. Luckily, the clerk didn't seem to require a response because she pushed her trolley on to the next desk.

Damn you, Nelson.

She couldn't very well yell at him when she hadn't asked him to keep quiet about it. Her heart dropped to the bottom of her stomach. What chance was there that this news would not be delivered to the whole office along with their mail?

Fat chance.

As if to confirm her suspicions, the next day Anna Mavis dropped by with a few barbed remarks of her own. She was already sore that Claudia had snaffled the Cornwall case, which she had thought was rightfully hers, and she was in no mood to be friendly.

'So I see you've got three cases already.' She looked down her nose. 'Seb must have a lot of confidence in you. Or did Cyril put him up to it?'

Claudia knew she was talking to a crocodile but her guilty conscience couldn't stop a flush of heat from invading her cheeks. 'I'm sure Cyril had nothing to do with it.'

'But everyone knows Cyril just dotes on his family. I heard you were related.'

'Distantly,' Claudia responded quickly.

'Must be,' Anna smirked, 'because Liam didn't think you were connected to Cyril Eddings at all.'

Liam was one of the lawyers she had recognised from university and she couldn't really blame him. She swallowed.

Well, this has to be a world record – two days on the job and I'm being exposed already.

Sweat broke out on her upper lip.

How can I spin this one?

'In fact, he said you and your family were in wine,' Anna went on, leaning her hip on the side of Claudia's desk with all the manner of someone who was going to stick around until she drew blood.

'Yes,' said a voice from behind her. 'Isn't it deplorable how some lawyers think running a B&B in the South-West will be that much easier than a full-time job.' Sebastian Rowlands entered their workspace like a prowling tiger. 'Cyril was very happy to see his niece return to the fold.'

'Seb.' Anna straightened and spun around, all a-fluster.

'Good afternoon, Anna.' Those dark eyes and flat mouth gave no warmth to the greeting. 'I see you've met Claudia. Don't let her relation to her uncle deceive you, we didn't take her on for that. She was recommended by Bianca Hanks.'

'Bianca Hanks?' Anna uttered weakly, like she'd just whispered the name of God.

'That's right.' His eyes ran over her person as though he were looking for something. 'Don't you have enough work, Anna?'

'I have mountains,' Anna tried to laugh but it came out somewhere between a gasp and a choke.

'Yes, I thought you wouldn't need that Cornwall case on top of everything else.'

'It wouldn't have been any trouble,' Anna whitened. 'I don't mind the pressure.'

'Still, the last thing I would want to do is overburden you,' Seb returned sweetly as he delivered the kiss of death.

There was a heavy pause as Anna's bitter gaze flicked quickly from Seb to Claudia, panic and accusation in her eyes. Claudia quickly looked away and Anna turned back to Seb.

'Er . . . thank you,' she squeaked tightly before scurrying off like a mouse into the scrub.

Claudia released a breath she hadn't realised she'd been holding as the man in front of her turned towards her, his dark eyes cutting a straight line into her brain.

'Making friends already, I see,' he observed.

Her smile was more wince than a grin, especially when she thought of what had passed between them earlier. Her silence did allow her a moment to fully take him in, however. It was the first time he'd decided to come into her workspace since she'd arrived. And honestly, she now thought it was worth the wait. The word that most adequately summed up his appearance was 'perfection'.

His suit was black, faultlessly cut to set off his tall, trim figure. The jacket was taut across broad shoulders, indicating muscle, and this was only confirmed by the certainty of his movements. They were as crisp and clean as his shirt. By contrast, his tie was a glossy blue net design. A statement, no doubt, that had just the right proportion visible above the buttons of his jacket. His cufflinks winked silver and his aftershave was subtle but effective, like a smoky hand that wafted out and caressed your throat. He was a work of art. There didn't seem to be a thread out of place and she found herself wondering the stupidest things.

How does he keep so fit when he works such long hours?
He must get up before five and go to the gym.
Or maybe he plays sport after work.
Probably rugby, he's certainly got the shoulders for it.
But then how does he find time to shop?
That suit is a masterpiece.
I wonder if he has a personal tailor?
Oooh, wouldn't it be great if they did skirt suits for women?
'Claudia.'
She blinked twice. 'Er, sorry, yes?'
He frowned. 'I asked you a question.'
Of course you did.
Heat flooded her face and her voice came out raspy. 'Would you mind repeating it?'
'Can you read up on the McCarthy file first?' he asked impatiently. 'We have a pre-trial conference next week and I'd like you to attend.'
'Really?' She sat up straighter. 'That's great. I'd love to.' And then realising she didn't sound as coldly aloof as the other

lawyers in the firm, quickly moderated her tone. 'I mean, I'll start getting our documents in order now, unless there was something else you wanted to talk about?'

'No.' He seemed amused by her sudden change in demeanour. 'I'd like to see what you can do. Bianca Hanks or not, you'll have to prove yourself to me first.'

His expression indicated that he didn't anticipate this challenge being easy. He walked off then, leaving her to breathe a sigh of relief. So that was it – her first real 'welcome to the firm' conversation.

Did she feel like a lawyer?

Hell yeah.

'Wow,' Nelson said without turning around. 'Bianca Hanks, eh? How many head honchos do you have in your corner? I'm counting three so far.'

'I think that's it,' she tried to say lightly, realising that he'd added Sebastian's name to Cyril's and Bianca's, which seemed like very wishful thinking.

Sebastian didn't like her or trust her and he meant for her to earn his respect. What she hadn't expected was for him to have her back with Anna. She simply couldn't imagine him not being pleased that she was getting her comeuppance. After all, she was sure as apples in pie that he didn't believe for a second that she was related to his boss. So why had he stuck up for her?

Perhaps he preferred revenge on his own terms.

As one week moved into the next, she began to grow more sure of it. She didn't see him much, but every time she did, she felt like the stakes to prove herself to him were getting higher and higher.

Sebastian Rowlands was as tough as any ancient Egyptian slave-master. He worked her to the bone and critiqued her best efforts with the diplomacy of a Middle Eastern Dictator.

He didn't like her formatting. He thought her sentences were too long. She didn't get to the point fast enough. Her arguments lacked credibility. She didn't quote enough precedence. And the list of his complaints went on.

The hardest part, of course, was not his words but his eyes!

He would stare at her just so, without saying a single word, and it cut far deeper than any verbal complaint. You knew he wasn't just disappointed in your work but in *you*. The very core of you.

Claudia Franklin was not good enough.

Her biggest problem was that she respected his opinion and craved his praise, hanging out for a kind word like a seagull waiting for a stale chip. She couldn't discount his criticisms, however. There were elements of truth in everything he said and she knew she needed the feedback. The best thing to have at this stage of your career was a good mentor – a role model to set you straight. Nonetheless, well into the second week she had to wonder if she was really being guided so much as bashed into a mould that was exactly to Sebastian Rowlands's liking.

It wasn't like she made friends elsewhere in the firm either. Cyril Eddings, for all his family devotion, made no further attempt to find out how she was doing, and this seemed to be proof to the other lawyers that her relationship to him was bogus. Basically, she'd set herself up a nice little posse of enemies without even trying, and they made her pay any chance they got.

She didn't have her own secretary, so had to rely on a pool of administration staff who served other lawyers at the same level as her. In turn, the secretaries took sides. They had formed their allegiances before she'd even introduced herself. And, suffice to say, they were not in her favour. Her work 'mysteriously' never seemed to rise to the top of any administrator's pile till very late in the day.

'Don't be too hard on yourself.' Nelson had tried to cheer her up. 'You're not the only one they punish. I'm sure someone else will rise to the top of the "most hated" list soon. These things tend to run in cycles.'

How reassuring.

Somewhere in it all, however, she did manage to fit in a visit to Peter Goldman in hospital. His room was watched over by a prison guard so she still had to get special permission from Casuarina to see him. She had phoned them earlier that day. At the time, Nelson had been out at lunch. Juliet had been seated at her desk but she'd had her earphones in so Claudia didn't think she heard anything that was said.

When she walked into Peter's room, he looked so pale and insignificant in the hospital bed she had to wonder why she had been so anxious about seeing him. After all, he was the one who had been bashed up, not the one who had picked the fight. White-collar criminals didn't know violence until it literally hit them in the face. The man was in his mid-forties, he had a slim bony structure and a rather large forehead further enhanced by his receding hairline.

He adjusted the bed into a sitting position using the remote control, wincing as he did so.

'Who are you?' he croaked, his eyes grey and watery.

'I'm Claudia Franklin.' She stopped half a metre from the bed. 'A friend of Bronwyn Eddings, and a lawyer from Hanks and Eddings.'

He dropped his head back into his pillow and grimaced. 'Your friend should have listened to me.'

'About what?'

'About giving the dog back. Elsa now belongs to someone else.' He nodded. 'Pass me that pad and a pen.'

Curious to see what he was going to write, Claudia passed him the hospital stationery. He scribbled an address down and tore it off.

'Take Elsa there.'

She glanced at the piece of paper. Above the address located in Northbridge was a name, The Quiet Gentleman.

'It's a pub,' Peter went on to explain.

It had to be the same place in Northbridge he'd mentioned to Bronwyn.

At Claudia's pointed look, he added, 'It's not dangerous, I promise you. It has a good reputation, besides being a public place. Go in the middle of the day if it makes you feel better and give Elsa to the manager. His name is Frank Jerome.'

Her eyes narrowed on him. 'And then what?'

'And then I can put this all behind me.' Peter frowned.

'Put *what* behind you?'

'None of your business.'

Claudia glared at him. 'It is very much is my business if it causes you to threaten my friends.'

'Look,' he glanced nervously at the doorway, where the guard was standing, 'Elsa and her pups are very valuable. They are part of a deal I made with someone else.'

Claudia frowned. 'A stud owner.'

'Yes,' he said tightly. 'Bronwyn was very helpful with caring for Elsa but now I think it's in her best interest to give Elsa back.' He leaned forward. 'Her *very* best interest.'

Claudia did not like the way he kept glancing at the guard by the door. The guard had his back to them but he was close enough to hear what they were saying. All her lawyer senses were on high alert. It felt like Peter Goldman was being cautious because he was talking about something illegal. She decided to try a different tack.

'The stud owner wouldn't happen to be Leon McCall, would he?'

If Peter had been pale before, he now had no colour at all. He pursed his lips together. 'I have no idea what you're talking about.'

'Bruce Carle is a friend of his, isn't he?' Claudia pressed. 'Seems to me like you've been in a bit of trouble with Mr Carle. That's why you're in here, isn't it?'

'Bruce Carle,' Peter began bitterly, 'is a brainless thug who –'

'Also happens to be a murderer.' Claudia tapped her foot. 'He's not scared of going above and beyond for his employer.'

Peter was silent.

'You're going back to Casuarina soon,' Claudia continued tentatively. 'What will Leon McCall do if he doesn't get his pups?'

Anger and perhaps fear made Peter Goldman foolish. 'It's too late, Leon knows Bronwyn Eddings has his pups. Bruce would probably have passed that on by now. He'll get Elsa back one way or another.'

Claudia's heart sank.

So Bruce had roughed up Peter to find out where Elsa was and Goldman had given up her friend's name.

Nice.

So what was she supposed to believe? Organised crime was after Bronwyn and her pregnant bullmastiff? It seemed like a little too much bad luck even for Bronwyn, who, let's face it, was always getting drawn in by people like this.

The other question was, why?

It did seem like an awful lot of trouble for one dog and its puppies. Why were they so valuable?

What was an illegal activity that involved dogs? Bullmastiffs in particular?

In this case, her past participation in animal rights protection stood her in good stead. Of all the sickening activities conducted to amuse the criminal mind, blood sports were her least favourite.

'Ugh! This is not about *dog fighting*, is it?'

The prison guard turned around and gave them both his full attention.

The sport was an abomination. Dogs raised in cruel conditions and made to fight each other to the death or face torture from their owners. Words could not describe the disgust she felt. So typical of the coward, to prey on innocents who couldn't protect themselves – to wage pain for pleasure or gambling.

Peter seemed to shrink into himself at her accusation. 'Don't be a fool. Elsa is not a fighting dog. You've met her, haven't you? She wouldn't hurt a fly.'

'Doesn't mean she can't breed with one, does it?' Claudia said. 'She's a nice big size, good breed for that sort of sport.'

Peter's eyes darted nervously once more towards the prison guard, who was starting to get very interested in their conversation. 'All conjecture,' he said to the guard rather than to her. Claudia ignored the remark.

'Was that your deal, Peter? Perhaps you owed Leon McCall money and you couldn't pay, so you let his stud mate with your dog.'

This explained the vicious-looking scar on Elsa's back. Peter refused to speak further. He kept his gaze firmly fixed on the window, which was not a very good avoidance tactic given it was closed and the blinds were drawn. She could completely see his weakness. The selfishness. The willingness to sacrifice the wellbeing of innocent animals to live to play again. He was a skinny, pathetic white-collar criminal who had taken too many shortcuts. He may not intentionally seek out violence but now it had come to collect him. As far as she was concerned dog fighting was worse than any other crime he was already in jail for, and if she could add it to his record she would in a heartbeat.

'Do you think that if you don't answer my questions you are safe from the law?' Claudia hissed. 'Just because you don't tell me what I want to know doesn't mean I won't keep digging until I incriminate you and anyone else involved in this disgusting sport you happen to be part of.'

She turned on her heels to go. It was only then that Peter called after her.

'Try your luck if you must. It'll get you nowhere.'

The second she got home that evening she called Bronwyn. Her best friend had to know what was going on. There was no way they could send Elsa back now. If anything, they had to somehow round up this dog-fighting ring. It was the only way Leon McCall would stop looking for what was owed to him.

It was way past dinnertime, so she didn't think she'd be interrupting a meal with her parents present. As it turned out, Bronwyn was in the middle of a poker game with Chris.

'When did your brother get to be such a flirt?' Bronwyn asked. 'He's far more outrageous than he used to be . . .'

'You mean when Jack was around,' Claudia said bitterly.

'I suppose so.'

'He's had to adapt to his wheels and I guess he reckons that means being larger than life. He doesn't mean half of what he says.'

'Oh, I know!' Bronwyn laughed. 'Considering I've seen him make the same comments to some of your mother's female restaurant staff. He seems to have turned into quite the Don Juan.'

Claudia rolled her eyes. 'Yeah, maybe, but that's not why I called.'

Bronwyn's voice turned serious. 'No, I can imagine. How did things go with Peter?'

'Not good.' She quickly outlined the interview and the conclusions she had drawn from it. When she was done, there was silence.

'Are you still there?'

'I think I'm going to be sick.'

Claudia shut her eyes. 'Just breathe. Count to three. And then you'll feel like helping me put these bastards away instead.'

As if on cue, Bronwyn burst out, 'There is no way in *hell* I'm handing Elsa over to anyone. He really had me fooled, Claud. He looked so devastated when he was telling me that his wife wanted to put Elsa down. I really believed him. I even felt sorry for him.'

'He probably was devastated!' Claudia responded bitterly. 'It's likely he was pretty scared about not being able to pay his debt. He had to complete the transaction to avoid the fury of Leon McCall. Hell, the guy is in prison and McCall was still able to get him bashed up.'

'Are you absolutely sure it's dog fighting we're talking about here?'

'No, that's just my suspicion. I need further proof and, honestly, I don't know how I'm supposed to get it.'

Bronwyn sucked in a breath. 'In the meantime, I've got organised criminals trying to locate Elsa. Claud, you've got to see if you can dig up more on this. What about that pub? Is that a lead of some sort?'

'Yeah,' Claudia bit her lip, 'I'll see what I can do. Can you sit tight for a little longer?'

'Sure, but should I tell your family about this?'

'Hold off.' The last thing she wanted was her blind father and brother in a wheelchair getting too brave. 'I'll see what I can dig up first.'

Unfortunately Claudia had absolutely no luck with her investigation on Bronwyn's behalf. The pub actually turned out to be rather nice. Not dark and dingy at all, with huge windows letting in a lot of light at the front. Just to be ultra-safe, she went to visit it one lunchtime during work hours. Using the local bus service, Northbridge was only a five-minute ride out of the city.

The pub had an immediate cowboy feel to it when she walked in the door. A polished dark wood bar ran the length of the left wall with timber floorboards and stools to match. All the spirits and wine were visible behind the bar on shelving that reached to the ceiling. Automatically, she searched for her family's label and was relieved not to see it there. She'd rather Oak Hills wasn't supplying a ring of animal tormenters if they could possibly help it.

As it was lunch hour, the pub was three-quarters full with a variety of patrons, from a wizened old man and his wife to a couple of guys in suits clearly from the accounting firm down the street. There were the usual 'no hopers' around the pool table, covered in tats and leather with no jobs to go to. There was also a bunch of young women enjoying a birthday lunch – at that table the alcohol was flowing freely.

Claudia went straight up to the bar where two men were serving drinks and taking orders for meals. She looked at the menu – a blackboard on the wall. The dishes were a little heavy for her taste but she had to order something. The man who walked over to serve her was in his early twenties. Dark hair, black T-shirt, jeans, heavy silver chain around his neck.

'I'll, er . . . I'll have the beef burger please.'

'With salad or fries?'

'Definitely salad.'

'Did you want a drink with that?'

'Um . . . a Diet Coke.'

'Sure.'

After she paid him, he turned to get her Coke out of one of the waist-high bar fridges and frowned.

'Hey, Frank!' he yelled up the counter, 'we're out of Diet Coke.' He turned back to Claudia. 'Is normal okay?'

She nodded hastily, glancing back towards the man he had addressed. A man who yelled out 'Noted, Jet' in response.

So that was Frank Jerome.

He was significantly older than the man called Jet, who was serving her. Probably early forties, with a gut that slightly sagged over his belt. The black T-shirt and jeans certainly flattered his figure much less. He wore his hair long and sported a beard. It was hard to say whether he looked like a dog-fighting ringleader, though who knew what a man with a fetish for animal abuse typically looked like? She supposed she couldn't straight-out ask him if he was or if he knew Leon McCall because that would break her own anonymity. As far as Leon and his guys were concerned, Bronwyn Eddings was their girl. Claudia Franklin wasn't featuring on their radar yet and she was hoping to keep things that way.

She ate her lunch quietly in a corner of the bar, spending the time observing the room, which, frustratingly, didn't turn up much. Frank and his mate ran a smooth bar, with the exception of the lost Diet Coke order. The patrons weren't acting suspiciously either and none of them had dogs with them.

After lunch, she headed out the back of the pub where the toilets were located and had a quick glance into the oily kitchen on the way through.

Apart from a few obvious hygiene issues that would horrify her mother, Claudia didn't think she could catch them out on anything else. There was one more door, right at the end of the corridor, which led outside to the back of the building. With a quick glance around to make sure no one had noticed her, she stepped over the threshold and into what seemed to be a private car park. It was bitumen right up the side of the restaurant, fenced all around and gated at the top – clearly a separate spillover car park that wasn't being used. Right by the door she had just come out of was a brick shed with a roller-door entrance but no windows. There was a blue skip bin sitting beside it, currently empty.

With another surreptitious glance about she tried the roller-door handle. Locked. This garage or storeroom was the only place she hadn't been able to check properly. If it was full of extra tables and chairs then she'd have to admit defeat, but if there were dogs inside . . .

She shuddered, remembering the horrific cases she had heard of in the news and read about on the internet. Dogs being chained up for hours on end, sometimes not fed properly, to bring out their aggression. Some owners injected their dogs with steroids to bulk them up or make them mad for a fight. She could not understand how anyone could tolerate this abuse, let alone inflict it themselves in the name of sport.

Urged on by these thoughts, she put an ear to the roller door, trying to hear movement.

'What are you doing back here?'

With a start, she spun around, her heart slamming against her ribcage.

'Er . . . Hi.'

It was Frank, with a garbage bag full of empties over this shoulder. He'd stepped out of the back door and was eyeing her crossly. Hastily, she shuffled away from the roller door.

'I . . . er . . . was just looking for the toilet,' she said quickly, hoping the tremor in her voice didn't give away the fact that her heart was beating so fast she was starting to feel light-headed.

'Well, it's not in there,' he snapped, walking towards her and dumping his load in the skip bin. 'It's back inside on your left.'

'Of course. I'm blind as a bat sometimes.' Smiling rather ineffectually under his steady glare, she hurried past him inside to the ladies bathroom. Passing through the swinging door, she swiped a hand over her damp brow as she caught sight of her frazzled appearance in the mirror.

That was a close one.

Here, she spent an obligatory five minutes pretending to use the facilities before making her way out of The Quiet Gentleman at a smart pace.

So much for cracking the case.

She had absolutely nothing to run with. Not even a yelp from a dog in need. The only thing that stood out, in fact, was the bad feeling that had taken up permanent residence in her gut. She knew she was onto something – she just wasn't sure what.

It was a shame that Leon McCall's dog-fighting ring wasn't the only crisis that she currently had to deal with. There was still Sebastian Rowlands and the copious amount of work he had piled onto her desk, the Cornwall case being her number one priority at the minute.

She'd hung on to these contracts for far too long. It was tantamount that she go through them with a fine-tooth comb for anything that might make Sebastian twitch even slightly. Late in her second week on the job, however, she was out of time. The document had to be submitted. Not to mention the pre-trial conference she had coming up with Sebastian later in the day. So that morning she emailed it to him for review and then started to prepare her files to take to the Perth District Court.

He strode into her open-plan office space an hour later. Her heart rate immediately stepped up a notch, as she was sure everybody else's did. Whenever Sebastian left his office it put everyone on high alert. She was glad that she wasn't the only one who seemed to be struck dumb by his instant ability to command the room.

He threw a printed version of her work down on her desk. She noticed it was riddled with red marks. There was no greeting, he cut straight to the chase.

'Work out the difference between "shall", "must", "may" and "will".'

She cleared her throat. 'I beg your pardon?'

'As you should,' he nodded. 'You use the words interchangeably and they all have completely different legal meanings. This contract is riddled with contradictions as you have drafted it. It needs to be redone.'

'But it's due tomorrow.'

'Then work late.'

A snigger sounded from across the room as he strode off.

She hoped his treatment of her didn't have anything to do with *her* treatment of *him* regarding Tom's fundraiser, which still had the occasion to plague her with guilt. She hadn't found a good time to apologise yet. They always seemed to be too busy or there were others in the room to overhear. The last thing she wanted was more gossip circulating about her.

Her fear was realised a few minutes later when she went into the kitchen to make herself a cup of coffee and overheard a conversation that was obviously meant to reach her ears.

'Oh, Anna,' said one of the secretaries, leaning against the counter in front of the microwave with all the air of a soap star, 'what *shall* I do? Where *will* I have dinner tonight?'

Anna had clearly caught on immediately by the size and slyness of her grin. She stirred her coffee and tossed her head. 'Jennifer, you *must* figure it out soon. Or you *may* just starve.'

Both girls tittered shamelessly as they walked out of the room, holding their steaming mugs.

Great! Just great. I'm not just the family fraud, I'm also the butt of every joke.

Fifteen minutes before they were due in court, Sebastian turned up at her cubicle again.

'It's time to go,' he said.

She was then caught in the uncomfortable scenario of having him watch her pack her briefcase. Already on the back foot, she couldn't stop her fingers from trembling slightly as she picked up a couple of slim files and shoved them into a black bag. She hoped he didn't notice, though she wouldn't lay bets on it. Sebastian's eye for detail was one of his many talents.

To her surprise, he broke the silence suddenly to say, 'I rang the client after I spoke to you his morning and bought you two days.'

He said the words as though they were torn from him against his will, and her body stilled. As much as she appreciated the reprieve the last thing she wanted from Seb was pity or leniency.

She'd rather he hated her guts and think she was a sassy pain in his arse, like the day she'd been hired, than this. She lifted her chin and said, 'Thanks, but I'll get it done tonight. It'll be on your desk tomorrow morning.'

He shrugged. 'Suit yourself. Got everything?'

She slung the bag over her shoulder. 'Yep.'

He gave her a long look and then said, 'Well let's go.'

Chapter 12

He could tell her that she didn't have everything – that she was at least a file short – but where was the fun in that? Claudia Franklin had been a thorn in his side from the day they'd met.

What annoyed him the most about her was her vulnerable facade. She *looked* so soft. So small, petite and fragile, like butter wouldn't melt in her pretty rosebud mouth.

Ha!

It would vaporise before it touched her tongue. She worked like a bull in Asian rice fields. It didn't matter what landed on her back, she carried it.

And maybe not as well as he would like just yet, but her legs (pretty as they were) hadn't buckled under the pressure and he couldn't be sure they ever would. As fragile as she looked on the surface, her insides were clearly lined with steel.

She was desperate to be a lawyer – a good one. Her determination was so potent he could smell it on her. And, frankly, the aroma was as familiar as his own skin.

So much for proving Claudia Franklin was a flake.

The girl did not give up.

She didn't cry either, which was damned strange. There was more than one female lawyer he'd brought to tears, and a few clients too, because his expectations were so high.

But not her.

She just kept going like a freight train.

Those blue eyes, that feminine honey-coloured hair that framed her pretty face. It gave him a pain in the chest he didn't recognise. No woman of her stamina should be so physically perfect. Her fragility was all a hoax. There was nothing he could undermine about Claudia Franklin. And it wasn't to say he hadn't tried.

After all, he had his pride.

'Really putting her through the wringer, aren't you?' Juliet had said to him that morning after his run-in with Claudia over the Cornwall contract.

Juliet was the only woman he permitted to walk into his office without announcement or appointment. *And* the only person, with the exception of Cyril, who was allowed to say anything even remotely disparaging to him. She knew far too many of his secrets for him to hold her to account for anything. The problem with secretaries was they were the person you spent the most time with. They witnessed it all and they knew everything about you. Your achievements, your faults, your failings and . . . the things you coveted the most.

He looked up. 'I assume you're talking about Claudia Franklin.'

'I've never known you to bully the juniors. That's more Jeffery's style.'

He winced. Jeffery Langton was a good lawyer, though hardly brilliant. He had been passed over for promotion year after year before finally making partner in the property team. His career struggle had made him merciless to his junior solicitors, paralegals and outside clerks, whom he believed should suffer as much as he had.

'You think I was too hard on her this morning?'

Juliet shrugged. 'Not at all. You just didn't need to do it in public. The other lawyers are having a field day with it.'

He swore inwardly. That hadn't been intentional. He didn't mind setting a hard pace for Claudia but he certainly didn't want anyone else doing it.

'Oh well,' Juliet shrugged again. 'As you've said, she's Cyril's niece. Her reputation will survive it.'

It was true. He had said that, at one point. Was it yesterday or the day before? He couldn't remember. His backing up of her story had taken on a life of its own. When he'd encouraged Nelson not to keep quiet about her lie, he'd done it for revenge. He knew word would get out and the speculation would start. He had wanted to make her nervous, see her flounder under the anticipation of discovery.

Yet somewhere between starting the cutting remarks and actually hearing them he'd lost the stomach for it. He had been unable to watch Anna trying to lay siege to Claudia on her third day and, knowing his endorsement would carry some weight, he had given it. Now he found himself constantly confirming her identity to his peers even though he didn't believe a word of it himself.

What's the matter with you, Seb?

Just yesterday he'd told Scott Cooper that Claudia had been at Cyril's daughter's wedding.

And on Tuesday, he'd told a secretary that Cyril had been so happy his niece was joining the team he'd kissed her.

But why should he!

You're an accessory to this lie if you don't shut up!

You're not only supporting her game, now you're bloody playing it.

The thought had kept him up late the night before, making him toss and turn in his empty bed. Her angelic smile taunting him as he finally fell into sleep.

Let her boat sink naturally, it's no responsibility of yours.

Only it was. For some reason, he couldn't think of Claudia Franklin as anything but his responsibility. So if her little boat on rocky water did sink . . . God help him, he wanted it to be on his watch.

Was it a perverse need to see her sweat?

Or a desire to shield her from other's eyes?

He had no idea, but it was exactly why he had decided to take her to the Perth District Court with him that morning, because if there was any day in the calendar to call Claudia's bluff, this was certainly it. Although now he wasn't too sure if the test he had picked for her wasn't too much. Perhaps, at the very least, she deserved to be warned.

They took the lift to the lobby and then exited the building to make the short journey on foot. It was only a block away from Hanks and Eddings. He strode with purpose, hands buried deep in his pockets. Her heels clicked on the pavement beside him, two strides for every one of his.

He knew he should slow down but the urge to put Claudia through her paces yet again was undeniable. He had fully intended to complete the journey in silence. But of course she was having none of that.

'I'm glad we have a minute alone.' She licked her lips. 'There's been something I've been meaning to say to you.'

Here we go.

He gave her no opening and continued to remain silent. As predicted she was unintimidated by this tactic that he used to unsettle the most hardened of businessmen.

'I feel like I owe you an apology.'

That got his attention.

'How so?'

'The other day, in the lift. I think I bit your head off without just cause. You're right, I don't know anything about you or your past and I completely misconstrued what you said anyway.'

'Yes,' he agreed. 'You did.'

'So,' she took a deep breath, 'I'm really sorry.'

He blinked.

Lawyers were rarely upfront. And female lawyers, never! They always held their cards close to their chest, played the game until the last second. Knocked the ball into someone else's court and waited. Otherwise, what did they have?

'In the spirit of honesty . . .' she began.

Honesty.

Yes, well, he supposed there was *that*, but last time he checked it was seriously out of fashion. Women, particularly, loved to keep him guessing. That was exactly why he specialised in flings, not long-term relationships.

'Cyril told me about your mum.'

Seriously?

'He shouldn't have,' he said bluntly. That man was really starting to get on his nerves.

'Well, I'm glad he did,' Claudia said slowly, her soft tones playing havoc with his nervous system. 'It's helped me to understand you better.'

The last thing he wanted was Claudia understanding him better. He never let anyone, let alone a woman ten years his junior, that close to him.

'I hope you feel enlightened.'

'I feel ashamed,' she admitted. 'You of all people would know what it's like to have your family torn apart and I just rattled off the other day like I know everything –'

He stopped her with a hand in the air. 'Don't try to turn my life into a soap opera, Claudia. What happened to me happened a long time ago. I was a child. I've moved past it since then.'

'But it's clearly left scars.'

He laughed. 'I wouldn't go that far.'

'You're obviously uncomfortable talking about it.'

'That's because,' he eyeballed her recklessly, 'I'm talking about it *with you*.'

It was a mistake to look in her eyes. It took all his willpower to tear his gaze away again.

'You don't like me.' She shrugged. 'I get that. But I'm hoping that will change . . . in time. Because despite everything, Seb, I really admire you. I want to do well in this job. I want you to be proud of me.'

The way she said those words, the shortened version of his name on her lips, made the hairs on the back of his neck rise. His heart flipped over in his chest and his fingers clenched tightly in the pockets of his pants. The temptation to let her in was so *strong*.

He sighed. 'What do you want from me, Claudia?'

'Your friendship.'

'I don't have female friends.'

'It shows.'

'Do you think that because you're Cyril's *niece* you can say anything you want to me and get away with it?'

She reddened and he knew he'd struck home. Could it be possible that Claudia was more ashamed of Cyril's mistake than happy about it?

Unlikely.

So he decided to remind her about why she should be. 'I wonder what would happen if Cyril discovered, just for the sake of argument, that his cousin Adriana never had a daughter called Claudia Franklin. What then?'

'What happened next would be up to Cyril,' she said quietly, unable to meet his eyes, as well she should.

'Friendship, Claudia, requires trust. And I don't trust you as far as I could throw you.'

Her head snapped up like a mouse trap. 'If that's what you believe, then why did you tell Anna that I was telling the truth, or Julie for that matter, or Scott Cooper? Why did you tell Helen in payroll if she wanted advice for her wedding she should ask me because I'd been to all the Eddingses' fancy do's?'

His jaw dropped at her sudden undercut that had squarely hit its mark. The smart-arsed little –

You walked straight into that one, my friend.

Her sucker punch had not only left him winded but strangely aroused. Her face was flushed with indignity, her eyes so startlingly bright in her delicate face that he just wanted to grab it between his palms and kiss her senseless. That would shut her up if nothing else. He shook the sensation away. The last thing he needed to feel for Claudia on top of everything else was attraction, particularly on a crowded street in the middle of Perth's central business district.

Come on man, get a grip.

'What's the matter, Seb?' she demanded silkily. 'Nothing to add?'

'You are playing a very dangerous game, Claudia,' he warned.

'That's why,' she patted his arm, 'I'm so happy to be playing it with you.'

He ignored the way her touch electrified his skin. It was time to teach this brass-faced fool a little lesson.

Game on.

The misgivings he'd had earlier that morning about today's session in court evaporated. In fact, he was going to take it up a notch.

'I think you should handle this next case on your own.'

'Really, you'd let me do that?'

His mouth hardened. 'I think you've proven that you're ready for it.'

'Thank you.'

By now they had reached the district court and he stepped ahead of her again to pull open one of the double glass doors. 'It's all yours.'

She walked in first, taking in the ambience of the slick modern decor, her nerves pricking slightly at the commitment she'd just made.

You just can't help yourself, can you, Claudia?
You shouldn't have spoken to him like that.

Throwing down the gauntlet had been a bad move, especially when all she'd really wanted to do was clear the air. After all, it had never been her intention to work for anyone under false pretences. She thought that if she'd just told him how much the job meant to her, he might have a little more understanding.

But no, of course not. He was as stubborn as a bull and even less forgiving. She had faults, but so did he! That's why she'd lost her temper. Yes, in a moment of weakness she'd let Cyril's mistake slide, but only because Sebastian had incensed her so much with his complete and utter dismissal of her skills as a lawyer. She'd wanted to put him in his place. It had been so nice to have someone on her side – someone who completely outranked him. She had never expected it to blow up to these epic proportions.

What are you going to do, Claudia?

Everybody was talking about it. Was she or wasn't she an Eddings? It seemed unclear how she was supposed to move on from here. She needed this job, for herself but also to help Bronwyn. Her best friend had organised crime after her, and she was counting on Claudia to find a way to bring a dog-fighting ring to justice before they found out where she was.

Geez, Claudia, you don't set yourself hard enough tasks, do you?

She could not see any suitable course of action. It was lose–lose no matter what angle she looked at it from.

Tell the truth: people gossip, lose reputation, job in jeopardy.

Uphold lie: people gossip, lose reputation, job in jeopardy.

Maybe it was only a matter of time.

He's not going to let what you said to him go, you know.
You wounded his pride.

Nobody made a fool out of Sebastian Rowlands and this was the third time she'd done it. She didn't think she could trust his sudden desire for her to handle the next case alone. However, as usual, her enthusiasm got the better of her. Maybe she could allay his suspicions by doing well on this case.

They walked across a wide foyer, heading for the designated meeting room. Their client, Bill McCarthy of McCarthy and Sons, was waiting outside for them. He smiled in greeting, rubbing his hands together.

'I have a good feeling about today,' he said. Claudia hoped his optimism was a positive omen.

Of all the cases Sebastian had given her, it definitely seemed the least complicated. They were representing an accounting firm who were suing Perth Domestics. This was a cleaning company who had damaged their office in Claremont by accidentally setting off the smoke alarm on the third floor. This, in turn, had activated the emergency sprinkler system, causing a burst pipe, fatal damage to their computer server and many work hours lost. The pre-trial conference was to discuss damages owing and perhaps settle the matter without going to trial, given the fault was so clear.

To Claudia it was a cut-and-dry case. It was obvious the cleaners had done the damage. It had occurred on their shift and security footage showed that they were the only ones in the building at the time. They were also the ones who had called McCarthy and Sons in the wake of the disaster, and their workers' cigarette butts had been found in an ashtray in the boardroom the next day. Further investigation showed that the particular cleaners who had been on the job that night were migrants, unable to speak English and unused to practices outside their own country – such as not smoking in an office building.

Her confidence in the case and herself was pretty high until she opened the door to the meeting room and walked in.

The first person she laid eyes on was Bianca Hanks.

Claudia stilled, unable to remove her hand from the door knob. It felt like it was glued there.

Bronwyn's mother was already seated on the left-hand side of the square table in the centre of the room. The pen that had been tapping the documents in front of her stopped as her gaze latched onto Claudia's face. The older woman pulled in a sharp breath. It was clear Ms Hanks had made two deductions in that split second.

First, that Claudia was working under Sebastian Rowlands, a job she thought she had tagged for her daughter.

And second, that she was the last to know about it.

Oh shit.

'Claudia, will you please proceed.' Sebastian's crisp command sounded behind her.

She started, removed her hand from the door knob and quickly advanced into the room.

Claudia hadn't seen Bronwyn's mother in a long time but nothing much had changed. She had the same shade of blonde hair as her daughter and also the same blue eyes. Unlike Bronwyn, however, there was nothing soft or inviting about her features. She was corporately handsome and sleekly stylish. Her hair was worn blow-dried straight, her make-up was bold. Her eyes narrowed behind black wire-rimmed glasses as Claudia crossed the room to sit as far from her as possible.

Not sure whether acknowledging they knew each other was a good thing or not, Claudia nervously and rather stupidly did something in-between. She lifted her hand to give a small wave.

Unfortunately, the slight twitch of her fingers accompanied by a half smile came across more comical than anything else – as though Bianca had lifted a blanket and found her hiding beneath. If the temperature in the room was cold before, it now dropped a further two degrees.

'Well, Claudia, this is a surprise.' Bianca's mouth seemed to form the words without her lips even moving.

In truth, the surprise was all Claudia's. Why hadn't she known that Bianca would be attending this case? The answer was simple. Because Seb hadn't *wanted* her to know.

You fool.
A case against Bianca Hanks!
She'll wipe the floor with you.

Claudia involuntarily cleared her throat, trying to keep her voice neutral, perhaps inspire Bianca to mercy. 'Lovely to see you again,' she said.

Bianca did not respond in kind. Instead, she turned to Seb in accusation. He addressed her smoothly enough, mentioning the lawyer Claudia had been expecting.

'Thank you for filling in for Margaret on such short notice.' He leaned over the table to shake her hand. 'I was reluctant to vacate the pre-trial conference.'

'Of course. It is, after all, in the best interests of our clients to settle this as quickly and cleanly as possible,' Bianca returned.

Claudia was at last able to turn her attention to Bianca's client – the owner and manager of Perth Domestics, Renee Ryder. She was a middle-aged woman whose fashion sense had not moved out of the eighties. Her white jacket was well endowed with shoulder pads and her red fizzy hair had been tied back in a satin scrunchie.

Suddenly, the door to Claudia's right opened to admit the registrar. He was a short, wiry man in a grey suit who strode in like someone who didn't have much time on their hands.

'Good morning, Counsel. Let's get down to business, shall we?'

It was like suddenly being tossed a cricket ball without yet being ready with the bat. There were so many thoughts flying about in Claudia's head – the top two being the fact that she hadn't expected Seb's revenge to be quite so swift or for Bianca to be part of it.

The registrar prompted her again.

'What do you have for me?'

'Er . . . thank you, Registrar.' Claudia nervously gripped her pen and looked at the notepad of dot points she had prepared earlier. 'Today I am here with my colleague Mr Rowlands and our client, Mr Bill McCarthy. As per our client's filed statement of claim, our client is seeking damages for the property damage caused by the defendant, Perth Domestics, on December twentieth last year. As pleaded, the claim relates to water damage to my client's building, its furnishings on the third floor, and computer server. My client is also seeking damages for consequential losses associated with lost work and time, relocation of the employees who worked on that floor and the rental cost of new premises . . .'

The registrar interrupted her impatiently. 'I have read your client's statement of claim – do you have anything to *add*?'

Claudia blinked.

Detail. Give him the detail. It was so open and shut . . . wasn't it?

'Registrar, as Perth Domestic's representatives are aware, we have photographs of the damaged areas as well as the cleaners' time sheets. Those timesheets demonstrate the cleaners were the only people present in the building at the time of the incident. We also have witness statements that the cleaners were smoking in the building just before the flooding on the third floor occurred. We believe this to be a cut-and-dry case, pardon the pun.' Claudia winced internally and decided to wrap it up. 'Our client has come in good faith to negotiate a resolution to these proceedings so as to save the parties the costs of a trial, and to unnecessarily avoid using the Court's time any further.'

The registrar nodded, turning his attention across the table. 'Bianca, your thoughts.'

The fact that he addressed the other lawyer by her first name dropped Claudia's confidence another notch.

Her adversary nodded. 'My client now acknowledges the damage and is willing to pay a fair amount in compensation to Bill McCarthy and Sons for their part in it.'

Claudia's spirits lifted.

There you go, your first instinct was right. She hasn't even tried to disprove you. You have a strong position. You've got this.

The registrar turned back to Claudia. 'And what do you believe is a fair amount, Ms Franklin?'

'We estimate the damages to be around seven hundred and thirty thousand. We are hoping that Mrs Ryder will agree to this figure or something close to it.'

Bianca clasped her hands together. 'This figure seems to be rather random. How have you come to this amount?'

Claudia sat up straighter in her chair. 'This is based on a number of quotes received from various tradespeople for repair and refurbishment of the premises. Also the time and work costs for the disruption, and additional building fees they have already incurred for relocation and temporary renting.'

'All right, and where are these quotes?'

'They are with the discovery documents.'

'And where are the discovery documents?'

'In our filing system at Hanks and Eddings.'

'You didn't think to bring them with you?' Bianca asked silkily.

Every part of Claudia's face froze. It was very easy to see in hindsight why she should have those documents with her. But in the rush to get over to court, to prove her case, all she had brought with her were her notes and the statement of claim. In preparing she had focused on proving causation and forgotten about demonstrating quantum. The documents a lawyer pulled together when they were opening a case, not closing it.

Rookie mistake.

The ultimate humiliation.

Words failed her. However, they were not needed. Bianca opened the thin beige folder in front of her. 'We have done our own research into the damage and losses of McCarthy and Sons. We estimate, based on our client's own quotes and calculations, that the appropriate figure is $175,756, precisely.'

Bianca pushed the papers across the table.

'But's that's not enough –'

Bianca held up her pointer finger for silence, and like a little kid told off by her classroom teacher, Claudia shut up.

'This figure may seem smaller because my client, while admitting some fault, does not wish to claim all credit for this disaster. Your client has complained that when the emergency sprinkler system came on, a corroded pipe burst over the server, causing fatal damage to it that would otherwise not be the case. This is not my client's fault. This would not have occurred if McCarthy and Sons had done maintenance on the sprinkler system in a timely fashion.'

She pushed a second document across the desk. 'I have another document here detailing a quote for the repair and maintenance of the building's emergency sprinkler system by a reputable contractor for Bill McCarthy and Sons. It is two years old and was never actioned.'

Corroded pipe.

How did I miss that?

Clearly, because McCarthy and Sons wanted to cover it up. But where was she supposed to go to from here, especially without those discovery documents on her?

'So unless you have figures to dispute mine, I think we should settle on $175,756.'

Like a sword through the heart, Claudia knew she was spent. So did Bianca's client. Unlike her lawyer, she was unable to hide her emotion and her lips curled with the gloating triumph of success.

The registrar pulled the papers towards him and perused them briefly. 'They seem to be in order and fair,' he agreed. 'Will McCarthy and Sons take the deal, or would you like a moment to talk with your client?'

Bill McCarthy made a sound somewhere between a choke and a snort, his gaze fixed on Claudia like he wanted to kill her.

She didn't blame him.

There were no more guns left in her arsenal. Though it cut her to the bone, for her client's sake she glanced at Seb for help. He seemed to be expecting it as his face was already turned towards her with raised eyebrows. She cast her eyes down in surrender. He opened the files in front of him.

'You'll have to excuse my associate. I didn't mention to her that I had packed our discovery documents. Though without reading them I can tell you that Ms Hanks's figures are grossly under the mark. McCarthy and Sons wish for an exact replacement of the existing carpet, which is a high quality brand known as Imperial English, currently available from only one carpet manufacturer in Australia located in New South Wales. It will need to be sourced and transported at a premium.' He drew Bianca Hanks's document towards him. 'This carpet seems to be of a generic variety, similar but not the exact replacement of that which was damaged. I suggest that our documents indicate an appropriate price. Also, two of the paintings in the foyer were originals, not prints, and are irreplaceable. Compensation for them is much more expensive than indicated here, as is the case with several other of Ms Hanks's items.' Sebastian clasped his hands together and looked up with a smile. 'And with regard to the corroded pipe, we acknowledge that there was indeed talk of fixing it. Perth Domestics knows this as they were asked repeatedly to clear out their storerooms so that a contractor could access damaged sections of pipe that passed through there. They did not do this, holding up my client's plans to start the work. We will, however, allow a small reduction in the settlement for not being more firm.'

He pushed their discovery documents across the desk to the registrar, making Claudia feel sick at her lack of foresight. The registrar went through the documents and nodded. Renee Ryder's face fell.

Stiffly, Bianca received the documents from the registrar and perused them herself. After that, there was a bit more haggling over a few minor points of contention. Claudia kept silent throughout it all, not trusting herself to speak.

I forgot documents.

I missed evidence.

How could I be so dumb?

In the end, Sebastian managed to settle the case at around five hundred thousand dollars, which was much more satisfactory to Bill than the paltry sum Bianca had initially suggested. It seemed clear now that her conversation with Seb earlier had been a big mistake. All she'd done was given him all her cards. And it seemed he knew exactly how to play them. What was worse was that the whole time they'd been talking, he had known they were meeting with Bianca Hanks. Perhaps he'd planned it. He'd always been suspicious of her. She wouldn't put it past him to pit her against Bronwyn's mum to see how she'd react.

When the registrar announced the case closed, Claudia rose numbly from her seat and they all began to file out. She and Bianca were the last to exit, and the older woman grabbed her arm just before she was about to pass through the door.

She turned bravely to face the firing squad.

'Where is Bronwyn?' Bianca demanded.

'Gone out of town.'

Bianca's eyes shot sparks. '*Where?*'

'She doesn't want you to know.'

'You will tell me immediately.'

Claudia had never been one to hold her temper in check, and, still sore from her earlier humiliation, she reacted more sharply than she probably should have.

'Bronwyn doesn't owe you an explanation and neither do I.'

'I'm her *mother*,' Bianca sneered.

'That's right. Not her keeper. She's a grown woman, Bianca. Let her live her life how she sees fit.'

'After today's embarrassing blunder, one would think you would learn to hold your commentary, Claudia.' Bianca released her arm in disgust. 'Your influence over my daughter has always been irritating but this time you have gone too far. Bronwyn has responsibilities here and no one appreciates her neglecting them.'

Claudia gritted her teeth, all desire to be respectful gone. 'That's where you would be wrong.'

'Explain yourself.'

'I know you would love to blame me,' Claudia returned bitterly, 'but this was entirely Bronwyn's idea and decision.'

'Really?' Bianca's tone could have cracked glass. 'It seems convenient then that the job that was meant for her has fallen to you.'

'I took nothing from her she wasn't willing to give,' Claudia retorted.

Bianca was buying none of it, and she stabbed her pointed finger inches from Claudia's face. 'I don't know how you stole my daughter's position, you presumptuous piece of work, but I will make you pay for that. Make no mistake. I will take great pleasure in removing you from the legal profession, and my daughter's life, for good.'

Claudia shuddered as she stalked out of the room, just in time to notice that Seb was still standing in the shadow of the doorway.

'Curious,' he said silkily. 'It would appear that the woman who gave you such a glowing recommendation doesn't even know that she did. It seems to me, Claudia, that this spirit of honesty you were talking about earlier is as fictional as the tooth fairy. Next time, don't try to draw me into your web, because I'm the spider, Claudia, not you.'

He turned and walked out then, leaving her feeling like a boxer who couldn't get off the mat after the referee had stopped counting.

Oh fuck, Claudia. You're in deep shit now.

Chapter 13

In the week that followed her arrival, Bronwyn made it her mission to discover exactly what was wrong with Oak Hills. And what a mission it was.

While outwardly agreeing that she should help with the business, Chris and Lydia actively put obstacles in her path.

'You sleep in, sweetie,' Lydia told her that first evening. 'No need to be up at sparrows with us. You'll be wanting a rest after coming off all that stress.'

It felt like she was being told that she was on holiday. And she supposed that, as a family friend, that had always been her place. It was what the Franklins were used to, what they were comfortable with. Yes, she had made the announcement that she was there to work. However, their acceptance of it was definitely still up for debate. Chris and Lydia would not admit it directly but she was positive that they were finding the concept just as difficult to digest as Horace was.

I don't know why you thought it would be so easy just to walk in and take Claudia's place. Even with her permission.

You're not family.

Why should they give you that much responsibility?

The large pot of tea, dish of homemade jam and plate of warm buttery English muffins that greeted her in the kitchen that first morning seemed to confirm it. Chris and Lydia were nowhere to be found. They had clearly already started work for the day and left her to relax. One of them, she suspected Lydia, had left her a note which read, 'Make yourself at home, sweetie. It's probably been a while since you've had any real food.'

It was true.

In the city she would have downed a cappuccino and breakfast bar by now, but still, it was clear that the note was code for *Stay here, don't interfere.*

She lowered herself into the tall-backed pine chair and stretched out a hand to grab a muffin. In all honesty, it was such a temptation to just sit there in the dining room in her PJs and gaze out the large window that overlooked the vineyard. What a gorgeous day. Not a cloud in the sky. She bit into her muffin and nearly died of ecstasy.

God bless country living.

When had life got so fast she didn't have time to stop and taste the strawberry jam?

Okay, Bronwyn, focus.

As cunning as Lydia was to ply her with food, she could not allow herself to be sidetracked. Claudia wouldn't. And she couldn't let her friend down, otherwise she'd land the Franklins in a worse mess. She'd taken away their manager with no replacement. It would be the final blow that killed their business. She nibbled nervously on her muffin. They had to let her help . . . one way or another.

The problem was, Bronwyn had never been big on confrontation or trying to force her way. She didn't think fast on her feet, she avoided people who disliked her and she was a chronic peacemaker who hated fighting more than anything else in the world. She laughed mockingly at herself as she poured a cup of tea, the steam rising out of the cup and filling the room with a delicious herbal aroma.

Why on earth did you become a lawyer then? You delusional person!

The answer to that question was completely wrapped up in her mother and what she wanted for her daughter's life. This was the first time in forever that she'd actually allowed herself the simple luxury of making her own choices.

So what are your strengths?

She grabbed another muffin, deciding already that she was going to eat three of them at least.

Well, you're reasonably intelligent.

Otherwise, she wouldn't have got through law and graduated in the top ten per cent of her class as her parents duly expected.

You're also stealthy.

She'd been hiding who she really was from Bianca Hanks, Robert Eddings and the legal profession for years.

And . . . you're so desperate.

She sighed. Yes, she was absolutely desperate to be somebody else – to be good at something else.

There was certainly enough to cut her baby teeth on here, if only somebody would let her. Perhaps her first mistake had been asking. One did not ask for trust, one earned it. Clearly, her first and most obvious method of attack was to start performing, which was far easier said than done. After eating her third muffin, she dusted off her fingers and ran back up the stairs to her room to have a shower. Donning jeans and a T-shirt, she pulled her hair back into a no-nonsense ponytail and motored out the front door.

The landscape stretched out before her, the ocean on the horizon. The heady smell of ripe, sun-warmed fruit hit her senses before she saw the swollen globes peeping from beneath large tri-pointed leaves. Bronwyn shielded her eyes against the glare of the sun as she crossed the top of one block of vines. The plantation was so neat, laid in stripes of green and brown – rich and vibrant. Insects and birds chirped and tweeted harmoniously from the vine. A golden whistler seemed to be the lead singer. He perched on top of one of the nearby trestles singing his little heart out, his bright yellow chest like a waistcoat for his stately olive-green back and wings. As soon as her shadow crossed his perch, he flew away. Bronwyn was sorry to see him go.

She knew from past visits that the bird was male. The female ones were so boring by comparison. Their feathers were a dull greyish brown and they were much shyer. For some reason, the thought made her think of her and Jack. He'd always been the golden whistler to her dorky insecurity. She did not want him back at Oak Hills. He'd just make things incredibly tense. The mere mention of his name had thrown Horace and Chris into such a dark argument the day before. And the awkwardness she still felt ran so deeply between him and her. She shuddered. Jack had not given a stuff about any of them for years. Having him stroll back into their lives now would just add insult to injury and toss this sinking ship right into the storm.

She had a niggling worry that Lydia had already sent the email she'd threatened to yesterday, and it had reached its destination. Jack had always been such an enigma. Hard to read, even more difficult to predict, though he always seemed to have her number. She remembered the day they met with a cringing embarrassment. She'd only been eighteen at the time, next to his twenty-three. He was the skilled winemaker while she was very much the shy, dull-coloured bird, hopeful to blend into the background. It had been her first night away from the family home in the city. She'd had no self-esteem to speak of and was totally in awe of her best friend's life, which seemed like Neverland. Everything at Oak Hills was magical – the surrounds, the house. And there was certainly one male resident who had never grown up.

Claudia had been out when she'd arrived, so Mrs Franklin had advised her to go exploring and get acquainted with the estate. It was late in the day and the sun had begun to sink.

A warm orange glow had spread fingers of light through the leafy vines on the path beside her. At the time the grapes had been plump and purple, ripe for the picking. The clusters were so heavy the vine drooped under their weight. The pose was almost seductive, like biblical temptation. That day a younger, more innocent hand had reached towards the vine. Curiosity and the sudden rush of the forbidden had made her brave.

I wonder if they just taste like ordinary grapes.

No one will miss it if I just try one.

'What do you think you're doing?'

She'd nearly jumped out of her skin at the sound of the voice. Quickly, she'd composed herself and spun around to register dancing green eyes and the flash of white teeth. At the time, Bronwyn didn't have much experience with men, let alone ones this good-looking. In blue jeans, a collared shirt rolled up to the elbows and broad-brimmed hat on his head, he looked much like a cowboy who had lost his horse and gun holster. Mischief was written all over his face. But then wasn't it always with Jack?

She'd pressed a hand to the middle of her chest. 'You scared me half to death.'

'Did I?' He raised innocent eyebrows. 'You looked so devious, I couldn't resist calling you out.'

She glared at him. 'I didn't mean any harm. I was just –'

'I know what you were doing,' he chuckled. 'Go on. Have as many as you like. They're good.'

Bronwyn put her hands behind her back, unwilling to let him patronise her. 'No, that's okay. I was only looking.'

'Come on.' He sauntered over to the vine, plucked a few, and before she knew what was happening had popped two in her mouth, his fingertips brushing longer than necessary against her lips. She jumped back, startled at the familiarity of his touch before he gave her a rather unsettling grin and put the rest of the grapes in his hand into his own mouth. She forced herself to eat, if only to free up her lips to speak. The skin puckered and burst between her teeth, filling her mouth with sweet, hot juice.

'This is shiraz,' he informed her. 'Our best crop yet.'

Her voice responded at last. 'It's good.'

'I know.' He hooked his hands in his pants. 'They're mine, after all. I'm Jack.' He tilted his head to look more closely at her. 'Who the hell are you?'

She shoved both hands awkwardly into the pockets of her jeans. 'Er . . . Bronwyn, Claudia's friend.'

He raised an eyebrow. 'I'm her older brother. She's never mentioned you.'

'Oh,' she responded, telling herself the uncharacteristic hurt she felt was an overreaction. As he continued to stare at her expectantly, she shuffled from one foot to the other, wondering whether she was supposed to somehow prove that she really did know Claudia.

Suddenly he lost his seriousness. 'Just teasing.'

It was the first of many times he used that phrase on her. She didn't know why he thought announcing it made it okay. If possible, it took it to the next level of irritating. However, just as a mixture of relief and annoyance enveloped her, someone else burst through the vines. A tall, leggy blonde with way too much hair and not enough skirt. She launched herself at Jack, throwing both arms around his neck.

'Found you!' Her voice was sing-song, high-pitched and definitely unaware that there was anyone else about.

What was this that she'd stumbled upon?

An adult game of hide and seek?

'Oh –' The newcomer belatedly seemed to register Bronwyn standing there. 'Who's this?'

'Bronwyn Eddings.'

To her surprise, Jack gave her full name without even blinking. 'My sister Claudia is forever going on about her and her family. Eddings this and Eddings that.' His lips quirked at her. 'You come from some real fancy digs, don't you?'

'Oh, I –' Bronwyn didn't know which was worse, to be completely anonymous or have her city reputation to live up to in the one place she thought she was free of it.

The blonde's hand seemed to tighten around Jack's neck as she gave Bronwyn a thorough once over. 'You don't look very fancy.'

Bronwyn felt her cheeks redden. She didn't. Skinny as a stick, no sense of fashion and glasses as thick as telescopes. She was the worst class of dork.

'Claws in, Becky.' Jack tickled the woman hanging off him, who giggled girlishly. 'She's our guest, after all,' he nodded to her. 'I'll see you at the house.'

The embarrassment she felt then jolted Bronwyn out of the past. She'd been nothing but a joke to Jack back then. She couldn't see how six years of no communication could have changed that much. As the flashback faded from her mind, the grapes in front of her came sharply back into focus. They were as heavy as the ones in her memory.

Vintage was almost upon them. It wouldn't be long before these succulent bulbs turned purple. Oak Hills needed a winemaker, and soon. Her first port of call would be to find out what they were doing about that . . . besides sending Jack emails, of course.

The gravel path she was on widened and the Oak Hills cellar door and restaurant came into view. It was an attractive building and clearly much better kept than the Franklins' residence. It was mostly stone and surrounded by an array of native trees that did much to emphasise the rustic style of the building. A cobbled path led up to the double doors, which opened into a large room accommodating floor-to-ceiling glass windows on one side. These looked out across the vineyard, giving the space an air of tranquillity. Polished dark timber floorboards supported a few burgundy-coloured couches and armchairs, set apart from the cellar door bar itself, which was a long 'S' shape. Stainless-steel spittoons sat in the curl at each end of the polished, chestnut-coloured counter.

She had expected to see a short Italian man called Marco, whom she had known since her university days. However, it was two strangers who stood behind the bar in black Oak Hills shirts. A young woman of slim build and perhaps Italian origin, and a tall gangly man with long fingers and dancing blue eyes. He was definitely the more charismatic of the two, and the first to capture her attention. He had one of those faces that was so alive it drew your focus immediately . . . that is, if his strong French accent and tendency towards theatrics failed to arouse your interest first.

'*What light through yonder window breaks?*' he quoted, stretching out his hand to her with all the drama of the Shakespearean tragedy from which he quoted.

It was so over the top that she couldn't help but giggle.

'Hi, I'm Bronwyn.'

'An angel come to relieve me of my boredom,' he corrected her. 'My name is Antoine.'

'And I'm Maria,' the girl beside him said. She had a shy smile and seemed uncommonly nervous at Bronwyn's arrival. 'I've heard so much about you from Chris.'

Bronwyn raised her eyebrows. 'All good, I hope.'

Maria's expression grew wistful. 'You're one of his oldest friends.'

'I guess I am.'

'Are you here for zee tasting?' Antoine drew her attention back to himself.

'Er, no,' she smiled. 'I'm here to work if someone will let me.'

'For shame!' he exclaimed. 'One does not beg for work. One avoids it. Look at me, I flirt for a living!'

She laughed.

'Come and sample ze wine. I'm sure I can teach you a few things you didn't know.'

'He is rather good,' Maria nodded, and stood back to let him do his thing.

'I'm better zan good,' Antoine rolled his eyes. 'I am *French*.'

He turned to grab four wine bottles off the shelf behind him, twining their necks between his fingers so he could carry them all in one go. When his back was turned she could see that his straight brown hair was tied elegantly at the nape of his neck with a black velvet ribbon. Her lips twitched. She didn't know when she'd last seen that hairstyle on a man but it certainly suited him.

Antoine spun back, placing the bottles on the counter. 'What shall I get you, mademoiselle? A fruity sauvignon blanc, a peppery shiraz, a full-bodied cabernet merlot or a woody chardonnay?'

'I'm sorry,' she shook her head, 'I've got to find one of the Franklins. I'm supposed to be taking on Claudia's workload.'

Antoine gasped. 'But you intrigue me. I was not aware Claudia was away. Lydia did not mention it, or you for zat matter, when she came in this morning.'

'Didn't she?' Bronwyn asked tentatively. It was very telling that Lydia hadn't said a word to the staff. It looked like her misgivings were not unfounded.

'No,' Antoine's eyes twinkled. 'Tell me, do you share Claudia's vision for the business?'

Bronwyn shrugged. 'I assume Claudia wants this business to be the best it can be and that's exactly what I want too.'

Antoine's mouth twisted. 'Ze best it can be in new markets – less prestigious ones.'

Bronwyn's heart sank. 'Oh no. We can't have that.'

Claudia hadn't mentioned this plan to her, and she wasn't surprised. She'd have known Bronwyn would be against it. If Claudia wanted Oak Hills to downgrade its reputation to survive then she was as bad as the rest of her family.

'Well, mademoiselle,' Antoine spread his hands, 'I'm afraid neither of us has a say.'

'I might if only Lydia and Chris would stop avoiding me.'

'Ah!' His eyes flicked wider. 'Zis explains why Lydia was

164

'ere at the crack of dawn. She never arrives before eight, unless she is avoiding something at home. Usually it is Horace but, surprise of all surprises, he came wiz her.'

'Great,' Bronwyn's shoulders slumped. 'They're teaming up against me.'

'I see, I see. Freezing you out, no?' He rested an elbow on the bench, leaning towards her. 'You are feeling zee pinch of her rejection, *chéri*? No matter.' He flicked away the offence with this hand. 'You must do what I do in crisis – turn to ze bottle.' He lifted one in front of him. 'Sauvignon blanc?'

Bronwyn chuckled. 'Isn't it a little early for wine?'

'Mademoiselle,' Antoine touched a hand to his heart again as though fatally wounded, 'it is never too early for sauvignon blanc. In fact, morning is ze best for fruity aromatic flavours, so crisp, so fresh. I dare you to give your day a lift.'

'I see you've met our resident backpacker.' A voice sounded behind them, startling Bronwyn with its unexpected sternness. She spun around.

'Chris?' she began uncertainly. He was eyeing them in irritation from the threshold. 'Hi, Bronwyn.'

She hadn't heard him come in, his wheels silent on the floorboards. 'Hi, Maria.' He turned his head to greet the woman Bronwyn had all but forgotten at the other side of the bar.

She looked up. 'Hi.'

At that point, Bronwyn expected Chris to make some outrageous comment, perhaps about taking them both out to dinner. He'd been a non-stop flirt since she'd arrived, and his cheekiness wasn't just limited to her. Instead he said, 'How are you?' to Maria.

'I'm good, thanks.' She nodded politely and said nothing more.

Something was off.

Antoine clearly thought so.

'Mademoiselle,' he protested. 'I would never put anything as uncouth as a backpack upon my person. I have a proper house. I have stayed there almost a year now.'

'My mistake.' Chris turned back to him and then said to Bronwyn, 'There are too many traditionalists in these parts trying to get some new world experience.' Then he smiled, some of his cheekiness returning. 'You're up early, Numbat. I thought you'd be sleeping in.'

'Not when there's so much to do.'

'You worry too much.' He wrinkled his nose. 'Take your massive hound for a walk. Hell, take me for a walk. Clear your head. You'll feel so much better.'

It sounded like another brush-off to her. 'So much better about what?'

'*Everything*,' he said with emphasis.

'I was actually hoping someone might get me into Claudia's office –'

'There's no way I'm letting you see how messy I am,' interrupted Chris. 'But maybe we can go for that walk after lunch.'

'But –'

'In the meantime, have a drink. Maria has just brought in some of our older reds, aged to perfection. Ant,' he said to the Frenchman brusquely, 'weren't you going to do a stocktake this morning?'

'Later, M'sieur.'

'Later would be now.'

He manoeuvred his chair into the storeroom after that, leaving Bronwyn startled by the complete change in his demeanour. 'I don't get it. He wasn't annoyed with me being here yesterday. I don't know what's come over him.'

'I'm sure it's nothing,' Maria said quickly.

'Do not let him bother you, *chéri*,' Antoine assured her. 'It is not you he dislikes but me.'

'Well, that doesn't make sense. Chris likes everybody. He's the easiest-going guy around.'

'Not when it comes to his brother.'

'Jack?' Bronwyn repeated. 'What do you know about Jack?'

'But everything, of course.' Antoine spread his hands. 'He was my friend in Bordeaux before he moved on to Carcassonne. When I came to Australia, Lydia hired me because I knew him. My friendship with his brother has always been a great trial to Chris, though he shuns it himself.' Antoine sighed. 'He thinks I am the guy Jack replaced him with.'

Jealousy.

She could believe that and even sympathise with it a little.

'Antoine, is Lydia still in the restaurant?'

'Oh yes. She is trying to sort out this week's menu.'

'Thanks.'

The restaurant was on the right hand side of the bar, after you passed through an area featuring a stack of wine giftware and souvenirs. Bronwyn trotted past these and through the double glass doors leading inside. She noticed that it had not changed much over the years. There was still a large flower arrangement by the door and no more than seven white-linen-dressed tables inside. The windows were wide with giant wooden shutters, which were currently open to let in as much light as possible and provide the subtle ambience of the view, which was no less than spectacular. The restaurant was and had always been Lydia's domain. While an excellent cook, she wasn't a chef herself. She mainly coordinated the staff, organised the functions and worked there in the evenings as the house's maître d'. Due to the fact that it had only just gone nine in the morning, the dining room was deserted. Bronwyn paused awkwardly on the threshold just in time, as there seemed to be an argument going on inside.

'You need to apologise to Chris,' Lydia was saying.

'Why should I?' It was Horace's voice. 'I haven't done anything wrong. It's him making all those assumptions.'

'Come now, Horace. When Jack took more interest in wine-making than Chris, there was an immediate division of your affections. You gave the lion's share to Jack.'

'It was completely misconstrued. I was passionate about furthering Jack's career. I didn't love him more. If anything, I was devastated by how he turned out.'

'And that's another thing.'

'Oh, don't start –'

'It wasn't just Chris's brother you sent away but his best friend, just when he needed him the most.'

'I didn't send him away. Jack didn't have to leave town. He did that of his own accord.'

'What did you think firing him and kicking him out of home was going to do? Jack wasn't going to work for any other winery in this area except Oak Hills. You knew that.'

'No, I didn't. Cocky as he was, he would have done anything to spite me.'

'Come on, you stubborn man. You can't be *that* blind.'

At Horace's deep sigh, Bronwyn took the opportunity to clear her throat loudly. After a moment, she moved forward. Lydia's face quickly transformed. 'Hello, sweetie! Did you enjoy your breakfast?'

'It was fabulous, thanks.' Bronwyn walked towards the table they were sitting at. Lydia was folding napkins.

Horace nodded coldly at her. 'Bronwyn.'

'So what are you up today?' Lydia enquired as though Bronwyn had a list of treats in store. 'It's a great day for the beach.'

Bronwyn shook her head. 'I was hoping to pick up where Claudia left off. I was wondering if I might check out her office, maybe get onto her computer and start fielding a few emails.'

'No,' Lydia shook her head, 'absolutely not. Chris and I were talking about it this morning and we've decided.'

Bronwyn's eyes widened. 'Decided what?'

'That we can't possibly impose our family problems on you.' Lydia clasped her hands at her chest. 'Don't give it another thought.'

'But –'

'I insist.' She turned to her husband. 'Horace, you really should take a leaf out of Bronwyn's book and just take some time off. Retirement is, after all, supposed to be the best part of your life. Think about it.' She gave him a meaningful look, stood up and then slipped through the swinging doors that led into the kitchen. Bronwyn caught a quick flash of the staff inside, madly engaged in preparation for the lunchtime rush.

'So,' Horace seemed wholly satisfied, 'they're shutting you out too. Welcome to my world.'

Bronwyn bit her lip. He was right, of course. She was definitely on the outside looking in. She knew what Claudia would do. Claudia would push and shove until someone gave in. But she wasn't Claudia. Fighting wasn't her thing.

She smiled. But allegiances were.

'Did you know Lydia's thinking of asking Jack to come home?' she blurted, before she could second-guess her decision to tell him.

'*What?*' Horace's voice cracked like a whip. 'She's going behind my back?' His tone was more question than statement.

'What else can she do?' Bronwyn tried to explain. 'The business needs a winemaker – someone you'll trust. You haven't done well with everyone else they've hired so far.'

Horace's eyes narrowed. 'She knows how I feel about this. Are you absolutely sure that this is what she wants to do?'

'It's not set in stone or anything,' Bronwyn reassured him. 'Jack hasn't agreed yet. However, Chris and Lydia were talking about it yesterday after . . .' She trailed off, hoping he would fill in the blanks.

He sighed heavily. 'After Chris and I had our disagreement.'

'They were just trying to find a way to fix things,' she said quickly. 'They think he is the only one who can.'

'Nonsense,' Horace snapped. '*I* can fix this place.'

Bronwyn carefully examined the nail of her pointer finger. 'Not when you're half blind, Horace. You need someone to be your eyes.'

She looked at him. He was still and silent, the expression on his face completely resentful, so she pushed home her point.

'Someone to tap into that extensive knowledge locked in your head. Someone you can work with to take control of this faltering business.'

He glared at her. 'Who are you suggesting?'

'I'm not suggesting anyone,' she shrugged, immediately turning to the fingernails of her other hand. 'Though now that you mention it . . .'

'Go on,' he said in resignation.

'I would be a good candidate.'

'You?' Then his shoulders drooped in defeat. 'All right, all right. I'll get you into Claudia's office, but we have to be quick before Lydia heads over there.'

Bronwyn dropped all pretence of indifference and threw her arms around him. 'You won't regret this, Horace. '

He seemed pleased by her sudden affection but pulled back a little and shook a knobbly finger at her. 'I better not. I know it's not much of a threat these days but I'm not letting you out of my sight.'

'I'll work harder for Oak Hills than I've ever worked in my life,' she promised.

He grunted. 'I'm doing this in protest. To keep Jack at bay.'

'Of course, I completely understand.' She smiled sweetly.

'Come on then,' he turned around crankily, 'before I change my mind.'

Chapter 14

Without further ado, the two of them hit the gravel path again, heading for the winery and office section of Oak Hills. Being the most industrial part of the estate, there was surprisingly nothing romantic about the winery. This was probably why the Franklins had chosen to surround it with tall gums. It definitely looked like a factory, consisting of a lot of steel tanks and structures. But the first thing Bronwyn noticed as they approached were the picking boxes – big purple plastic ones numbering in the hundreds, each standing at least a metre in height with a metre-square footprint. They were stacked on top of each other in columns of four. There was an empty green tractor parked nearby, a couple of huge warehouses in the background, and before her in various sizes were the fermentation tanks, their stainless steel bodies winking at her in the bright sunlight.

As they walked past the plant and equipment towards the brick office-building on the far side, Bronwyn couldn't help but notice how slow Horace moved compared to the last time she'd seen him. His disease really was taking its toll. Maybe she was wrong to enlist his help in preventing Jack from coming home. It would be a colossal shame if those two never worked out their differences.

Seeming to feel her pity, and clearly not liking it, he looked up with a frown to say crankily, 'Your dog has been chewing through our water hoses.'

'Oh, really?' Her nose wrinkled. 'I'm so sorry about that.'

'And digging holes in Lydia's vegetable patch.'

'Oh dear.'

'She also tore my shirt off the clothesline yesterday evening after you went up for your shower.'

Embarrassment and remorse reddened her cheeks. 'I'll buy you a new one,' she quickly reassured him.

'And a new clothesline too,' he grunted. 'It came down with it.'

'Seriously?' Bronwyn put a hand to her temple. *Damn!* She really needed to keep a better eye on Elsa. The plan had been to walk her twice a day but in her distraction she hadn't gotten around to it that morning. She had thought leaving her off-leash to roam the property would get rid of all that restless energy. Clearly, she was keeping busy.

Horace's face softened. 'I like your dog.'

Bronwyn turned to him in surprise. 'You do?'

He shrugged. 'She's feisty. I like feisty.'

'Me too,' she agreed, surprised at herself because it was probably the first time she'd admitted it as well. Elsa was really growing on her.

'Always wanted a dog like that but never had the time to get one.' Horace sighed. 'Now I have all the time in the world.'

'You should walk Elsa.' Bronwyn quickly pounced. 'She'd like that and so would I.'

'Maybe I will.'

They were silent for a moment.

'So . . . I know why I don't want Jack back, but why don't you?' Horace asked. 'Something happen between the two of you before he left?'

Great. She had thought she was in the clear after her chat with Lydia. Out of harm's way, so to speak. Of course, it would have to be the blind man who saw too much.

'You were the last person to talk to him before he left the country,' Horace continued to probe. 'What did he say to you?'

'You've asked me that so many times.' Bronwyn shook her head sadly. 'I've told you everything I know already, Horace.'

'Then why do I still feel like I'm missing something?' Horace cleared his throat.

Lydia was right. Horace just didn't get it. As a proud man himself, how could he have expected Jack to stay when he'd given him every indication that he wanted him to leave?

She was the only one who had begged Jack to stay, not condemned him, fired him and kicked him off the family property. She thought disowning one's child because they displeased you had died out in the 1950s. Even her parents hadn't subjected her to that, yet.

What the Franklins didn't know – not even Claudia – was that this wasn't the first time she'd wanted to leave law and run away to Oak Hills. Five years ago, when Chris had tragically lost the use of his legs, she'd wanted to help out then too – forget her career in the city and put down roots in Yallingup. Not just because the Franklins needed her, but because she was in love.

She remembered her last conversation with Jack as clearly as if it were yesterday. It had taken place in a rundown motel in Dunsborough – a one-bedroom apartment that had seen better days. She had knocked for ages because he hadn't answered at first. She, however, had been absolutely determined to reach him. The family she loved so much was splintering apart and she couldn't bear it. Finally he pulled open the door and her heart had gone out to him. He looked terrible, worse than she'd ever seen him . . . grubby T-shirt, old tracksuit pants.

He stank too.

He groaned at the sight of her, running a hand through his brown hair. 'What are you doing here, Numbat?'

'I had to check on you.'

'Well, you have,' he nodded abruptly. 'I'm fine. You can go now.'

'Isn't that usually my line?'

'I guess it's time for a change.'

He still hadn't invited her in, so she shuffled awkwardly from foot to foot. 'Look, I know you and I haven't exactly been best friends lately.'

He snorted.

'Or *ever*, for that matter,' she muttered. 'But I do think I'm about the only person right now who gets what you're going through.'

He folded his arms. 'Really? You get what I'm going through? I doubt it.'

She said, with simplicity, 'My family have *never* liked me.'

'Bronwyn –'

'There, you've made me say it. After all your teasing and nitpicking I'm finally admitting it to you. Isn't that what you've always wanted to hear?'

'No.'

She shrugged. 'It doesn't matter because the truth is, for you it's only temporary. The Franklins I know wouldn't let this beat them. I'm not leaving till I've helped you guys sort this out.'

'I think this is a bit beyond your clean-up skills, don't you?' he grumbled, but left the door open as he walked away. She stepped in tentatively.

The room was no more neat than Jack was. Takeaway containers that were days old lay strewn on the coffee table. The bed was unmade. The TV was on. The sink was full of dishes.

'Jack, what are you going to do?'

'I don't know but I can't stay here indefinitely.'

'No, you can't. Your mum is talking to your dad.' She walked around him, trying to catch his eyes, but he refused to look at her. 'I'm sure they'll both invite you to come back home very soon.'

'What if I don't want to go home?' he demanded. 'What if it's me who thinks I should stay away, not the other way around?'

She froze. 'Jack, don't do anything rash.'

'Where was that warning a week ago?' His fingers brushed over his unshaven whiskers, causing a rough rasping sound. 'Chris is going to be in a fuckin' wheelchair for the rest of his life with no hope of walking again.'

'There's plenty of guilt to go round. It's not all your fault, Jack.'

'You'd be the only person on the planet to think that.'

'Your dad is angry, hurt and pissed right now. He's not thinking straight. He's overreacting.' Everyone had heard the row between father and son when Jack had come home from the hospital the previous week without his brother.

'The thing is, Bronwyn,' his hands fisted, 'I don't blame Dad. I don't blame him for everything he said to me. He's right. I am reckless and I have ruined Chris's life, and for what? A great night out.'

He started to pace angrily. 'I wish he could take more from me than just my job and my accommodation. Leaving town is the best thing I can do right now.'

'Running away is never the best thing to do.'

'Bronwyn.' For the first time in their conversation he really held her gaze, and the glistening sheen in his eyes told her everything. She sucked in a sharp breath as he said quietly, 'Nobody wants me here.'

'I do.'

'Oh, for goodness sake.' He turned away, pressing his thumb and forefinger into his eyes. 'A week ago you never would have said that. It's pity talking. Besides, you don't even live here.'

'I could,' Bronwyn said quickly. 'I hate law. I don't want to work at the family firm next year. I could come here, help out, work with your family instead. I love you guys. You know that.'

He shook his head, a faint smile twisting his mouth. 'You always were the peacemaker, Numbat. And you know what?' He turned and nodded at her. 'You should do that. You should quit law because I know that's what would make you happy.' His mouth hardened. 'Chris would love having you here too. You should do that for him.'

'Chris is going to go through a very hard time. He's going to need a lot of support.'

'Then give it to him. You're the perfect person to do it.'

'What about you?'

'He hates me.'

'Don't be ridiculous.'

'I went to visit him at the hospital today,' Jack said curtly. 'The nurse wouldn't let me through. He doesn't want to see me, she said. What does that tell you?'

'Jack, he's just found out he'll never walk again. He'll be feeling all sorts of emotions. Anger is just the first. You need to give this time. People need a chance to process stuff.'

'It doesn't take long to process that he fell off the back of the ute because I swerved,' Jack growled. 'Deliberately. Everybody saw it. Including you.'

She wished she could deny it. He filled in the silence for her.

'I don't know why you haven't jumped on my case like the rest of them.'

'We all make dumb mistakes in life, Jack. I've screwed up more times than I can count.'

'Yeah, well we're not talking about your sense of fashion here, Numbat, we're talking about my brother's legs.'

'There's no need to get mad at me. I'm trying to help you.'

'I'm sorry.' Jack gritted his teeth. 'But you're looking at this through rose-coloured glasses as bloody usual. Dad wants me to go. It's not like I've got responsibilities at Oak Hills anymore. He's made sure of that. He wants me to prove myself elsewhere.'

'Then do that.'

He sucked in a breath. 'Oak Hills means everything to me. It's who I am. Do you think I want to work for a competitor just around the corner? The only option is to leave town.'

'Listen,' Bronwyn caught him by the shoulders, 'I've got to go home for a few weeks. My family wants to know why I've been MIA. Just hang on till then, okay? I'll sort out uni, my job and be right back. I can help you.'

'Always with the helping, Numbat,' he sighed. 'I never thought I'd be one of your strays.'

'You're not a stray.' She shook her head. 'But you do need me. I'll be able to talk Claudia round and once we've got her on side, maybe we can get your dad to give you your job back.'

He eyed her carefully. 'You're really going to quit law and come live in Yallingup?'

She took a breath. 'Yep.'

It was the closest she'd ever come to a declaration. How much plainer could she have got than that? Other than saying, point blank, 'Jack, I have feelings for you. I'd give up everything before I let you leave.'

In the moment that had followed she thought he'd got the message too, because he'd lifted a hand and brushed her cheek. It was the most tender expression of affection that had ever passed between them, with no trace of the teasing so-called 'brotherly love' he usually employed.

Her breath had hitched in her throat as she looked up into those sad brown eyes.

'Okay,' he agreed.

Then, dropping his hand, he moved away to the couch.

Having secured his compliance she didn't try to nag him further and left shortly after that to put the plan into motion. In fact, she drove back to Perth that very night.

At the time, she still lived with her mother, who had bought her father out of the family home. The decor in her bedroom had not changed since she was a teenager. When she arrived there and saw it, she couldn't help but reflect on how stagnant her life was. She was controlled by her parents' whims rather than her own. Especially her mother's. Her identity was Bianca Hanks's daughter, nothing more. She was completely two-dimensional. It had confirmed her belief that the leap she was taking was the right thing to do.

Of course, she had been stupid to think that her mother would make absolutely no objection when she told her about her plan the next morning over breakfast. Leaving law, forsaking the family firm to live and work in the Margaret River wine region was not just preposterous, it was *crazy*.

'Don't be a fool! After everything your father and I have done to get you where you are.'

What had they done, exactly? Apart from pressure her, browbeat her and withhold their love should she put one foot wrong.

'Where is this coming from?' Bianca demanded. 'It's that girl, Claudia, isn't it? And that family of hers. I always knew they were a bad influence.'

It didn't matter that Bronwyn had opened the conversation by trying to explain her clear unsuitability for the legal profession. Bianca remained convinced that there something more sinister afoot. After all, how could her absolute power over her daughter's decisions have faded so completely?

Bronwyn should never have given up talking to her mother. Leaving Bianca to her own devices and hoping that she got over it had been her biggest mistake. Bianca Hanks never let sleeping dogs lie. So of course she had gone digging for information she had no business knowing. She reported to her daughter a few days later that the man she was ruining her life for was gone.

Bronwyn had not understood at first. 'What are you talking about?'

'I'm talking about Jack Franklin. It's pointless throwing away your career for him when he's already left town.'

All the blood had drained from Bronwyn's face. 'What did you do?'

'Nothing but a simple test,' Bianca had informed her coldly. 'And Jack Franklin failed. He's not putting his life on hold for you. So I have no idea why you should do the same for him.'

Her mother was many things – devious, cold and mind-bogglingly efficient – but Bronwyn couldn't blame her if she was right.

'What do you mean?'

'When faced with the choice between you or the stellar job opportunity I secured him in France, he chose France.'

'You actually put it to him like that?' She was horrified.

Her mother had paused, her eyes narrowing. 'Of course.'

All the fight was snuffed out of Bronwyn then, her body limp and lifeless like a piece of driftwood.

'You don't understand . . .' Her voice trembled. 'We hadn't even spoken about being together. He didn't know how I felt about him. I wasn't going to push him. This was not why I was quitting law. It was never about that.'

'And now it never will be,' her mother agreed before walking out.

Bianca Hanks had gutted her daughter more completely than if she'd taken a knife to her stomach. The news had rendered Bronwyn speechless for days. She could not believe that her mother had so callously stepped in to a situation that she knew nothing about and not only ripped it from seam to seam but placed her daughter in one of the most mortifying situations of her life.

She didn't know what was worse: having someone tell Jack that 'little Numbat' was harbouring hopes of romance in the wake of his brother's tragic accident, or the fact that the knowledge had made him turn tail and run for the hills.

Green rolling vineyard-covered ones in Bordeaux, apparently.

She had still gone back to Oak Hills briefly to see Chris and offer what comfort she could. However, staying on indefinitely had made her feel sick after Jack's complete rejection. She had needed some space from Oak Hills and also some space from her parents.

She finally moved out of home, got her own apartment. She hadn't started at the family firm the following year but at Bantam, Harvey and Grey, where she told herself she might be able to stretch her own wings for a while.

She was wrong, of course.

The mantle of the Eddingses and the reach of Bianca Hanks touched everything in the Perth legal profession, and until she got out of law she was never going to be free of her.

So here you are . . . again, she reflected as Horace and the scenery around her came back into focus.

'You've gone awfully quiet.'

Horace's dry tone lifted her completely out of the reverie and she bit her lip nervously.

'Touched a nerve, didn't I?' He eyed her shrewdly.

More like six or seven.

'What did Jack say to you before he left?'

'Nothing,' she said bitterly. 'Not even goodbye or have a nice life.'

Horace's frown deepened. 'Everybody thinks I was too hard on him, but the truth is, I should have been harder earlier. His inconsideration knows no bounds. I gave him too long a leash here at Oak Hills and we all paid for it. Chris the most.'

'Don't get me wrong, Horace,' Bronwyn shook her head, 'as angry as I am at Jack for leaving, I'm just as mad with you.'

'What?'

'Do you know why I used come here so much when I was in uni? It was because my home was a wasteland. I couldn't bear to be there with parents who only wanted me for one thing – status. The Franklins represented real family to me. You guys were solid. You could count on each other, no matter what. And then you ruined it.'

'I ruined it!' Horace protested.

'Yes, you did,' Bronwyn said crossly, 'because you weren't there for your boys no matter what. You were judge, jury and punisher instead, and that's why this family broke apart.'

'For someone who is supposed to be a guest in my house, you've got an awful lot of opinions,' Horace growled.

'Get used to it.' Bronwyn shrugged. 'I'm turning over a new leaf.'

'God help us all,' he said, but when she glanced surreptitiously at his face, he seemed quietly arrested. Before she could contemplate it further they had reached the office block. Horace stopped to unlock the doors and let Bronwyn in.

The place was a mess.

If Bronwyn didn't know any better she'd say they'd been robbed.

There were five desks inside in a kind of open-plan arrangement. Chris, Lydia and Claudia had one each; there was a spare desk for the winemaker and a layout table in the middle. Paperwork littered the scene. Files were scattered on the floor, open ones on the desks, tools from the yard dropped by the door, and empty cleanskins on the central desk like they had actually been tasting produce while flicking through mail.

'It gets worse,' Horace nodded. 'Look at the bills on Lydia's desk.'

Bronwyn picked up the first piece of paper that caught her eye. 'You are fitting out the restaurant with fancy new candelabras? I thought you were supposed to be cutting spending, not investing in expensive upgrades. These are $150 a table.'

'According to Lydia, that is a saving.'

Bronwyn raised her eyebrows. 'How so?'

'We don't use as much power for lighting. Plus, they're on special.'

'*Say what?*'

'Half price,' Horace said tightly. 'So we're actually saving $150 a table.'

'She can't honestly believe that.'

'When we first got married it was endearing, but now that she's managing the budget, it's a nightmare.'

'I see. And Chris . . .' Bronwyn walked over to his desk, which she could barely make out under the layers of paper. Chris didn't seem to believe in filing, had no diary to speak of, and there was a stack of due dates and appointments written on various scraps of paper pinned to the walls.

There were wedding events coming up.

There were wine orders to fill.

Tours to prepare for.

Bottlers to line up.

Bronwyn's mouth thinned. 'This is going to take some time to sort through.'

It took her the balance of the week, in fact, just to get a list of priorities. Particularly as she was doing it on the quiet or whenever Horace could sneak her into the office. This wasn't as often as she would have liked and usually took some arranging. Despite the older man having committed himself to being her ally, he also spent a greater part of the time feeling sorry for himself.

The more they uncovered together, the worse the news got. Oak Hills wasn't just losing money. It *needed* money. Apparently the roof on the barrel room had to be re-tiled. The tractor's engine was on its last revs. Many of the picking bins were damaged and needed to be repaired or replaced. And that was just the beginning. Bankruptcy was nothing but a hop, skip and a jump away.

As soon as Horace found out that the damage to his business was worse than he had ever suspected, he spiralled into a depression that was difficult to pull him out of.

The week after, Bronwyn had much less success with him. Often during the day he would take long walks or disappear altogether, leaving Bronwyn high and dry. He seemed inclined to spend a lot of time with a man called John Maxwell, who Bronwyn didn't exactly count as good company. John owned the estate next door called 'Tawny Brooks' and back in the day had been more Horace's arch-rival than friend.

Now that the two men were freshly retired they both seemed to relate more to each other than anyone else and enjoyed wallowing in their mutual displacement.

She found them both the following weekend in Horace's leaky barrel room. Rows and rows of oak barrels on large steel racks filled the brick warehouse. A cackle of laughter had erupted from the far wall as she'd entered. When her eyes adjusted to the dim lighting she saw two old men sitting on the floor, their teeth stained red from the wine they were drinking. One was clearly recognisable as Horace, who lifted his glass to salute her. The other was John Maxwell. He was tall and weathered with wrinkly olive skin and greying facial hair.

'Horace, I've been looking everywhere for you,' Bronwyn complained, walking across the room and breathing in the cooler, fruitier air. It was laden with the aromas of oak and blackcurrant. An empty cleanskin bottle lay on the concrete between them. However, it looked like both men had graduated from bottle to barrel and were tasting straight from the tap.

Fantastic. He's drunk.

'This is my spy,' Horace slurred to John with a grand wave of his hand. 'Because of her I'm now aware of everything that's been going on.'

'And does that make you feel grateful or relieved?'

Horace choked. 'It makes me feel disappointed to know how far my children have fallen from grace.'

'All children fall,' John nodded sympathetically. 'It's about giving them the means to pick themselves up.'

Horace glared at him. 'Easy for you to say. You've got a pack of angels who have chosen to leave you in peace. My lot just want to stick their oars in any chance they get. They've ruined me.'

'Oh, I wouldn't go that far,' Bronwyn said crossly. She held out her hand to Horace's friend. 'Hi, I'm Bronwyn. Nice to meet you.'

He nodded. 'John Maxwell. Would you like a glass, my dear? We are sampling Horace's finest. And though it pains me to admit it, it's not too shabby.'

'Damn straight.' Horace lifted his glass in toast.

'Er, no, thank you. I'm kind of in a bit of a rush.' She looked meaningfully at Horace. 'You promised me you were going to get me into Claudia's office again today.'

'What's the point?' he demanded. 'You said it yourself yesterday. It's not just the people but the place that needs fixing. My bank account is dry. How about yours?'

'Well,' Bronwyn began thoughtfully, 'since you mention it –'

'Forget I said that.' Horace held his palm up. 'I've got my pride, after all, and you're already working for free.'

'Horace, if we're going to do this, I need you to stick with it. We need to get a plan. You and I need to sit down and brainstorm.'

Horace's eyes lit up. 'We can brainstorm in here if you want.'

'Over a couple more glasses perhaps?' Bronwyn put her hands on her hips.

'She's a woman after my own heart.' Horace nudged John. 'I don't know why neither of my sons snatched her up when they had the chance.'

Bronwyn felt herself redden.

Pretend he didn't say that.

'Careful, my friend,' John warned him, 'something tells me she's mad with you.' He elbowed Horace back. 'Look at her. Can't you see she's upset?'

Horace squinted. 'No. I'm nearly blind, remember.'

'Are you?' John hiccuped. 'I thought you said you were deaf?'

'No, that's you,' Horace chuckled. '*Obviously.*'

John laughed too. 'I guess you might be right. Should we make a toast then?'

'To what?'

'To losing our senses. I'm really quite enjoying it.'

They clicked their glasses, making Bronwyn want to bang their heads together as well. Luckily Adam, the winemaker from next door, turned up not two seconds later and offered to cart John back to where he belonged. Apparently Anita Maxwell was mad as fire because her husband had been MIA all afternoon. As soon they were both out of earshot, she turned crossly to Horace.

'Why are you doing this to yourself? Life shouldn't leave you along with your sight. You have a chance to make Oak Hills right again. Stop letting me down.'

The message must have got through because he grudgingly stayed by her side the rest of the afternoon, explaining various pieces of the Oak Hills puzzle that she was gradually unearthing from different areas around the office. The problem was, despite the pile of debris that needed wading through, there was still one crucial outstanding issue.

The winemaker.

The hiring was Lydia's task and so Bronwyn had steered clear of it until now. However, with the matter becoming significantly more urgent, she couldn't see how she could avoid challenging the Oak Hills matriarch again.

Her next opportunity to do so was at breakfast. Lydia told her she had hired a local who would be starting the following week. This was indeed a relief but when Bronwyn tried to press her for further details, she changed the subject.

'I heard you met John Maxwell a few days ago. Now there's a man who needs your help.'

Horace, who was also present, had lowered his paper. 'What are you talking about, woman?'

'Mrs Caffrey said he was enquiring in town after a lawyer. I'm surprised he didn't say anything when he met Bron the other day. Why don't I mention who she is next time he's here?'

Bronwyn frowned. 'I'd rather you didn't.'

'Nonsense, you should be proud of your family's connections.'

It was clear now more than ever that Lydia *really* wanted her otherwise occupied but just didn't want to be a bitch about it. Bronwyn didn't blame her. The last thing she wanted was to have a fight with Claudia's mother. However, maybe she couldn't avoid it.

After breakfast she wandered outside to check on Elsa.

This was the usual time of day she got to spend with her dog. She felt more protective than ever of Elsa now that she knew exactly the calibre of her owner. She had been totally taken in by Peter Goldman, but at least the upside was she might get to save Elsa and her pups from a lifetime of torment.

Not 'might', Bronwyn, you will.

Packing Elsa off to Leon McCall was not an option.

She gazed down at the pregnant canine. 'Hey, girl, how are you holding up? Babies coming out yet?'

Elsa scrambled up quickly from her prone position on the timber decking and shoved her head under Bronwyn's hand. It seemed like the expectant mother was putting on weight at an increasing rate lately.

Bronwyn looked at her sternly. 'I've heard you've been very naughty.'

Elsa barked and tried to jump on her but Bronwyn caught her paws before they landed. She was actually getting quite good at handling Elsa's rough displays of affection. 'Don't try to change the subject. I'm onto you. You've got to start being good or we're going to get into more trouble than we already are.' Grimacing, she put Elsa's paws down and stepped back, gazing out across the property. There was nothing like looking at a wide expanse of land to make frayed ideas knot together.

Suddenly, her phone buzzed in her pocket. It was Claudia's caller ID. She answered, 'Claud?'

'You haven't called your mother yet, have you?'

'My mum?' Abruptly she lifted her hand to her mouth. 'Oh no! I completely forgot.'

'No shit, Bronwyn.'

'Well,' Bronwyn frowned at her best friend's terse manner, 'I have a lot on my plate here, you know. And your family hasn't exactly been . . . transparent. Your mum and Chris are trying to hide problems instead of dealing with them.'

Claudia grunted. 'What did I tell you?'

'Yes, well, what you didn't tell me was your plan to downgrade Oak Hills's reputation to get on the lower end of the market. Claudia, that makes me very sad.'

'It would keep our business afloat.'

'I guess,' Bronwyn agreed reluctantly. 'For a few more years, but then what?'

'Well,' Claudia said cheerfully, 'I'm sure you'll think of something.'

'Thanks a lot.' Bronwyn sighed but was secretly pleased. 'I'm certain your mum's got Jack on board. She's trying to get me back into the legal profession. Found me a new client this morning.'

'Who?'

'John Maxwell.'

'Oooh,' Claudia pounced. 'Why don't you get the info and then toss the job my way? I'd love to tell Seb I'm bringing in clients *and* it'll appease my mum for you.'

Bronwyn's lips curled in amusement. 'Ambitious much?'

'Always! But that's not really the point, is it?' Claudia briskly moved on. 'It's not my mum that's our biggest worry, it's yours.'

Bronwyn had absolutely no trouble believing that. 'Has she threatened you or something?'

'I ran into her in court, she was opposing counsel.'

'Ouch.'

'She's mad, Bron. She's really frickin' angry. She wants me out of the legal profession.'

'Well,' Bronwyn tried to put a positive spin on it, 'that's not actually that bad. I'm enjoying being out of it. Don't tell me you want to swap back?'

'No. Do you?'

'Not yet.'

'Then tell me how to deal with your mother.'

'Do you think if I knew that I'd be in Yallingup?'

'So what you're saying is, I'm screwed.'

'Not necessarily.' She heard some papers rustling and clicking on a keyboard.

'Sorry,' Claudia apologised breathlessly. 'I gotta go. Seb's summoned me to his office. Can I call you back in five?'

'Sure.'

They hung up and Bronwyn went back to patting Elsa's head. It was typical how just the mere mention of her mother's name had the adrenaline coursing through her veins again.

'I can't go back to that world, Elsa,' she sighed. 'And neither can you. We need to be right here. Both for us and for Oak Hills. What do you reckon?'

Elsa pushed her head more firmly into Bronwyn's hands.

'Yeah, I know,' Bronwyn agreed. 'But that's what proving yourself is all about, isn't it? If I don't step outside my comfort zone for a minute I'll never find out who I need to be. And Bianca Hanks wins.'

Her phone buzzed in her pocket again and she immediately lifted it to her ear and said reassuringly, 'My mother can't touch you. Uncle Cyril calls the shots at that office now.'

'My dear Bronwyn,' came the sleek, steel tones of the woman who had raised her. 'You'd be very surprised about what I can do.'

Chapter 15

Bronwyn froze. 'Mum?'

'I don't know why you're so surprised to hear from me, darling. Did you think I wouldn't take offence after you completely ignored my instructions?'

'Mum, you didn't even ask me whether I wanted to work for Uncle Cyril,' Bronwyn tried to explain. 'If you had –'

'That question is irrelevant. Of course you do. What lawyer in their right mind wouldn't?'

'This lawyer.'

'You don't know what you want,' her mother snapped at her. 'You're too blinded by idealism. I know you think running away is very romantic but reality *will* sink in. As for installing that country hick from Backwater Creek in your family's firm –'

'Her name is Claudia Franklin.'

'I am fully aware of her name and her origins. That *family*,' Bianca's voice seemed to crack, 'has brought you nothing but problems for nearly a decade. How dare you foist her on your uncle. You need to cut that connection now, Bronwyn. Once and for all. And if you can't do it then I will just have to do it for you.'

For so many years, Bronwyn had kept a lid on her true feelings. Glossed over details, nodded her head while she thought something different on the inside. It was easier to pretend she agreed to spare Bianca disappointment, to avoid her anger and the fight that would follow. Anything to keep the peace. Bianca Hanks's will was like a tidal wave. Better to hide her little boat than face her head on.

This time, however, her chest was too full. Her ribcage strained against the force of her feelings.

'I'd like to see you try.'

'Don't test me, Bronwyn,' Bianca warned.

'Or what? You'll pull another stunt like you did last time? I'm sick of your manipulations and your power plays. The Franklins have given me more love and support than you and Dad ever have.'

Her mother gasped. 'You are delusional. I fed you, clothed you, gave you the best education, the best opportunities. Raised you to mix in the highest circles. How can you be so ungrateful as to toss it all back in my face?'

'It's not that I'm ungrateful,' she protested. 'It's the fact that *your society* is yours, not mine.'

Bianca Hanks snorted. 'Where are you?'

'I'm not telling you.'

'Of course you are. Give me your address.'

'I can't think of a single good reason to do so.'

'Stop playing games, Bronwyn.'

'This isn't a game,' she warned. 'This is reality. I don't want to be a lawyer anymore and this time you need to just accept it. I'm moving on to new horizons.' She blurted out the words and shut her eyes.

There was a stunned silence but no explosion.

The voice that came back to her after the pause was quiet and deadly. 'Are you out of your mind? You're an Eddings. You have everything going for you. You are cream of the crop. You are my daughter!'

'Really, because I feel more like your pet or your ornament or the picture you hang on the wall for your friends to see when they come over for dinner. Hey guys, look what I got, a lovely carbon copy of myself so that my legacy might continue.'

'It's not my legacy,' Bianca hissed. 'It's your father's. Your family name. Don't you have any pride? Your father will be devastated.'

'Maybe for one minute. Then I'm sure he'll put me out of his mind like he does the rest of the year.'

'I'm not done with you, young lady. And your father will hear about this.' The phone went dead.

She wasn't quite sure what this was supposed to signify, unless Bianca was implying that her relationship with Robert was going to disintegrate further. How you could reduce something that was already at zero was a mystery to her.

The honourable Justice Robert William Eddings was a judge of the Supreme Court of Western Australia who, like her mother, had started his illustrious career at the family firm. He had been the managing partner before his brother, Cyril, and far more of a tyrant. It was where her parents had originally met. Theirs was an office romance, though Bronwyn could hardly picture the clandestine meetings, stolen lunches or suggestive office memos that had probably *not* passed between them.

Her father was as straight down the line as they came. If anything, her parents' union had been more of a marriage of convenience. Perhaps not so convenient as the years went on. Her mother had harboured hopes he might pass on the reins of the firm to her when he left to pursue his dreams of becoming a judge. Divorce had shortly followed when he'd passed her over for his brother. Bianca's pride hadn't allowed her to stay under Cyril's rule and so she'd left to join the bar, a move that had only solidified her notorious cutthroat reputation.

Whatever the case, when Bronwyn called Claudia back later that same evening, she was not able to allay her fears.

'I really don't know what she's going to do. I don't think she'll say anything about you not being Uncle Cyril's niece. She would never besmirch the name of the family firm, which is hers as well. Then again, she and Uncle Cyril have never been on good terms.'

'Hmm,' Claudia murmured. 'I don't feel safe.'

Bronwyn agreed. 'You shouldn't.'

She had found it very difficult to fall asleep that night with so much flying around her head. In fact, oblivion had finally claimed Bronwyn in the wee hours of the morning so it was no wonder that she slept through her alarm clock.

She awoke a few hours later to the feeling of sunshine streaming across her face and sat up abruptly to glance at her clock. It was almost nine am.

Oh shit.

She threw back the covers, cursing her mother's name. The truth was, she was worried for both herself and Claudia. Bianca Hanks was a force to be reckoned with and all Bronwyn felt she'd done yesterday was load her mother's guns with ammunition. God only knew who she was going to fire at first. That said, if her mother was up to no good, then Lydia Franklin wasn't too far behind.

Against everybody's advice, Lydia wanted to bring Jack home. What better way to do it than with the element of surprise?

If that's her plan, you better be prepared, Bronwyn.

She couldn't wear her heart on her sleeve, that was for sure.

A sudden chill caused Bronwyn to stand up and rub the goosebumps on her arms. Abruptly, she walked into the walk-in robe to choose what she was going to wear for the day. There was no use procrastinating.

Might as well face the day head on.

Chapter 16

Jack Franklin had no idea if he was doing the right thing, but it sure felt like a good day for it. Sunshine streamed through the tree leaves, dappling the dash of his car and warming the knuckles of his right hand as it rested on the steering wheel. He drove unhurriedly up Rickety Twigg Road through a forest of Karri trees to his childhood home. The Karri rose up along the road like soldiers marking his entrance. How he missed their familiar watch – their long grey trunks unencumbered by branches until quite high up. There, their arms intermingled protectively over the road, giving him safe passage as he passed into their magical realm. Jack's mouth twisted.

If only it were that simple.

There was no security for him here.

Despite the picturesque tranquillity of the landscape, he knew he was travelling straight into the lion's den. There would be nothing but accusation waiting for him on the other side.

His mother had only contacted him because she was desperate. The business was going under, his father could no longer work, Claudia had finally given them all the finger and Chris, even with his determination, could not do it alone.

They needed him.

Ha! He didn't know whether to feel honoured or rejected that he was their last port of call. Neither his father nor his brother had tried to reach out to him these past five years, and the hurt in him ran deep. He knew he was no angel but hadn't he been punished enough?

The truth was, he'd known for months they were in trouble, before his mother had made contact to give him 'the news'. He had been biding his time. Oak Hills, with the exception of one other pretty face almost forgotten, had been the love of his life.

Fantasising about his return had been one of his favourite pastimes in France.

He'd just needed the perfect moment.

At long last it had arrived.

Oak Hills came into view and the sight took his breath away. It had been far too long. Nostalgia washed over him, drenching him in sadness. Blocks of vineyard rolled into the horizon: sauvignon blanc, chardonnay, merlot, cabernet, shiraz, pinot noir, chenin blanc. He licked his lips, remembering hot summer nights, a bottle of red between him and Chris as they toasted the fermentation gods for a good drop. He wound down the window as he turned into the Franklin driveway.

It smelled like earth and fruit.

Ocean and harvest.

Hell, it smelled like Australia, and that was an aroma he'd missed almost as much as his brother.

His heart ached when he thought of the years they'd lost. Chris was probably a different man now. How could he not be? An accident like that changed a person, permanently. They had to adapt, make do, get creative, stretch themselves to the limits of their ability. He shuddered in pain and guilt.

He wouldn't have had to if it weren't for you.

There was not a single day that went by that he didn't regret that night. For everything it had taken from them both. He had been stupid. There was no doubt about that . . . too much ego and not enough sense. When he looked back on his life as the playboy winemaker of the South-West, he had to admit he'd been out of control.

Nothing could touch him in those days.

He was Jack Franklin.

He had the women.

He had the wine.

And the Oak Hills throne was his inheritance. Well, his father had taken that privilege away in short order, hadn't he? Not that he didn't deserve it.

Everyone thought his exile had been a sudden decision, based on his responsibility for Chris's accident, and yes, that had been the straw that broke the camel's back. However, Jack knew that his father's displeasure with him had been brewing long before that.

Horace had disapproved entirely of Jack's attitude and lifestyle. He had wanted Jack to calm down, not only in terms of his social life but his way of thinking about his work. He was always having disagreements with his dad about how the winery should be run – because he knew best. It was only in his recent travels around France that he could see how his father had been trying to give him a well-rounded skill set.

Horace thought Jack was too experimental too soon – he had wanted him to perfect the Oak Hills 'tried and true' varieties before he started broadening their horizons. There had always been more tension between father and son than compliance. They were too much alike, too competitive. They should never have tried to work together. It had been a disaster from the start.

All the same, he missed him.

A lump formed in Jack's throat.

Don't be a fool.

The last thing he could afford to do was go soft on the old man now, especially given what he was here to do.

On a whim he bypassed the house and headed straight down the gravel track that led to the winery. It was early morning, so he was hoping for a look around before he woke anyone up.

Or maybe you just want to enjoy Oak Hills in peace for a second, before your father kicks you out all over again.

The large fermentation tanks sitting on steel platforms came into view. To his surprise, there was a bit of a commotion going on in front of the press and de-stemmer. This was a tank on its side, supported by a steel frame on wheels. It was mobile along a set of rails that ran directly under the fermentation tanks so that it could sit under any of them.

He recognised all three men in the argument. Two were from his childhood, the other from his more recent travels in France.

'Antoine.' He hailed the last individual. 'I see you've settled in.'

His French friend looked up with pure pleasure written large on his face. 'So you have come at last, your rescue is not needed. I'm winning ze fight.' He had a hose in one hand and was completely dry. His companions, by comparison, were soaked to the skin. They both spun around startled. 'Jack!'

The vineyard workers he knew as Nick and Bob came up to him, slapping him on the back and shaking his hand. 'What the hell are you doing here?'

He grinned back. 'Why the hell are you so wet?'

Bob glared at Antoine. 'Ant's having a little trouble with accepting his position.'

'My place is in ze winery, not ze yard.' Antoine shrugged. 'I am a winemaker, not cleaning staff.'

'You're actually a cellar hand, dickhead,' Bob corrected him. 'And you're supposed to go wherever you're needed.'

Ant flicked his hand at him, saying crossly to Jack, 'See how zey seek to belittle me? As though I'd let zis bother me. I know I was built for greater things.'

'That's right, Ant,' Nick smirked. 'You can carry ten times your body weight. So start connecting up that bloody hose.'

However, Ant was too busy warming to his theme. 'I must push past new horizons. Find my muse. Exercise my creative flair. Zis is my duty as an artist. A winemaker does not clean bins.'

'The only winemaker at Oak Hills is Horace,' Nick retorted, causing Jack to cough. 'Unless this smart-arse is intending to stay.'

'I'll let you know,' Jack agreed with a wink. 'In the meantime, I think I might take your problem off your hands.' He indicated Antoine. 'Do you want to come with me for a minute . . . er, Ant?'

'But of course.' Ant seemed to regard this as a win and his mouth curved into a smile of triumph, which he directed at the two indignant vineyard workers. 'Sorry to cut zis short. I will leave you to your business. My talents are required elsewhere.'

'Ant,' Jack said reprovingly.

'Oh, very well.' Ant's long fingers fluttered a dismissive wave as he joined Jack.

'Really?' Jack demanded as soon as they were out of earshot. 'When I asked you to come here, I expected you to at least try to blend in a little.'

'What?' Antoine regarded him, all innocence and intrigue. 'You think I do not blend in?'

'Well, if you've been busy throwing your weight around then of course not.'

'Your mother loves me,' Ant protested. 'I am ze sunshine in her day.'

'Only because you're her hotline directly to me. Where is she, by the way? Still in bed?'

'Possibly. Ze restaurant is not open yet.'

Jack nodded. 'I will see her first, I think. But tell me what's been going on here before I do that.'

'Ah, already pumping your spy for information. Ha!' Ant snapped his fingers. 'What about what you promised me? My time to shine, you said. A chance in the limelight. Where is my pinot noir? You cannot back out now.'

Jack rolled his eyes. 'Did I say I was backing out? You have to understand how delicate the situation is. My family is not going to like our plan.'

'Zey will get used to it,' Ant shrugged. 'Options are running out. I imagine zat is why your father has brought the lawyer in to dig through your family's files.'

'Lawyer?'

'A woman arrived last week after Claudia left.'

'Thick glasses, timid, shy, no sense of fashion?' Jack enquired quickly.

'Not at all,' Ant swatted his hand. 'She is gorgeous. Very elegant. And determined too. I imagine she will turn zis business on its head, should Horace let her have her way. No, I would not say she is shy at all.'

'Oh.' Jack shook the cobwebs from his brain. 'Of course.'

Silly of him to immediately assume it was Bronwyn. He hadn't heard from Numbat in years. He was probably just an afterthought in her life now – one of those unfortunate acquaintances she recalled if she thought hard enough about it. The last time he'd asked after her he'd been told she'd stopped coming back to Yallingup as often, and in recent years hadn't been at all. In fact, she was so fully immersed in city living that she'd grown into the daughter Bianca Hanks always wanted.

A shame, really.

She'd been such a sweet girl when he'd known her. In turn, he was sure she'd thought of him as an annoying, opinionated guy whom she could rely on occasionally, but not too much. He teased her a lot, and made fun of her insecurities.

Only because they were reflections of his own.

He could see that now.

She had wanted her parents' approval, and how he'd craved his father's trust. They seemed cut from the same cloth. She understood him. And had she but known it, their conversations, infrequent as they were, had started to make him think.

He couldn't pinpoint the exact day his feelings for Bronwyn had changed but there were certainly a few red flags – like the day he and Chris had eavesdropped on a conversation between her and Claudia. The girls had been sitting on the front porch discussing their big night out the day before. He and Chris had been about to walk out the front door when the conversation had suddenly turned down an interesting path. Chris had stopped walking and put a hand to Jack's chest. Not thinking much of it, and always keen for a little subterfuge, Jack had halted. After all, he and Chris had always been partners in crime.

'So I saw you talking to that cute guy by the bar,' Claudia was saying.

Chris looked over and met his eyes. Bronwyn was such a shy little thing. Neither of them had ever heard her talk about the men in her life. And frankly both of them simply assumed that she had none.

'He was okay,' came the noncommittal reply.

'What was his name?'

'George something or other.'

'He seemed to like you.'

'Yeah, I guess so.'

Silence.

He didn't know why but his whole body had tensed up, like a kangaroo about to jump, and he practically willed Claudia to ask her the next question.

'Come on, Bron, don't leave me hanging here. Did he ask you out or not?'

'Yes.' Bronwyn's voice seemed small and shy.

He had sucked in a breath and tasted something a lot like disappointment. In hindsight, he could also recall Chris's shell-shocked expression, but at the time had not thought much of it.

'And . . . ?' Claudia's teasing tone was starting to annoy him.

'I said no.'

His breath whooshed out in one gasp. So did Claudia's. 'Bronwyn!'

'I ran scared, okay? He was one of those big confident types and he just made me feel awkward and unworldly.'

'You make yourself feel awkward.'

'I just think I should go for someone younger, less experienced. George seemed like he'd been around the block half a dozen times. What's he going to think when he finds out that I've never kissed anyone before? At my age it's practically unheard of.'

Jack and Chris's gazes had immediately locked in gleeful enjoyment of this new piece of information. Chris had been about step through the front door again but this time it was Jack who pulled back on his shirt. He was curious enough to want to hear the rest.

Claudia sighed. 'He probably just thought you were picky and he was lucky enough to have made the cut.'

'He'd laugh at me. It's embarrassing.' Bronwyn groaned. 'He was too much . . .' Her voice seemed to strain. 'He was too much like Jack.'

His eyes had widened at the mention and Chris had flicked the back of his hand against his chest more like a 'way to go' than 'dumbarse'.

He couldn't return the sentiment, however. Her comparison of him and George didn't sit well for some reason, and something a lot like sadness sank to the bottom of his stomach.

'Hmm, well,' Claudia's voice clearly indicated her revulsion, 'I share your reluctance there. But how are you going to beat this hurdle if you don't put yourself out there?'

'Next time,' Bronwyn had murmured, or something that sounded very much like it.

The conversation had stuck with him for days. He started getting sick of his relationship merry-go-round, which was as meaningful as a chocolate bar for lunch – sweet, but only for the moment. After that it just left you feeling a little less healthy and a lot like you needed to change your diet.

Hastily, he pulled his mind back to the present, unwilling to go down that rocky road that had been partially responsible for the rift that continued to exist between him and his brother.

Speaking of whom . . .

'What does Chris think of this lawyer?'

'Taken with 'er, of course. Impossible not to be. Though still reluctant to give her too much information on the business. I don't blame him. Oak Hills is practically bankrupt. All zey are doing now is trying to stop the rest of Yallingup from finding out.'

'I see.'

By now they'd walked all the way to the cellar door and quietly entered the premises. Antoine went in first.

'What are you doing back, Ant?' Chris's voice came from behind the bar. 'I thought I told you you were needed elsewhere.'

A lump formed in Jack's throat when he heard the familiar tone and he quickly doubled his stride to get into the room. Then he saw him, sitting there in a wheelchair, his fingers resting lightly against the spokes. His face hadn't aged much. It still held that kind, good nature, the quiet determination, with only a couple extra lines. However, the sight of him in the chair . . .

It made it real.

Everything he'd heard.

The pictures.

It was strange seeing his legs like that, skinny and wasted. He couldn't take his eyes off them and felt tears forming. He blinked furiously.

For fuck's sake.

'Jack.' Chris's voice cracked in the dry air. '*What are you doing here?*'

He cleared his throat. 'I'm home, mate. I've come to help you.'

Chris lip curled. 'Too little, too late, *mate*,' he snarled.

His brother couldn't have hurt him more if he'd punched him in the face. Chris spun in his chair, so expertly that he left the room faster than Jack could walk.

'Zat went well.' Antoine clapped him on the back cheerfully. 'You must be glad to have got ze first meeting out of ze way. What shall we do now? Go out for breakfast? Celebrate?'

'Are you kidding me?' Jack returned tightly, feeling like someone had just sucked all the oxygen out of the room. 'You playing up on the job will make Chris hate me even more. Seriously, Ant, can't you be a little more sensitive?'

'Firstly,' Ant puffed out his chest and held up a finger, 'I'm a Frenchman. My heart bleeds with empathy every moment I am awake. Secondly, I do not take kindly to you copying the indigenous of these parts and calling me Ant. It is most insulting.'

Jack raised his eyebrows. 'There are worse nicknames and this one suits you.'

Ant snorted loudly.

'Anyway, I think I'll return to the house now and speak to my mum.'

'You might want to freshen up,' Ant flicked the comment at him pettily. 'You smell like three hours on the road.'

Jack grinned, his good humour returning. 'So is that French tact or just your empathy outdoing itself?'

'Bah! Why you Aussies must have no care for your appearance, I do not know. Zat is your impression. And I . . .' He looked down his long nose at him, 'always leave a lasting one.'

On this note, he walked away towards the bar, leaving Jack shaking his head. He left the cellar door shortly after and headed back to the house. With the vineyard all around him again the scenery lightened his step, but not completely. He had noted all the asphalt paths his parents had added to the property. The ramps going up into the winery and behind a section of the bar. There had been a lot of adjustments while he was gone and the sting of culpability and helplessness pricked him again.

It was all very well for them to say that he had abandoned them back then, but from his recollection it was far more like he'd been pushed out kicking and screaming.

Not that he was in any way downplaying the accident. He took full responsibility for that and had never known peace since. As his gaze stretched over the hill in the direction of the neighbouring property, Gum Leaf Grove, his heart shrank in his chest. No one lived there.

There was an old house on the land but it had been vacant for years. He shuddered to think what it would look like inside, probably a haven for wildlife. The land around the house had been leased to grape growers, so it had a vineyard that was mostly well kept. However, there was one section behind the house – a giant flat gravelly area – where he and his friends used to muck about as teenagers. He was told that when the house was occupied they used to run a casual drive-in for the locals there. There was no longer any trace of that movie screen but the car park certainly made a great place to meet up and hang out. Particularly if you wanted to smoke, drink or make out away from disapproving eyes.

As they grew older and became less interested in being delinquents and more concerned about just having a good time, Gum Leaf Grove had become the place to hold a party. He often wondered whether the owner knew about their frequent piss-ups on his land. Nobody ever came to tell them off. It was the perfect venue, BYO barbecue and esky. You could let loose without causing damage to anyone's home.

That was your problem, wasn't it?

You let too loose.

It was easy to do. Back then he'd thought the sun and the moon shone out of his own arse. He was always blowing off steam on women and booze and that night had been pretty run of the mill.

Oh, except for the part where he'd decided that he was in love with Bronwyn Eddings but couldn't ever have her.

He cringed when he thought of the mess he'd created that had ended in that tragic event; a mess that had been brewing for months because of his blatant insensitivity. Not just to Bronwyn but Chris as well.

He kicked a pebble with his shoe as he pulled his eyes away from Gum Leaf Grove to somewhere a little closer to home – the family's gazebo. It sat at the top of the hill overlooking the vineyard, white and hexagonal in shape with a traditional pitched roof of light brown tiling. Bronwyn had always loved that spot back when she was in uni.

She often went there to study all those years ago. The picturesque surroundings and the quietness of the countryside made it the perfect place to reflect and digest. It had also represented a great opportunity for him to catch her alone.

He used to get a real kick out of teasing her there. One time in particular would always stick in his mind. It had been during one of her study weeks, just before end-of-year exams.

As he sauntered up those gazebo steps for the fourth time in four days, he tried not to think too closely about why he enjoyed riling her so much. Bronwyn did not raise her eyes from *Torts: Cases and Commentary, Fourth Edition* but she did release a sigh when she said, 'Go away, Jack.'

He ignored her, of course, and sat down on the other end of the bench, an arm stretched across the back and one leg hooked up so that his ankle rested on his knee in a manner he knew she found irritating. She smelled like frangipanis and fig leaves but he didn't look at her just yet. Instead he turned his attention to a gorgeous metallic-blue wren hopping around in the flourishing bushes of red kangaroo paws that lined the sides of the gazebo.

'So where's Claud?' he asked. 'Why isn't she studying with you?'

With a groan she finally looked up. 'She doesn't need to. She's smarter than I am.'

He threw back his head and laughed. 'I love my sister to bits, Numbat, but she's not smarter. She's just knows when to take a break. Why are you so afraid of failing?'

'I'm not afraid of failing.' She tossed her head.

No, she wasn't, was she? Passing was in the bag. She was

afraid of was not being in the top two per cent, the cream of her class, as was expected of an Eddings.

'Hmm,' he murmured, keeping those thoughts to himself. 'So why not study at home if you don't want the company?'

She ignored him, as he knew she would. Why he liked asking her questions she had no desire to answer, he had no idea. Perhaps he enjoyed the leap of the pulse at the base of her neck too much.

'Come on, Numbat, you can tell me, I'm practically your brother! What's going on at home that makes you keep hiding out here every second weekend and on holidays?'

Her brother.

He'd rolled out that wagon one too many times and he wondered how much longer he was going to be able to make it stick.

'No particular reason.' Her tone was defensive. 'I just find home more stressful, that's all. It's . . . so peaceful here. I feel like part of the family.'

Jack picked up her textbook and flipped it over. 'So what are you going to specialise in? Torts?'

She gnawed on her lower lip. 'Maybe family law.'

'Family law?'

She wrinkled her nose. 'I know it can get a bit depressing, all the divorces you have to deal with . . .' She seemed to buoy herself. 'But it's the children. They are always the losers in situations like that and I just want to be in a position where I can protect their interests.'

'Like nobody protected yours?' He immediately wished he could yank the question back.

A little too deep, Jack.

She stuck out her tongue at him. 'Stop reading into everything I say. It just is what it is.' She took her book off him and reopened it to the page she was at.

'So you're not even going to take a five-minute break?' he teased.

'No.'

'What do you normally do for fun?'

She groaned at his persistence and clearly threw out the first answer that came into her head. 'I read.'

'So when you're not studying,' he squinted at the ceiling of the gazebo, 'you read. Wow. Bit of wild child, aren't ya? Haven't you got a boyfriend or something?'

'No.'

And then, dumbarse that he was, he brought George up.

'What about that guy you met in Margaret River last time you were here? Isn't he taking you out?'

She turned her head quickly, realising for the first time that he was studying her as intently as she had been studying *Torts* ten seconds earlier.

'How do you know about him? Have you been eavesdropping on my conversations again?'

'It would help if you girls didn't giggle so loudly,' he returned gruffly.

'That was a private conversation.' She was blushing bright red and clearly wondering just how much he'd heard.

'Don't worry, I didn't hear it all. Just the first bit,' he lied, and should have ended the conversation there. A decent man would have, but not him. 'So he's not your boyfriend?'

'No.'

'Why not?'

She glared at him. 'Why is that your business?'

He shrugged, his eyes twinkling. 'Because I'm asking.'

'He just wasn't my type, all right.'

He gave a bark of laughter. 'You have a type. Numbat has a type!'

'Of course I do. Doesn't everybody?'

'I don't.'

'Yes, you do.' She shook her finger. 'Curvy, blonde and easy.'

'True,' he grinned, 'but I'm not opposed to other shapes

and sizes. Even you wouldn't be half bad if your eyes weren't so big and you didn't have so many freckles.'

She gasped and self-consciously touched her face.

'Don't do that.' He captured her hand and pulled it away. 'I was just teasing.'

'About my eyes or my freckles?' she asked in a small voice.

He leaned in close, squinting at her face as though trying to make up his mind, and suddenly got lost in her eyes. Big blue orbs, deep and mesmerising. He was also enjoying the sensation of her breath on his face and her hand still in his. He watched in fascination as heat infused her face, building slowly from the base of her neck, parting her pretty pink lips like a blatant invitation. If he really was trying to count every freckle on her face, he was going to find it difficult to see them soon.

She yanked her fingers out of his, moved right over and opened up *Torts* a second time. 'Stop it, Jack. You're not funny.'

No, not funny. Just fascinated and quite suddenly taken by a need to have more of her. 'You've never been kissed,' he stated matter-of-factly, almost like a note to self rather than engaging her opinion.

Heat scorched her face. She gasped. 'You *did* eavesdrop on the whole conversation! Liar!'

'Even if I hadn't, it's as plain as –'

'The freckles on my face? Yeah, yeah I get it, whatever. Go away. You're really starting to annoy me now.'

'Bron, how old are you now? Nineteen or twenty? You gotta do somethin' about that.'

She lowered the book. 'Since I last checked there's no age limit on a first kiss.'

'No, but if it's stopping you from dating people you really should get it out of the way.'

She blew her fringe out of her face. 'Oh, for Pete's sake. Haven't you got something better to do?'

He felt his expression sour. 'I would if Horace would just bloody let me.'

'He'll come around.'

'He's a micro-manager. He watches everything I do and gives me no freedom at all.'

He stood up, the move motivated by frustration and flung his hands up to clasp the back of his head. 'He's driving me mad.'

'Like father, like son.' She snapped her book closed, shoved it in a bag that held a couple of others and stood up too.

'Where do you think you're going?'

'I'm trying to study and I'm not getting anything done.' She looked at him pointedly. 'I might as well see if I can find Claud. Maybe we can test each other or something.' She hugged her books to her chest. 'I'll see you round.'

'Hey, Numbat, before you go . . .'

Maybe it was that he was piqued she could dismiss him so easily that made him do it, he really wasn't sure, but when she turned around he cupped her face with two hands so she had to look at him.

Her eyes darted worriedly. 'What are you doing?'

'Helping you out.'

On her gasp of outrage, he captured her conveniently open mouth and proceeded to kiss her in a fashion that brothers would never use on sisters. He had half expected her to pull away immediately and when she didn't, he lost the point of the whole exercise . . . *if* there was one. He pulled her closer, devouring her softness and her honesty like a lifeline. She felt good. So good. And he didn't want to let her go.

When he did finally lift his head and step back they stood there for a moment staring at each other in shock. For once, he was speechless and it was because he had just realised he had gone too far with his teasing this time.

She slapped him, the sting of her palm hot against his face. 'That was mine to give!' Her chest heaved with emotion.

'I wanted it to be special and sweet and real and you just . . . you stole it from me! You're a jerk, Jack. A big fat jerk!'

His eyes rounded. 'Bron –'

'Sod off, Jack!' She hooked her bag over her shoulder and tore off into the vineyard.

They hadn't spoken for days after that and the awkwardness of it all had stretched between them like a sticky piece of Blu-Tack. He'd had no idea how to fix his blunder. And then she'd gone back to Perth and he'd thought that maybe it could all be brushed under the carpet – the next time she came to town they could pretend like nothing had happened. Of course, Chris, *damn him*, had noticed something was up and had immediately demanded an explanation.

'What's going on between you two? Why were you both acting funny just before she left?'

And because at the time he was so completely self-absorbed, so wholly incapable of seeing past his own nose, he'd told him. No fluff on it either. Just the unvarnished truth. It was his brother, after all, and they'd never kept secrets from each other in the past. So he hadn't seen any reason to do so then. What he hadn't realised was how Chris would react to his honesty.

He had punched him in the face.

Nearly broken his nose too.

There was certainly enough blood on his shirt to show for it.

'What the hell!' he cried reeling back. '*What'd ya do that for?*'

'You're a bastard.'

'Okay, I know.' He held up his hands palms up. 'It was a dumb thing to do. And I've been sorry ever since, but I don't know . . . There's something about Numbat that makes me lose my head.'

'No shit,' Chris snapped, his fists clenching by his sides like he was getting ready to hit him again.

'*What's the matter now?*'

'You must know I like her.' His eyes flashed fury like Jack had never seen before. 'And then you go and do *that*.'

He gaped at his brother. 'I had no idea. You never said anything.'

'Isn't it fuckin' obvious?'

The problem with having too much luck with women was that you never tried subtlety anymore. It just took too much time. Chris, on the other hand, was a master at it. It was, after all, the gentleman's way. Jack suspected that if you really were looking for a long-term relationship you had to spend some time on the emotional side of things. However, as far as he could see, from day one Chris had firmly set down roots in the 'friend zone' and grown a bean stalk that had led to absolutely nowhere. Spurred on by this fact, Jack shook off his shock and glared at him. '*No*. It's not obvious. You haven't even asked her out, for crying out loud.'

'I'd been working up to it,' Chris had returned in anger.

'How?' he remembered sneering as he wiped the blood from his nose on his sleeve. 'It's not rocket science, Chris. You just ask the bloody question.'

'It's more complicated than that and you know it,' Chris threw at him. 'She's Claudia's best friend. Hell, she's *our* friend. She's here all the time and she thinks of us as brothers.'

'Not anymore,' he'd responded, a little too cruelly.

'How can you be so callous? She's not one of your two-week flings, Jack. You can't do shit like that to her.'

'Who said I thought of her as a fling?'

'Well, you can't mean to go after her for real.'

'Why not?'

Chris's eyes shot sparks as he literally rolled on his feet with rage. Words seemed to fail him, and so Jack had filled in the blanks.

'Because she's yours?' he suggested quietly. 'Who's the neanderthal now?'

'Why are you doing this to me?' Chris had spluttered. 'You

could have your pick of women and often do. It's not like I get in your way. Why do you have to go after the one woman I like. She's not even your type!'

Because I don't want you to have her.

As soon as the thought had entered his head it had refused to budge. The challenge was out of his mouth before he could stop it.

'Who says I didn't like her first?'

Chris had gasped. 'I don't believe you.'

'Believe it or don't believe it, I don't care. But if you think I'm going to back off to spare your feelings, think again. *Contemplating* asking her out isn't a claim, Chris. It's not even a head start. It's nothing.'

'You want to make this a competition,' Chris said darkly, 'fine. Have it your way. I don't think she'll go for you anyway. Not after what you've pulled. The truth is, Jack, you don't get what you want by stealing it. I hope one day you learn that.'

And then he'd marched off, never knowing how poignant his words would prove to be.

Bronwyn hadn't returned to Yallingup for six months. When she did, he'd made every attempt to make up for his earlier impulse, just short of bringing it up. In hindsight, he realised the best thing he could have done was apologise and then try to move on. But no, that Jack Franklin, that idiot from half a decade ago, was far too sure of himself. He apologised to no one and so, despite his efforts to befriend her, Bronwyn had remained distant at best.

Of course, Chris was not so encumbered. And it was beginning to dawn on Jack that for all his expertise with women he had effectively boxed himself out of the market. He didn't know the first thing about friendship with a woman. Real friendship – the kind that led to love. The last thing he wanted or expected was his brother to swoop in and start wooing the first woman he'd given half a damn about, but that was exactly what happened.

Good old dependable Chris. Sensitive to a fault. He couldn't see how Bronwyn would not eventually fall for his brother. He was just the sort of man for her. The honest truth was, Jack knew he was losing.

Jealousy was a terrible, green-eyed monster that didn't allow you to think straight, and it had followed him to Gum Leaf Grove the night of the accident. The usual suspects were present. Chris, some of the vineyard workers and a couple of cellar hands. The twist was, Chris had invited Claudia and Bronwyn to join them. The surprise was . . . they'd accepted. It was a rare victory that never would have occurred had he raised the invitation himself. The knowledge had made him mad and moody, which was probably why the fight with his father had been inevitable as knock-off time approached.

'You're irresponsible and reckless. You spend more time organising your next social event than looking after the business.'

'Is the business failing, Dad?' he'd demanded. 'Am I losing us money? Sales have never been better. People love my wine.'

'Overconfidence is not a virtue.'

'Neither is constantly looking over your shoulder. Can't you just calm down? You're stressing me out.'

'*I'm* stressing *you* out? I heard you're going out again tonight.'

'So what?'

'Last week, you punctured two tyres on our ute from driving it off to Gum Leaf Grove. That property is not safe. Besides the fact that you're trespassing there with an Oak Hills vehicle. Get some responsibility!'

It had probably been one of the worst things to say to him in the mood he was in. What do you suppose he'd done? Taken that exact same ute off to the party they'd organised that night. Driven himself, Chris, Claud and Bron in it, just to spite his father.

Stupid arrogant fool.

When he looked back on those days, all he could see was mistakes. One after another. Dumb, pig-headed, couldn't-see-the-forest-for-the-trees oversights that in the present day just made him want to close his eyes and cringe.

His brainlessness, however, hadn't stopped at the ute. With Chris winning the race for Bronwyn's affections, he'd been nothing but a brute to him all evening and everyone had noticed, including the girls.

'Get a grip, Jack,' Claudia had scolded him when Bronwyn and Chris had walked off to get more drinks from the esky. 'What's up with you? You're terrible to be around tonight.'

He'd taken a swig from his beer, unable to put his dissatisfaction into words. Mainly because it was disappointment in himself. It didn't help matters when some of the boys had suggested doing donuts with this father's ute on the gravel.

What a great idea.

Nothing helped a foul mood more than doing something to make things worse. The fight he'd had with his father that evening hadn't even occurred to him as he'd jumped behind the wheel, adrenaline pumping, freezing out things he didn't want to think about. And if Horace's disapproval had featured on his radar, he probably would have thought 'so much the better'. His dad needed to loosen up before he turned to stone.

As the revelry escalated, some of the boys jumped in the tray to hitch a ride, and that was fine too.

Then two things happened.

At the same time.

And only one of them was witnessed by everyone.

Chris had been standing in the tray and had yelled out, 'Hey, Bron, look. No hands!'

As Bronwyn had turned around, Jack had swerved. Chris had gone flying straight out the tray and smacked into a tree. His back never stood a chance.

What no one else had seen was the pair of glowing eyes in the undergrowth, a kangaroo poised to jump into the path of his vehicle. That was why Jack had suddenly turned his wheel just when Chris cried out. And yeah, he'd saved the animal and ruined his brother's life, but none of this had anything to do with Bronwyn.

Nothing.

He had not swerved to show Chris up, though in the days that followed there was no persuading Chris otherwise.

Waiting for the ambulance had been the longest fifteen minutes of his life. Chris was out cold and Jack had no idea if it was better to stay or get him into the back of the ute and drive him to the hospital himself. Everybody had advised against moving him, though it had taken nearly all his willpower just to sit there, Claudia on his left, Bronwyn on his right. His sister had been beside herself, sobbing her heart out. Bronwyn's expression had been frozen as she stroked Chris's arm.

'Hold on, Chris, we're getting help.'

He couldn't remember a time in his life when he had been more tormented.

He shook the memory off, even now wanting to get as far from it as possible. There was no use in reliving the past. What was done was done. All he could do was try to atone for it and seek forgiveness. He had hoped that five years on, Chris might be more ready to listen to his side of the story. However, it looked like the battle to be heard was still ongoing.

Keeping his gaze averted from both the gazebo and the direction of Gum Leaf Grove, at last the house came back into view. It looked older and more worn than he remembered. Grabbing his travel bag from the car, he trudged slowly up the front steps and found the front door was unlocked. Nothing much had changed in that department.

He pushed it open and walked in.

'Hello? Hello? Mum?'

No one responded to his call and a quick reconnaissance of the lower floor showed him that everybody was out at the winery. The house was empty.

He thought about his father as he climbed the stairs. Horace had probably expected him to return crawling in on hands and knees, begging for forgiveness. Not there to provide the rescue. There was a certain satisfaction in that.

Fate had a weird way of sorting everyone out.

He walked into his old bedroom and was pleased to note his mother had not changed much about it. The few personal items he had left behind were still on the shelves. There were some of Claudia's clothes tossed over a chair, but otherwise it was mostly the same. Eagerly, he dropped his suitcase and stripped off his shirt, discarding it where he stood.

That had to be a good sign, right? His father hadn't ordered that the house be scrubbed of all things 'Jack'. So there was at least some chance he'd expected him to return.

He pushed down his pants and jocks and stepped out of them, walking towards the bathroom door, never thinking it would open before he got there.

Bronwyn Eddings stepped out of the shower, naked as the day she was born, but certainly not as innocent. Despite her slender frame, she had curves in all the right places and skin as creamy and golden as a freshly plucked apricot. Her semi-wet hair was swept up in a tousled pile on her head, though a few strands had escaped to caress her damp shoulders. Arousal shot straight to his groin as her pretty pink lips formed a large 'O' of surprise.

'Jack!'

'Bronwyn!'

'You're naked!'

'So are you!'

He stumbled back, tripping over the bags he had dropped in the centre of the room and landing squarely on his arse. 'Ow!'

'Damn! Are you okay?' She ran forward, her lovely bits bouncing everywhere.

No! He was not okay!

Especially if she happened to notice what was going on downstairs.

'I'm fine.' He leaned left, trying to drag the doona off the bed to cover his person.

Unfortunately, from the angle at which he was trying to drag it the cotton quilt was quite heavy, especially covered in cushions, and was refusing to budge from the bed.

'Here, let me help you,' Bronwyn said. But as she went to pick up the soft cover, he gave it an almighty yank and ended up with not just the doona on him but an armful of delectable, soft woman as well.

'Oh,' said Bronwyn as her body grazed the length of his. The shock of it fried all his senses and he groaned loudly.

'Sorry!' she cried. 'Did I hurt you?'

'Bronwyn.'

'Yes?'

'Get off me, right now.'

'Of course,' she squeaked. 'No problem.'

She threw the doona away and leapt off him, flashing her perfect little butt in the process. Ducking over to the other side of the bed, she grabbed the white dress he had noticed earlier hanging over the desk chair. In one swift movement, she threw it over her head and dragged it down her perfect form.

He lay there exhausted, with the doona over his privates. His heart was beating so fast it felt like he'd just run four hundred metres at a dead sprint. Slowly, he sat up and met her eyes, which were twinkling at him mischievously. It didn't matter that they were now mostly decent. He felt more vulnerable in this moment than he had ten seconds ago.

'So.' She clasped her hands together under her chin as a slow grin curled her mouth. 'You're looking well.'

That was the last straw. Who was this sexy, confident woman who took things like that in her stride, and what the hell had she done with Numbat? He struggled clumsily to his feet, holding the doona together with one hand at his hip.

'What are you doing in my bedroom?' he demanded angrily.

'*Your* bedroom?' She raised her eyebrows and put her hands on her hips. 'It hasn't been your bedroom in five years.'

'That's beside the point,' he growled. 'It's still got all my things in it.'

'Well, I'm sorry but I'm living in it now.'

'Since when?'

'Since just over two weeks ago,' she retorted. 'You got the email from your mum, I take it.'

'And all the messages she left on my phone. There was no mention of you. Though things with the business sounded pretty dire.'

She tossed her head. 'We're handling it.'

'We're?'

'I'm helping out.'

He snorted. 'Like you offered to five years ago? Forgive me if I don't have much faith in your word.'

Her body stilled and for a moment he thought he caught a glimpse of the old Bronwyn, the young girl he'd fallen in love with all those years ago. 'You aren't seriously calling me out on that, are you?' she demanded. 'When you were the one who abandoned us first.'

He deliberately ignored this comment. 'Unless Claudia's suing Dad for negligence, I think we can manage without you, Numbat. Especially now that I'm back. Won't your mother be missing you?'

She folded her arms. 'That nickname is a bit worn out, don't you think? I'm not the same person you left behind, Jack. Times have changed.'

'Yes, they certainly have.'

Chapter 17

The shock of seeing his face again had almost poleaxed her.
Thank goodness he had fallen over first and saved her the
embarrassment. When she had decided not to wear her heart
on her sleeve, she had thought she'd at least be wearing sleeves
at the time.

He looked different. Older, maybe. And he had facial hair –
that rugged, castaway look that made her breath catch in her
throat. All the same, she hoped telling him that times had changed had effectively conveyed that her feelings for him had well
and truly dried up, even if she wasn't so sure on the point herself.

To her irritation his eyes wandered across her body appre-
ciatively, as though he hadn't looked enough. 'You finally
filled out.'

She felt her face heat and resolutely gathered her defences.
Half a decade ago, this statement would have left her a
babbling, stuttering mess, but not today. 'Nor am I as shy and
naive as I used to be. I've had a very promising start to a law
career and met slipperier snakes than you, believe me.'

*And been ripped off by most of them, but we won't be
mentioning that part.*

He seemed to be rather annoyed by this statement, whether with her or with himself she wasn't too sure. 'Yeah, I can see that.' His eyes narrowed upon her. 'It would seem the name *Eddings* suits you a lot more than it used to.'

She lifted her chin. 'Well, after you left I did return to the fold.'

'I hope that wasn't to spite me.'

She gave a laugh that broke in the middle. 'When are you going to learn that the world doesn't spin based on your movements, Jack?'

He shrugged, causing a rippling effect across his bare chest that had her mouth dry in an instant.

'The truth is,' he said with a gentle sigh, 'I have a lot of regrets about the way we left things.'

'Do my ears deceive me?' She folded her arms. 'Are you actually apologising for not saying goodbye?'

Old Jack would never have done that.

'People change. Do you think you're the only one who's grown up?'

The way he said it, slowly and quietly, made her heart jump into her throat, so much so that she could hear the echo of its beat in her head.

'I'm sorry I left you hanging. When I received the offer for a job in Bordeaux –'

She cut him off, turning away to the window. 'It's all right, Jack. You don't need to explain.'

The last thing she wanted to do was review his conversation with her mother. She was sure the French opportunity had been very attractive and if there was nothing to hold you back, why shouldn't someone like him take it? She walked towards the window and the scenery outside seemed to soothe her somewhat. There was the ocean on her horizon, stretching her mind and smoothing away the ache in the bottom of her heart.

'It was the right thing for you to do,' she added tightly.

He was silent, and when she turned back around it was to find him studying her intensely.

'Of course.' A muscle in his cheek flinched. 'Turned out to be the right thing for everybody, didn't it?'

Not for Chris.

Not for your mum.

Not even for your dad.

She didn't say any of that though. It wasn't her place. That was between him and them, and if he found solace in being a bastard then who was she to disagree?

'So what *are you* really doing here?' he asked.

As if what she said before couldn't possibly be true. She blew on her fringe and tried a different tack.

'Claudia and I have swapped places.'

His eyes widened. 'Come again?'

She took great pleasure in copying his flippant tone of old. 'We thought it might be fun. I was over law and she was over the Franklins.'

He nodded. 'That I can believe. But you do realise a move like that isn't sustainable, right?'

'Why not?'

She hated how shrewd his gaze was. 'If you want to feel comfortable in your own skin, Bronwyn, you need to find a place and calling of your own and stop riding on everybody else's coat-tails.'

She felt like he'd slapped her. What he said was true. More than anything else in the world, she needed to carve out a life for herself. All the same, she folded her arms defensively.

'This is different. Claudia has put me in charge of fixing this place.'

'What right does Claudia have to put you in charge? This is Dad's business.'

'And, little though you care,' she returned sarcastically, 'he's half blind and retired. Besides, he likes me helping out. He trusts me.'

The only person who does.

'Well, you'd be one up on me then, wouldn't you?' Jack

returned bitterly. 'Honestly, Bronwyn, what this place needs is a winemaker. And in this room, that's me.'

'Your father's not going to like it.'

'I don't think he'll have much of a choice. Mum has hired me back.'

She figured as much; however, it was still a blow to hear it.

He put his hands on his hips. 'I don't think the question is whether I'm staying, but whether you are.'

He was right, of course. She was still the outsider looking in. Not one of the family, although trying to be. She could contribute, but only if they let her. It wasn't a job. She wasn't being paid. There was no future in any of it. It was like being a band groupie on some perverse holiday away from her old life. It wasn't anything real . . . unless she could make it so.

Even as realisation struck, an idea flew in with it. Suddenly she knew what to do.

'Well?' Jack enquired.

'I'm not going anywhere.' She put her hands on her hips. 'And just so we're clear, you'll have to sleep in Claudia's room.'

'If I can find the bed.'

'Your problem, not mine. In the meantime, I better get going. I've got a lot to do today.' *And I need to speak to Horace urgently.* 'So if you don't mind?' She did a little twirl and pointed with her finger, indicating he should leave.

'All right,' he responded in resignation.

'Er,' she said cheekily, 'you're not taking my doona with you.'

He had begun to turn but his eyes returned to hers, narrowing suspiciously as though calling her bluff.

When she folded her arms and stood her ground, he shrugged. 'Fine.' And he flung the bedding back on the bed. It took all her willpower not to gasp at the sight of him, fully unclothed in all his masculine glory. He stooped low, swiped his jeans off the floor and pulled them on.

Discreetly, she released her breath.

'Oh, by the way,' he said as he headed for the door, 'before you go out I'd put on some underwear first. You can see everything when you stand in front of the window like that.'

She jumped out of the light, her hands immediately going across her body.

'So you haven't completely lost all your shyness,' he noted. 'Good to know.'

His wicked chuckle echoed all the way down the hall.

Chapter 18

You would have thought that after their little run-in with Bianca Hanks at the Perth District Court, Claudia Franklin might have pulled back her attitude a little or at least acknowledged the hit. However, much to Seb's chagrin, all she did was put her head up and soldier on. He couldn't help but admire that just a little. After all, she had most of the firm's junior lawyers after her blood, Bianca Hanks wanting to crush her under her heel, and then there was Seb – the hard-hitting boss who wouldn't allow her to breathe.

'So how's my niece *really* going?'

The door to his office swung open, breaking Sebastian's train of thought. The man who had put them all in this mess in the first place strode in, all business and efficiency, before parking himself in the visitor's chair.

'Good morning, Cyril,' Seb responded dryly.

The managing partner of Hanks and Eddings did not look happy. 'Is it? I hadn't noticed.' He crossed one leg over the other and rested his right hand on his knee. 'Just got off the phone from that bloody ex-in-law of mine.'

'Let me guess, Bianca Hanks.'

'The one and only.'

To be honest, Bianca's animosity towards Claudia did worry Seb. That woman had more influential connections than fingers and toes. She could do some real damage if she was left unchecked. He was already certain she had some equity in the Hanks family trust and hoped she didn't mean to use it. She definitely didn't have any day-to-day say at the firm, but come financial-reporting time she could make herself a real pain in the arse if she wanted to.

'Wants me to fire my niece,' Cyril announced as though to punctuate this concern.

Sebastian stilled, surprised that the primary emotion he felt in that moment was disappointment. 'I thought Bianca specifically recommended her,' he said, even though he knew that this, among other things, was just another lie in Claudia's elaborate portfolio.

'Ha!' Cyril snorted. 'Her recommendation, or should I say demand, was for me to hire her daughter.'

'Bronwyn Eddings.'

Seb hadn't seen Bianca's daughter in years but he had met her. She'd done some work experience at the family firm in her final year of university. After some disagreement with her mother, though, she had decided to take a job somewhere else. He'd heard she'd started at Bantam, Harvey and Grey, which was by no means less reputable. However, Bianca's daughter had never struck him as the kind of lawyer who was going to make waves.

'I know Bianca has an agenda,' Cyril shrugged. 'But I've always liked Bronwyn and never approved of my brother's attitude towards her. He isn't a family man. He's like you.'

Seb raised his eyebrows at the reproving comment but said nothing.

'Anyway,' Cyril continued, 'the point is, I was going to do it. Then Bronwyn rang a few days before her interview and recommended Claudia instead.'

'So have you hired Claudia as a favour to Bronwyn or to spite Bianca?'

Cyril smiled. 'Perhaps a little of both.'

Sebastian groaned. 'Is it really wise of you to pick a fight with Bianca again? Honestly, when she left the firm I thought we were through that phase.'

'Can I help it if that woman brings out the worst in me? She put me through hell for years, almost putting a wedge between me and my brother, which we have never truly recovered from.'

Sebastian was under no illusions about that, given he'd been there to witness most of the fallout from Bianca's scheming. The woman was a psychopath who moved people around her chessboard like they were playing pieces in her game of life. He looked up at Cyril, whose chin was buried in his chest. The man was staring steadfastly into his lap as though watching a reel of past gripes. Their fight for the top position at the firm had been the stuff of legend.

'The problem with Bianca Hanks,' Cyril remarked slowly, 'is that she wants the best of both worlds. You can't be at the bar and have a say in the family firm at the same time. She obviously thought she'd be able to do that through her daughter.'

'Do you think Bronwyn is aware of this?'

'Of course she's aware of it,' Cyril scoffed. 'Why do you think the poor kid's disappeared and sent a decoy in her place?' He smirked. 'Bianca must be spitting mad knowing that my niece is taking the place of her daughter, only cementing my family's clout further.'

'Cyril, I know Claudia is not your niece.'

Cyril raised his eyebrows. 'Really, how?'

'Because I'm not an idiot.' Sebastian gave him a pointed look. 'That's why you hired me, remember? Way back when. It worries me that you are placing too much trust in a girl chosen at random by the daughter of your worst enemy.'

Cyril gave an indulgent titter. 'Not at random, I assure you. Do you think my thirst for revenge has in any way reduced my responsibilities to this firm, or to you, my son?'

It felt like a fist had grabbed hold of Seb's heart and squeezed it. Cyril didn't refer to him as his son often, but when he did it never failed to floor him. They never spoke of their relationship. Sebastian often felt too overwhelmed by it. It was unbelievable that this man had given him so much, for no apparent reason, and expected nothing in return.

'We both know who I want to take over the firm when I leave,' Cyril said quietly.

His eyes widened. 'Cyril –'

'Don't get me wrong,' he shook his finger, 'that won't be anytime soon but I need something more from you, Sebastian.'

'What?' Sebastian sat back in his chair. 'Is this the part where you give me a lecture about my morality again?'

'Maybe so. You're a brilliant lawyer, Seb. However, if you continue down the path that you're on, it's going to eat you alive. Exactly as it did Bianca Hanks.'

Sebastian couldn't help it, he rolled his eyes. 'You're over-dramatising.'

'You think so?' Cyril shrugged. 'I've been in this profession longer than you have. I know what it does to the best of us, including my own brother. If you let law become your life, with nothing else of meaning in it but this firm and this office, you might as well die right now.'

Sebastian laughed. 'Whoa. That's a bit extreme, isn't it?'

The older man shrugged again. 'Spending a lifetime solving other people's problems so that you don't have to look at your own is no way to live.'

'So what?' Sebastian's eyes lit in amusement. 'You're giving me a problem to focus on?'

'I like Claudia.'

'That doesn't mean you need to call her your niece.'

Cyril sighed. 'You're really going to insist on taking all the fun out of this, aren't you?'

'Absolutely. This lie you've started . . .'

'And you've encouraged,' Cyril added shrewdly.

'Is out of control.'

'Not at all. It's actually your fail-safe,' Cyril explained, 'because I know you don't trust her.'

Sebastian threw up his hands. 'How has that anything to do with it?'

'One day, she'll tell you that she's not my niece and that's the day you'll know you can.' Cyril put his palms up. 'No, that's okay. Don't thank me.'

'It's never going to happen, Cyril.' Sebastian glared at him.

'You don't know that.'

'And you don't know her. She's a smart-mouthed, cunning little fox with a backbone like a steel rod. I've tried to break her, believe me.' He gritted his teeth. 'But her ambition is probably just as high as Bianca's. Is that really what you want around here?'

'Or what you don't want around here?' Cyril countered. 'Claudia is a life lesson you need to learn, Seb. I think it's been smooth sailing for a little too long.'

'I have no idea what you're talking about.'

'Then understand this.' Cyril stabbed a finger at him. 'I want you to protect *my niece* at all costs from Bianca Hanks.'

'And how do you expect me to do that?'

'Bianca wants her buried. So let's unveil her talent.'

'You want me to give her more responsibility.'

'Exactly.' Cyril stood up, buttoning his jacket. 'Send her to court on her own.'

'On her own?'

'Let her spread her wings. Give her every opportunity to excel. I want Bianca to know that she doesn't intimidate me in the slightest.'

Claudia couldn't have forged a better path forward than if she'd planned it herself, and this worry sat with Seb long after Cyril left his office. What did they really know about this girl other than the fact that Bianca hated her because she'd ruined her plans to install her personal puppet in a place where she no longer had much sway?

The girl was ruthlessly ambitious and too confident, almost to the point of arrogance.

Only like every other lawyer in the building, he reasoned, and then frowned as he recalled the scene he had involuntarily witnessed earlier that week.

Not quite.

He had been sitting in the conference room waiting for his nine o'clock to show up. The door was open, so he'd had a clear view of the stationery area just outside, where Nelson and Claudia were reordering documents currently spewing out of the printer.

Nelson was sweating as usual, his forehead gleaming with the damp sheen as his eyes wandered worriedly over the text he was reading.

'I just don't know how I'm going tell him.' He looked up at Claudia. 'He's going to be really mad. Which is not good considering he's also one of those scary, burly types. He speaks really loudly cause he's a farmer. I guess he must be used to yelling across fields. Now he'll be yelling at me for my miscalculation.'

Claudia laughed. 'What's the problem, Nelson? What are you so scared to tell him?'

'The stamp-duty expense is going to make this land transfer jump by a huge chunk. The client is going to freak out.'

'Give me that.' Claudia snatched the document out of his hands, skimming the main section at the top. 'He's transferring it to his brother, right?'

'Yeah but –'

'And what's his brother going to use it for?'

'More of the same, I imagine.'

'Then I think you can get a stamp-duty exemption,' Claudia mused, and passed his contract back to him.

'Really?' Nelson's face lit up and he glanced at the document again like it was a completely new animal.

'Yep,' Claudia nodded as she returned to the printer. 'If it's being transferred between family members and has been used for farming for at least five years prior, and will be used for farming purposes post sale, then I think you're okay.'

'Really?'

'Sure. Check the WA *Stamp Act 1921*. I think it's somewhere in section 75.'

'How do you know that?'

'Er . . .' Claudia seemed to hesitate. 'I tend to just retain useless random facts.'

'Hardly useless,' Nelson sighed. 'You're a life-saver, Claud. Thanks.'

As Nelson walked off, Sebastian's appointment arrived, allowing him to get up and shut the door. However, recalling this scene now, he realised that the conversation was significant in two ways. It revealed that:

a) Claudia was probably as smart as she advertised herself to be.

b) She hadn't minded helping Nelson.

In an office where any upper hand got you one step closer to promotion over your peers, none of the junior lawyers ever shared knowledge. They were too busy pretending they knew exactly what they were doing to offer any tips to their colleagues. She was either very confident in her own ability or simple kindness was just second nature to her.

Perhaps it was a bit of both.

He also liked that she was so passionate about her clients. Most lawyers got very annoyed if they had to explain any concept more than once to their client, especially if the advice was simply to settle. Some clients would dig their heels in, hankering for their day in court to bring the bad guys to justice. Justice was sometimes a very large price to pay, especially for a retired old lady.

Claudia spent a whole morning on the phone to Mrs Herman, soothing the older woman's indignity and explaining the concept to her until she was satisfied enough to accept it. Anna Mavis would have dismissed her opinion and told her to just let her do her job. Mrs Felicity Herman may still have got a good outcome this way but she would have left the firm always feeling like she could have done better.

Whatever the case, witnessing Claudia's generosity made him uncomfortable.

It was all right when she was just the smart-mouthed, over-ambitious lawyer who was always underfoot. Then he could dismiss his growing attraction to her as a physical problem easily pushed to one side. Liking her, however, was completely unacceptable. How could he like someone he didn't trust?

She was masquerading as Cyril's niece, for goodness sake, and working for someone else on the side. Juliet had overheard her talking to Casuarina Prison at least a couple more times. He knew about that off-the-books meeting she'd had with a certain Peter Goldman late last week.

And then there was Bianca Hanks.

Anyone who could make an enemy out of her so easily was in over their head.

So what was Claudia up to?

Or Claud, as Nelson was now calling her. His protégé's familiarity sent an irrational streak of jealousy straight through his body, causing him to grit his teeth and draw his keyboard towards him roughly.

He was sure that Claudia's immediate knowledge of the stamp-duty waivers for farming land had something to do with her own history. Didn't she say she'd run a vineyard at some point? The wine he'd sampled at Seashells came from Oak Hills, a brand he recognised immediately. A quick google search showed that the winery had not been doing so well in recent years though. He had to wonder what strife Claudia had walked away from.

Another search under the name Peter Goldman didn't make him feel any better. The man's crime and conviction meant nothing to Sebastian. However, he noticed that the firm representing him had been Bantam, Harvey and Grey.

Bronwyn Eddings.

Unease rippled through him and could not be stilled. Was there a connection between Peter Goldman and Bronwyn Eddings? Was Bianca's daughter the one running and not Claudia? From whom? Claudia, Peter or her own mother? Whatever the case, the house of straw she was holed up in was about to blow down. If not by him then someone else. He resolved to comply with Cyril's wishes, but with caution. There was no telling who the big bad wolf would turn out to be.

Seb went by Claudia's desk that afternoon to break the news about Cyril's wishes. She was certainly pleased to hear it.

'Really? You want to give me more responsibility?' Her eyes lit like stars, an expression that was entirely infectious if one was inclined to let it get to you. 'But I thought –'

She cut the sentence off before she could utter it, her eyes darting about in confusion.

'You thought what?' he enquired silkily.

'I thought after our case at the Perth District Court last week, you might want to dial it back.'

He swore inwardly. *She's not trying to be honest again, is she?*

His gaze took in the curve of her cheek, those dark lashes against her pale skin. How did anyone so strong manage to look so vulnerable? He looked about the open-plan office and watched the way interested eyes quickly glanced away. Not wanting to make the same mistake as last time, he said gruffly. 'I think we'll finish this in my office.'

Then he walked away. He heard her get up and follow him but didn't turn around until they were both behind closed doors. He felt the air whoosh out of his body as soon as they were alone, in a space so quiet he could hear the pulse of his own blood. Not that they were safe from prying eyes. Their body language could still be scrutinised by everyone on the floor. That was the drawback of glass walls.

'I'd like to explain what you overheard at court the other day,' she said softly.

It would be so easy to be drawn into her web, given how good she was at weaving it. He resolutely shook his head to clear his mind.

'There's no need.'

'Surely you're wondering how I managed to get a recommendation from Bianca Hanks without her knowledge,' Claudia suggested.

'Actually, no, I'm not,' he said, in perfect truth, and strode away from her to sit down behind his own desk. 'You manipulated Bronwyn Eddings into speaking for you.'

Claudia gasped. 'Bronwyn Eddings is my friend.'

Sebastian's eyes narrowed. Was she?

From what he knew of Bronwyn Eddings, she was nothing like her mother. He'd never forget the day she'd looked after one of their clients – a chronic shoplifter and mother of infant twins. The woman had arrived for her appointment late, frazzled and pushing a pram containing two screaming babies. So what had Bronwyn Eddings done? Sent the woman downstairs to get a coffee and a breather while she rocked her kids to sleep in the boardroom. He supposed it was a nice gesture, well-meaning and even slightly practical. It could have been just fine had the shoplifter come back up after ten minutes. However, the mother didn't reappear for her meeting until five o'clock that evening. Bronwyn Eddings had been beside herself and Cyril . . . well, Cyril had been about to call social services.

The girl was too trusting. There was no doubt that if someone as smart as Claudia Franklin had managed to play on that trust . . . He frowned.

She got you to be an accessory to her lie, didn't she?

And she's working some angle on Bronwyn's last case.

Yet even as he sat here thinking about Claudia's possible deceit, his eyes had sketched a path from her hip to her ankle and he'd mentally noted that he had never seen a more stunning pair of legs in his life. Whoever said men couldn't multi-task was a moron.

Oblivious to either of these thoughts, Claudia Franklin lifted her chin and eyeballed him. 'As I told Bianca, I did not coerce Bronwyn to leave town. She left of her own accord.'

'Frankly,' Seb shrugged, 'it doesn't matter what I think. You may believe I have some sort of vendetta against you but honestly,' he dipped his head, 'I'm leaving that particular joy to Bianca Hanks.'

'B–'

He held up a hand for silence. 'Please don't burden me with any more of your "honesty". The truth is, Claudia, you are currently nothing more than a bone between two dogs.'

She blinked. 'I don't follow.'

'Cyril and Bianca,' he said curtly. 'They are using you to sort out their differences and I just happen to be the poor fool who has to facilitate the argument.'

'Oh.' She seemed stunned and moved to sit down in his visitor's chair. 'What differences?'

'Did I ask you to sit down?'

'No, I guess not.' She quickly stood up again.

'You don't have time to sit down. My priority is obvious. Cyril wants his niece to shine. So next week you're going to be all the colours of the rainbow. Do we understand each other?'

Much to his disappointment, she looked absolutely delighted. 'Does that mean I get to go to court?'

'As many times as you can.'

'Can I still come to you for advice?'

'You may have to,' he returned dryly. Her happiness was by no means diminished as she left the room.

His was.

Cyril may not be worried. However, Claudia Franklin was an enigma that he couldn't fully grasp and his attraction to her was starting to grate on his patience. He had always been able to separate his physical needs from the business. The two had never clashed so completely before. It got too messy because, let's face it, his affairs usually ended badly. Woman always seemed to expect more from him.

And that just wasn't something he could give.

Claudia's forthrightness was refreshing, and so was her enthusiasm. Her ripper-sharp tongue excited him in more ways than one. He wanted her.

Badly.

He couldn't deny it anymore.

However, that didn't make it right . . . Or possible.

She was too young for him, too idealistic, and she was his subordinate. Even he had to recognise the unethical nature of taking advantage.

She was definitely better off with Tom from the coffee shop, a man whom she would have dancing to her tune with a snap of her pretty fingers. Tom would expect their mutual attraction to lead to a relationship. And their romance would probably be sweet and uncomplicated.

Touching her would be a mistake. Liking her, entirely dangerous to his peace of mind.

Claudia liked to be upfront but only when it suited her. Cyril was right. He didn't trust her and didn't plan on doing so anytime soon. Claudia would get a legal-system education, but only on his terms.

And as for his ridiculous attraction to her, he'd never let a woman get the better of him before, so why on earth would he start now?

Chapter 19

The week after her confrontation with Bianca Hanks, Claudia wasn't sure whether the woman had done her a favour or was setting her up for a fall. Her standing at Hanks and Eddings was better now than it ever was. True, no one else was happy about it except maybe Cyril Eddings, but he was a ball firmly in her court. When Bianca Hanks had announced her intention to bring Claudia down, she never thought she'd be so lucky as to fall under his protective wing. *An enemy of my enemy is my friend*, the saying went. Or uncle as the case may be. All she had to do now was cement her position by performing well.

Razzle dazzle.

Sebastian Rowlands, however, was a snake in the reeds. She could feel his eyes on her sometimes and knew that should she put one foot wrong, he was all but ready to pounce. Despite this he gave her, as promised, her first case to handle in court alone.

'It's not a difficult one,' he instructed. 'The hearing is merely to obtain consent orders. You just need to hand up to the judge a signed minute of consent orders.'

She was excited and not really that nervous. He'd been more than generous by giving her a file that was very straightforward. All the work had been done. Both parties involved had already negotiated and signed their agreement. Unlike her other high-profile case against Bianca Hanks, she couldn't imagine how anything could go wrong.

She fronted up at court early to make sure that she had all her ducks in a row before she went in. This was probably her first mistake, because Bianca Hanks happened to spot her there loitering in the foyer. Much like a scene in a corny cartoon, their eyes met across the room and Bianca's narrowed menacingly.

Claudia knew that this was what Cyril wanted. He was parading her blatantly; letting Bianca know that he would not be ordered about by someone who no longer worked at the firm, let alone controlled it. Yet doubt still put a tremble in Claudia's knees. If Cyril lashed out, then how could Bianca not be expected to retaliate? She was half afraid that Bianca was going to come up and threaten her again, but the woman seemed to look beyond her at someone else who was entering the court. She turned her gaze away from Claudia and then walked straight past her. Claudia's heart sank. Bianca was conversing with the judge who was about to take her case, just like they were old friends. Probably because they were. She shook his hand and gave him a smile that could beguile a rattlesnake.

What is she saying?

Judge Hickles laughed, his yellow teeth flashing wickedly before he turned and walked into the judge's chambers. Bianca glanced at her briefly before walking out of the court. Neither smile nor frown crossed her features, which made Claudia clutch her file all the tighter.

Don't let her get to you.

It's a simple case.

Short of breaking the law she can't have it overturned.

Claudia knew she was fully prepared. Since her last lesson in 'What Not To Do', she had remembered to bring all the required documents with her. In the walk over she had also mentally gone through the rituals. Where and when to stand, when to sit down, who talks first, correct greetings and callings. The last thing any young lawyer on their first appearance alone wanted to do was commit a faux pas that would have court staff giggling behind their hands for the rest of the day. Stories like that travelled up and down the Terrace like free community newspapers, and there wasn't a single corporate player who didn't want a bite of someone else's humiliation. The most precious commodity to a lawyer, other than their smart phone, was their ego.

In terms of visual presentation, she was quietly confident. Her business suit was freshly pressed. Her make-up was matt, not glossy. Her fingers might be trembling slightly as she lined up the papers on the desk in front of her but at least there was no jury to her right to observe this, given it was a civil action. The public gallery was also mostly empty. She hadn't expected it to be full, given the completely standard, run-of-the-mill task at hand.

At the appointed time the bailiff, a man dressed in black with crowns on his lapels, asked all to rise. As they did so, Claudia heard a knock-knock behind the judge's desk and then the door was opening. Judge Hickles strode out in sweeping black robes and took a seat at his bench facing her. His expression was one of impatience. He tapped the desk with his hand as he sat down.

Everyone else followed suit but Claudia remained standing. She cleared her throat.

'Ms Franklin for the plaintiff, Your Honour.'

Judge Hickles nodded almost gleefully, like a serial killer who had just opened the door to his basement and waved her in.

She forged ahead, anyway. Straightening both her shoulders and her jacket, she took a leap of faith.

'Your Honour, today I have a consent order to hand up for your consideration that is signed by the parties, by the plaintiff Mr Michael Lewis and by the defendant Ms Lavinia Becker. If you agree that everything is in order, Your Honour, the proceedings will be disposed of.' She held the orders out to the bailiff who took them and handed them to the Judge's Associate, who then handed them up to His Honour. Judge Hickles perused them with a wrinkled brow.

There was a prolonged silence and Claudia stood uncomfortably, hands resting on the lectern before her. Finally Judge Hickles looked up from the document he was reading.

'And where is Lavinia Becker?'

Why is he asking me that?

'Er . . . sorry, Your Honour?' she said, hoping she'd misheard the question.

He shuffled the papers on the desk and said once more, 'Where is Lavinia Becker?'

A fleet of questions raced through Claudia's brain at lightning speed.

Am I supposed to know that? Is she supposed to be here? Should I have shot her an email? 'Er . . .' she blinked, 'I don't know where she is, Your Honour. I represent Michael Lewis.'

'I am fully aware of who you represent,' Judge Hickles tossed at her impatiently. 'But does Lavinia Becker know about this hearing?'

'Ah,' Claudia clenched her fist behind her back. *Stay confident.* 'Yes, Your Honour. She's a party to the action.'

He put her orders down, folded his arms and looked at her from his lofty position. She felt the eyes of everyone in the court upon her and Seb's own voice in her ear, 'Shine with all the colours of the rainbow,' making her self-esteem sink like a little stone to the bottom of the river.

'How do you know that she knows?' the judge smirked.

'I . . .' she swallowed. 'I just presume so.'

After all, she signed the bloody document!

He clasped his hands together on the desk in front of him and raised an eyebrow. 'If Lavinia Becker does not know of this hearing, doesn't that go against her natural justice?'

Panic seized her by the throat and lifted her at least a couple feet off the ground.

Shit! What is natural justice?

Wasn't that in Administration Law at university?

Damn it, I only got seventy-two per cent for that unit.

I could easily have missed something.

Hang on! This is a civil case. What's that got to do with Admin Law?

Judge Hickles was smiling down at her, the sheen of his yellow teeth destroying all hope that she had any chance of answering the question correctly. 'What would you have me do, Ms Franklin?'

'I . . .' Claudia swallowed and glanced at the bailiff, who immediately averted his eyes. With a sigh of defeat she said in all humility, 'I guess I'm happy to be led by the court.'

'You guess?' Judge Hickles's tone was sugary-sweet.

Claudia cleared her throat. 'I am happy to be led by the court.'

'All right.' The judge folded his arms. 'Outline for me exactly the orders you seek.'

Given she had already handed over the orders to him and she had not thought that it was imperative for her to memorise them or make a copy, she could only stammer quickly.

'It's what is written in the document, Your Honour.'

A snigger came from the back of the court.

'Are you saying that you don't know what is written in the document you have just given me?'

'No, Your Honour. But I've only read it once. I can't remember specifically –'

He cut her off. 'So you are telling me, Ms Franklin, that you neither know for sure or specifically where Lavinia Becker is, what is written in this document and how to proceed further in this matter without guidance from the court.'

Claudia wanted to die.

A stake through the heart, lightning bolt from heaven, falling down a crack through the earth – she honestly had no preference at this point except for it to be over.

How did I get here?

'Perhaps,' Judge Hickles suggested silkily, 'it would be best if we were to adjourn this matter for another time when you are more prepared or you can send someone more senior to handle it for you.'

'Yes, Your Honour.' She bowed her head.

The judge hit his hammer, the bailiff asked all to rise, and Hickles walked out, leaving Claudia standing knee-deep in shame, watching her dignity retreat out the door with him.

Well, now you know Bianca's power.

Mortified, she collected her things quickly and turned to go. A movement in the public gallery caught her eye, making her look up. Claudia's feet stalled. Sitting there, legs crossed, one hand resting lightly on her knee, was Bianca Hanks. An expression that was neither apathy nor triumph but something in-between featured on her hard face – almost as though to feel victory over someone who held no more significance than an ant was beneath her. She did, however, wait patiently for Claudia's mouth to drop open before she stood up coolly and left with the rest of the spectators.

As though I needed confirmation.

Claudia was out of the courtroom like a shot.

The only thing left to do now was return to the firm in disgrace and wait for the story to follow her up the Terrace. Anna was going to love it. And Seb . . . she didn't like to think of the disappointment she would read in his face.

If she could read his face at all.

She didn't know why she found any of the aspects of his personality appealing. Or why the room seemed to buzz with electricity every time they were in it together. The physical attraction she had felt for him in her first week on the job seemed to be getting worse. It didn't matter how many times she told herself it was inappropriate. He was her boss. Her nemesis. And at least ten years older to boot. There was something about him that made her sizzle and choke whenever he walked into the room.

Perhaps it was the soft spot she had for the 'wounded soldier' in him. She couldn't imagine the impact being abandoned at a police station at age six would have on a person – about the way they'd feel about themselves. The way they related to others. No doubt it coloured all of his decisions. It was no wonder he was so jaded.

In fact, he was the direct opposite of any man she'd ever dated before. The good-natured country larrikins whom her father had always looked upon with distrust couldn't hold a candle to Sebastian's sophistication.

When she'd made this life swap with Bronwyn, one of the things she had wanted to sort out was her love life. Be free. Start dating again.

Meeting Tom at Costello's that first week had seemed like a step in the right direction. He fulfilled the wish list she had outlined to Bronwyn. Blond, smart, easygoing, funny and good-looking.

He was everything that Sebastian was not.

Oh, except for the good-looking part. Sebastian had that in spades. Dark and broodingly dangerous, he was a charismatic magnet.

The second time she'd gone to Costello's Tom had flirted with her again, and she knew if she came in a third time he'd probably ask for her number. So why hadn't she been back?

If you're holding out for a second look from Sebastian Rowlands, don't bother!

She winced. If he even knew what was in her head right now he'd laugh in her face. To Sebastian she was nothing more than a junior lawyer, and a painful one at that. Besides, it wasn't like he was relationship material. Word around the office was that he was the love 'em and leave 'em type.

What makes you think you'll be the woman to change his mind?

She wanted to kick herself in the shins.

Come on, Claudia. It's nothing but fantasy and you know it.

As she walked back into Hanks and Eddings, she hastily reined in her thoughts. It was time to focus on the job. Nothing else.

'What happened?' asked Nelson when she arrived back. 'You look terrible.'

'My case was adjourned. I'm going to have to go back.'

'A whole morning wasted,' Nelson nodded grimly. 'Seb won't be pleased.'

For this reason, she decided to get breaking the news to him over and done with, even though sticking her head in the door of his office unannounced was considered tantamount to a death wish.

'Er . . . Seb, can I talk to you for a minute?'

He was standing by the window, looking out at the view rather than at her. He sighed. 'All right, come in. Shut the door.'

She did so, her senses immediately going on high alert. The air around her seemed to thicken.

For goodness sake, just tell him and make your exit.

'I was unable to have the consent orders made.'

Finally, he turned. 'Why?'

She told him exactly what happened.

'Where are the consent orders? May I have them?'

She stilled. The Judge never gave them back.

And I forgot to ask for them!

Just when she didn't think her humiliation could get any greater, a new level of hell opened up – full. Panoramic. Humiliation. She cringed. 'Judge Hickles has them,' she moaned. 'He never gave them back.'

'I see.' He walked across to his desk, unbuttoning the jacket of his suit as he pulled out his chair and sat down. The simple action caused the pulse at her throat to leap.

You've never been into suits. It's lads all round. Get a grip, girl.

He looked at her curiously. 'Why are you still standing?'

Well, maybe because after several attempts at sitting in your presence I've always been told not to.

She said nothing, however, and parked her bum.

He raised an eyebrow. 'Did I say you could sit down?'

What the?

'Oh, I –' She was going to stand up again when he waved a hand. 'Claudia, I'm just messing with you.'

Wait, he's joking around with me? We do jokes now? When did that happen?

Given his expression was blank of any humour or amusement she wasn't quite sure how to take all this.

'You are?'

'I'm messing with you to illustrate exactly how easy it really is.' This time his lips did curl into a smile. It lit his face from within too and made her heart stop for one delectable moment as she admired it. 'Judge Hickles was messing with you.'

'He was?'

'It's one of his favourite pastimes. You will notice that he never actually said that anything you had said or presented was wrong.'

'No, I guess not.'

'He just posed a lot of questions. A lot of unnecessary questions I might add. The correct response would have been to simply hold your ground and be confident in why you were there rather than being led willy-nilly off the beaten track. Like just now, you should have said, "Stuff you, Seb, I'm sitting down."'

She grinned. 'That does have a very nice ring to it.'

'In future, Claudia, simply stick to your plan. Court appearances are one part smarts, one part acting. Forget you don't know everything because you can never admit it. Do you understand?'

She nodded. 'Perfectly.'

She couldn't help but recognise that, despite Sebastian's poor bedside manner, he did give her good advice. As a boss he was hard but he was also fair – it was no wonder all the lawyers in the office coveted her position. There was no way that she was going to waste this opportunity.

'Should I get on with the Jackson dispute? Or was there something else you wanted me to work on first?'

He spun in his chair to access the low shelving against the wall behind him. 'I'll just check,' he said, flicking through a stack of case files that were sitting there. While he was doing so she took the liberty of casting her eyes around his office, which she could only note was sparse. There were no photo frames depicting his friends and family, or even something ornamental that doubled as a paperweight. Two walls were glass, but the other two formed an L-shape around his desk and could have supported a painting, or some piece of artwork that reflected his personality. One of the walls was half-covered by a sturdy looking bookcase, on the other hung both his degrees in non-descript black frames – one in law, the other in commerce – as well as his admission certificates to the Supreme Court and to the High Court. She noted that he was not messy. His books were all neatly positioned, mostly by size rather than author or subject. His paperwork was neatly piled or filed. Even his coffee mug sat precisely on a steel coaster. It was clean, black and void of coffee.

Did Sebastian have any life outside work?

She knew he had no female friends.

But what about male ones? Apart from Cyril . . .

'Claudia.' Her eyes refocused on the man in front of her. He was holding out a file.

'Your mind has a tendency to wander at the oddest moments,' he observed dryly.

'Sorry, I was just thinking,' She took the file and licked her lips. 'Are you coming to the fundraiser at Costello's on Thursday morning?'

'No.'

'Half the office is going.'

He stood up, buttoning his jacket. 'I don't see how that is any concern of mine.'

'You might find it fun,' she suggested with a smile. 'Life can't be all work and no play.'

He walked around his desk to observe her, leaning back on the edge of it with folded arms. 'I don't doubt that. In fact, I'm surprised you're so keen on having the whole office crash your date with Tom Rubin.'

For some reason the husky sound in his voice, the way he was looking at her, put images in her head that shouldn't be there.

'Oh, it's not a date,' she clarified hastily.

'Why not? He seems like just the sort of naive do-gooder perfect for you.'

'*Naive?* As opposed to your startling sophistication, I suppose,' she said, before she thought better of the words. She felt herself going red with embarrassment, her heart fluttered against her ribcage like a deck of cards.

You bloody idiot.

He was silent for a moment as he steadily regarded her. The air swirling around them, tainted with the taste of the forbidden; the electricity so hot it burned her.

Don't say anything else. Don't say anything else.

You'll just make it worse.

He stood up from the desk and his height dwarfed her, his body invaded her personal space.

'I don't date,' he said quietly. 'Not to say, if given the chance, I wouldn't use you, hurt you and discard you.'

If given the chance?

What did he mean by that exactly?

245

She slowly raised her eyes to his and the need she saw there scorched her like the flame of a torch, causing her insides to liquefy and pool at her feet.

'Stick with Tom Rubin,' he rasped.

When she continued to stand there in shock, he added, 'If you don't mind, I'd prefer to get on with my next case now rather than plan your social life.'

'Of course,' she squeaked in mortification before dashing out of there faster than a rabbit with her father's bullets screaming over its head.

Chapter 20

Damn!

She'd completely taken the wind out of his sails again and he'd said far more than he'd meant to.

It was the fault of that damned RSPCA tin she'd had sitting on her desk since last week. That's what had put him in this mood. He never would have said anything if his willpower hadn't been so sorely tested just the day before.

Juliet had mentioned that a stack of brochures from the RSPCA about the abuse of animals had been couriered across with the tin, so he'd been unable to stop himself from dropping by her desk to conduct his own cross-examination.

'Is there a reason why you're looking into animal cruelty, Claudia, or has this always been a hobby of yours?' he'd asked.

Her expression had grown uncommonly dark. 'I became a lawyer to fight for the innocent.' She looked up at him. 'Who is more innocent than those who cannot defend themselves?'

He had been taken aback by the conviction in her words. It was a truth so often forgotten by the profession. Why were they all here after all? To seek justice for the innocent, not just animals but all those who had been victims and could not speak for themselves. How easily his peers lost sight of this, distracted by the search for money, power, status and the admiration of their fellow lawyers. Under his steady gaze, her expression suddenly cleared, like the sun coming out from behind a raincloud.

'Were you hoping to make a contribution, Seb?' She picked up the tin and shook it with a smile. 'For a gold coin donation I'll give you a sticker as well.'

He'd had no such thought in his head, but after that stirring speech how could he possibly say no?'

Well, he should have.

Honestly, the girl was like a Venus fly trap, drawing you in with the sweet scent of her nectar and then snapping shut when you least expected it.

Reaching into his pocket and removing his wallet, he'd withdrawn a two-dollar coin. After slotting it into the tin, he'd turned around to find that she was standing up with a roll of stickers in her hand. Before he could protest, she'd reached out and pressed a round message to the lapel of his jacket. At the touch of her hand his words immediately dried up.

She smoothed her thumb across the words 'I love animals' and then looked up at him.

'There you go.'

Unlike many other lawyers in the firm he had never suffered from stage fright. One of his greatest skills was always having something to say, even if it was only to give him time to fight another day.

Then, however, he'd had nothing. He was speechless, like a teenager flirting with a girl for the first time.

All he'd been able to do was clear his throat and walk off. He'd worn that bloody sticker for the rest of the day too, as though to prove he was completely immune to its symbolic meaning. It had finally found a home in his bathroom bin that night. The sight of it in the morning, however, had been a reminder of his vulnerability.

How dare she get under his skin.

How dare she ruin the perfect order of his life.

How dare she confuse him this way!

It was no wonder he'd said what he had when she'd invited him to Costello's while comparing him to her latest love interest.

It was a warning, as much to her as to himself. Now, though, the cat was out of the bag. And it made them awkward around each other. So he did the only thing a man in his position could do.

He'd loaded her up with more work.

The busier she was, the less she'd bother him.

On Thursday morning, when he decided to go into work early to hide because he knew everyone was going to Costello's, he realised that maybe he'd gone a bit too far.

The office was more or less dark apart from a dim light that came from the main open-plan area. Someone had either stayed all night or come in early like him. He was about to walk past the area when he heard the gentle sound of snoring. Stepping out of the hall, he strode into the space, casting his gaze around the room.

There she was, forehead in the crook of one arm, fast asleep. The other hand was stretched out in front of her, clutching the last document she had been working on. He twitched it out of her hand and ran his eyes over it. She had incorporated all the corrections he'd suggested earlier that week and finessed it further.

'Hmm, this isn't half bad.'

'Huh? What? Say again?' Claudia's head flicked up and she jerked herself into an upright position, wincing at a pain in her neck. She rubbed bleary eyes and smudged her mascara as she squinted up at him.

'Seb, is that you?'

His heart lurched at the sound of her sleepy voice. Thank goodness no other staff were in the office. They would have a field day with this one.

'Yes, it's me. What are you doing here, Claudia?'

'Er . . . working.'

'I hate to contradict you, but you were actually sleeping.'

Claudia sat up straighter and waved a dismissive hand. 'It was only for a few minutes. Just a little pick-me-up to help me power ahead.' She slid one palm over another in a whooshing motion.

'Right,' he said, eyeing the drool on the corner of her mouth with some amusement.

She smiled. 'What time did you say it was again?'

'I didn't. But it's six am.'

She swallowed hard. 'Oh.'

'More than a few minutes, wasn't it?' he remarked dryly.

'Maybe,' she said quickly, and then brightened. 'On the plus side, I finished drafting that letter you wanted. It's –' She began to pat down the desk for the document she'd been holding a few seconds ago. He could see the panic on her face at its disappearance and took pity on her.

'It's okay, I was just reading it.' He handed the document back to her and then drew a tissue from her desk box and held this out as well.

Her eyes darted to it but did not take it. 'What's that for?'

He pointed at her chin, but when she continued to look confused, he wiped the drool from it himself, screwed up the tissue and chucked it in her wastepaper basket.

'I look terrible, don't I?'

In his eyes, she looked adorable. Honest, unsophisticated and real. He was so used to women dressing up for him. Coiffed and groomed to within an inch of their life, to spend no more than a week in his company. And here was Claudia, her makeup smudged, her hair fuzzy and her shirt once again not quite buttoned correctly, the swell of her lace-cupped breast just visible beneath her shirt. All he felt like doing was ripping off his own jacket and pulling her into his lap.

A muscle jerked in his cheek as he silently studied her.

'I'll take that as a yes.' Claudia licked her lips nervously and he followed the movement of her small pink tongue with interest. 'Not to worry.' She stood up hastily. 'I'll just need a few minutes in the ladies bathroom, a coffee. Okay, maybe two coffees, a Berocca . . .

'And a packet of Mentos?' he suggested.

'Do you have some?' Her eyes rounded eagerly.

'Claudia, you're going home, where you will take the morning off, at the very least. I'll drive you there myself. Where do you live?'

'Oh.' She quickly shook her head. 'There's no need for you to do that. I'll just catch the bus after the breakfast at Costello's this morning.'

'By all means, if you want Tom Coffeeman to see you looking like this.' He took his phone from his pocket, snapped a shot of her, and then handed it over.

She glanced at the screen and gave a startled yelp.

He turned and walked out of the open-plan area back into the hall. 'Grab your things and try to keep up. We're leaving.'

He heard the clicking of her shoes on the tiled floor behind him as he entered the foyer and jabbed at the button on the lift. She fell in beside him.

'Listen, about the other day, in your office.'

Really? He'd been hoping to avoid mentioning that.

'I want apologise about giving you the wrong impression. I really wasn't implying that I – that we – that somehow –'

'Because that would be highly inappropriate,' he suggested.

'Exactly,' she agreed, clearly glad he'd filled in the blanks.

'Claudia,' he sighed. 'You don't need to apologise. It wasn't entirely your fault.'

'You mean,' her mouth dried, 'you think I'm attractive.'

'Very.'

It took her a moment to digest this.

So he added with some amusement, 'Most of the time.'

He was relieved when the lift doors opened and they stepped in. It was a perfect opportunity to end the conversation.

But when the lift doors closed, she reached up and pulled the pins out of her messy hair. He suspected she did it because they were falling out anyway, although watching her thread her fingers through the silken strands had him holding his breath.

The lift doors opened.

Thank God.

They entered the executive car park reserved only for partners of the firm. It was completely empty except for his own car – a quietly stylish silver Audi sedan. Claudia's lips curled slightly at the sight of it, but she said nothing.

He unlocked the car with his remote and they both hopped in. She broke the silence briefly to give him her address, which wasn't really that far from their offices at all. It was exactly the sort of residence he expected a successful young lawyer of moderate means to have: a two-storey apartment block in the heart of Subiaco, which overlocked some gorgeous gardens and a community swimming pool. When he drove up into the brick-paved driveway he had expected her to simply grab her handbag and hop out; however, the slight gasp that escaped her lips caused him to pause.

'What is it?'

'My front door is open.'

'What?' He followed her gaze to the second storey. This was accessed by a flight of stairs on the side of the building. A wide balcony gave means of entry to three front doors, embossed and labelled with metallic gold numbers three, four and five. Number four was open.

She got out of the car and so did he. 'I'll come with you,' he said.

She didn't seem to hear him but he followed anyway as she hurried up the stairs. He grabbed her arm before she could walk over the threshold, taking in the state of the apartment in a glance.

'I'll go in first. Make sure they're not still here.'

She nodded.

The place had been ransacked. There was not a single piece of furniture that had not been overturned. Her belongings lay strewn across the floor. Framed pictures were off the walls and on the floor. Even the cushions from her couch had been pulled out of their covers. The apartment was small, only two bedrooms. He was through the entire place in less than a minute before returning to the main open-plan living space. She stood there clutching the back of the sofa, not in shock but in anger.

His eyes narrowed. 'Was there another reason you stayed at the office all night other than work, Claudia?'

Chapter 21

Her gaze flew to his. 'You think I was expecting this?'

He folded his arms. 'You just don't look that surprised.'

She wasn't. If Leon McCall's men were actively looking for Bronwyn, wouldn't their first port of call be an apartment search for clues? In fact, she was amazed it had taken them this long.

'I've been thinking of upgrading my security,' she responded evasively.

'So your all-nighter wasn't an avoidance technique?'

'How could I possibly know I was going to be broken into?'

Where on earth was this coming from?

'It doesn't look like you've been broken into so much as taught a lesson.' His dark eyes glittered as he scanned the room. 'Anyone you know got it in for you?'

She shuddered and rubbed arms that were suddenly covered in gooseflesh. There was a list.

Bianca Hanks.

Peter Goldman.

Bruce Carle.

Leon McCall.

Anna Mavis.

Geez, Claudia. You might want to start your own 'I hate Claudia' club. It could be a real revenue raiser.

'Er . . . I can't really nail anyone down in particular,' she replied, distractedly casting her eyes around the messy room looking for missing items. He put a voice to her concerns.

'Has anything been taken?'

'I don't think so.' Though she would be hard pressed to say for certain, given she didn't own the place. The main items of value in the room, like the TV and the glossy wood-carving on the bookshelf, were still there. A glance across to the kitchen told her that all removable kitchen appliances were also still in place. Whoever had been here seemed to have been either searching for something or just wanting to rough the place up a bit. Clearly the hunt for Bronwyn and Elsa was still on. Not that she thought there were any clues lying about that indicated that Bronwyn was in Yallingup. Bronwyn had abandoned everything, including her car, taking Claudia's ute for transport. As far as anyone could tell, her best friend had disappeared off the face of the earth.

The only clue she left behind is you.

Swallowing hard, she looked up at Seb, who was watching her closely. She tried to keep her expression neutral. He was not fooled.

'So what's really going on here, Claudia?' He leaned against her kitchen counter.

'What do you mean?'

'Well, I've been into every room in this apartment and this place isn't yours, is it? It belongs to Bronwyn Eddings, Bianca's daughter. I can see her mail here on the kitchen counter and there's an open suitcase that I presume is yours on the floor in the bedroom.'

'I'm house-sitting,' Claudia returned tightly.

'I think you're playing a very dangerous game and you've just found out you're in over your head.'

Claudia laughed. 'Boy, you do have a vivid imagination.'

'Where is Bronwyn Eddings?'

'She doesn't want anyone to know.'

'Seems awfully convenient to me.'

'What exactly do you mean by that?'

'From where I'm standing it looks like you've stolen someone else's identity.'

'Are you expecting to find Bronwyn's body stuffed in a linen cupboard somewhere, or have you already looked?' Claudia demanded angrily. 'Honestly, I've never met a more judgemental person in my life. This is like our first meeting at Seashells all over again.'

'I didn't actually check your linen cupboard,' he said quietly.

'How careless of you,' she snapped. 'Perhaps you'd like to do so now.'

He sighed. 'If I thought you were capable of killing someone I would have already called the police.'

'Funny you should mention it,' She hugged her arms to stop herself trembling, 'I was just about to do that myself.'

His expression softened slightly as he watched her.

Oh, for goodness sake, stop looking at me like that. We just agreed that anything between us is inappropriate.

He straightened and walked towards her, invading her personal space. 'I never thought I'd see the day you were scared by something.'

She averted her eyes. 'Of course I'm afraid. What do you think I am? Made of steel.'

'Maybe a little.'

Sebastian's eyes had always been intense. But usually they were focused on a document or a computer screen or a client. It was impossible not to feel absolutely stripped bare when they rested on her. After all, wasn't his attention to detail the best in the state?

Inappropriate. Inappropriate. Inappropriate.

She sucked in a quick breath and looked away.

'Claudia, I think it's about time you took me into your confidence.'

'I beg your pardon?'

'I want to know everything.'

'I'm not quite sure what you mean.'

'Put it this way,' he folded his arms. 'I already know half the story, so you might as well tell me the rest.'

She bit her lower lip. 'What do you mean you already know half the story?'

'There's not much that goes on at Hanks and Eddings that doesn't get back to me,' he responded grimly. 'I know you've been to see an inmate of Casuarina Prison. I know it's something to do with Bronwyn. So you might as well come clean about the rest.'

If she was honest, it would be a relief to unburden herself. She'd been carrying this pressure all on her own for a while now. He might even have some advice.

She curled her hair behind one ear, trying not to be affected as his eyes followed the movement.

'Okay, so I think I might be in a little smidgen of trouble with . . .'

'Who?' he pressed.

'Leon McCall.'

'*Leon McCall?*' His eyes widened.

'Don't forget the smidgen part,' she added hastily, lifting her thumb and forefinger in front of her face.

'I don't think there's any such thing when it comes to Leon McCall,' Sebastian said sternly. 'Do you know what that man's allegedly responsible for?'

'I have a fair idea,' Claudia grimaced.

He seemed to brace himself. 'You had better start from the beginning.'

'Okay, so back in uni, Bronwyn and I were best friends. We lived in each other's pockets.' She paused to think on this a second. 'Actually, her mostly in my pocket because she hated her life. In recent years, though, we haven't seen much of each other because of this whole debacle that went down in my family about five years ago with my brothers who –'

He held up a finger. 'Maybe not that far back to the beginning. Perhaps you can skip forward to present day.'

'Right.' She nodded. The problem was he was making her nervous. Sebastian's confidence was sexy enough. His concern was intoxicating.

'The long and the short of it is,' she tried again, 'Bronwyn needed a sabbatical from law, so she left town to work on my family's vineyard. I wanted to get back into law so I marched in and took her job. With her permission, of course,' she added quickly.

'Of course.' His tone was as dry as toast.

'It was a great plan from both our perspectives and it would have been perfect –'

'Naturally.'

She tilted her head. 'Okay fine, except for all the issues she's having with my family and all the problems I've been having with –' She broke off.

He tucked in his chin and looked over his nose at her. 'The problems you're having with . . . ?'

Claudia swatted her hand. 'Perhaps I should just stick to the two main characters, otherwise this is getting far too convoluted.'

'So it would seem.'

'Anyway, it would have been perfect *if* Bronwyn hadn't adopted Peter Goldman's dog, Elsa, and taken her along to Yallingup.'

'Right.' Sebastian inclined his head slowly. 'And what does that have to do with Leon McCall?'

'Elsa's pregnant with pups. According to Peter they belong to Leon. They made a deal to settle a gambling debt Peter couldn't pay. He wants those pups back.'

'What does Leon McCall want with a bunch of pups? No, let me guess.' He shut his eyes as though seeking patience from a higher power. 'You've stumbled on a dog-fighting ring.'

Claudia nodded. 'That was my first conclusion.'

'Of all the things to be involved in,' Sebastian groaned. 'Couldn't you have picked a simpler, less violent crime?'

Claudia put her hands on her hips crossly. 'That's not on me. It was Bronwyn who –'

'Who seems to have got off scot-free while you're here cleaning up her mess? I'm surprised that Peter didn't just tell Leon where to find Bronwyn.'

'He doesn't know,' she said quietly. 'Nobody does, except me. And now you.'

He ran a frustrated hand through his hair before eyeballing her again. 'You know what this means, right?'

When she was silent, he spelt it out for her. 'Leon, or more likely some of his associates, have just searched Bronwyn's apartment. They've come up with nothing, except for the fact that she's got a house-sitter. They'll be back, Claudia. This time when you're home. They'll want to ask you a few questions, and not politely.'

She swallowed. 'I suppose it's possible.'

'Don't be a fool,' he threw at her. 'It's *certain*, and they're not going to take no for an answer next time.'

'So what would you have me do?' She threw her hands up.

'Pack up your suitcase, you're moving out.'

'But I have nowhere to go.'

'I'll take you to a hotel. There are plenty in the city, near our offices.'

'That is *completely* unnecessary.'

He met her eyes again, then grabbed her by the shoulders. 'Claudia, that Goldman bloke is in the hospital. Do you really want to end up there too? These guys are bloodthirsty meat-heads. Think about who you're dealing with here.'

She licked her dry lips, her body aware of his closeness. She knew she should be concentrating on the danger she was in, but somehow it didn't really seem that significant when compared to the fact that he was holding her, albeit none too gently.

'*Claudia?*' he urged again, clearly noticing that once more she'd tuned out.

'Okay, fine,' she agreed, 'you're right. I don't particularly want to end up in hospital.'

'Go have your shower and get your things. We're going now.'

'But –'

'While you're sorting yourself out, I'll call the police and get them down here. I'm pretty sure your little private investigation is now a public one.'

He let go of her shoulders and pulled out his phone, already scrolling through numbers. A warmth spread through her chest. Her heart thudded dangerously fast but there was something else there too that she didn't quite understand. A growing awareness that she'd never experienced with another man before.

'Seb?'

'Yes?' he said as he lifted the phone to his ear and glanced back at her.

'Thanks.'

Something unreadable crossed his face before it settled into a self-mocking smile. 'I'd say no problem, but I have a feeling this situation is going to be fraught with them.'

He wasn't wrong.

What neither of them had counted on was the Swedish aeronautic sky show being in town that weekend. They'd been setting up on the esplanade and along the foreshore all week for the demonstration in the sky across Saturday and Sunday. Perth was abuzz with the free show. It was going to be huge. They tried three hotels in the city and they were all full.

'Let's go back to the office,' Seb suggested. 'I think it'll be faster if you do a ring around from there, rather than me driving to every hotel on the map.'

However, when they walked into Hanks and Eddings, Cyril was waiting for them in Sebastian's office. Sebastian had called Juliet earlier, letting her know why they'd be late.

'What's this I'm hearing?' Cyril demanded as he shut the door to Sebastian's fish tank and turned on Claudia. 'You've been broken into? Your apartment ransacked?'

'Yes,' Claudia wrung her hands in embarrassment. 'It's nothing really.'

'Nothing?' Cyril's eyes swung to his right-hand man. 'Sebastian?'

Sebastian strode with purpose to his desk and sat down. 'It is no longer safe for Claudia to stay in her apartment, but we're having a little difficulty getting her into a hotel at the moment with the aeronautic show in town.'

Cyril's eyes shot shrewdly from one to the other. 'If it's not safe, then she shouldn't be alone. You should stay at Sebastian's place, my dear.'

Sebastian dropped the phone handset he had just picked up. It bounced off the desk and towards the floor, pulling the rest of that unit with it with an almighty crash.

'*What?*'

However, Cyril wasn't addressing him. 'Sebastian has a giant house with a guest bedroom on the lower floor. Honestly, I don't know what he does with all that space.' He clapped Claudia jovially on the back.

'I – I couldn't possibly –'

'Yes,' Sebastian agreed, turning dangerously large eyes on Cyril. 'She couldn't possibly. Wouldn't it be better if she stayed with *family*? As I recall, you have quite a few guest bedrooms yourself.'

'You know,' Cyril nodded, 'that was my first thought but my daughter is in town with her husband and kids. It's a full house. Your place is much better.'

'Cyril –'

'Sebastian, you assured me that you would protect my niece at all costs.'

'This has nothing to do with Bianca Hanks,' Sebastian growled.

'Where is your sense of charity?' Cyril censored him. 'I will have no more argument. Come, my dear,' he put an arm around Claudia's startled shoulders, 'let's get you a coffee, you must be quite shaken up.'

Chapter 22

Discovering Bronwyn Eddings naked in his bathroom was a development Jack hadn't prepared for. When he'd heard that she'd taken up her position at the family firm five years ago, he figured she was gone from Yallingup for good. Her mother was a force not to be toyed with and, in his opinion, shy, sweet Bronwyn had never been equipped to win that battle.

This Bronwyn, however, was neither shy nor sweet.

She was fiery, passionate, wilful and, without a doubt, smoking hot.

She'd always been pretty. Beautiful in that soft, ethereal way that brought out a man's protective side. This afternoon he'd all but completely combusted when he found himself with an armful of delectable wantonness pressed against his chest.

She had changed, but in ways that only made things ten times worse. He thought time had healed his need for her. That the distance he'd put between them had allowed him to get on with his life. Yet seeing her now, especially in this way, made him realise that all he'd done was put his feelings in a box to be opened later.

The lid had popped off with a bang that morning and made him wish he'd asked his mother or Claudia more questions about Bronwyn over the years. He'd figured if he just put her out of his mind, it would be easier to get her out of his system.

Ha!

It felt as though he'd only left yesterday. The emotions churning in his stomach were just as strong. The day he'd decided to leave he'd taken a very black and white view of his situation. In hindsight, he realised that perhaps he should have fought harder to be heard. But when your family, the people you turned to in a crisis, shut you out as completely as his had, who else could he turn to?

He knew, after the accident, that Bronwyn had wanted to help him. The irony of it all. She hadn't even realised she was the reason Chris hated him so much. That's how innocent she was. When she'd left to go back to Perth to quit law, he'd tried to get into the hospital again to see Chris. This time, he had been successful by circumventing reception and stealthily peeking into every room in the hospital until he'd located the right one.

When he walked in, Chris was lying in a bed that was adjusted upright so that he could look out the window. His skin was an awful, pasty white. Jack would never forget that. There were scratches on his face and a deep cut on his arm, where Jack could make out the neat black stitches. Chris looked worse than terrible, he looked almost like a vampire who hadn't found prey in several days.

Chris had turned his head, sensing the extra presence in the room, and his expression had darkened.

'What are you doing here?'

'Chris, I had to see you.'

'Now you have, so *leave*.'

'Why are you doing this? Why are you blaming me? How can you honestly believe that this is what I wanted for you?'

'You weren't thinking about me,' Chris snarled. 'You were thinking about Bronwyn and how I was finally going to make headway with her and you couldn't stand it. So when you heard me call out to her . . .'

Jack's eyes widened and his jaw dropped. 'Chris, I saw a kangaroo. I was dumb. I swerved. It wasn't about showing you up, it was –'

'Don't lie to me. You forget how well I know you, Jack. How far I've seen you go. You've never had any respect for anyone else. All's fair in love and war, right?'

Jack had felt the blood drain from his face.

Chris's observation of his character at the time was true enough. He'd never been very discriminate in his dealings with women. He figured they knew what they were getting themselves into. If they got hurt, it was their fault, not his. Don't buy what you don't need, in his book.

'But you're my brother –' he began.

'That's what makes this even worse,' Chris threw at him. 'Maybe you didn't mean for me to get this hurt. Perhaps it was a miscalculation on your part. It doesn't matter. The intention was still there. Dad is always going on about how reckless you are and he's right.'

'Chris, I promise you –'

'There is no promise that you can make that will give me my legs back.' Chris gasped. 'I'll never walk again, thanks to *your ego*.'

'Chris –'

'I'll never walk again!' Chris repeated and his eyes had begun to glisten as the gravity of what he was saying dawned on him again, like a recurring nightmare. Jack had felt himself reacting in the same way. He'd immediately stepped forward, wanting to take his brother's hand.

'Mate –'

He'd been so overwhelmed he hadn't realised that sometime during their conversation, Chris had pushed the red button on the side of his bed. A nurse popped into the room just before he reached Chris's side.

'Is everything all right?'

'I asked for this man not to be admitted,' Chris said to her. 'Will you please show him out?'

'Of course,' she agreed.

'Chris,' Jack had begged, 'don't do this. Let me help you.'

'How can you? When I don't ever want to see you again. Right now it would be better for me if you just dropped off the face of the earth.' His brother had turned his head away and the nurse had gently pulled Jack from the room.

That was their last conversation before he'd seen him again yesterday, five years later, in the winery.

He should have fought longer and harder for Chris's forgiveness. Or tried to explain to him again what had happened that night. He probably would have if that letter hadn't arrived from his dad the next day.

It had been in a non-descript white business envelope without a stamp. Someone had clearly dropped it off personally. The staff from the motel had left it on his bed after they'd cleaned the room while he was out. This was no mean feat given the mess he'd left it in. If he hadn't been a local boy, no doubt the owners, Mike and Louise, probably would have kicked him out sooner. Depression did not make him a very good tenant. Depression didn't make him a very good anything.

The note from his father was unsigned, short and to the point.

After all you've done, don't you think it would be better for everyone if you just left? Please take advantage of this opportunity and the ticket I have bought for you and allow your family time to heal. Especially Chris.

Attached to this note was a plane ticket booking and an offer of work from an extremely reputable winery in Bordeaux. It was an area that his father had worked in when he was in his early twenties, still sowing his wild oats. He must have obtained the job through his various connections there. It was a startling opportunity. The kind that people waited years for and that rarely came their way. Yet Jack felt none of the excitement he should have as he'd held the letter in his hand. The plane ticket alone said it all. He glanced at the date, a week from today. It was one-way only. His father wanted him gone that badly and didn't care when he came back.

If at all.

It was like a knife slash across the chest.

Kicking him off the property hadn't been enough – his father had to kick him out of the country as well. He must have gone to the hospital and spoken to Chris. His brother's words rang in his ears.

At this point, it would be better for me if you just dropped off the face of the earth.

Perhaps they'd even hatched this plan together.

He sat on the note for a couple of days, waiting for someone to call him – either to take it back or tell him it was untrue. Perhaps his mother, asking him to ignore his father's order. Or his sister, wanting him to stay and work things out. Finally, he'd bitten the bullet and gone to see his dad at Oak Hills in a one last-ditch effort to make amends.

He'd found his father in the tearoom next to the lab. He was staring at the blackboard nailed to the far wall, hands clasped behind his back, rocking on his heels. The board was old and really should have been replaced years ago, perhaps with one of those electronic white ones that could do display dumps on a mini printer attached to its base.

Nobody, it seemed, had wanted the upgrade. The board was a piece of Franklin history, prized almost as much as a good vintage. The wooden framing was scratched and discoloured and the duster looked like it would put more chalk on the board than take off.

To an outsider the blackboard seemed to display a table of unrelated numbers, acronyms and dates. But Jack knew that it was the pulse of the winery. It told the winemaker where his grapes were, what they were mixed with, which fermentation tank had them and how long they had been there. It was both recipe and schedule, status and timeline. It was Horace's lifeblood and until a week ago it had been Jack's as well.

Horace did not turn when Jack entered the room. His eyes remained fixed upon the board, but he did speak.

'If you're here to demand your job back, think again. I have made up my mind. I don't want you here.'

Jack gritted his teeth. 'I'm sorry for what I did.'

'I don't doubt it.'

'I shouldn't have taken the ute. I shouldn't have been doing donuts with it and I shouldn't have allowed my brother to get on the back when I did so.'

'No, you shouldn't have.'

'I don't understand. How many more times do I have to say it before you believe me?'

At last Horace had turned around. 'I believe you, Jack. But this time, I need more than just words from you.' He stabbed his finger at him. 'You've gone too far this time. I'm too angry, too deeply disappointed. You have irrevocably changed Chris's life and now I want to irrevocably change yours!'

'I realise . . .' Jack licked his lips.

Horace waved aside what he was about to say. 'I know you will say whatever necessary to placate me, but the truth is, you need space from this place. I am not giving you your job back. Not yet.'

'Dad –'

Horace Franklin's face was set. 'I want you to learn from this, Jack, and this is the only way I can see you doing that.'

Jack stared at him in shock. Did he really think that he was that far gone that he hadn't already learned his lesson the second his brother had hit the ground?

'So this is where we're at?' he said tightly.

'This is where we're at. This family needs time to heal.'

267

He flinched. 'So you're all in agreement about this?'

'Your mother is too upset.' Horace had shrugged. 'And I don't want to bring her down further by hashing this out, but I have spoken to Chris. We had both hoped you would have got the message by now.'

'Oh, I got your message,' Jack returned bitterly. 'And if that's what you really want, then fine.' He backed away. 'Tell the others I said goodbye.' He spun on his heel and left.

A few days later he'd flown out to France. No one had turned up at the airport to send him off. No one had rung him to say goodbye. Perhaps his father was waiting until the date and time of the flight had passed to tell the rest of the family about his plan. If they could all disown him so completely, he wasn't going to ring up and thank them for it.

As for Chris, he prayed he didn't mess up his chances with Bronwyn over this. The girl was going to quit law, move to Oak Hills and make everything perfect again. Fingers crossed Chris let her. From this perspective, it was better that he was out of the picture. He didn't know that he could honestly watch their happily ever after. The least he could do after taking away Chris's ability to walk was let him be with the woman they both loved.

And so he'd gone.

France had taken a long time to get used to. It was colder there and there was the language barrier as well, but he'd made it work. Hell, he'd more than made it work. If he was completely honest, there had been a point when he'd started to get caught up in the atmosphere of the place. Bordeaux was the wine capital of the world, steeped in history and tradition. They'd been making wine there since the eighth century, and Jack couldn't help being overrun by a desire to inhale everything around him . . . if he couldn't actually taste-test it, that is.

He managed to make friends with a few locals, which had certainly made life a lot easier.

Antoine, in particular, would never let him feel sorry for himself. The Frenchman was as outrageous as he was ambitious and he'd pulled Jack right out of his apathy and into ambition. The job his father had found for him was with Antoine's family – Beauchene Wines. Over a barrel of Bordeaux Sauternes, he and Antoine had bonded. Both were winemakers, both searching for something more. It seemed fitting to discuss their dissatisfaction with the world over the infamous sweet wine that was made with partially rotted grapes.

Nonetheless, at the end of the day, Jack hated living someone else's life in France. Oak Hills was his home, his birthright. It was where all the people he loved were. Even if they didn't love him back.

Antoine had wanted a break from tradition. He'd also wanted Australian women, sun, surf and chardonnay to die for. Unlike Jack's family, Antoine could trace his back generations, twelve to be precise. Family feuds and rivalries were a way of life for him and he was unimpressed with Jack's stories from home. He regaled him with more outrageous tales of his own ancestors, who, as far as Jack could see, loved as much as they betrayed, in true French style.

'Zis gripe you have with your father, to me, it is so insignificant, I do not know why you are here, unless to assault my ears further with your dull complaints.' Antoine's long fingers had flicked at him in dismissal. 'Go back to Australia, teach him a lesson. Reconcile with your brother and kiss ze woman you love *adieu*. There are more fish in ze sea, let me assure you.'

For Jack, this was not the insult it was meant to be but the kick up the bum he desperately needed. He had stopped and taken real stock of his life. Did he really want to be the irresponsible disappointment who spent a life of exile working on someone else's winery just because his father said so?

No.

He wanted what he'd always wanted.

Oak Hills.

France was no more than a detour on his life journey. He had to go back.

So for the next five years, Jack had worked like a slave. He'd started in Bordeaux, exploring the region completely, getting to know the French obsession with *terroir* – the set of environmental factors that affected a grape variety's epigenetic qualities, and the basis for wine regulation in France. He studied everything from the simple but delicious everyday table-wine to some of the most expensive and prestigious drops in the world.

When he was done with this, he'd worked his way through Burgundy as well, in the valleys and slopes to the west of the Saône River, where all the best vineyards were. Gaining experience here with exotic grape varieties he'd never worked with before, such as gamay and aligoté, just to round off his skills.

Antoine had come with him 'just for laughs' and had fallen in love with the red varieties made from pinot noir, and a variety of women as well.

He deplored Jack's lack of interest in the scene after dark. 'Why do you not come with me zis time?' he asked. 'There are plenty to go round.'

'Because you always take the good ones,' Jack had lied jovially. He was more interested in reading as many French wine journals as he could lay his hands on. His womanising ways were over and Ant had coined him the 'Monk of Aquitaine'.

Ha! If only Bronwyn had seen him there.

He had dated a few women but his heart hadn't been in it. It was still sitting somewhere on the south-west coast of Australia.

Sometimes he and Antoine worked together, sometimes they worked in neighbouring vineyards. Whatever the case, they were a force to be reckoned with. When they returned to

Bordeaux they gave a talk together at Vinexpo, regaling other experts with their experiences – comparing and contrasting methods used by the different wineries they had passed through.

At that point Jack had known he was ready to return. His bank account told him the same story. Given his frugal lifestyle, limited social life and his tendency to split accommodation costs with Antoine, he'd amounted quite a sum for himself as well as a good reputation.

The old Jack might have bought himself a flash car, gone on a holiday to Hawaii and worked his way through the female beach population. This Jack, however, got financial planners involved, invested in the stock market, and doubled his earnings. He was ready not only to return to Oak Hills but to take it by force if necessary, and Antoine was his willing partner in crime.

When he'd first arrived in Bordeaux, Jack had sent his family a few impersonal postcards, saying he was doing okay in his new job, hoping to break the silence at least. They had never responded. When he moved on to Burgundy, however, he had given them a call. Luckily, his mother had picked up the phone.

'Oh, Jack, thank God. Where are you?'

'I'm in Burgundy now, Mum, on the Côte d'Or. It's amazing.'

'Well, you must send me your address this time, otherwise I have no means to contact you.'

He gave her his email instead as he was always on the move. All the same, he couldn't help but be further incensed by his father's continued churlish behaviour. He may have still been refusing to speak to him, but that he hadn't bothered to pass on Jack's whereabouts to his mother was just cruel. No wonder he'd heard nothing from them when he was in Bordeaux.

He and his mum had spoken for a long time that first phone call. She had apologised for her behaviour after Chris's accident, wishing that she'd taken more of a stand in what

271

was going on between him and his father than focusing all her thoughts on Chris.

'You needed me too and I didn't realise it.'

After that, he'd maintained a fairly regular email relationship with her. Claudia sometimes sent him a picture or two as well, but nothing came in from Chris or his father. He heard about their news indirectly though the female members of his family. He'd seen photos of the property and a lovely Christmas picture of them sitting round the table out on the patio, tucking into his mother's famous coleslaw, fresh garden salad and the garlic prawns his father always cooked on the barbecue. This was served, of course, with Horace's semillon sauvignon blanc – a lively, zesty blend that just cried out for the foods of summer. Seeing their glasses raised in toast over the spread made him long desperately for home. Family. Australia.

Several times his mother had tried to entice him back and more often than not he'd been tempted. Yet the last thing he wanted to do was return as a second-class citizen, only to be shunned again.

When his father had retired and the problems at Oak Hills had followed, he knew that his time was approaching. All he had to do was wait a little longer, and they wouldn't be able to refuse his help.

Antoine not only thought 'zis plan is genius', he'd wanted to be a part of it. So with his mother's help he had sent the Frenchman off to Oak Hills as a spy. When the time came, they would buy Oak Hills together. He didn't want to wait for an inheritance, not that he counted on still being in the will.

His father was no longer in any position to refuse to sell. And the truth was, deep down, Horace Franklin didn't really trust anyone else with his estate except for the man he had personally trained. If Jack had to humiliate him to get his way, he'd do so. Especially after everything Horace had put him through the last five years.

Of course, whenever he'd imagined his homecoming, Bronwyn Eddings had never featured.

When Claudia had first written to him, she'd told him that Bronwyn was living it up in the city, working as a lawyer for a prestigious firm and becoming horrendously successful. He could see the thread of envy in her note and knew that his sister wasn't too pleased about carrying the majority of the family responsibility.

She was angry at him for having left. She could only see his motives as selfish. To escape the drama, to further his own career and to not have to deal with the permanent damage he'd done to his own brother. If only it were that simple.

Many of her letters were borderline accusatory.

It was why he never told her anything of his plan to return, because he wasn't sure how she'd react. Maybe if he had he would have known more on the Bronwyn front, because it seemed Claudia had a plan too: escape to the city and install her best friend in her stead. It was the craziest thing he'd ever heard. Though, he had to admit, pretty ballsy.

The Bronwyn he'd seen today was a lot different to the one he'd known way back when. She still had that fragile quality that suggested if you were too rough with her, she'd break. One conversation, however, had showed him that she was far stronger than she looked.

His first week at Oak Hills was a testament to that. His mother was the only one who welcomed him with open arms. That first night at dinner, both his father and brother were absent from the table.

Chris, apparently, was on a date.

What the?

His father's absence was a little more mysterious and a lot more insulting.

It was just him, Bronwyn and Lydia sitting around a gorgeous lamb roast – his favourite dish as a child – accompanied by a selection of chargrilled vegetables and a bottle of gutsy shiraz.

'Try not to take their absence too much to heart,' Lydia said. 'After all, I did spring you on them. They are still trying to get over the shock.'

'So who is this woman my brother is dating?' he asked, with a quick glance in Bronwyn's direction for any signs of jealousy.

However, she only appeared to be half listening as she forked a piece of broccoli and put it in her mouth. How on earth did she make *that* look sexy? He averted his gaze to take in his mother's reply.

Lydia was tapping her chin thoughtfully. 'I'm really not sure. He takes out a lot of different women, I've stopped keeping track.'

Jack started. 'Seriously?'

'Yes. Though it never goes anywhere,' Lydia complained. 'I think he sabotages himself on purpose.'

'Yes,' Bronwyn piped up with a smile, 'he likes to keep his options open.'

'Strange.' His throat tightened. 'I always thought he was a one woman kind of guy. Are you sure he's not just running interference?'

'Running interference how?' Bronwyn's nose wrinkled.

Lydia smiled shrewdly. 'I think what Jack is trying to say is that perhaps Chris is trying to make you jealous.'

Bronwyn turned a delicious shade of pink that had his heart rate jump a notch.

'Chris pays me no more attention than he does your sous chef or her apprentice. He's a flirt. He doesn't mean anything by it.'

'Are you sure about that?' He smirked.

Bronwyn tossed her head. 'I'd think I'd know if a man really liked me or not.'

Jack laughed.

'What's so funny?'

'You.' His lips continued to twitch. 'Can you pass the pepper please?'

She laid her hand on it, her eyes sparkling crossly. 'Not until you tell me what you mean by that statement.'

He shrugged. 'Only that Chris has liked you since the day he met you and you friend-zoned him.'

'I *what?*'

'You know,' Jack explained, 'that place women put the nice guys in their life so they can turn to the bad boys.'

'And by that are you referring to yourself?' she demanded, clearly fuming.

'Hey,' he raised both palms, 'you jumped there, not me.'

Lydia cleared her throat to break up the fight. 'In case either of you are interested, Chris likes Maria.'

'Maria?' Bronwyn repeated.

Jack blinked. 'Who is Maria?'

'She started working here after you left.'

'She's a cellar hand,' Bronwyn said thoughtfully. 'Really quiet and shy. She's the only female around here Chris *doesn't* flirt with.'

'Exactly.' Lydia smiled.

Bronwyn nodded, understanding. 'Oh, I totally get it now.'

Jack did not get it at all. 'I'm not following.'

'There's something you need to understand about Chris, my love.' Lydia turned to him. 'Ever since the accident he's been so determined not to let it best him, not to be given any special treatment, that he thinks that anyone who does must be pitying him.'

Jack thought guiltily of Bronwyn and his naive notion that Chris would somehow find a way for them to be together with him out of the picture. His brother had so much to deal with that year. Romance was probably the last thing on his mind. And now . . .

'He thinks of himself as a faulty package,' he said.

His mother nodded. 'He doesn't go for long-term relationships because he doesn't think he has the right to one.'

Jack felt his gut twist into a knot and he suddenly wasn't that hungry anymore.

You did this.

You did this to your brother.

'So what about you?' His mother broke into his thoughts. 'I hear French women are very beautiful.'

'They are.' He shrugged.

Bronwyn drained her glass in one gulp. 'Could someone pass the wine please?'

Lydia handed her the shiraz. 'Why didn't I get any emails about all the fancy foreign ladies in your life? You can still tell your mother those things, you know. I won't judge.'

He choked.

Bronwyn splashed wine beside her glass as she was trying to pour it. 'Er . . . can I get a napkin?'

Gratefully, he reached towards the silver holder and got one to her.

'So,' Lydia rested her hand in her chin, 'keep talking.'

'Yeah,' Bronwyn agreed, taking huge gulps from her fresh glass. 'Why not give us more details?'

'I hadn't realised I'd given you any,' he protested, not wanting to reveal his true identity as the 'Monk of Aquitaine' at this point, particularly after witnessing firsthand Bronwyn's confidence with her body.

It was funny how France, reputably one of the most romantic places on earth, had turned Jack Franklin from playboy to workaholic. Or maybe it was his state of mind that did that. Maturity, he supposed with a slight smile, had to arrive sometime.

His mother misinterpreted his expression.

'I see. Well, don't tell me then.' She paused. 'Have you spoken to your brother yet?'

'Very briefly.' He nodded. 'It didn't go well.'

'You have been gone for five years,' his mother pointed out.

His top priority was to reconcile with his brother, though he wasn't exactly sure how he was going to do this. Especially with the added pressure of keeping on top of the vintage as well. Earlier that same afternoon he'd done an inspection of the vines and noticed they hadn't taken the chardonnay off yet. In his opinion, it was at least a day overdue. The block wasn't Oak Hill's star crop but that didn't mean they should give it any less consideration. Horace Franklin, however, was nowhere to be found. He couldn't believe his father was being this irresponsible out of spite.

'What about Dad?' he enquired of his mother. 'Where was he today? We need to harvest the chardonnay as soon as possible before the grapes get too sweet.'

Bronwyn cleared her throat. 'He, er . . . was with me. We had a few things we needed to discuss.'

His eyes narrowed on her in exasperation. 'Look, I know you mean well, but this year's chardonnay is going to be in some serious trouble if we don't get those grapes off the vine in the next day or so.'

'Way ahead of you.' She patted his hand, sending goose-bumps flying up his arm. 'I've organised a harvesting machine after talking to the vineyard manager. It's all going down, two am tonight.'

He had to, begrudgingly, give her this win. 'Good, but do we have everyone organised for tomorrow?'

The day after harvest was always a mad rush. It required everyone on the property to muck in for the huge task of crushing, de-stemming and pressing the grapes – basically the extraction of the juice so it could be placed in the tanks or barrels for fermentation.

'Everybody is on standby,' Bronwyn assured him, 'so make sure you get to bed early tonight.'

It was a pretty cheeky order from her, given she was sleeping in his bed; in his nice mind-clearing room, sparsely furnished and comfortably neat. By contrast, he had to sleep beneath a floral pink doona he'd picked up off the floor, next to a mountain of clothes and a desk overflowing with books, half of which he was sure Claudia had never read. After all, who would want to sit through such titles as *Custody Battles Gone Wrong*, and *Issues Facing Tax Law: Cases and Commentary*, just for fun? Certainly not him. Just looking at her leisure pile was enough to give him a headache.

He shovelled the last of his food into his mouth. 'What about the actual harvest? Won't I be needed –'

'No, you won't,' Bronwyn said quickly. 'Your dad is going to supervise that. He's out talking to the guys now.'

He ground his teeth as she started collecting their plates. The harvesting tractor was actually very efficient and he was confident that his father would not have to do much. The machine enabled only two men to harvest a complete block of vineyard in just a few hours. The tractor was built high so that it straddled the wine trestle. It basically shook the vine as it drove over it so that the fruit fell on a conveyor belt that could sort grapes from leaves and twigs, before dropping them into the tractor's storage unit. It wasn't that he felt the need to be present. It was more that he had been told in no uncertain terms not to be.

He barely slept that night. The floodlights in the field made sure Claudia's bedroom never completely settled into darkness. Combined with the noise of the harvester, most people unused to the situation would not have blamed him. However, if he was honest, it was neither of these things that kept him up. Generally, he was one of those sleepers who, if he was tired enough, could sleep through anything. In this instance, unfortunately, his brain just would not switch off. Bronwyn had definitely disrupted the balance of power and he wasn't sure what to make of it.

Eventually, he gave up on trying to sleep and decided to go for a walk. He flung off Claudia's pink doona with satisfaction and pulled on a pair of jeans hanging over the back of her desk chair. A T-shirt over the head and he was ready to leave the room.

The house was dark and he didn't turn on any lights as he

crept down the stairs. They creaked the whole way, just as he remembered. He smiled wryly to himself. Good thing the harvester was in action or he might have woken the others.

He swung open the door to the front of the house and walked out onto the porch. Stretching his arms to open up his lungs, he breathed in deep the flavours of crop. It was a warm and balmy February night, perfect for a harvest and a good walk. The harvest lights glowed brightly in the distance, making the sky seem black by comparison. On any other night he wouldn't have been able to count the stars.

'All right,' a resigned tone came out of the darkness, 'I give up. Why are you really here?'

Jack turned around quickly, and as his eyes adjusted to the darkness he saw his brother sitting in the shadows of the house. The first thing to catch his eye was the glint of moonlight against silver wheels as Chris rolled out so that he could see him better.

A pang tore at his heart when he laid eyes on him, and also a sense of pride. His brother held his head high, his back straight, his powerful biceps on display because of the T-shirt he was wearing. There was nothing weak about Chris. He had conquered his disability.

'It's good to see you,' he said to his brother.

'I wish I could say the same.' Chris's face was hard like stone, his mouth a flat line.

'I was hoping that time might have mellowed your anger towards me.'

'Without an apology,' Chris snapped, 'there can be no forgiveness.'

Jack frowned. He'd told Chris about the kangaroo but his brother, it seemed, still clung to his own truth. 'What do you want me to say, Chris? I'm sorry I fell in love with her. I'm sorry that I wanted her as much as you did.'

Chris's face contorted as he turned away. 'If it were only that –'

'It *was* only that!' Jack threw at him. 'Oh, I admit in the beginning it was a competition. A fight to the last man standing and I was all in, but I didn't cross the line that you think I did.'

'I only have your word.'

'Yeah, you do,' Jack responded bitterly. 'And you've chosen not to believe it. God only knows why. I'm your brother, damn it! Why would I ever set out to deliberately hurt you?'

Chris's jaw set. 'The thing is, Jack, you never set out to deliberately hurt me but you always did.'

'With Bronwyn?'

'No, with *everything*!' Chris's voice rose a notch and he had to take a breath or two to calm himself down. 'You were the favourite son.'

'What?'

Chris gritted his teeth. 'Don't play dumb, Jack. You know what I'm talking about.'

'No, I don't.'

'You were the one who inherited all Dad's talent. His knack with wine. His passion for making it. You were good-looking, sought after by the ladies, admired by your peers. Dad gave you every opportunity he could and you took it like it was your due,' Chris remarked bitterly. 'Did you ever pause to think about what I was doing during all that?'

Jack looked at him stunned, so guilt-ridden that he actually had nothing to say. He'd been far too self-absorbed back then to think about Chris's endgame. He knew his brother hadn't been into the actual winemaking process. He was more business oriented and had done a degree in marketing and management at university. Jack had naturally assumed Chris was planning to use those skills in the winery.

'You've always been interested in doing the marketing for Oak Hills,' he began uncertainly. 'Haven't you?'

'No,' Chris retorted. 'I've always been interested in getting the hell out of here. Out from under your shadow and making my own way. While you were establishing yourself as the heir apparent, I was planning my exit strategy.'

'Where were you going to go?'

'I don't know,' Chris shrugged. 'The sky was the limit . . . back then. After you left, everything fell apart. I got stuck.'

Jack pushed his hands roughly into the pockets of his jeans. 'That's not true. Look at you, Chris. You didn't let your disability beat you. I have nothing but admiration for the way you've handled it.'

'It's not just that.' Chris's mouth twisted. 'Dad needed us. Me and Claud. When you ran off to France he was devastated.'

'Hardly,' Jack scoffed.

'You weren't here,' Chris threw at him bitterly. 'If I thought being the second son with no gift for wine was bad, the disabled one he'd passed you over for was even worse.'

It was Jack's turn to get angry. He stabbed a finger at his brother. 'That's utter bullshit.'

'I'll tell you what's bullshit.' Chris rolled forward. 'Your fucked-up attitude. You keep saying you're my brother. That you'd never do anything to deliberately hurt me, and look what you did, Jack. You put me in hospital, and even if that wasn't your fault *as you claim*, afterwards you just left. Do you have any idea what I was going through? Any idea at all? I needed you back then, Jack. You were my best friend and where were you? Living it up in France, that's where!'

Jack rolled on the balls of his feet in fury. 'Living it up? Ha! Hardly. I was there because you sent me there. You and Dad!'

'Don't be ridiculous,' Chris protested.

'How can you get angry at my lack of consideration when you never wanted it?' Jack threw up his hands. 'Do you have any idea how hurt I was when you both conspired to kick me out of the frickin' country?'

'What?' Chris paled.

'You keep going on about how Dad loves me more,' Jack spat. 'What a joke! After how he treated me.'

'I have no idea what you're talking about.'

'How many times did I come to visit you at the hospital before I left? How many times did you turn me away?'

'I don't remember,' Chris shrugged. 'You may recall I was going through a lot at the time. Can you blame me if I didn't have time to think about your sensitive feelings?'

'All right then,' Jack threw at him, 'what about when I did manage to break through security? You told me that you never wanted to see me again.'

Chris lifted his chin. 'And I didn't, not then.'

'Right.' Jack nodded in satisfaction. 'Which is why it came as no surprise to me when Dad sent me a note explaining how you all wanted me to go. It also included a job offer in Bordeaux and a plane ticket to get me there just in case I was too busy begging to stay to organise one myself.'

'You're mistaken,' Chris responded weakly. 'Dad would never go that far.'

'Well, he did. So don't go on to me about how I abandoned you, when you told me to drop off the face of the earth and then had Dad send me a ticket to do so.'

'Jack –'

'Look, I'm sorry about your legs, and I'm sorry that I wasn't here when you were trying to get used to that blasted chair, but that wasn't from a lack of wanting to be. France was fuckin' lonely until I got myself a sense of purpose.'

Chris's jaw seemed to set. 'And what purpose was that, Jack? Wait till we're down and out and swoop in to gloat?'

'No.' Jack glared back. 'I just want to be part of what you and Claudia are starting to take for granted. This family, this vineyard and this lifestyle. Oak Hills is in my blood and this time you guys can't turn me away because, like it or not, you need me.'

Chris gave a mocking laugh. 'We've always needed you, Jack. It was just never in your best interest to notice before.'

On these words, he wheeled himself back into the house.

Chapter 23

She hadn't meant to eavesdrop on the conversation. It had just sort of happened when she slipped downstairs to make herself a cup of tea. With the harvester at full steam outside and the small victory she'd won over Jack that evening still buzzing in her brain, she'd found it impossible to sleep. She was filling the kettle with water when she'd heard the faint sound of voices coming from outside. Plugging the kettle in, she'd left the kitchen to see who it was by walking into the living room.

Shrouded by darkness, she could see easily out of the large bay windows to where Jack and Chris were talking on the porch. To be honest, she was relieved at first to see them together. It was about time they settled their differences. They couldn't go on with this silent treatment. It wasn't good for either of them when it was clear, even to a toddler, how much they loved each other.

The windows were open and the light curtain was billowing gently with the faint sea breeze. Their voices wafted in clearly.

'What about when I did manage to break through security? You told me that you never wanted to see me again.' Bronwyn sucked in a breath, startled to hear such anger and hurt in Jack's voice.

She glanced at Chris, whose face was grimly set in the faint lighting from the field. 'And I didn't, not then,' he croaked.

'Right,' Jack said. 'Which is why it came as no surprise to me when Dad sent me a note explaining how you all wanted me to go. It also included a job offer in Bordeaux and a plane ticket to get me there just in case I was too busy begging to stay to organise one myself.'

Bronwyn's hand flew to her throat as Chris put a voice to her thoughts.

'You're mistaken. Dad would never go that far.'

'Well, he did. So don't go on to me about how I abandoned you, when you told me to drop off the face of the earth and then had Dad send me a ticket to do so.'

Oh crap!

Bronwyn hastily returned to the kitchen. She turned off the kettle and made her way straight back up the stairs. That conversation had just turned her world on its head.

Did she hear it right?

Jack thought his dad had given him the opportunity in Bordeaux.

She shut the door to her bedroom and began to pace the floor. He said something about a note. A note with a plane ticket and a job offer. It was from her mother, no doubt, but she mustn't have signed it if Jack didn't realise it was from her. And if that were true, then her mother had lied to her about seeing Jack face to face . . .

She sank slowly onto the bed, her fingers trembling in horror. She had been manipulated into doing her mother's bidding yet again.

Bianca Hanks had not spoken to Jack five years ago.

He didn't know anything about Bronwyn's feelings for him. He didn't even know that that job offer in Bordeaux was anything do with her or her family.

He thought . . .

She threw herself back on the doona, a hand to her forehead.

He thought his own family had wanted him gone. No wonder there was such a rift between them all.

Shit, Bronwyn! This is all your fault.

She closed her eyes in disgust at the unfathomable damage her mother had caused. Damage she probably didn't even know the half of. All she had wanted to do was make her daughter stay in law. She bit her fingernails as her thoughts flew in all directions.

All this time, all this awkwardness.

You've been so embarrassed over nothing.

He didn't reject you. He didn't even know you had feelings for him.

Still doesn't.

Her significance to him in this whole debacle was actually non-existent. It was all in her head and the cost of that mistake was huge.

Her mother had destroyed his relationship with his family. She sat up abruptly.

You are going to have to tell him what really happened.

Even as the thought formed in her head, another flew in the back door.

Wait!

What was she going to tell Jack when he wanted to know why he had been singled out? Why her mother had thought that if he was gone she wouldn't come back to Oak Hills?

She chewed her lower lip. Number One Humiliation Street. Her infatuation with him was going to come out after all. Her embarrassing unrequited love that he wasn't even aware existed. She massaged her temple.

The situation only got worse the more she unravelled it.

Then, of course, there was the plan she'd set in motion the afternoon before, which made everything that much worse. Jack would not be pleased with the development, and had she known how much her family had taken from him already she might have thought twice about it. But now it was too late, her offer was out there. And if she was really honest with herself, did she want to take it back?

Yesterday, when Jack had gone off to settle into Claudia's messy bedroom, she had tracked down Horace. The old man had been talking to the harvest tractor driver in the yard – discussing the pros and cons of machine harvesting and whether it really produced the same standards as hand-picking. She was sure Horace was gathering support for a debate he was going to have later with John Maxwell, whose organically grown vineyard had never seen a mechanical clipper in its life.

'Horace, can I talk to you for a minute?' she had asked.

After the driver wandered off and she had his full attention, she'd cut to the chase. 'I want to buy into Oak Hills.'

'Huh?'

'You need money and I've got money,' Bronwyn tried to explain. 'Not immediately available but certainly in time if you agree. I've got assets and investments that can easily be liquidated. I'm happy to sell my apartment in Subiaco, which will fetch me a good profit, and I have shares in the Eddings Company Trust, which I'm sure I can cash out –'

'Whoa, whoa, whoa.' Horace held up his hands. 'Where is this coming from? Why do you want to do this?'

Bronwyn had licked dry lips. 'Because you're in trouble and I'm sick of the way things stand. I don't just want to be the resident groupie anymore. I want you guys to take me seriously. I want a real interest in this business and for you to have a real interest in me.'

Horace smiled. 'That's fair, I suppose.'

'I know I'm still green, but don't you think what I've contributed so far has proven my passion about the winery?'

Horace considered this with a laugh. 'Bronwyn, anyone who could go through the pile of unfiled documents on Chris's desk without a word of complaint must have a passion for this business.'

'So . . .'

'It's not just my decision,' he shrugged. 'I will have to talk to Lydia about it. If we are going to reduce the share we leave to our children she will want to have a hand in that.'

'Okay,' Bronwyn agreed. 'I'm willing to wait on your answer.'

And she was. However, in light of the fact that Jack was here to claim his rightful place, she was doubtful that he was going to be happy about it.

Under the sting of his rejection, she'd been happy to show him the 'New Bronwyn'. Yet now that the truth had been revealed, all she wanted to do was give her mother a piece of her mind.

So what's stopping you?

Harvest.

It was probably the worst day to be making a private phone call. Everybody was up at sparrows to help process the grapes that had been taken off the vine that night. She could already hear people moving downstairs. In an hour, it would be all on.

The hopper had to be filled. This fed the de-stemmer and crusher. After that they prepped the press and when it had done its business, the must (or grape juice) had to be pumped to the vats or fermentation tanks. Then the lab tests were done and the juice chilled right down. The winery was a bustle of noise, tractors and people. Staff from the cellar door were helping out too. She worked solidly all morning and then thought she'd catch five minutes for herself behind the barrel room to make the call.

When she made her way over there, however, a couple of others appeared to have had the idea first. Chris and Maria were conversing under the open roller door, so Bronwyn stopped before she rounded the corner.

'In four weeks my visa runs out and I must return to Italy.'

'In four weeks,' Chris repeated, seemingly at a loss. 'It seems like only yesterday you started.'

'Yes. I wanted to speak to you about my resignation.'

'Of course.'

'I have really loved working here,' she began uncertainly. 'I have really enjoyed working for . . . you.'

Bronwyn crossed her fingers.

Come on, Chris. Read between the lines.

Unfortunately, his response was polite and impersonal. 'We have really enjoyed having you too, Maria. You make a good impression on our customers.'

'Thank you, but I just wanted to say –' Maria cleared her throat as if coming to the point with some difficulty.

'Yes?' Chris prompted her.

'How much I . . . admire you. Particularly how far you've come since your accident –'

'Thank you, Maria, but there's no need to go on.' His voice was stern, cold even. 'My accident is, after all, a personal matter.'

Bronwyn slapped a palm to her forehead.

'Of course. So sorry to have intruded.' These last words were said in a mumbled rush and Bronwyn heard Maria's footsteps retreat a little.

'Maria, wait!'

At last.

'What will you do when you return to Italy?'

'I'm not sure.'

'I've always wanted to visit Italy.'

'Then you should,' Maria said quickly. 'Don't let anything stop you.'

And then she'd walked off, almost running into Bronwyn as she came around the corner.

'Oh, hi,' Maria murmured in embarrassment and quickly walked on. Chris rolled forward to see who she was talking to and Bronwyn twiddled her fingers awkwardly at him as Maria disappeared. He seemed unaffected by her presence, though his lips curved into a smile.

'Hey gorgeous, what can I do for you?'

'Don't you "Hey gorgeous" me!' She shook her finger at him. 'What's going on, Chris? Can't you see she's mad for you?'

'What? Who?' Chris blinked. 'You're not jealous of Cathy are you, because I swear to you nothing happened on our date Monday. In fact,' his smile went lopsided, 'I helped her pick up somebody else. It was all a crock.'

Bronwyn put her hands on her hips. 'It always is. Except for Maria. So get your bloody act together and do something about it.'

Chris abruptly lost his smile. 'Honestly, I don't know where you're getting these ideas from, but in case you didn't quite *overhear properly*, Maria is going back to Italy. There's no point.'

'You've never been one to give up.' She looked pointedly at his legs. 'Ever.'

'Where is this coming from?' His eyes narrowed. 'Have you been talking about me with Jack?'

She baulked at this suggestion. 'Absolutely not. Though there is something you should know.'

He wheeled forward at the seriousness of her expression. 'Jack leaving the way he did isn't what you think. It's my fault. I hope you can forgive me.'

'What's to forgive?'

'Jack left because he got a plane ticket and a job opportunity from my mother.'

Chris blinked, his hands tightening on his wheels. 'I don't understand.'

'He thought you guys wanted him gone but it was actually my mum.'

'But –' Chris frowned. 'Why would your mum want Jack gone? It's nothing to do with her.'

'Well, yes it was, sort of, at the time.' Bronwyn shoved her hands in the pockets of her jeans. 'I was going to quit law and move to Yallingup to be with your family.'

'And Jack.' Chris's mouth twisted.

Bronwyn reddened. 'How did you know?'

'It's Jack,' he shrugged ruefully. 'I always knew.'

'Are you angry?'

'Yes. No.' He threw his hands up in the air. 'I don't know what to think anymore. I'm angry at myself more, I guess.'

'Why?'

'Because of what I put him through, what I put myself through. All the negative things I said before he left. I was jealous, you know.' He winced. 'Still am. I've always felt like I got the short end of the stick.'

'You didn't.' Bronwyn put her hand on his shoulder. 'You just got a completely different stick. If you stopped comparing yourself to Jack and just asked yourself for a change what you wanted, then maybe you'd realise that the only thing holding you back is you.'

'That's a lesson you've learnt this month, isn't it?' He smiled at her affectionately, shaking his finger. 'Don't think Mum and I haven't noticed you lobbying the old man. Very cunning indeed.'

She blushed.

'Not that we blame you after we both tried to shut you out.' He grimaced. 'You've actually done a really great job replacing Claudia. Better than great. Yesterday I went into the office and actually saw my desk. It's only been three years!'

Bronwyn shrugged modestly. 'I enjoyed sorting out all your paperwork.'

'Then you're completely welcome to keep doing it.' Chris laughed.

'I hope that ends up being a really long time,' Bronwyn grinned. 'I really do want to be part of this business.'

'I believe you.' This time his smile was absent of flirtation. 'And I hope you get your wish.'

As he rolled off, Bronwyn also hoped that what she had said regarding Jack had at least partially sunk in. She wanted the brothers to reconcile. It would be a crying shame if they never found friendship again.

As for her mother, she doubted she would ever forgive her.

Surprisingly, it didn't take long to get hold of Bianca Hanks once Chris was out of earshot. It was the middle of the day, so she was almost sure she'd be in court, but Bianca picked up the phone after two rings.

'Ah, so at last you have come to your senses,' Bianca purred in satisfaction. 'Has your friend been complaining to you of my cruelty?'

Bronwyn tossed her head. 'Not at all. Claudia can hold her own. I'm just ringing to inform you that I know what you did five years ago with Jack Franklin. You didn't even speak to him, did you?'

Her mother was silent a few seconds too long. 'I don't know what you're talking about.'

'You lied to me so I would be too humiliated to do anything but accept what you wanted.'

'I honestly can't remember what happened.' Bianca seemed unperturbed. 'Is there a point to this conversation?'

'That's it?' Bronwyn gasped. 'That's all you're going to say?'

'What do you except me to say?'

'Maybe an apology or something? You estranged Jack from his family.'

'Jack Franklin is not my concern. You are.'

'Not anymore,' Bronwyn said firmly. 'You're never going to be able to have that sort of power over me again. I'm selling my apartment. I'm cutting all ties with the city and with you.'

Bianca sucked in a breath. 'There's no need to be so rash. If you want to take a break, fine, but why sell your apartment?'

'I'm buying a share in the Oak Hills Winery.'

'Oak Hills Winery!' Bianca Hanks repeated. 'That's where you are, isn't it? Where you've been hiding. What a fool I am. I don't know why I didn't think of that before.'

'Yes, well I have always loved this place,' said Bronwyn, 'and it's always loved me in return.'

'Are we back to how much I never loved you?' Bianca was contemptuous. 'If I didn't love you, I wouldn't care what you did.'

'Well, perhaps I'm a bit over your brand of love.' Bronwyn sighed. 'Goodbye, Mother.'

She hung up, completely dissatisfied with Bianca's complete indifference to the havoc she had wreaked in the lives of others. It wasn't until much later that Bronwyn realised the cardinal mistake she had made during the phone call.

Bianca Hanks now knew exactly where she was.

Chapter 24

After his dysfunctional conversation with Chris, Jack found it no easier to get back to sleep when he returned to Claudia's room. As a result, when he finally left his bed, he was tired and cranky. Not a good combination for an intense day of crushing and pressing. It didn't help that Ant was in such good spirits.

'So have you spoken to your father yet?'

'No.'

'Why not? It's best we make our move as soon as possible, is it not?'

'Depends.'

'Depends on what?'

Jack ran a rough hand through his hair. 'Look, I'm angry with Dad but I'm not here to make things worse. I'm here to show my family that they need me and get them back on side.'

'I think showing your father how serious you are about zis business will do that.' Ant seemed unperturbed. 'I wish you would stop resting on your hands, Jack, and make our offer. I have been doing ze tastings in the cellar door with zat brother of yours, who hates me by ze way, and I am done. I *need* to get back to ze winemaking. My body craves it like a smoker craves cigarettes.' He threw his hands in the air. 'I do not know why you continue to allow me to suffer these agonies of the suppressed artist!'

'All right, all right,' Jack agreed with smile. 'I'll see what I can do.'

As he finished the sentence he saw Bronwyn enter the winery yard and his mind went blank. She looked so wholesome, even in that ratty old T-shirt and pair of jean-shorts. He couldn't help but acknowledge how she fit right in. He could barely even imagine her in a corporate suit, strutting the Terrace with files under her arm. This was where she belonged.

'Good morning, Jack,' she greeted him, rather formally. She seemed worried and he wasn't sure why that was. His senses went on high alert.

'Hi, Bronwyn,' he said. 'Are you helping out today as well?'
'Where else would I be?'

'She wishes to be by my side, toiling in the Australian sun,' Ant announced, much to Jack's annoyance.

'Hi, Ant,' she giggled, with a warmth Jack did not like.

'How do I compare thee to a summer's day?' said Ant. 'Thou art more lovely – '

She blushed but shook her head. 'You seriously need to update your reading material, Ant, but thanks.' As she walked on to help some others who were raking spent grape stalks from the crusher, Jack turned to his friend.

'Seriously, what are you trying to do here?'

'Light ze fire under your arse.' Ant tipped his hat at him. 'Because if you don't get a move on, you are going to miss ze boats. All of them.'

And with a wink, he sauntered off. Jack could now completely understand why all the other cellar hands wanted to use Ant's face for target practice.

Nonetheless, he did decide to bite the bullet and talk to his father. His mother tried several times during the day to draw them together. She brought out a cart at lunchtime full of ham-and-salad rolls and bottles of ice-cold water. It was a far cry from the images in European movies where the vineyard workers all sit around a huge table having a massive lunch and drinking a rustic red by the gallon. That sort of carry-on in the Australian heat would probably cause most of the workers to pass out.

After a hard morning's work, with much of the day still to go, the emphasis was always on a light meal with plenty of non-alcoholic fluids. Lydia made Jack pass his father a roll, hoping it might get the conversational ball rolling. Then she pushed the cart away to a group of others, leaving them alone.

'That woman is a mastermind,' Horace said to Jack as he took the roll. 'She knows exactly what she's doing all the time.'

'Dad, we need to talk.'

'Yes, we do.' Horace nodded.

They walked away from the winery towards a large gum tree and sat down on the patch of grass under it. Elsa was already laying there, tongue hanging out as she panted. She'd been feasting on skins that had dropped out of the press all afternoon. As a result, much to the amusement of the crew, and to Bronwyn's horror, she was drunk as a skunk, stumbling around the work-site before partially passing out under the tree.

Horace chuckled, briefly passing a hand between her ears. 'Had enough, eh? You're not supposed to get pissed when you're pregnant, you know.'

She stood up unsteadily, swaying slightly on her feet before trotting off back towards the winery.

'Oh well,' Horace swatted his hand, 'she didn't need those brain cells anyway.'

They sat down under the tree, each biting into the rolls, both reluctant to be the first to open the floodgates.

'I thought you would come home sooner,' Horace said at last.

'Why?' Jack looked sideways at him. 'When I was so unwelcome?'

Horace gave a deep sigh. 'The accident affected us all in a lot of ways. For me it was a wake-up call. I blamed myself.'

'Well, that was *completely* obvious,' Jack responded sarcastically. 'I suppose that's why you told me it was all my fault and kicked me out of the country.'

'Now that's not true.' Horace shook his head. 'I did not kick you out. All I wanted was for you to take stock. To wake up and smell the roses. I should have been harder on you boys and instead I let you run wild. Trespassing on our neighbour's property. Throwing parties. Messing with the equipment from our business.'

'You don't need to give me the same lecture I got from you five years ago. I've punished myself enough since then without you rubbing more salt into the wound.'

'I know.' To his surprise, his father agreed. 'So why are you here now, Jack? Have you come back to gloat? My eyesight is half gone, the winery is in a shambles. Did you want to point out how I couldn't do it without you?'

Jack swallowed. It was exactly why he was there. And now the revenge seemed so petty and fruitless because, if he was truly honest with himself, what he'd really come home for was family.

'Let me help you,' he croaked. 'I have money and you need it. Let me buy into the business.'

His father looked at him. His eyes were watery and bloodshot. Jack had to wonder how clear his face must be in his father's field of vision.

Horace's flat expression did not change. 'I've already had another offer.'

Jack started. 'What?'

This cannot be happening.

'Bronwyn has offered to buy into the business as well.'

'You can't be serious.'

'I'm perfectly serious. That girl has been a godsend to us these past few weeks. And at least I know I can trust her. She's never abandoned us when times got tough. Quite the opposite actually.'

'You're really going to sell part of Oak Hills to Bronwyn Eddings?'

'I haven't decided yet.'

'What does that mean?'

'It means,' Horace polished off his roll, 'I haven't decided which of you I trust more with the labour of my life. The drop-out lawyer who has a passion for grapes, or the prodigal son who returns without so much as an apology.'

'Why the hell would I owe you an apology?' Jack growled angrily.

'Well, if you haven't figured that out yet, then I don't know why you came back at all,' Horace threw at him, and then stood up and stormed off.

Jack was left kicking the dirt in frustration.

Well, that went well.

After this less than successful conversation with his father, Jack found himself at point non plus and was not quite sure how to go on. He had never anticipated that he would be in competition over his birthright with Bronwyn Eddings of all people.

The drop-out lawyer, as his father called her, was proving to be a force to be reckoned with and an Achilles heel all at the same time. His feelings for her, he had to note, were being stirred up like the sediments at the bottom of his father's fermentation tanks, infusing the rest of the wine with new flavour. It was difficult seeing her again, and noting, moreover, that Chris had no claim on her.

Her face and manner brought back such memories. The way she had always crushed his ego, made him think deeper than himself and set him on a path that had taken him all the way to France and back. The old Bronwyn he might have trusted, even opened up to.

But this new woman was different. She was too sure of herself, too confident, sexy as hell . . . and on a mission to steal his inheritance to boot.

Living with his family again was also bittersweet. The smell of his mother's cooking brought a rush of memories. His brother's clothes on top of his own in the laundry basket reminded him of how close they used to be. His father's boots, sitting on the porch next to the broad-brimmed hat that hardly ever left his head, gave him such an ache in the chest.

Some things never changed.

Others definitely had.

Dinner that night was an exercise in awkwardness. Chris and his father were out of excuses, so when his mother put a tray of lasagne on the table they reluctantly took their places. In the past, the evening meal with his family had always been loud and opinionated. Everybody interrupting everyone else – butting in to be heard, joshing the speaker or adding two cents' worth. Silence was unheard of.

In this case, however, his brother focused solely on his meal, responding concisely when Lydia asked him how things had gone in the cellar door that day when everyone else had been at the winery. Horace commented briefly on how good the lasagne went with his cabernet merlot, but probably wished he hadn't said anything because Lydia immediately pounced on him.

'That puts me in mind of something. You forgot to take your medicine today.'

'Well, I was pretty busy,' Horace grunted. 'Why didn't you come out and grab me?'

Lydia rolled her eyes. 'It's not my job to chase you about. I was busy making sandwiches for the troops. What you need, Horace, is a mobile phone.'

'Eh?'

'Then I can get you whenever I need you.'

Horace looked so horrified Jack had to cough to hide his smile.

'I don't want no newfangled rubbish hooked up to my arse,' Horace swore.

'It's hardly newfangled,' Lydia insisted. 'Back me up here, Chris.'

His brother tapped his chin. 'People have been using them for over twenty years.'

'You know, I think I'll get one too,' Lydia seemed inspired. 'Maybe we can get a two-for-one deal or something. I hear they do packages now.'

Horace shook his head firmly. 'I'm already losing my eyesight. I don't want a brain tumour as well.'

'There's no evidence they cause tumours.' Lydia frowned and then her eyes lit up with a sudden thought. 'What about bluetooth? You'll love it.'

'Blue what?' Horace was flabbergasted.

'It's hands-free,' Lydia replied with an air of superiority. 'And it doesn't have to be blue. I hear you can get them in a range of colours.'

'Because all a man needs in his life is rainbow-coloured teeth and no hands. What are you on, woman? I swear to God you're enough to drive a bloke mad. Give me the pill box. I'll take anything you want.'

Jack, Chris and Bronwyn all grinned at each other as Lydia triumphantly got up from the table to get Horace's medicine. For a second it was just like old times. Then Chris seemed to remember first. His smile faded and Bronwyn dropped her eyes. Lydia returned to the table and Horace took his pills. They were all silent once more until the meal ended and a tightness developed in Jack's chest. Would things ever be the same again?

The following morning he locked himself in his father's lab under the pretence of testing their produce. He only had a few simple tests to do, so unfortunately it wouldn't keep him busy for very long. In all honesty he had been concerned that they'd picked the chardonnay a little late, so this analysis wasn't a complete waste of his time. He poured a portion of distilled water into a glass beaker, shoved a pH probe into it and set it down on the bench. Standing back, he looked around for his pipette and as he did so heard a short rap of knuckles against wood.

He turned to find Bronwyn standing on his threshold. So she'd found him despite his bid for space.

'Hey, Numbat, you're up early.'

She shrugged, shoving her hands in snug-fitting jeans that showed off her shape to perfection. She'd pinned her beautiful blonde tresses back. He'd didn't like her hair as much like that but he could definitely run with it if he had to. Especially with all that lovely neck exposed.

'I had to see you about something,' she said.

'Is this the part where you apologise for trying to steal my inheritance?' he said, probably a little too harshly.

'So your father told you about me wanting to buy in.'

'You mean steal.'

She put her hands on her hips. 'I'm not trying to steal anything.'

'Well, sure looks like that from where I'm standing. I wonder if you've told Claudia about it. After all, it's her inheritance as well.'

Bronwyn bit her lip. 'No, I haven't told her but I don't think she'd be against it. I'm trying to save this business, not take it away from you guys.' She paused as though searching for the right words. 'Jack, you *know* me.'

'Do I?'

'Yes,' she hissed. 'You know how much I love Oak Hills and how much I've always wanted to be part of it.'

'Which explains why you went off to the city for five years,' he accused. 'Weren't you just boasting to me a few days ago about what a good lawyer you are?'

She sighed. 'Yes, but that was just a defence mechanism. Claudia is the good lawyer, Jack. Not me.'

'Then why didn't you come back when you said you were going to? Five years ago, you were quitting law to be with Chris.'

She blanched. 'Not to be with Chris.'

'You said you wanted to help and I thought you two were finally going to get together.'

'Me and *Chris*?'

'Yes, Bronwyn,' he said impatiently. 'You two have always been perfect for each other. Knowing that made leaving that much easier.'

Bronwyn ran a hand across her brow. 'Of course.'

He turned away from her, frustrated with a conversation that was simply turning in circles. He located his pipette further down the bench and picked it up.

She broke the silence first. 'There's a reason I didn't come back and I'm guessing it's not what you think, but you need to know the truth.'

He was interested but tried not to let it show, moving instead towards a beaker of chardonnay must. He added ten millimetres of must to the distilled water he'd prepared earlier.

She marched up to the bench and stood beside him. 'Jack, look at me. This is important.'

Then he made the mistake of doing just that, turning his head and catching those deep blue eyes and the sprinkling of freckles across her nose that swamped him with so many memories. For a moment he could do nothing but stare back.

'What are you doing?' she murmured.

What am I doing again?

A flash of recollection jolted him. 'TA test,' he blurted, picking up his mixture and moving it to a second bench where another piece of equipment stood waiting.

'A what?' She followed him.

'Titratable acidity test. You might want to stand back a bit.'

Just for my peace of mind.

'Why?'

301

He positioned a tall glass burette containing a clear solution over the beaker and indicated the substance it contained. 'When I add this to the wine there may be a small explosion. I'd hate for your clothes to catch on fire and burn off, especially after what happened the last time I saw you naked.'

'You're kidding, right?' Her eyes were wide.

He nodded gravely. 'Yes, I am.'

'Argh.' She shot him an exasperated glare. 'Are you ever serious? About . . . about *anything*?'

'Life's too short.'

And I'd rather avoid talking about you and Chris.

He took a deep breath and turned his back on her again, slowly dripping the sodium hydroxide from the burette into the beaker, watching his pH probe until the reading he wanted appeared. 'You've gotta take the good times when you can.'

'No, Jack,' she said harshly, 'you need to fight for them, otherwise you're just swept away by the bad ones.'

He sighed. 'Still can't help lecturing me, can you, Numbat?' He turned around. 'You need to loosen up. Kick off your shoes. Let down your hair.' Before he thought the action through, he reached out and unclipped the hair claw holding her knot in place. Her hair rapidly untwisted and whisked across her pink cheeks and around her shoulders. All in all it looked much better, but as she stood there staring at him like the Statue of Liberty with her torch blown out, he realised that maybe he'd gone too far.

That was not cool, man! Not cool.

'Just a thought,' he said quickly. He put her clip on the bench and spun back to his beaker. Grabbing a pen, he scribbled down the reading from the burette on his notepad. The silence behind him was palpable.

Finally, he heard her snatch her clip off the bench. His peripheral vision caught her retwisting her hair in short, sharp movements. When she was done, her voice came out tersely.

'There's something you need to know about what happened five years ago. My mother wanted me to stay in law that badly that it *she* sent you the plane tickets and the job offer in Bordeaux and the note explaining it all.'

'No.' He turned around, shaking his head. 'My dad sent me those things.'

'You've got it wrong, Jack,' Bronwyn said firmly. 'It was my mother.'

Jack stilled, his throat dry. 'So you're saying my dad didn't want me to leave town?'

'No.'

'He had no idea where I went till I made first contact?'

'Yes,' she confirmed breathlessly.

That can't be right.

'It doesn't make sense. Why would your mother think that getting rid of me would keep you in law?'

Bronwyn took a deep breath, her eyes wide and glistening. 'Think about it, Jack.'

'I am,' he protested. 'Nothing is coming to mind.'

She threw up her hands. 'Because I was in love with you, *you idiot*. She knew a rejection from you would send me flying back to her, and it worked.'

He gazed at her in complete and utter shock. 'But Chris –'

She shrugged. 'I guess neither of us got what we wanted.'

Hope caused his chest to fill and expand. 'Why are you telling me this now?'

'Because I don't want you to resent your father and brother for the rest of your life. They don't deserve that when it was all my mother's doing.' She raised her chin. 'So now that I've sufficiently humiliated myself for your family's benefit, I better get back to it.'

'Back to what?' he demanded. Anything to stall her from leaving his side.

One eyebrow flicked up as she lifted her hands to make the quotation marks. '"Stealing" your inheritance, of course. Good luck, Jack. You're going to need it.'

And then she was gone.

Chapter 25

Personally, Bronwyn had had a gutful of Jack Franklin.

Since he'd arrived, all he'd done was rock the boat. Chris was on edge. His mother was worried and his father couldn't decide what to do about the future of Oak Hills, which, unfortunately, was now very closely linked to her own. The competition for Horace's winery had begun and she fully intended to win.

It wasn't like she wanted all of Oak Hills, just a small part so that she could feel like she was contributing to something she was connected to. Her best friend would still receive a sizable inheritance and so would Jack and Chris. She didn't know what the big problem was.

Unless, of course, Jack preferred that she marry Chris to receive her share rather than legitimately buying into the estate. She cringed when she thought of their conversation the day before and how he had gone on about how perfect she was for Chris and how glad he had been when it seemed like they were going to get together.

Argh! The delusion.

She could still recall the shock on his face when she'd admitted she'd actually been in love with him.

He was absolutely dumbfounded.

Like she'd just showed him an alien in his Year One class photo.

Her mother shouldn't have wasted so much money on getting Jack off to France. A few more weeks in Yallingup and he would have rejected her himself. It was perfectly clear that he'd never thought of her in a romantic way at all. And to top it all off, he'd had her earmarked *for his brother*.

The confusion she was feeling now, these feelings his return was stirring up, had to be ignored. Otherwise she was just setting herself up for the rejection she didn't receive five years ago. Hadn't he just returned from a smorgasbord of beautiful, sophisticated French women? In the wake of that party, why would he even look twice at her?

She had to concentrate on what was important.

Winning Oak Hills.

Not Jack Franklin's heart.

With this is mind, she decided to focus on building her strengths. Jack's was obviously winemaking so she'd steer clear of that. Her strength lay more in organisation, people and staying on top of things. So far she'd been in the background, helping Horace sort out the chaos in the office. Now, however, she thought it was time to move into the foreground. She wanted to try her hand at serving in the cellar door, get to know a little more about the product she was promoting. So that morning she reported there as soon as it opened at ten o'clock.

Ant was very pleased to see her. His eyes lit up. 'You have not forsaken me! My life is complete.'

'It is?' Chris appeared from the storeroom and Bronwyn quickly covered her embarrassment by explaining the situation.

'Would I be able to help out here for a while? I want to know more about how you guys do the tastings. Would you be able to show me?'

Ant blocked her view of Chris.

'I would be more zan delighted.' He flicked the counter several times with the white cloth that had previously lay folded over his shoulder, thus removing any imaginary specks of dust. 'Ze art of serving wine is a talent zat has been bred into my family for generations. A skill zat, fortunately, can be learned if the pupil is apt and eager.'

Chris rolled his eyes, grabbed a glass from under the counter, put it on the glossy top, and tipped in one inch of white wine from a bottle he had near at hand. 'In other words, grab a glass and pour.'

Bronwyn laughed.

'Ugh!' Ant shut his eyes in revulsion. 'Ze oaf's manners are as simple as his T-shirt.'

'I happen to like this T-shirt.' Chris glared at him.

'I'm sorry,' Ant's eye's widened, 'do you wear that colour for fashion?' Behind his hand, he said to Bronwyn, ''Tis worse than we thought!'

The demonstration continued much like this for the rest of the morning. At first, she just hung back and watched Ant and Chris do it. She wasn't afraid of pouring wine. That was the easy bit. It was the questions that stressed her out.

Luckily, there were cheat cards on the counter. These were meant for the wine tasters, but Bronwyn found herself reading them and trying to memorise bits and pieces. Most customers, however, didn't want to talk so much as taste, and the 'wine wankers', as Chris called them, preferred to talk to each other rather than the bar staff.

'Spotted any yet?' Chris asked her with a grin.

'Not yet,' she returned his smile, knowing from her uni days that you could definitely pick them out of a crowd.

A few days and a couple more shifts later, she spotted two. They approached the bar in a leisurely fashion, pausing over the merchandise in the store, muttering to each other softly, as they surveyed all before them with a critical eye. Having completed a preliminary inspection they finally approached the bar.

Bronwyn clutched the bottle she was holding to her chest as the taller of the two looked down his long nose as her.

'Surprise me,' he murmured and then threw a smug smile at his appreciative friend as though it were private joke shared between them.

She put two glasses on the counter and served them each an inch of cabernet merlot.

The tall man swirled the contents of his glass, taking in the colour, a rich ruby-red. 'Oh, this is elegant,' he noted.

'Very fine.' His companion agreed before they both sank their noses into their glasses to take an extended sniff.

The taller man closed his eyes.

'Interesting character . . .' he nodded. 'Deep . . . but approachable. Very approachable. Tell me,' he said to Bronwyn, 'did Horace Franklin have a hand in this or was it another winemaker?'

Bronwyn decided to play the safe card. 'Horace Franklin has a hand in all our wines. He is never far from the heart of the winery. It's his lifeblood.'

This was true enough, but the wine wanker studied her carefully as though looking for evidence of fault.

His companion lay his glass on a slight angle against a white napkin he had removed from his pocket. 'There is remarkable clarity here. I do like a wine which is distinctive immediately with unmistakable qualities.'

Interesting character, deep, distinctive.

Bronwyn's lips tilted. 'Our wine is exactly like the man who makes them.'

'Intriguing,' said one of the wine wankers. 'I heard that Horace Franklin is retired.'

'Yes, we have a new winemaker now, his son. He's incredibly talented.'

'Indeed?' he responded, and both men finally lifted their glasses to taste. They pursed their lips, pushing their tongues against the rim as they sucked an infinitesimal amount of fluid into their mouths. Bronwyn had to wince at this rather uncomfortable looking start. They did not appear to be bothered by it, swirling the fluid across their tongues much like she did with mouthwash.

'Sensuous,' the first man exclaimed at last. 'I like it. So intense upon the palate.'

'Middle or after?' his companion enquired.

'After,' the taller man announced. 'A full-bodied, well-balanced wonder with definite structure.'

With an air of superiority and a waggle of black bushy brows, the second man flicked his glass. 'You don't think it's not a little *austere* . . . a bit short on the finish?'

'Not at all, not at all,' the first man responded, returning his friend's look with his own haughty expression. 'Can't you taste the wild berries in it?'

'Blackberries,' Bronwyn murmured, tentatively, because in actual fact she had absolutely no idea.

His companion snorted indignantly. 'More like cherries.'

'I also detect vanilla.'

His friend glared at him. 'Nougat, you mean.'

'Nutmeg.'

'Turkish delight!'

'Licorice!'

The nostrils of their pointy noses flared in challenge before they plunged them back into their glasses and moved away from the counter. She turned to Chris, who was stocktaking at the back of the bar. 'I think I've had my first wine wanker encounter since I got here.'

'Count yourself fortunate. I know I'm going to have a bad day when a whole tour bus of them arrives.'

'Is there really that much to be said about wine?' she mused. 'I mean, people say they can taste all these different flavours but at the end of the day all the winemaker puts in the barrel is grapes, right?'

'And an insane amount of skill.'

Chris's expression closed slightly and she knew exactly who was behind her. She had to wonder how long he'd been standing there.

'Jack.' She spun around. He was leaning against the counter, one arm up bent at the elbow, hip out, and that lopsided smile that made her heart drop out of her chest and rattle around her kneecaps.

'I thought you handled them really well, particularly that part about the new winemaker being incredibly talented.' He grinned. 'Did you mean that, I wonder?'

'No one doubts your skill, Jack,' she shrugged. 'It's your attitude that pisses people off.'

There was a chortle from Chris behind her.

'All right, all right.' Jack glared at them both. 'There's no need to gang up on me. Especially since I'm here to give you a message you definitely don't want to miss out on.'

She put her hands on her hips. 'And what would that be?'

'I'm pretty sure your bullmastiff's just gone into labour.'

'What?' Bronwyn threw down the white napkin she'd been holding. 'Chris, I think I've got to go.'

He laughed. 'Sure. I'll see you in a bit.'

She walked straight out the double-doored entrance to the cellar and down the gravelled path with Jack hot on her heels.

'Hey, slow down, you've got plenty of time. It's not like the pups pop out that quickly. It'll be a few hours before she starts pushing.'

'Still, I want to be there every step of the way,' Bronwyn insisted, not slowing her pace at all. 'Is she distressed?'

'No.'

'How did you know she was going into labour then?'

'She started shivering a couple of hours ago and she hasn't moved from that nest of blankets you and Mum made up for her.'

'And you're only just calling me now?' She nearly slipped on the gravel as her feet sped up. She should have stuck to one of Chris's asphalt paths.

'Bron, calm down.'

'Why is it that you're always telling me that?' she grumbled.

'Because you take everything too seriously.' His hand slipped into hers and the complete opposite of calm ricocheted through her chest like the pinball in a slot machine.

'What are you doing?'

'Holding your hand.'

'Why?'

He paused. 'So you don't fall down.'

She removed her hand from his. 'I'm fine,' she swallowed. 'It's just . . . my first time, having puppies, that's all.'

They entered the house, walked straight through it and out the back door into an enclosed patio, where Lydia was hovering over Elsa. The room was light, bright and warm because the walls only rose to waist height, and then it was windows all round. Elsa was whining slightly as she lay on her nest of towels and blankets in one corner.

'Ah! There you are.' Lydia turned around to greet them. 'She's definitely going into labour. If we'd known this was her final week of pregnancy we should have been taking her temperature. Then we could have been more prepared.'

'Really?' Bronwyn bit her lip. 'Should I call a vet?'

'I already have,' Lydia nodded. 'She's on standby if there are any problems.'

'Standby?' Bronwyn yelped. 'We're doing this ourselves?'

'Honey, over ninety-eight per cent of dogs deliver their pups without complications or assistance. She's going to be just fine.'

'Are you sure?'

'Positive.'

'Now,' Lydia dusted her hands, 'I'd love to stay and watch, but as you know we've got that wedding on tomorrow and the staff in the restaurant are feeling the pressure.'

Bronwyn's face dropped even further. 'You're not going to stay and help me?'

'I'll just be down the end of the driveway if you need me. Besides,' Lydia looked slyly at her son, 'Jack will be here.'

'Huh?' The man himself, who had been kneeling on the blankets and gently rubbing the back of Elsa's neck, looked up in surprise.

'It's not like you're harvesting another block today, is it?' Lydia threw at him. 'You can make the time.'

'But –'

'Have fun, you two!'

'Great.' Bronwyn threw up her hands as his mother walked out. She had noticed in the last day or so that the ice in the Franklin household was starting to melt. Chris and Jack were talking again. Not with complete freedom, but at least there was no longer silence at the breakfast table. She was glad she had confessed to both brothers exactly what had happened with her mum. However, seeing them bonding again had certainly raised Lydia's hopes, and the Franklin matriarch seemed to be making it her mission to include Bronwyn in their reconciliation.

Bronwyn turned to Jack with a sigh. 'What are we going to do now?'

'Watch Elsa give birth, I imagine.' He stood up and folded his arms.

Easy for him to say.

This was just the sort of thing that was way out of her comfort zone. She knelt down beside her dog. Elsa whined again, shivered violently and then vomited on her bedding. 'Oh shoot! You poor thing.' She wrapped up the towel filled with vomit and pulled it away from the rest. Elsa's belly tensed near her hands. 'She's having contractions.' Her gaze flicked over her shoulder at Jack. 'Have you ever done this before?'

'Delivered puppies?' he asked.

'No, milked a cow. What do you think?'

He shrugged. 'I may have witnessed one dog of a different breed doing this under someone else's supervision, but –'

'Oh good.' She breathed a sigh of relief. 'So you're an expert then.'

'I wouldn't go that far.'

'Well, *pretend*!' she insisted. 'Because I'm freaking out here.'

'Bronwyn –'

'I know,' she sighed, 'calm down.'

He grinned and picked up the dirty towel. 'I'll get rid of this and get some more.'

She threw him a grateful look as he walked out, and lay a soothing hand on Elsa's head. Her dog didn't push her snout into her palm like she usually did, but only passively accepted the caress.

'It's okay, girl,' Bronwyn said firmly. 'You're going to be just fine. I'm right here. I'm going to get you through this. Me and Jack.'

Jack re-entered the patio with a new towel just in time to hear the promise.

'Okay.' She stood up, dusting her hands by her sides. 'So what else do we need for this? Maybe some plastic bags, rubber gloves? Scissors to cut the cord?'

'Er . . . I don't think we do that. It's not a human birth.'

She wasn't listening. 'Oh shit,' her eyes widened. 'Should I be boiling some water?'

'Why on earth would you need to boil water?'

'That's what they always do in the movies, isn't it?' Bronwyn explained. 'Whenever someone is having a baby at home, someone always boils some water.'

He came forward, grinning ruefully as he knelt down to lay the towel. He ran a hand down Elsa's back. 'Okay, so I don't know what movies you've been watching, but I don't think I've seen them.'

'No,' she stuck out her tongue, 'they wouldn't be your sort of movies.'

'Not enough intelligent commentary?' He smiled.

'No, not enough guns.'

He sighed. 'Guns do make for good action sequences.'

She knelt down beside him. 'We're completely moving off topic here.' She swiped her hand down in a cutting motion. 'Focus.' She bit her lip. 'Will there be a lot of blood?'

'Not unless she needs a caesarean.'

Her eyes widened to saucers. 'You can do that?'

'No,' he laughed, 'I can't! We'll definitely be calling the vet by that stage. But there's honestly no need to start panicking, Numbat. We've got this.'

'I'm not panicking.' She tried to moderate her tone but then ruined it by jumping up. 'I think I *will* get a bucket of water. The unboiled kind.'

'Okay,' he nodded. 'That's probably a good idea. I'll get more towels. And that rubber glove idea might not be a bad plan. The pups are a little icky right after birth.'

So after they rushed around for five minutes collecting the various items that they thought might be needed and returned to Elsa's side, it was all a bit of an anticlimax because nothing happened for over an hour. The two of them were left just sitting there on the towels, stroking Elsa's back as she whined uncomfortably from time to time.

The last thing Bronwyn had expected was to spend the afternoon sitting on the floor with Jack, especially after the chaos of the last few days. There was the harvest, the extraction and her 'I used to be in love with you' confession. Yet here she was, happily hanging out with Jack and a pregnant dog.

Unable to handle the silence, she had to say something. 'So how are you and your dad? Have you spoken to him about what I told you yet?'

'So you think I owe him an apology too, do you?' Jack returned dryly.

Her gaze flicked to him in surprise. 'He said that to you?'

'Yeah.' He ran a hand through his hair.

The vulnerable expression on his face made her chest ache.

'And I guess in light of everything you told me, I can see why he might.'

'He thinks you abandoned the family. Nobody knew where you were, Jack. And you didn't make contact for months.'

'Yeah,' he nodded. 'It's hard to wrap my head around it. I've been operating in this place where nobody gave a damn about me for so long, it's hard to accept that I was wrong.'

She licked dry lips. 'Change is hard. So is starting again. Trust me, I know.'

He hung his head. It was a humble Jack, one she was seeing more and more every day since his return. 'I'll have to talk to him again. Explain everything. Tell him what you told me.'

'I'm sure he'll get it. You both thought you'd been abandoned. It'll take forgiveness on both sides.'

'It'll be harder with Chris,' said Jack.

'Why?'

'Because I'll always feel guilt where he's concerned.'

'I think everybody will,' Bronwyn shrugged. 'Don't forget, I was there too. Drinking, partying, yelling from the sidelines. It's not like Claudia and I told you two to stop behaving like morons. And it was Chris's fault too.'

Elsa whined and Bronwyn quickly reached over and patted her belly. 'Stay brave, girl. Stay brave.'

'You always know exactly what to say, Numbat.' He smiled ruefully at her.

She rolled her eyes. 'Not always. We both know I've made some massive stuff-ups in my life . . .' She swallowed. 'Some poor judgement calls. I mean, that thing with my mum, with you, the plane ticket . . . I'm so embarrassed.'

'Don't worry about it,' he assured her. 'It's ancient history.'

'Ancient history.' She repeated it more to convince herself than him. If it was that much in the past, then why did she feel awareness spreading through her chest? Why did watching his hand gently stroking Elsa's coat put a lump in her throat and a restlessness in her bones?

'There's a lot of water under the bridge,' Jack began. He seemed nervous for some reason and she couldn't fathom it.

'A lot of messed-up stuff that went on five years ago. Dad's not the only person I need to apologise to. I treated you pretty badly too, Bron. When I think back on how much I teased you.'

'Yeah,' she pushed his shoulder, 'you did. You were hell to be around sometimes.'

He pushed her back. 'Because you were so easy to rile.'

'Well, I got over that.' She looked away.

'You did. And I need to tell you something.' He didn't meet her eyes. 'Remember that time I kissed you?'

She licked her dry lips, and didn't look up either. 'Yes.'

How could I forget?

'It was your first kiss,' he said softly. 'And I was a dick and I ruined it and I didn't apologise.'

'Yes.' She wasn't going to help him out at all.

'Well, I want to apologise now. And I want to tell you why I did it.'

This time when he spoke he turned towards her, pinning her eyes with his so she couldn't look away. He reached out and grabbed her hand, sending her blood pressure through the roof.

'The first kiss is one of those milestone moments in life. It's like one of those things that stays with you for good. You always know who it was with, what time of day it was, where it was. It's like, twenty years from now you could be sitting around a table at a party somewhere and someone asks you, "So who was your first kiss," and just like that,' he snapped his fingers, 'you're right back in that moment, no matter where you are. I guess I wanted to be that guy. I wanted to be that person that your mind flies straight to whenever you think about your first kiss. No matter where you were or who you were with. I . . . I wanted to stay with you forever.'

Bronwyn's jaw slowly dropped open. Of all the things anyone had ever said to her, in her entire life, that was top ten. No! It was simply number one. The most gorgeous, sweet, romantic thing anyone had, *hands down*, ever confided in her.

'Say something.' His shoulders slumped.

Elsa grunted, her stiffening leg caught Bronwyn's eye and she turned her head just in time to see the dog's vulva dilate. A glistening package was only just visible at the opening. She gasped. 'Shit and biscuits! We're having a baby!'

They both turned to Elsa, who whimpered gratefully and then turned her head to lick at herself before pushing again.

'It's coming!' Bronwyn cried.

'Come on, girl,' Jack encouraged. 'You're doing good. Keeping going.'

It was now absolutely clear that the first puppy was on its way out, the fluid-filled amniotic sack beginning to protrude as the pup's head emerged. A couple of pushes later the puppy, still wrapped in placenta, rolled onto the towels.

'What do we do now?' Bronwyn asked, quickly shoving her hands in some gloves.

'No, wait!' Jack put a hand on her shoulder. 'You have to let Elsa do her thing. This is the way she first bonds with her pups. We can't interfere yet.'

'Right.' Bronwyn held her breath.

They watched in fascination as Elsa bit the umbilical cord off and began to lick her puppy clean of its sack, actually eating some of the afterbirth to get it off. It wasn't the easiest thing to watch but it was so natural. The baby curled up under this rough licking but submitted to it, its eyes still firmly shut, its little black paws up protectively around its face as it took its first breaths.

'It's so cute,' Bronwyn exclaimed.

Elsa nudged it with her nose towards her nipples. The wayward pup didn't seem to understand.

'I think we can help out here,' said Jack and carefully knelt, picking up the pup. 'Come on, little guy.' He moved its face against its mother's nipples. As soon as it felt Elsa's straining teat, it immediately latched on.

'Oh, Elsa.' Bronwyn patted her dog's head. 'You did so well. That was amazing!'

'She's not done yet.' Jack grinned at her.

'How many more, do you think?'

'I don't know,' he shrugged. 'Could be as many as fifteen!'

Bronwyn gasped, feeling vaguely sick. 'Seriously? Elsa.' She turned to her canine friend again. 'I want you to know, I have so much respect for you.'

Elsa whined.

'I think number two is on its way,' said Jack.

After that, Elsa birthed a pup every half hour or so until she had nine miniature dogs in varying shades of black, brown and tawny fighting for an available nipple. Bronwyn had since washed the first one by dabbing it gently with a towel wet with warm water. She picked him up, stroking his velvety fur as Jack cleaned another.

'I can't believe all these little guys were inside her. She sure carried them well. What should we name them?'

'Oh,' Jack raised his eyebrows, 'so I get a say, do I?'

'If you want one,' she responded shyly.

'I'd name him Shiraz.' He indicated the one she was holding.

She rolled her eyes. 'Let me guess, these others are Merlot, Pinot and Cabernet.'

'How'd you guess?' He lifted the one he was washing so she could see its wrinkled little face. 'Don't forget about sweet little Chardy here. Bright, zesty and the colour of French oak.'

She laughed. 'All right, you've convinced me. But we've still got to come up with another four grape varieties for the others.'

'That shouldn't be too hard.'

She picked up another puppy and nuzzled it. Its rough little tongue tentatively licked her cheek. Her eyes flew to Jack's. 'Did you see that?'

'Yeah,' his lips twitched, 'we'll call him Champagne. Looks like he's a flirt already.'

She laughed. 'Thanks for doing this with me, Jack. I know we haven't seen eye to eye lately with the whole buying into Oak Hills thing.'

He gave a deep sigh and put the puppy down. 'It's not that I don't want you to be part of all this. It's just that . . .'

'What?'

He raised his eyebrows at her. 'What do you think is going to happen if I stick around and you stick around and we all work together as one big happy family?'

'I don't know.' Bronwyn shrugged, standing up, dusting her hands against the sides of her jeans. 'Maybe we'll pull Oak Hills out of trouble and back into the limelight. You're good at the creative side and I'm good at the organisation side. Chris and your mum have the rest covered. Your dad won't have to worry anymore.'

'No, Bron,' Jack also stood up, 'that's not the sort of complication I'm talking about.'

'Then what?'

He reached over and took her face between his palms. His mouth took hers in a kiss so sweet her body literally melted. It was like sailing into a harbour after decades at sea.

Is this really happening?

She lifted her hands to place them on his firm shoulders as his arms wrapped more firmly around her, his lips a bruising crush under the strength of his feeling.

Yep, he's real.

She kissed him back with all the pent-up angst of years of wanting. Not really caring, in the moment, how it ended.

And then it did.

A cough in the room caused them to break apart.

'Well,' smiled Lydia, hands on hips. 'About bloody time!'

Chapter 26

If there was one way to give yourself a reputation as a slut around the office, showing up every morning in Sebastian Rowlands's car and leaving with him every night would have to be up there.

It didn't matter that Juliet had put it around that Claudia's home was under siege. Criminal gang lord Leon McCall was after her bacon and a little organisation called the police had been called in to do a full-blown investigation.

Ha!

The investigation, *full blown* as it was, had led absolutely nowhere. The police had combed Bronwyn's ransacked apartment for fingerprints and found none. They'd interviewed Peter Goldman and elicited no more information from him than Claudia had.

They did manage to contact his ex-wife, Freya Goldman, in Melbourne.

But the only thing she had to add was, 'Peter Goldman is a lying, gambling, manipulative bastard who deserves what's coming to him,' which, frankly, Claudia had known already.

With Claudia and Sebastian's help, the police did manage to secure a search warrant for The Quiet Gentleman. A couple of days after the break-in at Claudia's apartment they searched the property, including the shed out the back. They found floodlights on stands and pieces of temporary fencing; the kind of equipment that might be used to light up an arena in the middle of the bush for a dog fight. However, much to Claudia's disgust, they made no arrests because apparently the evidence was not solid enough.

'You're not thinking rationally,' Sebastian had explained to her. 'Lights like that can be used for other things. They said they used them for when they had functions that spilled into the back car park.'

'And the fencing?'

'For the same thing.'

'When did they last have a function like that there?' Claudia scoffed. 'Believe me, the pub is not that popular.'

'Maybe that's something we can look into,' Sebastian had agreed. 'But in the meantime you need to be more objective about this and less emotional.'

It was difficult not to be with the smears against her name at work. Anna Mavis was having a field day. And the problem was, she wasn't actually completely off base.

The tension at her place of residence was . . . well . . . tense.

Sebastian owned a two-storey townhouse in Leederville. It was stylishly masculine and sparsely furnished. His bedroom was on the top floor while he had given her the guest one on the ground level. She had her own bathroom and toilet so there was absolutely no danger of them running into each other naked, no matter what her work colleagues might think.

What they did share was the kitchen. And that was more than enough.

At work she could exile Sebastian to the business side of her life. He made no entrances into her personal world except in fantasy, which of late she had managed to curtail quite firmly.

However, that first night when they'd walked into his home, he'd shrugged off his jacket and pulled off his tie, tossing them both on the couch in front of the kitchen. Sebastian was always so neat and precise, to see him even in slight disarray made her mouth immediately dry. He didn't seem to notice her discomfort and walked straight into the kitchen, pulling a couple of takeaway menus from on top of the microwave.

'So what do you want for dinner?'

'Really?' She wrinkled her nose. 'Haven't you got any real food we can work with?'

Automatically, she went over and opened his fridge. He stepped forward as though to stop her and then halted, obviously realising it was too late.

His fridge contained five items.

A bottle of Oak Hills Chardonnay.

A bottle of Oak Hills Semillion Sauvignon Blanc.

A bottle of Oak Hills Pinot Gris.

A bottle of milk.

A tub of margarine.

Her eyes widened and flew to his. She was both surprised and pleased to see something that looked suspiciously like a flush emerging from the base of his neck and moving up his throat.

She smiled. 'I think we're going to need more than that.'

He coughed. 'Yes, I believe so.' She swiped his keys off the counter where he had dropped them and passed them to him. 'Come on, we're going out again.'

'What?' his eyes narrowed. 'Where?'

'Grocery shopping. You may be able to live on that but I can't.'

'But it's already seven o'clock. What about dinner?'

'I'll rustle something up when we get back.'

'Is this absolutely necessary?' he demanded. He pushed one of the menus forward. It was for an Italian restaurant that did home delivery. 'This place is very good.'

'I'm sure it is. But then we'll have today's problem tomorrow. Besides, what will I have for breakfast in the morning?'

He opened his mouth and then shut it again. 'All right. You win. Let's go.'

They found themselves back in his car. He had not put either his jacket or his tie back on and had run a hand through his black hair, leaving some strands sticking up slightly. She smiled secretly out the window. It was nice having the upper hand for a change.

He took her to his local, a small independent store with quality, fresh produce. At least he had good taste. The one thing Claudia couldn't get over with city folk was their complete lack of care for their digestive system. No matter how rushed she was, she always made time for a good breakfast. Snagging a trolley on their way in, she started in the fruit aisle, immediately hovering around the berries. The brightly coloured fruit, so plump and juicy, smelled like home. Her interest in them was clearly shared by the woman beside her, who was examining a punnet of strawberries.

'They look so good, don't they? Like they were just picked this morning.' Her child, a little boy, who was sitting in the front section of the trolley, noisily blew bubbles into a juice box.

'They do, don't they?' Claudia agreed, her hand hovering between the raspberries and the blueberries. Sebastian had walked on to the apples. He'd placed three pink ladies in a bag and then returned to place them in Claudia's trolley.

'How about some berries?' she said brightly.

'I don't need any.' He shook his head. 'But feel free to get some for yourself.'

She frowned. 'Yeah, but I kind of wanted to get a selection.'

'What are we going to do with a whole bunch of berries?'

Good point.

She brightened. 'We could have smoothies for breakfast. With yogurt and milk. You'll love it. Totally healthy. Berries are a superfood.'

He gave her a long look. 'Are you sure we have time before work? I think a bowl of cereal is just fine.'

'Where's your sense of adventure?'

As if to punctuate this question, the toddler in the trolley giggled and squirted Sebastian with his apple juice.

'Oh no!' cried his mother. 'I'm so sorry.' She reached into her handbag for two tissues and passed them to Sebastian, who quickly began to wipe his now soiled designer shirt.

'That's all right,' he said with a sigh.

'Kids are so unpredictable,' she confided to Claudia, and then said with a wink, 'but I'm sure you two will work that out when you have your own.'

Sebastian choked, dropped the tissues he'd been using and hastily bent to pick them up. As he did so the kid kicked him in the face.

'Ow!' His hand went to his eye.

'Oh, shoot!' said the boy's mother. 'Wasn't I just saying. Felix! Naughty!' Felix giggled as Sebastian stumbled back in pain.

Claudia covered the laugh that fought to escape her mouth. 'Are you okay?' She reached out and grabbed Sebastian's face, drawing it towards her.

'I'm fine,' he muttered.

'Let me see.'

He took his hand away from his eye and she noted there was no damage. It looked a little red and watery but otherwise perfectly fine. Both eyes were now trained on her face and then her lips. She was finding it a little difficult to look away. He reached up and warm hands tightened around her wrists, drawing her hands down.

'Perfectly fine.'

'Yes. So I see.' She cleared her throat and finally managed to break eye contact.

'Oh good,' said the woman beside them. Her voice somehow seemed far too loud and bright for the moment. 'I better leave you two to get on with it before I do any more damage.'

As she rolled on, Sebastian regarded her steadily. 'Let's just get this over with, okay?'

Claudia picked up a punnet of raspberries and put them in the trolley. They moved around the store and managed to buy a selection of meat and veg without further spills or violence. They got to the checkout and Claudia was beginning to think they were home and hosed until the lady with the little boy moved into the line behind them.

She grinned. 'Don't worry, Felix has finished his juice box.'

All the same, Sebastian took one look at her and pushed past Claudia. 'I'll pay,' he said, but before he presented his credit card to the assistant, her till started beeping loudly. While they were all trying to figure out what was going on, the manager and assistant manager appeared from nowhere. One of them was carrying a giant hamper, which they placed in front of Sebastian.

'Congratulations!' they announced grandly. 'You are our one thousandth customer!'

'We are?' Claudia's eyes rounded.

'Can you get in closer to your partner for the photo?' The assistant manager was holding a camera.

'No photos please,' said Sebastian, just as Felix's mother shoved Claudia into him and the assistant manager snapped the shot.

'Oh, that's just lovely,' the mother exclaimed. 'A nice end to your day, wouldn't you say?'

'Wonderful,' Sebastian responded dryly, shoving the giant hamper none too gently into the trolley and heading straight to the car park without watching to see if Claudia was following.

'So that was fun,' Claudia began tentatively as they hopped into his car.

'Like getting a tooth pulled.'

She turned her face to the window so he wouldn't see her smiling. 'Can't wait to see what's in that hamper.'

When they got back to his townhouse, Sebastian went

straight upstairs to have a shower. She didn't blame him for wanting to change out of his juice-stained shirt. However, when he came downstairs for dinner afterwards, she had to do a double take.

Sebastian Rowlands in a suit was eye catching, powerful and incredibly charismatic. However, Seb in a T-shirt and jeans made her weak at the knees. It was like meeting the man for the first time. With all his armour off, he actually looked approachable – vulnerable even.

She could totally curl up on the couch in front of the TV to watch a movie with this guy.

Careful, Claudia.

He's still your boss.

Still off limits.

One thing was becoming clearer and clearer every day. It wouldn't take Seb long to break her heart. She was looking for a real relationship. The kind her parents had. By his own admission, he didn't do that sort of thing.

Sebastian Rowlands didn't date.

He didn't have girlfriends.

He didn't have relationships.

He had affairs – very short, intense ones. Much like the image he'd conveyed to her in his office the other day.

'I would use you, hurt you and discard you.'

Is that really what you want?

If being in town was supposed to sort out her love life, then Sebastian Rowlands was the last thing she needed.

She turned her attention back to her meal. She had to stop thinking about him like this. A happily ever after between them was completely impossible. The trip to the grocery store really hadn't helped her frame of mind.

While he'd showered, she'd kicked off her shoes and put two fillets of fish in a frying pan with a light crumb. When he came out she was sipping her father's semillon sauvignon blanc in front of a plate of fish and a fresh garden salad. She'd plated a portion for him as well and put it on the other side of the table next to napkins and cutlery.

'I have to admit,' he said as he sat down, 'this does look fantastic.'

'Totally worth being kicked in the eye for?' she teased.

Reluctantly, he smiled, making her heart skip a beat. 'So what was in the hamper? I'm sure you opened it the second we walked in.'

She winced. 'Do you really want to know?'

'Why not?'

She got up and brought the basket over, taking the bits out one by one. 'His and hers towels, a selection of nuts, biscuits and fruit, two coffee mugs, a box of chocolates, champagne and dinner for two at . . . wait for it . . . Seashells!'

He snatched the envelope off her. 'Give me that. You can't be serious.'

His expression of horror as he pulled the voucher from its pink sleeve only caused her to laugh harder.

'Come on. We've got to go out as much as we can now before we have kids! Remember?'

He slapped the envelope down on the table and picked up his fork. 'You're really enjoying this, aren't you?'

She shrugged. 'Call it revenge for thinking I had Bronwyn stuffed in a closet.'

'That's an exaggeration.' He looked at her reprovingly. 'I didn't honestly think that. I just find it very difficult to read you sometimes.'

'You find *me* difficult to read!' She gasped. 'You're not exactly an open book.'

He raised an eyebrow. 'What do you want to know?'

Everything.

The word whispered across her heart, both startling and alarming her. When had her fascination with Sebastian Rowlands turned into something more? Before she could stop herself, she asked, 'Well, what do you *really* think about kids? Do you want to have some one day?'

He didn't answer immediately and she knew that she'd overstepped the line again.

Good one, Claudia.

And then he surprised her.

'I've never considered myself a family man. The hours I work are too long and I don't think you should ever commit to something like that unless you're willing to put in a hundred and ten per cent.'

'Is that because you were a foster kid?' she asked quietly.

'Maybe. Moving from family to family was never easy but I did get used to it.'

Used to it? How could anyone get used to being told that their home was no longer their home? That they had to move on, again? It would have been awful. Never really belonging anywhere, never having a constant in your life – making it difficult to trust anyone but yourself. No wonder he was the way he was.

Guilt seized her.

From the moment they'd met, she had never been completely honest with him. She was masquerading as Cyril Eddings's niece, for goodness sake. He probably thought she was trying to play him for a fool like she had been doing with everybody else.

She didn't want to participate in these games anymore. Not when he'd opened his house to her on top of everything else.

'I'm not Cyril's niece.'

The piece of fish on the way to his mouth stalled before he slowly lowered his fork. 'What?'

'We're not even related. He made a mistake.' She rushed the words out. 'I just went along with it to show you up because I was mad at you for being too arrogant.'

'Am I supposed to apologise now?' He raised an eyebrow.

'For being too arrogant? No, you can't help that.'

'I don't know whether to be relieved or insulted.'

'It wasn't my point,' she shrugged. 'Cyril's mistake and my encouragement of it is my bad behaviour, not yours. When Bronwyn got into trouble, it just got out of hand. It seemed too risky to tell the truth after that.'

'Why are you telling me now?'

'Because,' she put her hand over his, 'I want you to trust me and I want to trust you.'

A pin-drop could have been heard in the silence that followed. He pulled his hand away.

'Okay, what did I say wrong now?' she asked in resignation.

His eyes returned to his food. 'You didn't say anything wrong, Claudia.'

'You're angry with me.'

'No.'

'You're disappointed.'

'Not really.'

'Then say something, at the very least that you forgive me?'

'What's to forgive?' he snapped. 'I never thought for one second you were Cyril's niece.' Abruptly, he pushed his plate away. 'So how are things going with Tom?'

'Tom?' She blinked at his sudden change of subject.

'He must have been disappointed when you didn't show up at the Costello's fundraiser.'

'Honestly, I wouldn't know,' she returned crossly. 'I haven't seen him recently.'

'Why not?' The way he said it was almost accusatory.

'I don't see how that's any of your business.'

'Good,' he finally approved. 'Because you and I aren't friends. You staying here, that was Cyril's idea. And as much as I wouldn't like to see you in any trouble, by general rule I don't do rescue or go out of my way for anyone other than my clients.'

'Of course.' She tossed her head flippantly though her heart ached from the rejection. 'I know that.'

Abruptly, he stood up, taking his half-empty plate to the sink. 'If I were you, I'd focus your energy on Leon McCall and putting that dog ring away. That's certainly what I intend to do. The sooner we can get you back to your own place, the better.'

With that, he left the room to go upstairs and didn't come down again till morning.

So much for that movie.

It was hard to sink all your energy into an investigation that was going nowhere but she tried anyway. Over the next few days she took her lunch break at The Quiet Gentleman. She detested their food and the place was too rowdy when all she really wanted after a hectic morning was to gather her thoughts. Nonetheless, she knew that now it was all about watching and waiting. They were at a complete dead end in terms of the investigation. If they wanted to catch these crooks, they had to observe them slip up or leave a clue that was more telling than all the rest.

She did notice that Jet, Frank's young protégé, had his hand bandaged the last time she went in. A dog bite perhaps? When she questioned him about it as much as she dared, he didn't go into any details though.

'This?' He raised his hand. 'Nothing that won't heal.'

'How'd you do it?'

'By being stupid.' He grinned and would say nothing more.

Apart from that, the hour-long vigils gained her no further insight, unless she was hoping to make Frank believe she had the hots for him. Several times he caught her watching him and gave her a slow wink. She nearly gagged on her burger.

Seb was not impressed when she was back from lunch late on Friday either. Even less happy when he found out where she'd been.

'All you're doing is giving them someone to be wary of. If they know you're watching, they'll just be more careful.'

'Maybe, maybe not.' She lifted her chin stubbornly. 'Today I noticed one of the guys had an injury on his hand, could be from training a dog.'

'Or he could have cut himself in the kitchen,' Seb retorted.

Claudia tossed her head. 'Don't stress. I'm pretty sure Frank has no idea who I am, except one of his regulars, of course.'

'You don't know that,' he said sternly. 'You need to be cautious. The police said most of the time they take these guys out investigating some other crime, like illegal drugs or domestic violence.'

'Great,' Claudia fumed. 'So you're saying they catch them by fluke.'

'They are very hard to spring. Most of the dog fighters will not be notified of the time and venue of a fight till half an hour before. A text message will go out to all interested parties and then it's on. It's not like there will be a memo you can stumble upon a week in advance. They are very careful. They have to be.'

'Well, isn't that why we should be on their tails every second?'

He tilted his head. 'I think the point is, you can't be, Claudia. You're wasting your time.'

You could say defeat almost conquered her until Bronwyn's photo text messages had starting popping up on her phone the following day. Elsa had had her babies and they were *gorgeous*. Bronwyn sent a picture of each of them cradled in the palms of two hands. They were a range of browns from light to tawny with cute black snouts and such large eyes. Their fur was wrinkled and looked velvety to touch. She wished she could have been there to welcome them into the world.

She called Bronwyn immediately after receiving the pictures. 'They are so cute!'

'Aren't they just?' Bronwyn gushed. 'And so affectionate already. I'm holding one on my chest right now and she's snuggled right in.'

Claudia's heart melted. 'What are we going to do with them all?'

'Honestly, I don't know.' Bronwyn whispered. 'I guess it's a bit much to be asking your parents to take on the responsibility of housing nine dogs. But I love them all so much already. They need to have a good home.'

'Absolutely,' Claudia agreed. 'And we'll make sure they do. I'm certain there will be some locals who are interested in having a new pet.'

'For sure,' Bronwyn agreed. 'We just have to keep them safe.' There was a pregnant pause. 'Claudia, the very thought of . . . of –'

'Don't say it.' Claudia shut her eyes. 'But I do think it's time you warned my parents and brothers. Knowing the babies have probably been born will make Leon more desperate than ever.'

'Sure. How are things coming with McCall?'

'Not well,' Claudia sighed. 'But I don't want to ruin your moment with bad news.'

It was exactly why she hadn't told Bronwyn yet about the break-in at her apartment or the fact that she'd moved in with Sebastian Rowlands.

At least, that was the reason she *told* herself she hadn't said anything to Bronwyn.

The truth was slightly more complicated. The problem with Sebastian was that he was becoming a rather all-consuming fixture in her life. And she was afraid, very afraid, that she was beginning to like it just a little too much.

Chapter 27

Life after kissing Jack was a notebook of questions.

She really wasn't too sure what to make of it and didn't want to get her hopes up. When Lydia came in and interrupted them, they had no chance to talk afterwards. Lydia had wanted to know all about the delivery of each of the puppies. By the time she had held and cooed over every single one, Horace and Chris came in, also keen to view the new arrivals. The romantic moment she and Jack shared melted into a family gathering.

Not that she begrudged them this. It was about time, in her opinion. Claudia called as well, gushing over the photos she'd sent her. However, after they rang off, Bronwyn knew if they really wanted to keep the puppies safe, they needed to bring everyone into their confidence.

'Er . . . guys,' she said, as she nervously rubbed Shiraz's back, 'there's something I need to tell you.'

The news that Elsa was a breeder rescued from a dog-fighting ring did not go down well.

'Did you say Leon McCall's involved?' Lydia demanded.

'Shouldn't we call the police or something?' Jack's eyebrows twitched in concern.

Bronwyn waved it away. 'Don't worry. The police are already involved. They're doing a full-blown investigation in Perth. Claudia's keeping tabs on it.'

'My daughter's involved in this too?' Horace was not happy.

'She actually knows more than me,' Bronwyn admitted. 'The important thing is to just keep these little guys a secret until the crims are caught.'

'We can definitely do that.' Chris nodded.

Jack folded his arms. 'It's also a matter of keeping an eye on who's coming and going from the property.'

Horace agreed. 'We have to be careful.'

As unpleasant as the subject was, it was great to see the family all in one room interacting at last. Almost like before, but not quite. There was still a lot of anguish in their eyes. Especially when Horace and Jack spoke to one another – like there was a thread of something else, something unspoken.

It gave her hope, however, that telling the truth about what her mother had done had really helped Jack. She could tell he wanted to talk to his dad about it, and the sooner he got it off his chest, the better. So when the opportunity came, she suggested they go on a walk together.

'Horace, weren't you saying that the sauvignon blanc is almost ready to come off the vine?' she asked.

'I haven't been out there today yet.'

'Then you should go now with Jack.' Bronwyn threw him a pointed look. 'He'll want to be part of the decision.'

Jack had met her eyes for a long moment. She saw both gratitude and hesitation there. 'That would be good.'

He and Horace left the room, leaving Bronwyn, Lydia and Chris with the newborns.

'Horace has asked me what I think about selling you a slice of Oak Hills,' Lydia said. 'What do you think, Chris?'

Bronwyn held her breath.

'If you're asking me whether I mind,' Chris shrugged, 'the answer is no. We've both seen what a great addition to the team Bronwyn makes.'

'Yes, I'm sorry I was a little reluctant at the start, love,' Lydia apologised. 'I was trying to get Jack back to town and I didn't want you to upset those plans. You and Chris were both so against the idea.'

'Can you blame us?' Chris demanded. 'It hasn't been smooth sailing.'

'But it's been worth it.' Lydia turned to Bronwyn with a wink. 'Right?'

Bronwyn bit her lip. 'Lydia, I'm not sure what you think you witnessed just now but I wouldn't set much store by it. It is Jack, after all.'

'Have I missed something?' Chris asked.

'Jack kissed Bronwyn,' Lydia announced. 'They're getting together.'

Chris clutched his heart. 'The betrayal!'

Bronwyn waved her hands in denial. 'I don't know that we're *getting together*.'

'You don't want to be with my son?' Lydia asked crossly.

'Playing fast and loose,' Chris announced archly. 'I never expected this of you, Numbat.'

'No,' Lydia folded her arms, 'neither did I, because the world can see you're more than half in love with him.'

Bronwyn felt her face heat up and knew she'd turned bright pink.

'Yes,' she agreed. 'I am. But is he in love with me?'

When she thought back over the conversation leading up to the kiss there hadn't been much talk of that. She didn't think her heart could take it if all Jack wanted was a fling. She would like to think she was smart enough now not to get her hopes up too high. Jack was a playboy fresh from France and a bevy of gorgeous women he'd surely left behind there. She had stupidly admitted yesterday that she had once been in love with him. That would have given his ego a nice little boost. Now suddenly he was turning on all the charm. Her heart sank.

Is he just trying to have a bit of fun with me like he always used to?

She swallowed hard, not wanting to believe this but struggling to find evidence against it. She thought of the sweet things he had said to her during Elsa's labour, the story of their first kiss.

I wanted to stay with you forever.

In hindsight, away from his distracting presence, the words seemed almost too good to be true. Jack was an accomplished flirt who had perfected the art of the chase.

Was she just another conquest, conveniently placed in his path? He seemed to think that the two of them working together would inevitably lead to an affair. Was that based on his feelings for her, or his skills at seduction?

She had no idea.

If she had hopes that he would come to see her later that evening, they were soon dashed. He stayed out late with his father. The two of them didn't come home till after she had gone to bed. And while she understood that the conversation they were having was more than five years overdue, she couldn't help but worry that it was also a very convenient excuse for Jack not to have to explain himself.

Oh for goodness sake, Bronwyn!

It was just one kiss.

One little moment of nothing. Couldn't she just treat it as such, rather than making it such a big deal in her head? Didn't she have more important things to worry about?

As it turned out, she did.

The next morning she rose early and went downstairs to check on Elsa and her pups.

They were gone.

All of them.

Telling the family had clearly not improved security much, though she could hardly blame them when they'd all been asleep. Her included. The flyscreen in one window of the patio had been ripped from the frame. The dogs had not escaped.

They'd been taken.

Her heart leapt into her throat. She felt a rage so deep it burned her soul.

There was no way Leon McCall was getting away with this.

And so the chase began.

Chapter 28

Four days after Claudia moved in with Sebastian, one day after her last fruitless lunch at The Quiet Gentleman, five minutes before noon at Hanks and Eddings, Claudia received a phone call from the brother she had not spoken to in years.

'Hey, Claud.'

'Jack? So you finally got around to calling me.'

'Yeah. So how's it going?'

'Don't you dare pretend like this is not a big deal.'

'Okay, I won't.'

'You're a complete jerk and you know it!'

'Yeah, I do.'

'Leaving us high and dry and tearing off to France.'

'That's not exactly how it went down but I don't have time to explain right now.'

'Like hell you don't,' Claudia returned crossly. 'I hope Bronwyn's sticking both her feet into all your plans. You thoroughly deserve it.'

'I wish she was.' Jack's voice was too serious for her liking. 'But she's gone, Claud.'

'What? Gone where?'

'Drove off a few hours ago. I'm calling because I was hoping she was with you.'

'What do you mean? Why would she be with me?'

After the conversation they'd had last night about the dogs she couldn't imagine Bronwyn suddenly wanting to leave Oak Hills. Something must have happened.

'The dogs are gone.'

'*What?*' Claudia repeated.

'All of them. They're missing. Someone has stolen them.'

Claudia's blood ran cold. '*When?*'

'Last night. They were taken right out of our back patio. The flyscreen was cut right down the middle. There're tyre tracks out the front of the house. They came prepared, as though they knew exactly what they were looking for.'

Claudia clutched the phone, her knuckles turning white. 'That's because they *did*.' She swore.

'You think this is Leon McCall's handiwork, don't you?'

'So Bronwyn told you.'

'Yeah, she told us everything, except that she was going to take off this morning,' he responded crossly.

'She's probably on her way here.'

'To do what exactly?' Jack demanded. 'Where are you with the investigation?'

She gave him a brief rundown, which wasn't much.

He was silent for a moment. 'I'm coming to Perth too.'

'We don't need you.'

'Yeah, like all those times you didn't need me when you were teenagers.'

'Ha!' Claudia threw at him. 'Believe me, that ship has sailed. I stopped relying on you a long time ago.'

'Maybe you did,' he said softly, 'and I'm sorry for that. But right now it doesn't matter because I'm helping you out whether you like it or not.'

'Save yourself the bother.'

'I'm coming to Perth.'

'You're not welcome here.'

'It's too late, I'm calling from the road. I'd have to say I'm about two hours behind Bronwyn, who should be in Perth within the next half hour.'

Claudia chewed on her lower lip. 'She's probably out of her mind with worry about those dogs.'

'Exactly. You should have seen her with them yesterday. She adores those pups.'

'Don't worry, I'll calm her down.'

'And then what?'

Claudia ground her teeth. 'And then we'll go after Leon McCall to get our dogs back. I hear he likes playing poker at The Crown. Maybe we can win them back. I'm pretty good with cards.'

Jack groaned. 'Now this is exactly the kind of bacon-brained plan I thought you might cook up. You two better wait till I get there.'

'Maybe.'

'I swear to God, Claudia, if you try to stop me from helping you, I will tear your front door down.'

'You don't know where I live,' she said smugly.

'But I do know where you work,' he responded just as smugly.

She put a hand on her hip, entirely frustrated with him. 'Oh, for goodness sake, Jack. Since when do you care?'

'Since I've decided that I'm in love with Bronwyn,' he said gruffly. 'I can't let anything happen to her.'

This announcement did cause Claudia to pause.

Wow, Bronwyn! You have been busy while my back is turned.

'Jack, if you dare hurt my best friend, I'll make you wish you were never born.'

'Believe me, she's more likely to hurt me. Has she said anything about me to you?'

339

'Actually, no,' Claudia replied crossly, not sure who she was more annoyed at – Bronwyn for not confiding in her or him for asking her to betray a confidence she didn't have. 'Don't worry, as soon as Bronwyn gets here, I'm going to be asking her all about it.'

'Give me your address, so I know where to find you.'

'It's not necessary.'

'Let's leave that up to Bronwyn.'

'All right, *fine*.' She blew on her fringe and gave him Seb's address. He muttered 'Thanks' and then the dial tone sounded in her ear.

'Typical.'

She tried to call Bronwyn's mobile but it was turned off. There was a text message that Bronwyn must have sent earlier though.

Coming to Perth. Will explain when I get there.

The problem was she still hadn't told her best friend that she'd moved in with Seb. She tried to tell herself it was to do with timing, but it was more like embarrassment. How did she begin to tell anyone about her relationship with a man that she didn't quite understand herself? If she didn't get in touch with Bronwyn soon, there was going to be an issue. Bronwyn was still likely to show up at her apartment, which remained the ransacked mess she'd left four days ago.

Pulling out her phone again, she quickly texted: *Don't go to your place. Call me as soon as you get this.*

She didn't hold out much hope that Bronwyn would turn on her phone before arriving in Subiaco though. She checked her watch. It was half past twelve. Sebastian and a couple of company executives had been shut up in the boardroom all morning. They still hadn't broken their meeting for lunch yet and she couldn't afford to sit around and wait till they did. Quickly, she sent Seb an email that he could find on his computer later and stood up to go. Just as she turned into the foyer of the floor, she bumped into Nelson. He was returning from his break.

'You're taking a late lunch, Claud. Under the pump again?'

'My best friend is in trouble,' she blurted. 'I've got to leave.'

His eyes widened. 'Oh no, anything I can do to help?'

'Cover for me with Seb, will you? I don't know if I'll be back this afternoon.'

Nelson paled slightly but firmly nodded his head. 'Of course.'

Claudia took the lift downstairs and then headed to the bus stop. When she arrived at Bronwyn's apartment she tried calling her friend's mobile phone again but it was still turned off. Frustrated but willing to kill a little more time, she started packing away the items strewn on the floor of the living room.

Half an hour later, the room was nearly tidy and her best friend still had not shown up.

Okay, now you're worrying me.

She could imagine exactly what was going through Bronwyn's head. It was the same images that had plagued her since her phone call with Jack. Her fingers trembled as she straightened the books on the bookshelf. Those pups were innocent, adorable and so loving. She'd seen the photos. Bronwyn had had the joy of actually holding them in her arms and seeing them born into the world.

The very thought of them in the hands of someone as cruel and heartless as Leon McCall put a heavy dread in her chest. She couldn't bear the thought of them being trained to be brutal killers. Taught to thirst for blood, to maim or be maimed. To fear their owner rather than love them.

Those pups had to be rescued.

Even as these frantic thoughts ran through her mind, a text message from Bronwyn finally came through.

No worries. Am at Quiet Gentleman. Meet me here?

Panic hit Claudia directly in the chest as she gripped her phone. Idealistic Bronwyn clearly thought she might be able to reason with the crooks.

341

Don't do or say anything till I get there! She texted back, then, grabbing her key, slammed the door on her way out.

I hope I'm not too late.

Chapter 29

Claudia was not at her desk.

Nelson said she had taken off early, and Seb was not happy at all. It was ironic. Cyril had been prophesising for nearly a month now that when Sebastian finally stumbled upon the right woman he would be delirious with joy.

What a pile of rubbish.

Seb was at the point where he was pretty sure that Claudia was the right woman. She was smart, she was funny, and she brought out his caring, protective instincts like an army of soldiers marching over a hill. And she was gorgeous – drop dead, in-your-face, can't-stop-looking-at-her beautiful.

But that didn't mean he was happy. Far from it.

It had been fine when she hadn't been honest with him. He could put her in the same basket he'd placed all the other women in his life, including his own mother. There was no need to take it further. He could keep his distance without the confusion he was experiencing now.

But Cyril, in his wisdom, had built in a fail-safe. A test, if you will, so that Seb would have to admit that Claudia was different.

I know you don't trust her.

One day, she'll tell you that she's not my niece and that's the day you'll know you can.

It was difficult reliving that moment, where she'd sat across the table from him, placing power over her life squarely in his hands. The power to destroy her career and her reputation in the blink of an eye. She'd given it all to him.

I want you to trust me and I want to trust you.

Could it get any more cliché than that? So what was expected of him now? Much to his disgust, he strongly suspected it was a leap of faith. If he really was in love with this woman, then he couldn't just trust her, he had to trust it.

This was a concept he was definitely not prepared to deal with. Cyril's so-called bubble of joy was most likely to pop in his face.

It was no wonder that when he discovered her email upon returning to his desk later that afternoon, he was less than satisfied.

'Hi, Seb,' it read. 'I'll see you at home later tonight. Bronwyn's back in town. She may need my help. I have to go find her. Claudia.'

He wished she hadn't just taken off like that. He couldn't be pleased with the fact that she was intending to spend time with the one person currently on Leon McCall's most-wanted list.

Couldn't she have gotten him out of his meeting? Taken him with her, so he could make sure she was safe?

Why would she do that, Seb?

It's not like he was her husband, or even her boyfriend.

She was his housemate, and a very reluctant one at that. Unable to concentrate on work any longer, he packed up his briefcase and left the building, heading for his car and home. Hoping she'd be there already when he arrived.

She wasn't.

He collected the mail from his letterbox before he walked in. As he set it on kitchen counter he noticed in horror the image of him and Claudia on the front page of the local community newspaper.

'Young couple wins Harley Supermarket's 1000th customer competition.'

It was the kind of photo you hoped never saw the light of day. Claudia clearly looked like she'd been flung into him. Her face was pressed sideways into his arm, screwing up her mouth and nose. One arm was out as though trying to catch something for balance. His expression was one of shock – his mouth open like a frog catching flies and his eyes as wide as jar lids. If that wasn't bad enough, he looked a wreck. Hair standing on end. Juice on a shirt with no tie. It was a nightmare.

How many people have seen this?

He didn't get the chance to contemplate it any further because the doorbell rang.

He definitely wasn't expecting anyone, and Claudia had a key. Angrily, he marched over to the front door and yanked it opened. A man he did not recognise stood there.

'Whatever you're selling, I'm not interested,' he said, and would have closed the door had the other man not wedged his foot in it.

'I'm not selling anything. I'm here to see Claudia.' The man frowned. 'Who the hell are you?'

Seb relaxed his grip on the door and slowly re-opened it. 'Not that it's any of your business, but I'm Sebastian Rowlands.'

'Never heard of you. Where's Claudia?'

Sebastian's eyes narrowed. There was so much he didn't know about Claudia's past and the thought that this man was an ex-boyfriend come to reconcile with her shot hot jealousy through him. 'Now that really is none of your business,' he snapped.

'I'm her brother, Jack,' the man threw at him. 'So it's every bit my business if she has a stranger in her house.' As relief washed through Sebastian's body, Jack managed to push past him into the main living space.

'This is not actually Claudia's house,' Sebastian turned. 'It's mine. I'm helping her out while her friend Bronwyn's place is unavailable.'

Jack's eyes widened as he picked up the community paper on the kitchen counter. He gave a low whistle. 'Geez, what happened here?'

Sebastian snatched the paper away from him.

'So you're her boyfriend then?' Jack demanded. 'Funny, you don't look like her type.'

'I'm not her boyfriend. I'm her housemate,' Sebastian continued on stiffly. 'Why are you looking for her? Is she in trouble?'

'Not yet.' Jack glanced around. 'But she was supposed to be here. Bronwyn too.'

'You know Bronwyn Eddings?' Seb's interest was picking up.

'Yes,' Jack announced. 'She's my . . .'

'She's your . . . ?'

'My housemate,' Jack finished lamely. 'I have to find her.'

'I see.' Sebastian noted he was warming to the man. 'Why the urgency?'

'I'm afraid she's about to do something stupid. Her dogs went missing last night.'

'Wait,' Sebastian held up his hand. 'Dogs? There's more than one?'

'Her dog had her litter and they were all stolen right out of our back patio.'

Sebastian's stomach lurched.

Leon McCall had made his move. Jack was right – Claudia and Bronwyn were about to do something rash.

The question was, was it too late to stop them?

346

Chapter 30

Claudia wasn't too sure what to expect when she rocked up at The Quiet Gentleman that evening, but it certainly wasn't the sight that greeted her. Her friend, more than a little tipsy, at table number five with a bunch of empty glasses in front of her. Claudia quickly weaved her way through the furniture and sat down, giving Bronwyn a tight hug.

'I'm so glad I found you. Are you okay?'

'No.' Bronwyn's eyes filled with tears as she lay her head on Claudia's shoulder. She reeked of alcohol.

'Bronwyn, are you drunk?'

'Yes. No. Maybe a little.' She reached up, pinching thumb and forefinger. 'Turns out I'm not very good at reconnaissance.'

'What were you trying to do?'

'I was going to question our lovely friend Frank over there,' Bronwyn slurred. 'But every time I went up to the counter, I chickened out and just ordered a drink instead.'

Claudia's eyes roamed over the glasses on the table. 'Seems like that amounted to quite a few times.'

'I know!' Bronwyn groaned. 'And to make matters worse, their house white is *shite*. If they weren't a bunch of sick-minded criminals, I might be tempted to give them my Oak Hills business card.'

'You have an Oak Hills business card now?'

'Oh yes,' Bronwyn nodded brightly. 'I got them made up for Jack and Horace too. All part of drumming up business.'

'I see.'

'You know,' Bronwyn slurred thoughtfully, 'I *am* feeling much braver than I was when I first came in. Perhaps I should just try one last time.'

'Oh no you don't.' Claudia firmly pushed her back into her chair. 'It's too dangerous, Bron. You don't just go up to a criminal and ask them whether they stole your dogs.'

'I wasn't going to ask him *that*.' Bronwyn swatted her hand. 'I'm not that naive. I did have a bit of a plan.'

'Really?' Claudia raised her eyebrows. 'What?'

Bronwyn's eyes widened slightly at her own genius. 'I was going to flirt with him a little. You know, like they do in Bond films and hope that maybe once we got to talking . . .'

'He might take you off into a back room and assault you?' Claudia suggested.

Bronwyn frowned. 'There's no need to be so negative. I thought he might confide in me something meaningful. After all, I'm much better at this whole seduction thing than I used to be.'

'Seduction thing?'

'Illicit affairs.' Bronwyn moved her hands as though she was magicking a puff of smoke.

'Bron, I have no idea what you're talking about.'

'Yes,' Bronwyn agreed sadly, 'neither do I. It was something Jack said to me yesterday.'

'Jack's a tosser.'

Bronwyn sighed. 'Not all the time.'

'He's here, you know.'

'He's what?' Bronwyn perked up.

'Came after you. I imagine he's at my place by now.'

'Really?'

'Really.' Claudia sighed. 'Come on, let's get you out of here. Live to fight another day, eh?'

'But Elsa, and Shiraz and Merlot and . . .' Bronwyn's eyes were filling with tears again.

'Yes, yes. We will find them. You have my promise on that.' Claudia helped her up, glancing around surreptitiously to make sure no one was watching them too closely.

'Sorry,' Bronwyn winced. 'I need to go to the toilet.'

'Okay,' Claudia agreed on a sigh. 'We'll do that first.'

They headed out to the ladies room and while Bronwyn went in to relieve herself, Claudia happened to be well positioned to see what was going on in the back car park. And what was going on was very interesting indeed!

A couple of men had the shed open and were packing a small trailer with the lights and the fencing.

The hairs on the back of Claudia's neck rose to razor-sharp points.

Could it be . . . Was there a fight going down tonight? She got out her phone and snapped a quick photo of the men before Bronwyn came out of the bathroom.

When she did, she pulled her friend at a fast pace towards the front door. Bronwyn tripped unsteadily on her feet, knocking against Claudia's shoulder as she pulled her across the street.

'What are you doing?' Bronwyn slurred. 'I can't walk that fast, and come to think of it, I don't think I should be driving.'

'Don't worry, I will,' said Claudia. 'Where's your car? I took the bus over.'

'It's just there.'

By lucky chance, it was conveniently placed just in front of the entrance to the side car park. From the front seat, they could see whoever was driving in or out of The Quiet Gentleman.

'Great spot, Bron.'

'I thought I did a terrible job of parking the car though,' Bronwyn giggled. 'And that was *before* I was drunk.'

'Don't sweat it. Nobody's good at parallel parking,' Claudia said distractedly as she focused her gaze on the car park.

Her palms were starting to perspire as she positioned herself in the driver's seat, wondering whether what she was about to do was really such a good idea.

Stuff it! This is the only way to catch them.

Bronwyn had sat back in her seat and closed her eyes, but when Claudia didn't start the engine, she opened them and looked over. 'Is it just me, or are we not moving?'

'We're waiting.' Claudia nervously licked her lips.

'For what?'

'For the trailer packed with equipment that's going to the dog fight to drive out of that car park.'

Bronwyn sat up straight. 'What are you talking about?'

'I'm going to show you how real reconnaissance is done, girl. Are you in?'

Bronwyn rubbed her temple. 'I'm not sober enough for this.'

'I could leave you behind.'

'No way!' Bronwyn pursed her lips. 'But shouldn't we tell someone?'

'You're right.' Claudia whipped her phone out of her pocket and dialled the number of the only man she trusted.

'Claudia, where are you?'

'Seb, I think a dog fight is going down tonight. They are packing up a vehicle at the pub. I'm going to follow them.'

'Claudia, under *no* circumstance are you to go on your own.'

'I'm not on my own,' she smiled. 'Bronwyn is with me.'

Bronwyn turned and gave her a clumsy-looking thumbs up. Cringing slightly, she gave the thumbs up back and focused her gaze ahead again. She didn't think it would be wise to mention that Bronwyn was drunk.

'Bronwyn will need just as much protection as you,' Seb began.

Probably more.

'You –'

'Don't worry,' she interrupted him, 'I'm not going to need it. I'm not even going to get out of the car. Trust me. Once I'm close enough to see where it is, I'll text you the address and you can get the police involved. I just thought I'd give you a heads-up so you're prepared.'

'Claudia –'

'Keep your phone on, okay?'

'*Claudia* –'

'Can't talk now. They're pulling out.'

She clicked her phone off and turned on the engine just as the ute and attached trailer bumped gently out the driveway of The Quiet Gentleman.

Bronwyn clapped her hands. 'I feel like I'm in *NCIS*. Let's get these bastards!'

As Claudia turned the car out into the street, Bronwyn's body swayed with it and she hit her head on the window. 'Ow!'

Claudia eyed her with misgiving. 'Er . . . maybe you should just try to sit back and relax. Sober up a bit.'

'I'm fine. In fact, I'm really quite pumped about this. It's a shame we don't have any weapons.'

'Bronwyn,' Claudia said firmly, 'we are not getting out of the car. This is purely recon.'

'Of course,' Bronwyn smiled, 'although I do have some hairspray in my handbag. Do you think that works as well as pepper spray?'

'*Bronwyn.*'

'Okay. No getting out of the car.'

Just as she finished speaking, Claudia's phone buzzed again. Bronwyn fished it out of the centre console. 'It's Sebastian Rowlands.'

Claudia shook her head. 'Don't answer it. He just wants to talk me out of this. Switch it off, will you.'

Bronwyn did so and put the phone back on the dash. 'I just have one question.'

'Yeah?'

'Why did you call Sebastian Rowlands of all people? I thought you hated the guy.'

Uh-oh.

Claudia felt heat infuse her face. 'Er . . . hate is a really strong word.'

'I knew it!' Bronwyn flicked a finger at her. 'You have the hots for him, don't you?'

'I –'

'Geez, Claudia. If you're not even going to admit it to me, then it must be serious.'

'It's complicated.' Claudia frowned, making a right turn as the trailer two cars ahead of her did so. 'For a number of reasons,' she winced, 'particularly as I've started living with him as well.'

'*You've what?*'

'I didn't want to say anything,' she groaned, 'but your apartment was broken into last week and Seb felt that if I stayed there I wouldn't be safe. So I moved into his place.'

'Really?' Bronwyn's eyes widened. 'Who suggested that?'

'My uncle.' She lifted her hands briefly off the wheel to make quotation marks around 'uncle'.

Bronwyn frowned. 'Uncle Cyril didn't think it was inappropriate?'

'It's only supposed to be temporary and Sebastian has a big house.'

'So, how are you finding it?' Bronwyn prompted again, when she said no more. 'The co-habitation, that is?'

'It's hard.'

'Because he's your boss?'

'And because I think I'm falling in love with him.'

'Well,' Bronwyn spread her hands reasonably, 'if you're worried about seeing someone you work with, just change jobs.'

Claudia grimaced.

'You're already in hot water at Hanks and Eddings with everyone thinking you're Cyril's niece. Why not make a fresh start somewhere else, where there won't be any stigma attached to you? We both know you can make it anywhere, Claud.'

'Thanks for the vote of confidence. When this Leon McCall debacle is over, I might just do that,' Claudia agreed. 'But it won't solve my problem with Seb.'

'Which is?'

'He's just not boyfriend material.'

'How do you know?'

'Because he *told me*.'

'Oh.' Bronwyn was finally stumped.

'He might as well have said, "Quit while you're ahead, sweetheart."'

'Then maybe you should. After all, there are stacks of good-looking, successful men out there.'

Claudia nodded reluctantly. She was absolutely right, of course. No point in putting her life on hold for something that was never going to happen.

'Good point.'

The dog fighters made a left turn, this time on to the main freeway. It looked like they were heading south. Claudia tried to stay at least two cars behind. She had absolutely no idea about tailing technique but she figured out of plain sight was probably a good move.

'So,' she said carefully, 'I've been hearing some weird things from Jack.'

'Like what?'

'Like he said he's in love with you, and you're going to hurt him.'

Bronwyn's gaze swung to her and she shoved Claudia's shoulder, causing the wheel in her hands to jerk a little left. 'Really, he said that?'

'Hey! Careful!' Claudia laughed, swerving back. 'We don't want to draw attention to ourselves.'

'Right,' Bronwyn said dismissively. 'But he *said that*?'

'Yeah, he really did.' Claudia threw an amused glance at Bronwyn. 'I take it these feelings are returned.'

Her friend's eyes were looking a little teary. 'Yes, but I've just . . . I've just been so scared it's not real. Do I believe him, Claudia? I mean, *you know* Jack.'

'Don't I ever!' Claudia nodded. 'Stand by your guns, Bron, and if it's real, he'll definitely come to you.'

Just as she finished speaking, the vehicle they were following turned off the freeway and the scenery around them became less suburban and more semi-rural.

'Take note of the freeway exit,' Claudia said to Bronwyn. ''Cause we'll need to give that to the police.'

'Yep,' her best friend nodded. Luckily, Bronwyn was starting to sober up a little now, or perhaps it was Claudia's own tenseness affecting her.

Suddenly the ute ahead slowed right down and pulled off onto a dirt track marked with a rusty old sign, Hero's Parade.

Claudia raised her eyebrows. 'I hope that sign is talking about us.'

She pulled the car onto the shoulder of the road just before the turn-off. They watched the other car and trailer disappear through the trees. There was not a house or a residence in sight.

'Should we follow now?' Claudia asked her best friend.

Bronwyn leaned forward in her seat, peering through the trees, trying to catch even a glimpse of the vehicle they'd been following. 'I don't know. We don't know how far that road goes in, and then what if they see us? I think it's too risky.'

'Yeah, you're right.' Claudia nodded. 'Besides, I think we've pretty much arrived. They've got to be having the fight in that bushland right? It's the perfect place.'

Bronwyn mouth twisted. 'Yeah, the perfect place.' She took Claudia's phone off the dash and passed it to her. 'Call your boyfriend.'

'He's not my boyfriend.' But Claudia took the phone off her anyway and switched it on to call Seb. However, when she found his number, the line would not connect. She pulled the phone from her ear and eyed the signal bars at the top of her screen.

'Damn it! We're in a blind spot,' she cried. 'There's no signal out here.'

Bronwyn shook her head. 'That can't be right. We're not that far out of the city. What about if you try it outside the car? I'll try mine too.'

They exited the vehicle, waving their phones around trying to get a signal. So focused were they on what they were doing, they didn't see another car approaching until it was too late.

A silver Mercedes Benz pulled up on the road beside them. The tinted window slid down like a Hollywood reveal.

Bronwyn's arms dropped to her sides as she looked at the driver in shock. '*Mum?*'

Bianca Hanks removed her sunglasses and eyed her daughter with equal surprise. 'To be quite honest, Bronwyn, I had no idea you could be this resourceful.'

Chapter 31

The shock of seeing Bronwyn's mother on the side of the road was completely trumped when a second later they heard barking from within her vehicle.

Bronwyn gasped. 'Elsa!'

The honey-brown bullmastiff was panting heavily against the back passenger window, creating a large moist fog on the glass.

How on earth did she get you to stay in your seat?

Bronwyn raced towards the door just as Bianca hit the central locking button on her dash. The door was secure by the time she got there and pulling angrily on the handle was useless. She slammed a fist on the window, as Elsa barked excitedly. She peered beyond the happy canine and saw a full cardboard box also on the back seat.

'You took my puppies!' she cried.

'So you didn't know,' Bianca smiled. 'And here I was crediting you with having put it all together. Oh well, I guess I'll see you later then.'

On these words, she wound up her window and drove on, her wheels kicking dust in Bronwyn's face.

'*What is going on here?*' Claudia cried as she stumbled up beside Bronwyn.

'I don't know,' Bronwyn turned around. 'But I'm sure as hell going to find out.' She raced back to their car. 'Who's driving? Me or you?'

'I better.' Claudia nodded. They created their own cloud of dust as she spun the wheels down the dirt road after Bianca Hanks.

'What is your mum doing with those dogs?'

Bronwyn clutched the dash in front of her as she perched as far forward on her seat as her seatbelt would let her. Her knuckles were going white as her eyes remained fixed on her mother's car.

'Revenge obviously, or some lesson she wants to teach me,' she ground out. 'I wouldn't go back to law so she had to find some way to coerce me.'

'By stealing your dogs in the dead of night?' Claudia rolled her eyes. 'Sounds a little extreme.'

'My mother is not above extreme.' Bronwyn sucked in a breath. 'She was the one who got Jack to go to Bordeaux. He didn't abandon you guys, you know. He thought he was being kicked out of the country.'

'*No.*' Claudia refused to believe it. 'That doesn't make sense.'

'It's a long story,' Bronwyn sighed. 'But, to cut it *really* short, Jack thought your dad kicked him out of the country. Only it was my mum who sent him a ticket and a job offer. She did it just to make sure I stayed in law and didn't move to Yallingup, which was kind of my idea at the time.'

'Okay,' Claudia took a hand off the wheel briefly to shake a finger at her, 'you are definitely leaving parts of that story out. Do you mean to tell me that you've been in love with my brother all this time and you've said nothing to me till now?'

Bronwyn winced.

'We are going to have some serious words after this, let me tell you.'

'Definitely later,' Bronwyn agreed. 'Right now, we really need to focus on what my mother plans to do next.'

Claudia's nose wrinkled. 'What I still don't get is how she knew where to steal the dogs from. I mean, we were so careful about keeping your whereabouts a secret.'

'It was me.' Bronwyn looked sheepish.

'What was you?'

'I blabbed. I told her where I was when I rang up to yell at her for interfering in my life, and Jack's too, for that matter.'

'Looks like she's still interfering,' Claudia commented dryly as she swerved to miss a pothole. 'You don't think she's in cahoots with Leon McCall, do you? I mean, your mother can be cruel, but she's definitely not a criminal. '

Bronwyn shook her head firmly. 'There's no way she'd put her license to practice law in jeopardy. She *loves* what she does.'

Far more than me, anyway.

'So if we're not going to a dog fight,' Claudia mused, 'where are we going?'

Even as she posed the question, the road ended suddenly in a clearing – a massive oval in fact. Their mouths dropped opened as myriad colours and sounds and smells assaulted their senses – tents, stalls, people, candy floss, rides, music and . . . lots and lots of animals. Dogs, cats, rabbits, guinea pigs, snakes, fish in bags. There was even a camel being led around with an Arabian carpet on its back.

Claudia's foot fell off the clutch and the car jerked and stalled.

They were at a fair.

The Great South-West Pet Show, apparently. There were flags and banners flying everywhere in red, white and yellow.

Well I'll be damned.

Clearly they'd just taken a shortcut through a national park to reach the showgrounds. Frank and his men were setting up the lights and fencing off to one side. There was an elevated stage there and heaps of people were laying out picnic rugs in front of it to watch. It looked like whatever was about to take place on the stage was the main event of the day. They needed the lights because it might continue after dark.

A car behind them tooted noisily.

'Quick, drive over to the car park.' Bronwyn pointed in the distance. 'I can see it over there. My mum too.'

Claudia tried to follow her instructions, although the car park was a nightmare to navigate. Narrow lanes, horns tooting, cars parked both legally and illegally, kids running dangerously across the bitumen. Literally every man and his dog were there.

'I don't understand,' Claudia cried as she circled the block yet again. 'I was so sure, Frank, Peter and Leon were all connected. I never factored in your mum at all.'

'Maybe she's not involved with them. My mum could be acting completely under her own steam.'

'So do you think Leon McCall is still after you then?' Claudia asked.

'He very well could be,' Bronwyn cringed and then spotted a space. 'There!' she pointed urgently for Claudia's benefit.

It wasn't a car park. More like a vacant patch of grass and gravel close to the kerb. Everybody else was illegally parking though, so Bronwyn figured why the hell not.

'I'll pay the fine,' she offered, just in case Claudia had a problem with it.

'We'll go halves.' Claudia swung in to the spot.

They jumped out of the car, making it back on foot to where they'd seen Bianca parking earlier. Bronwyn had not expected to find her mother still there, however good old Elsa had had other ideas. The large bullmastiff had wound its leash around Bianca and pinned her up against the side of her car, front paws up on her chest.

'Get off me! Get off me! You stupid dog,' Bianca cried, her features contorted in both terror and desperation. Elsa responded by licking her face from chin to hairline.

Claudia and Bronwyn skidded to a halt in front of them, taking it all in with frank enjoyment. The box of puppies was on the ground at Bianca's feet – clearly dropped there if the dent in the side was anything to go by. Luckily, the dogs had all stayed in the box.

'Help me!' Bianca turned frantic eyes upon her daughter. 'Don't just stand there!'

Bronwyn folded her arms and Claudia made no move to step forward either. They grinned at each other instead. Bronwyn couldn't recall a time in her life when her mother had ever needed her help. Let alone been completely at her mercy. She was going to milk this for all it was worth.

She turned back to Bianca. 'I think we need to have a little chat first.'

Elsa licked Bianca's face again, lapping at her cheek like it was an ice-cream.

'Ugh! Ugh!' Bianca cried. 'Make her stop.'

'Sure,' Bronwyn replied. 'I just want your agreement on a few points first.'

'Anything.'

'One, you will stop antagonising my friend Claudia and endorse her position at Hanks and Eddings. Two, you will accept my decision to live and work in Yallingup without any more manipulations calculated to change my mind. And, three, you will return those dogs to me immediately.'

A shadow flicked across Bianca's features. 'I can do that, of course, but I can't see why you would want to hide the dogs from a man as dangerous as Leon McCall.'

Bronwyn was surprised by two things. First, that her mother actually cared about what happened to her and second, that she knew about Leon's involvement. She hesitated.

'Claudia,' she turned to her friend, 'let's get Elsa off her.'

'Right.'

Together, they pulled Elsa back and the dog dropped to all fours.

'Good girl,' Claudia encouraged her as Bianca spun around, untangling the lead.

'Thank you!' Bianca exclaimed as she deposited the end of the lead in Bronwyn's outstretched palm.

'Now,' Bronwyn prompted, 'explain to me what you know about Leon McCall's connection to these dogs.'

'He owns the puppies but wants their mother too after Peter attempted to double-cross him.'

'Peter attempted to double-cross him?'

Bianca sighed. 'Your client made the big mistake of giving his dog to you for safe-keeping. Nobody, I suppose, could have predicted you would quit your job and disappear so suddenly without a care for anyone but yourself.'

'Oh yes,' Bronwyn snapped, 'because this is all about me being selfish.'

Claudia stepped forward. 'Hold up, hold up, hold up.' She held up her palms for their attention. 'How are you connected to Peter Goldman?' Her gaze fixed on Bianca.

Bronwyn's mother shrugged. 'I'm not. I honestly couldn't care less about Peter Goldman or his gambling debts. My concern is for my client.'

'Who is?' Claudia prompted.

'Linda McCall.'

Bronwyn gasped. 'Leon's new wife.'

'Exactly.' Bianca raised her chin. 'I've been handling her defamation case. But that aside, she's quite the animal lover. Those prize pedigree puppies were Leon's wedding present to her. You can imagine how angry he was when they just disappeared.'

'And Peter Goldman got the brunt of it . . .' Claudia tapped a finger thoughtfully to her chin.

'When they found out Bronwyn had them, they did come to me,' Bianca admitted. 'Both of them, Leon and Linda. I had a meeting with them in my office just a couple of weeks ago.' She averted her eyes. 'I must admit, Leon does have many interesting suits filed against him and almost every member of his family. Having his business would be an excellent windfall for me.'

'But you didn't tell him where I was,' Bronwyn whispered.

'Of course not,' Bianca scoffed. 'I am still your mother, after all.'

They looked at each other long and hard. It was strange seeing her mother in this new light. She had always thought of her as one hundred per cent ruthless, but maybe now she could shave off ten per cent.

Bianca examined the knuckles on the back of one hand. 'I did think, however, that your recklessness deserved to be punished and those dogs ought to be returned. If not for my business advancement, then your own safety. So I stole them . . . er . . .' she amended, 'paid a grape picker to do it for me.'

And there's the other ten per cent.

'Who are you meeting with today?' Claudia's eyes narrowed on her mother.

'Linda,' Bianca replied. 'She will be very pleased to finally receive these dogs.'

'As will you, when her husband gives you more of his business,' Claudia suggested.

'Exactly.'

Claudia turned to Bronwyn with raised eyebrows. 'What do you reckon?'

Bronwyn looked down at Elsa, who hadn't stopped tugging on her lead since the conversation had started. The dog looked back, a smile in her eyes, as her panting tongue dripped drool on the hot bitumen. How could she lose this dog now? True, there was no horror story in Elsa's future. Linda McCall was obviously not an animal torturer of any kind and Elsa would be treated well. If only she, Bronwyn, had not grown to love her.

Leon had only wanted the puppies for his wife originally. Perhaps they could come to some sort of arrangement.

Bronwyn licked her lips. 'I think I'd like to talk to Linda McCall myself.'

Claudia sighed. 'I was afraid you were going to say that.' She picked up the box containing the puppies and said to Bianca, 'We'll take it from here if you don't mind.'

Bianca inclined her head regally, smoothing her crushed skirt with her palms. 'Be my guest. Linda is in the biggest tent next to the stage. You can't miss it. Give me a call when you have a result. I'd like to know the final outcome.'

'We will,' Bronwyn agreed, 'but I hope our other agreements still stand.'

'Yes,' Bianca assented grumpily. 'They do.'

Her mother held her gaze for a second longer than necessary before turning away to get into her car. As she started her engine, Bronwyn's heart felt a little lighter. Was it possible that her mother was finally going to accept her for who she was?

As Bianca drove away, Claudia nudged her. 'So, shall we do this?'

They took off towards the main tent and hadn't been walking long before a man selling dog ears on headbands started harassing them. 'Buy one, get one free. Pay another two dollars and get your free glow-in-the-dark stick for the talent show tonight.'

'Talent show?' Claudia laughed.

'Look, they're putting a banner up.' Bronwyn pointed.

Sure enough, Frank and some other guys were hanging the words 'Linda McCall's Pet Talent Show' across the front of the stage right next to the giant white tent they were heading for – clearly this was backstage.

'Hey, watch it!' cried a fat woman in a hot-pink sequinned leotard as they entered the tent. Claudia, still carrying the box of puppies, had almost run into the woman's greyhound. The animal was wearing a very similar-looking leotard and walking on its hind legs with a ribbon on a stick in its mouth. It let it go, dropped back to four legs and barked loudly in protest.

'We're trying to have a rehearsal here,' the woman growled at her.

'I'm so sorry,' Claudia apologised, momentarily taken aback by the pandemonium all around. Bronwyn didn't blame her. There were three parrots playing a ditty on some tin cans to her right, a cat dressed in a clown suit balancing on a ball on her left and a host of other horrors directly in front of her. Involuntarily, her fingers tightened on Elsa's leash and she wound it more securely around her wrist. The last thing everyone needed was a cat amongst the pigeons.

They weaved their way through the crowd until finally, right at the back of the tent, they found her. Linda McCall was stationed in an area obviously set aside for the event organisers. There were costumes hanging on racks against the wall and two long bench tables where a panel of ladies were taking registrations of the performers.

Unquestionably the trophy wife, Linda was dressed in a showy floral summer dress that displayed plenty of leg and a generous amount of boob. The transition from swimsuit model to kept woman was as clear as kindergarten maths on a chalkboard. Her blonde curls were far too well formed to be natural and her bronze skin definitely came out of a can.

When she saw what they were carrying, she was pleased to greet them. 'Well, what do we have here?'

'Hi,' Bronwyn held out her hand, 'my name is Bronwyn Eddings. I believe these puppies are yours.'

'Bronwyn Eddings,' Linda purred. 'It's nice to finally meet the woman who has led me on such a merry dance these past few weeks.'

Bronwyn bit back the retort that was on the tip of her tongue. Only politeness and a little sucking up were going to get her anywhere at this point. She had to play this very carefully.

'I'm sorry if my leaving town was an inconvenience to you. I had no idea what plans Peter had for the dogs.'

Linda raised her eyebrows. 'And you didn't think to ask him?'

'He never gave me much of a chance to,' Bronwyn returned.

'Yes, well, I never liked him either.' Linda waved her hand dismissively. 'But Elsa did win a big prize last year for her breeding. And when Peter owed Leon that gambling debt . . . well, she was a means to wipe the slate clean. My husband has such a bad reputation in Perth, you know, but,' she nodded her head earnestly, 'he's really not that unreasonable.'

'No doubt,' Claudia murmured dryly.

Bronwyn, however, had had enough of Leon and Peter. All she wanted to do was cut Elsa's ties to them once and for all.

'The thing is, I have grown rather attached to Elsa while she has been in my care and, if possible, I'd like to buy her off you.'

'Is that so?' Linda eyed her with some interest. 'I completely understand, of course, being a dog lover myself.'

'You do?' Hope buoyed in Bronwyn's chest.

'Of course,' Linda responded brightly. 'However, Elsa's not for sale.'

Bronwyn's joy deflated. 'Everyone has a price,' she said slowly.

'What am I to do with more money?' Linda tittered. 'In case you haven't read the news, honey, I'm loaded.'

Bronwyn winced at her crassness. 'Not money then,' she suggested. 'Is there anything else I can do for you to secure Elsa's ownership?'

Claudia shot her a worried glance, but Bronwyn didn't care. Elsa had changed her life. She had given her the chance to become who she wanted to be. In her opinion, that was worth anything Linda demanded.

'Well,' Linda rubbed her chin thoughtfully, 'now that you mention it, there is *something* I'm in need of right at the minute.'

Chapter 32

First impressions had not given Jack a very high opinion of Sebastian Rowlands. The man was wearing a suspiciously pink business shirt with a very fine check print. It was uniquely tailored to his slim, fit body and suited him perfectly. However, Jack had never been one to keep up with trends and witnessing fashionable perfection, particularly on a guy, immediately had his back up.

Honestly!

Was this really the kind of man his sister wanted to date?

Mr Hot-Shot Mega-Star with his supercool haircut and winking silver cufflinks? Jack couldn't remember the last time he'd been clean-shaven, let alone that neatly pressed. And his shoes, as far as he was aware, had never seen one lick of polish in their life . . . unlike Sebastian's, which seemed to reflect the light.

In fact, he was quite sure that most of Sebastian's brain power must be sucked away by the time-consuming process of staying in vogue. So he was quite surprised and rather pleased when the man abruptly hung up on his third connection with Claudia's voicemail and said, 'We're going to have to go after them.'

'I thought you'd never ask.'

It was clear from the phone conversation he'd overheard earlier that the women were together, they were doing something stupid, and weren't going to listen to reason.

'Where are they?' he demanded.

'On the road somewhere,' Sebastian swore, throwing his phone down on the kitchen counter. 'They're tailing those criminals.'

'Okay, which criminals?' Jack held up his hands for clarification. 'Leon McCall, Peter Goldman, some random dog fighter?' He scrunched his hair in frustration.

'I see somebody's taken you into their confidence.' Sebastian's lip curled sardonically.

'Claudia told me everything.' Jack groaned. 'Except where to find her if she goes missing. If they are on the road driving and they've turned their phones off, how are we supposed to locate them?'

'We can't,' Sebastian shrugged. 'We'll just have to find someone who knows where they are going instead.'

'And how are we supposed to do that?'

'There's a pub called –'

'The Quiet Gentleman.' Jack nodded. 'Yes, Claudia told me, but I thought it was a dead end.'

'A fight is going down tonight. Somebody there has got to know something.'

Seb turned around and began to walk towards the front door, swiping his keys off the hall table as he wrenched it open. Parked out the front of the house, in an open car port, were two cars. Sebastian's sleek and stylish silver Audi stood next to Jack's rundown old ute. There were insects and mud sprayed all over the front bonnet and the side-view mirrors were hanging off from their hinges.

'Er . . . we'll take my car,' Sebastian announced firmly.

He opened the door and got in. Jack hesitated and then climbed into the passenger side. 'So that's how you're playing it, is it?' he asked ruefully.

'Playing what?' Sebastian revved the engine and backed smoothly out of the drive.

'Your car's better than mine?'

'I don't recall saying that,' Sebastian murmured as he pushed into the higher gears and flew effortlessly up another street. 'However, if that's the conclusion you've come to . . .'

'Just so you know,' Jack glared at him, 'you're the one in this car wearing the pink shirt.'

'True,' Sebastian laughed.

They arrived in next to no time at The Quiet Gentleman, and Jack couldn't help but reflect as they left the vehicle and walked across gravel to the front door that the pub was far from aristocratic. It was your typical Northbridge dive, old and in need of a scrub from top to bottom.

'Nice place,' he commented sarcastically as they walked in.

'It has a certain charm.'

Jack scanned the long bar. It was presided over by only two people, a young man in a black T-shirt with his hand bandaged and an older woman in her fifties. 'Are we going to buy a drink?'

'No, let's try a more candid approach,' Sebastian murmured. 'The guy with the bandage is the one we want. He's most likely to know something about the fight.'

'Why would he tell us?'

Sebastian's smile was crooked. 'We're going to be very persuasive.'

Jack nodded and rolled up his sleeves. 'I like your style.'

Sebastian gave Jack's flannelette shirt, 'seen better days' jeans and brown work boots a sideways glance. 'Somehow I doubt that very much.' He stepped forward. 'Follow my lead.'

'Good evening, sir,' Seb said to the man with the name tag 'Jet' on his black T-shirt.

Jet put down the glass he was wiping. 'What can I get you?'

'Nothing.' Sebastian shook his head as he removed a white card from his wallet and placed it on the dirty bar. 'My name is Sebastian Rowlands and I am a lawyer from Hanks and Eddings. This is my client, who has a serious complaint about the running of these premises.'

Jack set his expression as Jet's nervous eyes flicked over him.

'We were wondering if we might have a word with you, in private.'

Jet cleared his throat. 'Er . . . I'm not the owner. Frank is away at the moment.'

Sebastian flicked an imaginary piece of fluff from his cuffs. 'That's all right. We're happy to have a preliminary discussion with you, which you can relay to Frank when he returns.'

'Er,' Jet swallowed, 'okay.'

'Given the sensitivity of the issue,' Sebastian informed him in a lowered voice, 'I don't think you would want the rest of your patrons to hear what my client has to say.'

Jet hastily came out from behind the counter and said, 'Follow me.'

He took them into the back office, shut the door and turned around. At that moment Jack grabbed him by the shoulders and pushed him up against the back wall.

'All right, now tell us where your boss is *right now.*'

'What the hell is going on here?' Jet glanced from one to the other.

'Just answer the question,' Jack hissed.

'I don't know where Frank is,' Jet responded quickly. 'He never said where he was going tonight.'

'Really?' Jack glared at him. 'And I suppose you don't know what all the equipment he took with him is going to be used for either.'

'No, I don't.'

'Humans lie,' Sebastian murmured, 'computers don't.' While Jack held Jet pinned against the wall, he removed the phone that was conveniently sticking out of the side pocket of the barman's jeans.

'All we need is this.' Sebastian turned on the phone.

'Hey!' Jet finally thought to struggle against Jack's hold but his squirming was to no avail.

'What does it say?' Jack barked impatiently over his shoulder. 'Does it give a location?'

'There are a lot of messages here,' Sebastian remarked grimly.

Jet's face was now going red with fury. 'That's my private business. You've got no right to go through my things!'

'Very true.' Sebastian shook his head as he scrolled through text messages. 'By the way, how did you cut your hand?'

Jet glanced down at it briefly. 'In the kitchen with a knife.'

'Really. Do you have any pets, a dog perhaps?'

'No. My apartment wouldn't allow for that. Not that I like animals.' Jet grimaced.

'Does Frank have any dogs?'

'Not that I'm aware of.' Jet shrugged but at Jack's stern's glare he quickly added, 'But I could be wrong. It's not like we're close or anything. We don't hang out after work.'

'Do you know Leon McCall?'

Jet blanched. 'You mean that criminal guy who's always on the news? You guys work *for him*?'

'No,' Sebastian informed him, 'and clearly neither do you.' He sighed, putting Jet's phone down on a nearby bench and turning to Jack, 'Let him go. He doesn't know anything.'

Jack slowly released the man's shoulders. '*Great*, so what do we do now?'

'Leave this bar, that's what,' Jet stabbed a finger at him, 'before I call the police.'

Jet quickly marched to the bench and snatched his phone up, shoving it once more into his back pocket. As he was doing so, Seb and Jack's phones both buzzed simultaneously. It was a message from Claudia.

I need you! Hurry.

The words were followed by a list of instructions on how to get there.

They both glanced up.

'My message is from Claudia,' said Jack. 'Is yours?'

'Yes. You're in luck, Jet,' Seb said to the waiter. 'We're leaving. Make sure you keep my card. You never know, you might need it one day.'

Under Jet's stunned gaze, they both filed out.

'Seriously?' Jack muttered as they crossed the bar at a smart pace.

Sebastian shrugged. 'Business is business, after all.'

They reached the double-doored entrance to the building and walked out. '

So it looks like we're going south,' Jack commented.

'Yes,' Sebastian grimaced. 'Almost to Mandurah. It's going to take us nearly an hour to get there. I just hope we're not too late.'

Jack felt his muscles tensing up at the mere thought of it. 'I hope those two didn't get out of the car.'

'As I'm sure you're aware, the problem with your sister is that even when her brain advises her to do one thing,' Sebastian mused, 'her heart gets in the way.'

'Is that what happened with you?' Jack demanded shrewdly as they headed back towards the car.

Sebastian gaze snapped up quickly, then he looked away. 'I have no idea.'

'Just what are your intentions towards my sister?' Jack demanded.

'My *intentions*?' Sebastian responded with a mocking smile. 'My intention is to get her home safe and sound.'

'And after that?'

'If she's safe and sound,' Sebastian said quietly, 'then that will be completely up to her.'

Chapter 33

For so long Seb had prided himself on not letting anyone hold him back. What he'd never counted on was that person being himself.

His body shuddered. He couldn't bear it if anything had happened to Claudia. Or, God forbid, they didn't arrive in time.

Luckily, Claudia's texted directions were fairly easy to understand. He had been half afraid they would be incomplete and he'd get lost. However, forty-five minutes after he and Jack Franklin left The Quiet Gentleman, they turned off the freeway and found the quiet dirt road just where Claudia said it was.

Relief, however, was short-lived. The dodgy hidden track led straight into bushland. He gritted his teeth. Great! The perfect place for murder, rape, dog fighting and any other crimes Frank and his men had on their minds. It was at this point he really wished he didn't have such a good knowledge of the criminal psyche. He could do without all those past cases in his head.

In turn, he could feel his companion tensing up beside him as the car jumped and bumped when he turned off the smooth road onto red gravel. Jack clutched his left armrest tightly, his face set and his eyes fixed intensely upon the road ahead. It was twilight. And while not dark yet, the light was definitely fading. Seb couldn't imagine a worse time for a couple of unarmed women to be chasing criminals.

'If Claudia's all right,' Jack murmured, 'I'll kill her myself.'

'Get in line, my friend,' said Seb. 'Get in line.'

Just when he couldn't get any more tense, the road ended abruptly on the side of an oval.

What the – ?

A wave of colour and commotion blasted his senses. A fair! He abruptly killed the engine and both men stepped up out of the car in a daze to take in the scene before them. As Seb's left hand slowly pushed his door closed, 'How Much is that Doggie in the Window?' erupted brightly over the loudspeakers that seemed to be dotted everywhere. Surely this was how Charlie had felt when he'd arrived at Willy Wonka's Chocolate factory.

As if to add proof to this statement, two persons, one dressed in a large ginger cat suit and the other as a huge black-and-white Snoopy detached themselves from the crowd and headed in their direction. Seb couldn't move, overwhelmed by the surreal nature of it all. The ginger cat was lugging a black suitcase while the dog seemed to be breaking into a sprint before launching itself at Jack.

'Jack! It's me, silly,' Snoopy protested when his startled travelling companion took a giant step back.

Bronwyn whipped off her large headpiece.

'Bronwyn,' Jack cried, immediately grabbing her by her large plastic shoulders. 'Are you all right?'

'Of course.'

'But what are doing?'

She rolled the large dog head under her armpit. 'Dressing up as a dog, obviously. We're giving out flyers for the talent show that starts at six tonight.'

Seb's mind reeled. 'Talent show?'

'You guys will love it.' She grinned at both of them in turn. 'I believe one of the acts involves a dog who can drive a motorbike.'

What the fuck is going on here?

'Where's Claudia?' Seb demanded.

'I'm right here.' The ginger cat came up to the group, dropped the suitcase and removed her own head. Claudia smiled brightly at him as she tried to smooth down her static hat hair. 'How's it going?'

'How's it going?' Seb repeated through his teeth. The fear and worry morphing into an anger that permeated up through his ribcage. '*How's it going!*'

Claudia's giant ginger paw touched his arm sympathetically. 'Are you okay?'

He ignored the question. 'Where is Frank?'

She shrugged. 'Probably still setting up lights with the other guys. Who knows how late the show will run into the evening.' She slapped a palm to her forehead. 'Oh, did I forget to mention it? Turns out he's *not* a dog fighter.'

'No shit!' Seb responded.

Luckily at that point Jack jumped in. 'Seriously, Claudia, you had us both tearing down the freeway to get here in time because of your text message. I'd be surprised if Seb doesn't have a few speeding tickets for it.'

'Well, it's all for a good cause,' Bronwyn piped up. 'You are still preventing animal cruelty. Just indirectly. All the proceeds for the fair go to the cause.'

'Yeah,' Claudia told her brother, 'isn't it fantastic? We found Bronwyn's dogs too.'

'My mother had them.' Bronwyn looked at Jack. 'Would you believe it was her who took them?'

'Yes.' The winemaker replied. 'Not trying to get herself some leverage again, is she?'

'Something like that.' Bronwyn smiled. 'But I told her where to go. I'm not going to let anyone come between us again.'

He drew her into his side, dog suit and all. 'I'm glad we're finally in agreement about something.'

Seb turned away in disgust to the ginger cat who was eyeing him innocently. 'If there are no criminals, or dog fighters, or life-threatening situations, why am I here?'

'Oh!' Claudia jumped as though she'd just realised she was late for an appointment. She turned around, got down on her knees and unzipped the suitcase, explaining as she went. 'The dogs all had to be given back to Leon McCall's wife, Linda, who, would you believe, the dogs were actually meant for the whole time.' She rolled her eyes. 'Bronwyn, however, wants to keep Elsa so we agreed to help Linda out of a jam in order to earn the ownership. After we spoke to her, that's when I sent you guys the text message asking for help.'

'And what kind of help would that be?'

'Her mascots didn't show up and she had no time to hire new people. So we're it. We have to put on these costumes and hand out flyers. This one is yours.' She stood up, holding a white-feathered, half-plastic creation with a giant orange beak.

By this stage, the anger in Seb's chest had crept up through his neck and was pounding a hole in the top of his skull.

'Let me get this straight,' he said in a dangerously quiet tone. 'You called me here with all the urgency of a dangerous criminal intervention because you want me to dress up as a *chicken*?'

Claudia's body jerked at the inflection on the final word, her two paws huddled together under her chin as she eyed him with some concern.

'You're really not okay, are you?'

'*No, I am not!*' Seb threw at her. 'Do you know how terrified I was for you? How out of my mind with worry I was for your safety?'

Claudia winced. 'Er . . . I'm guessing . . . a lot?'

To her surprise, and his own, he grabbed her round the waist and pulled her into full body contact. The bulky cat suit became just another annoyance in his long list of grievances. He finally had her in his arms and there was all that fur in the bloody way. It set him off again.

'How could you run off to round up a dog-fighting ring all on your own like that? Are you completely insane?'

'I told you,' she made no attempt to get out of his hold, 'I had Bronwyn with me.'

She glanced over at her friend. 'Bronwyn, back me up here.'

However, it appeared Bronwyn was now far too busy kissing Jack to provide any real assistance. She did offer a rather distracted thumbs up but otherwise didn't break her lip lock with Seb's road-trip buddy.

Claudia blew on her fringe, 'Really? That's all you got, Bron? Jack, get off her.'

A hand under Claudia's chin returned her attention to Sebastian. 'Look at me, I'm still lecturing you.'

She raised her eyebrows. 'We're not at work right now, Sebastian.'

'Don't call me Sebastian, you've never had a shred of deference to me in your life.'

'How true.' Claudia inclined her head with a slight smile. 'But you were right when you judged me guilty of wanting a meaningful relationship. I like you, Seb. There, I admit it. I like you more than I should but I need more than you're offering.'

'How do you know what I'm offering?' His eyes ran over a face that had hooked him from the beginning, along with her irrepressible quick wit and edgy intelligence.

'I thought I was going to lose you,' he said softly. 'I couldn't bear the thought.'

He felt her body shudder in his arms, her eyes widening as she gazed up at him in adorable confusion. 'I thought you didn't do rescue or worry?'

'And then I met you,' he growled. 'You make me want things that I never cared about before. As much as I try, I can't seem to get enough of you, Claudia.'

She didn't get to respond because he kissed her with a passion that had been held at bay for far too long. His hand pushed into her hair, angling her mouth for the most intimate contact. His heart seemed to lift out of his chest when she responded completely, clinging to him as though she too had just found home after a long journey.

'So,' he murmured when he finally lifted his mouth. 'Would you like to go on a date sometime?'

'Sure,' she said breathlessly, and then bit her lip. A cheeky dimple peeked in her left cheek. 'There's just one more thing I need to clarify.'

'What?'

'You're still going to dress up as the chicken, right?'

Chapter 34

One Year Later

Sitting in front of a huge platter of Horace's famous garlic prawns, Jack's semillon sauvignon blanc in her glass, while Lydia mixed the dressing into freshly made coleslaw, Bronwyn reflected that life couldn't get much better.

That year's vintage had been a cracker – record sales and the best-tasting wine she'd had in a while. The wine wankers had been out in force and she'd encouraged them every step of the way. Now all they needed was James Halliday to pop round and give them the five stars she knew they deserved. She was working on that and also pushing Jack's wines into Perth's most popular shows. Antoine had finally got his pinot noir and was making a name for them with that well.

Bronwyn had not regretted her move to Oak Hills one iota, nor buying into a company she had loved for the last ten years. Working there for the past twelve months had been one of the most rewarding experiences of her life. A life she couldn't imagine without Jack Franklin in it.

He was the man who had helped Oak Hills to thrive and flourish again.

The man she loved.

Who loved her in return.

She'd never forget the day he'd declared it. Her in a dog suit, in the middle of a fairground, her best friend arguing with her now–significant other just over to their right. Who needed drippy candles and chocolates – that was what you call romance!

'I don't care that it all turned out to be sham. There's a lesson to be learned in this,' he'd said sternly. 'If you want to go chasing after dog fighters, you take me with you. I'm one of those protective types.'

'Are you, Jack?' she had asked. 'You're not just bored after coming home from exotic France?'

He groaned and grabbed her by shoulders. 'Isn't it obvious how I feel about you?'

'No.'

'I love you, Bronwyn. *Always have*. Just never thought I stood a chance against Chris.'

Bronwyn sucked in a breath. 'I never thought of Chris that way. Never. It was always you, right from the beginning.'

'What about now?' he'd demanded. 'Do you love me right now?'

'Yes.'

'Then we've got everything we need.'

And he was right.

Since that moment they were exactly where they needed to be. She looked across the table at Horace. His health was still fading but his face was definitely not as grey as it had been when she'd first arrived at Oak Hills. You could say that after he had reconciled with Jack, it had given him a new lease on life. As she observed him, he was busily engaged in giving Sebastian Rowlands the third degree.

'Why haven't you been here to visit me before? If you want to date my daughter, you need to get my approval first.'

'*Dad*,' Claudia protested. 'Leave him alone.'

'Well, he's been dating you for over a year now and this is the first time I'm meeting him. I want to know what he's been hiding, apart from a ten-year bloody age gap and a pink shirt.'

'I told you you shouldn't have worn that,' Jack said with a shake of his finger from across the table.

Sebastian's lip twitched.

Claudia glared at Jack and then turned back to her dad. '*Nothing*, Dad. He's hiding nothing. We've just been busy.'

'My apologies, Horace,' Sebastian smiled ruefully, slinging an arm across Claudia's shoulders and drawing her into his body. 'Honestly, I wish I could have come and seen you sooner.'

'Well, what the hell has Claudia been so busy with?' Horace demanded.

'Turning me into a better man, of course.'

Claudia grinned at him. 'Good answer.'

Bronwyn loved the way Claudia was with Sebastian. There was no doubt in her mind that they complemented each other perfectly. When they had decided to date properly, Claudia had moved back into Bronwyn's place and quit her job at Hanks and Eddings. Losing her position there actually hadn't been a great sacrifice. Working at a different but no less prestigious law firm had given Claudia the confidence to prove herself away from the sniping about her being an Eddings. She also got to do more pro-bono work for an animal-rights charity, as one of the partners in her firm was a strong environmentalist. 'Uncle' Cyril had been sad to see her go, but smugly satisfied at her new relationship with Seb. Apparently he was taking complete credit for this development.

Her mother also seemed to be keeping her word. There was no more interference from Bianca's side of things. Yet Bronwyn suspected that she was far too busy with all the new work coming in from Leon McCall to be concerned about small fish such as Claudia and herself. In any case, if worst came to worst, she was sure Elsa was still prepared to protect her if Bianca decided to cause any more trouble.

And if not Elsa, then Seb would step up to the mark. Claudia still had that ridiculous photo they'd taken of the four them dressed up in their South-West Pet Show costumes sitting on her mantel in Perth. Seb had made one disgruntled chicken. But if that didn't say 'I love you' then Bronwyn didn't know what did.

By now, Lydia had finished mixing the coleslaw and was handing out plates. 'Has anyone heard from Chris? That boy is such a poor correspondent.'

Bronwyn gave a secret smile. This observation fit right in with his talent for disorganised paperwork and over-scheduling, but as it happened she did have news. 'You mean you haven't seen the photos?'

'What photos?' Lydia asked.

'He sent some photos of him and Maria in front of the Trevi Fountain just last night. It looks amazing.'

Chris's adventures overseas really did inspire her. For a man in a wheelchair, he certainly made the most of life. She was so proud of him for that, but especially that he'd finally let Maria love him. Sometimes, she reflected ruefully, the hardest thing in life was allowing yourself to be vulnerable. But it could also be the most rewarding.

'I've seen 'em,' Jack helped himself to a plateful of coleslaw. 'And I've gotta say, I'm pretty jealous.'

'I'm glad he's enjoying himself,' Lydia commented as she took a portion for herself. 'But I do miss him terribly. I hope he doesn't mean to migrate to Italy permanently so that we never see him again. Or worse, do a five-year stint there the way Jack did in France!'

'Well, he'll have to be here this time next year.' Jack put a hand on the back of her neck and she turned to meet his laughing eyes. 'Cause I'm going to need a best man.'

Lydia's fork clattered to her plate and she squealed. 'You're getting married!'

Bronwyn tore her gaze from Jack's twinkling eyes to meet the expectant looks of the family. She held up her hand on which a diamond ring winked officially. 'We got engaged last night.'

'And you didn't tell me?' Claudia cried, jumping up from her place at the table and racing around to her seat. 'As the best friend, I should have known at least a couple of hours before anyone else.'

Bronwyn stood up and hugged her. 'We wanted to tell everyone at the same time.'

After that, there was nothing but talk of weddings. When, where, and what she might be wearing. The boys soon got bored and went off to play cricket on the lawn. Elsa raced around between them, barking cheerfully every time someone hit the ball.

As Lydia stood up to clear away the dishes, Claudia reached out and grabbed Bronwyn's hand.

'I gotta say, Bron, when you first suggested we should swap places I never imagined it would turn out like this.'

'Why?' Bronwyn smiled. 'You don't think my grass is greener?'

'Well, it wasn't at first!' Claudia retorted. 'It was just like you said. Bloody awful.'

'So was yours,' Bronwyn pulled a face. 'The truth is, it was never about swapping our lives exactly. It was always about making the most of our own.'

'So,' Claudia said with a slow wink, 'what you're really saying is, the grass *is* greener on the other side, but *only* if you water it.'

Bronwyn threw back her head and laughed. 'Absolutely.'

Acknowledgements

It's been a very busy year! Along with writing a book and caring for four children, I had to move house as well. There are so many people I have to thank for helping me get through it all in one piece.

My family, of course, leads the pack. Mum, Dad, Shirley, Steve, Aunty Moira, Uncle Richard, Jacenta, Tim, Lena and Ang. Thanks for everything. Not just for the babysitting to give me more time to write but for helping with the move and the renovations as well. We couldn't have achieved it all without you.

To my critique partners, Karina and Nicola. You were the ones who kept me sane. Ladies, your reassurance and support meant so much to me. You both knew exactly when I needed a confidence boost. Thank you so much.

My warm appreciation to our nanny Elysha, who worked extra hours whenever I needed it. I was so thankful for your flexibility and enthusiasm. You are a pleasure to have in our home. Thank you also to my mum and sister Jacenta, who provided extra babysitting especially when my deadline was looming dangerously close. You guys were lifesavers.

As for the actual story itself . . . where would I be without my gurus?

Thanks firstly to Ben Gould, vineyard owner and winemaker for Blind Corner – birthplace of delectable, organic and sustainable wines with unique and diverse flavours. Ben has been such a wonderful source of information over the years and has been so generous with his time. Thank you so much for all your help and for agreeing to read random chapters without a murmur of complaint.

Special thanks to Andrea Jennings, my legal eagle; I sincerely hope you don't find any mistakes in my work! And if you do, I take full credit for them. You were such a great sounding-board for all of Claudia's court dramas. Thank you so much for your time, your war stories and your advice. I had such fun throwing plotlines at you and you were such a good sport about it. Hugs.

Thanks to everyone at Random House who worked on this book with me, especially my publisher, Beverley Cousins, editor, Kathryn Knight and publicist, Jessica Malpass. Thank you for getting behind yet another of my books with so much enthusiasm.

Thank you also to my wonderful agent, Clare Forster, for all your support and advice behind the scenes.

To my husband, Todd. You have been so patient, so understanding and so supportive. At the end of the day, you have put as much into this book as I have. Love you so much.

And finally, my kids. Luke, James, Beth and Michael. Yes. Now mummy will take a long break. Let's go out!

The Maxwell Sisters
by Loretta Hill

All families have their problems. No more so than the
Maxwells of Tawny Brooks Winery. Situated in the heart
of the Margaret River wine region, this world-renowned
winery was the childhood home to three sisters, Natasha,
Eve and Phoebe.

Today all three women are enmeshed in their city lives
and eager to forget their past – and their fractured sibling
relationships. Until Phoebe decides to get married at home . . .

Now the sisters must all return to face a host of family
obligations, vintage in full swing and interfering in-laws who
just can't take a hint. As one romance blossoms and others
fall apart, it seems they are all in need of some sisterly advice.

But old wounds cut deep. Somehow, the Maxwell sisters
must find a way back to one another – or risk losing each
other forever.

**From the author of the bestselling *The Girl in Steel-
Capped Boots* comes a heartwarming romantic comedy
about three extraordinary women on a journey to find
love and rediscover family.**

The Girl in Steel-Capped Boots
by Loretta Hill

Lena Todd is a city girl who thrives on cocktails and cappuccinos. So when her boss announces he's sending her to the outback to join a construction team, her world is turned upside down.

Lena's new accommodation will be an aluminium box called a dongar.

Her new social network: 350 men.

Her daily foot attire: steel-capped boots.

Unfortunately, Lena can't refuse. Mistakes of the past are choking her confidence. She needs to do something to right those wrongs and prove herself. Going into a remote community might just be the place to do that, if only tall, dark and obnoxious Dan didn't seem so determined to stand in her way . . .

Loretta Hill's bestselling debut is a delectable story of red dust and romance, and of dreams discovered in the unlikeliest of places . . .

The Girl in the Hard Hat
by Loretta Hill

To tame a bad boy you will need:

a. One hard hat

b. 350 sulky FIFO workers

c. A tropical cyclone

Wendy Hopkins arrives in the Pilbara to search for the father who abandoned her at birth. So getting mixed up in construction site politics is not high on her 'to do' list.

But when she takes a job as the new Safety Manager at the iron ore wharf just out of town, she quickly becomes the most hated person in the area. Nicknamed 'The Sergeant', she is the butt of every joke and the prime target of notorious womanizer, Gavin Jones.

Giving up is not an option, though.

For, as it turns out, only Wendy can save these workers from the coming storm, find a man who wants to stay buried and . . . put a bad boy firmly in his place.

From the author of *The Girl in Steel-Capped Boots* comes another funny and deliciously romantic tale of a woman in a man's world.

The Girl in the Yellow Vest
by Loretta Hill

'We can't choose who we fall in love with. It could be our best friend . . . or our worst enemy.'

Emily Woods counts cracks for a living. Concrete cracks. So when her long-term boyfriend dumps her, she decides it's time for a change of scenery. Her best friend, Will, suggests joining his construction team in Queensland. Working next door to the Great Barrier Reef seems like just the sort of adventure she needs to reboot her life . . . until she realises that Will is not the person she thought he was.

Charlotte Templeton is frustrated with the lack of respect FIFO workers have for her seaside resort. But picking a fight with their tyrannical project manager, Mark Crawford, seems to lead to more complications than resolutions. The man is too pompous, too rude, and too damned good looking.

As both women strive to protect their dreams and achieve their goals, they discover that secrets will come out, loyalty often hurts, and sometimes the perfect man is the wrong one.

A scintillating romantic comedy, set on the beautiful Queensland coast, from the author of the bestselling *The Girl in Steel-Capped Boots* and *The Girl in the Hard Hat*. The perfect summer read!